PENGUIN CA

Selected W

ROBERTSON DAVIES (1913–1995) was born and raised in Ontario, and was educated at a variety of schools, including Upper Canada College, Queen's University, and Balliol College, Oxford. He had three successive careers: as an actor with the Old Vic Company in England; as publisher of the Peterborough *Examiner*; and as university professor and first Master of Massey College at the University of Toronto, from which he retired in 1981 with the title of Master Emeritus.

He was one of Canada's most distinguished men of letters, with several volumes of plays and collections of essays, speeches, and *belles lettres* to his credit. As a novelist he gained worldwide fame for his three trilogies: *The Salterton Trilogy*, *The Deptford Trilogy*, and *The Cornish Trilogy*, and for later novels *Murther & Walking Spirits* and *The Cunning Man*.

His career was marked by many honours: He was the first Canadian to be made an Honorary Member of the American Academy of Arts and Letters, he was a Companion of the Order of Canada, and he received honorary degrees from twenty-six American, Canadian, and British universities.

JENNIFER SURRIDGE worked in various administrative positions for many years before joining Robertson Davies for the last three years of his life as his research assistant. In 1996 she and Mrs. Davies formed Pendragon Ink, where she is general manager. Pendragon Ink looks after Davies's literary legacy. She has edited *The Merry Heart* and *Happy Alchemy*, and is working on editing and annotating Davies's voluminous diaries.

Also by Robertson Davies

NOVELS

Tempest-Tost

Leaven of Malice

A Mixture of Frailties

Fifth Business

The Manticore

World of Wonders

The Rebel Angels

What's Bred in the Bone

The Lyre of Orpheus

Murther & Walking Spirits

The Cunning Man

SHORT FICTION

High Spirits

CRITICISM

A Voice from the Attic

ESSAYS

One Half of Robertson Davies

The Enthusiasms of Robertson Davies

The Merry Heart

Happy Alchemy

ROBERTSON DAVIES

Selected Works on the Art of Writing

Edited and with an Introduction by Jennifer Surridge

PENGUIN
CANADA

PENGUIN CANADA

Published by the Penguin Group

Penguin Group (Canada), 90 Eglinton Avenue East, Suite 700, Toronto, Ontario, Canada M4P 2Y3
(a division of Pearson Canada Inc.)

Penguin Group (USA) Inc., 375 Hudson Street, New York, New York 10014, U.S.A.
Penguin Books Ltd, 80 Strand, London WC2R 0RL, England
Penguin Ireland, 25 St Stephen's Green, Dublin 2, Ireland (a division of Penguin Books Ltd)
Penguin Group (Australia), 250 Camberwell Road, Camberwell, Victoria 3124, Australia
(a division of Pearson Australia Group Pty Ltd)
Penguin Books India Pvt Ltd, 11 Community Centre, Panchsheel Park, New Delhi – 110 017, India
Penguin Group (NZ), 67 Apollo Drive, Rosedale, North Shore 0632, Auckland, New Zealand
(a division of Pearson New Zealand Ltd)
Penguin Books (South Africa) (Pty) Ltd, 24 Sturdee Avenue, Rosebank, Johannesburg 2196,
South Africa

Penguin Books Ltd, Registered Offices: 80 Strand, London WC2R 0RL, England

First published 2008

(WEB) 10 9 8 7 6 5 4 3 2 1

Some of the pieces in this collection were originally published in the following books by Robertson Davies: *Merry Heart, Happy Alchemy*, and *One Half of Robertson Davies*.

Manufactured in Canada.

ISBN-13: 978-0-14-305567-9
ISBN-10: 0-14-305567-4

Library and Archives Canada Cataloguing in publication data available upon request.

For

Rosamond and David Bailey
with love

Contents

Stratford

Making Speeches

Youth

Age

Canada

Introduction

by Jennifer Surridge

Robertson Davies wrote in most forms: plays, novels, diaries, articles, book reviews, play reviews, editorials, children's and adult short stories (including ghost stories), television plays, libretti, an oratorio, poems, and speeches. The greater part of this collection is made up of my father's speeches, which he delivered throughout his life, beginning when he moved to Peterborough, Ontario, in 1942. By that time he had graduated from Oxford in England, worked as a professional actor, served as literary adviser to Tyrone Guthrie at the Old Vic Theatre in London, and taught theatre history at the Old Vic School.

When Davies made his first speeches, he assumed too much of his audience and spoke of his subject in too difficult a style. He soon became aware of the problem and, with practice, included his listeners by using devices such as "as you know" and then explaining the reference. He would also make light of some subjects, and insert a joke to break the concentration a little. (Given his early humorous writing, many audiences assumed he would be funny, but sometimes they were nonetheless taken by surprise.) Davies was a popular lecturer and speechmaker; he routinely attracted a large crowd and had more invitations than he could possibly accept. He rarely used the same speech twice, as he usually wrote a new one for the particular audience he was addressing and the occasion being celebrated. He would write the speech some time ahead of the date, practise it beforehand, and make sure it fit into the required time frame.

In addition to the speeches I've gathered here, I've included a poem, a hoax, and three articles; all these works have been taken from *One Half of Robertson Davies*, *The Merry Heart*, and *Happy Alchemy*. Within each of the sections I've ordered the works chronologically in order to reflect the development of my father's writing style. If the introductions to the individual pieces seem to have been written by different people, this is quite right. The ones from *One Half of Robertson Davies* are by Davies, *The Merry Heart* are by Douglas Gibson, and *Happy Alchemy* are by me. And although the overarching theme of this collection is the art of writing, Davies's work cannot be forced to conform to an arbitrary theme, as many of his fans know. Davies thought of writing as his principal work and would become uneasy if away from it for too long: If not actually at the typewriter, he was writing in his head. He never regarded any other work he did as important, and with every novel hoped that someday he would write a really good book. It would seem he got his wish.

The introduction to individual pieces feature some selections from Robertson Davies's voluminous diaries. He kept a diary most of his life, but became serious about it in 1960, writing every day (or filling in later if he missed a day). He used the diary exercise to clear his mind of day-to-day happenings so that he could go deeper into himself to do his imaginative work. He began writing the diaries by hand, but after 1970 he turned to the typewriter, as he was getting cramp and felt that his handwriting was deteriorating. I am currently engaged in transcribing and annotating his diaries and, since an author lives a lot of the time in his head, the process is giving me insights into his life and thoughts that I would not have had otherwise. This is a great treat I never imagined I would experience. My father asked that his diaries not be published until he had been dead for twenty years, and I am keeping to his wishes, but I don't think he would mind the snippets that I've used to illuminate the circumstances in which these speeches were given.

When he was asked to compile the collection *One Half of Robertson Davies*, he noted on January 19, 1977:

Feel low and I do not think it is the cold, or 'flu, or whatever I have. It is one of my old fits of melancholy, of greatly reduced energy, of heaviness of spirit. However, I had to pull up my socks and lunch at Fernando's with [Douglas] Gibson of Macmillan, & the sales manager, whose name for the moment escapes me, although I have met him several times. Upshot of the lunch is that they want to do a book of some of my speeches and occasional pieces, and think it will sell; want to call it *A Davies Festival* which I am not sure I like; want a theme which takes from it, as much as possible, the reproach of being a book of reprinted pieces, and this should not be difficult, as nothing I shall include has ever been in print before.

Later, when the publicity photo for the book was done, he wrote: *"to Peterson, the photographer, at 10, and have pics taken for cover of* One Half; *I am wrapped in black velvet, lit very much from one side, and mugged 48 times...."*

I leave the reader with my father's thoughts on the writing and delivering of speeches—works "written to be spoken"—in his preface to *One Half of Robertson Davies:*

"The tongue is one half of a man: but the other half is the heart." I have always liked that proverb, because it does honour to the faculty of speech, and it is speech as much as anything that divides man from the lesser creation. Without it, we should have no abstract thought, probably little memory, and therefore nothing much in the way of foresight. Speech can be developed into a form of art, and thus puts some artistry within the grasp of every man. And, as the proverb makes clear, speech is a means of revealing what is in the heart. In offering this book to the public as one half of myself, I certainly mean to imply that the other half, of necessity, goes with it.

All my life, it seems to me, I have been making speeches, or telling stories in public, and it has always been my desire to bring tongue and heart into an equal partnership. I cannot pretend that I have always succeeded, but I have done my best. When I have failed, I hope that the heart was the senior partner, for I know what abysses of folly await those speakers who rely on the tongue for more than it can give.

This book is composed of pieces that were written to be spoken, and in all of them the qualities of speech are apparent. What is meant to be heard is necessarily more direct in expression, and perhaps more boldly coloured, than what is meant for the reader. The speaker must seize the attention of his audience, and take care not to tax it extremely, or be too sure of his welcome. So, when you read this book, will you please try to hear it, and to think of it as something said to you. A couple of centuries ago no such request would be necessary, for then everybody heard what they read, and at an even earlier time in history they spoke it aloud. We all know the story of the Renaissance cardinal who was compelled to suspend his studies because he had lost his voice. Nowadays we all have to read so much that we read very quickly, and teachers of reading condemn what they call "verbalization," as if those who practiced it were the kind of people who followed each line with a forefinger, and wetted a thumb when they turned the page. But there are great rewards for the verbalizers; they hear everything they read spoken plainly and expressively in the halls of the mind—those halls that can so readily become noble forums, splendid theatres, cathedrals or chapels, palaces or woodcutter's cottages. And they know that the ear—even when it is the mind's ear—is a surer judge of prose than the scampering, skipping eye.

Because these pieces are, in the main, speeches, I decided not to cut out those passages at the beginning of each in which I have, so to speak, made my bow to the audience, paid it a few compliments, and thanked the Chairman. These are necessary decorums of public speaking, and to leave them out would be to do precisely what I am determined not to do—that is, to pretend that I am offering you something to read, rather than something to hear. And, to let you in on a speaker's secret, it is in such passages that he tries out his voice (because he is always fearful that it may have deserted him during the Chairman's introduction) and winds up his courage to a point which makes it possible for him to speak at all. Because, you see, the poor wretch is nervous.

Speakers' nerves affect them in various ways. Some tremble, some become frenzied. I lose all confidence, and suffer from a leaden oppression that makes me wonder why I ever agreed to speak at all; the Tomb and the Conqueror Worm seem preferable to delivering the stupid and piffling speech I have so carefully prepared. But there is no escape; speak I must, and I need a ritual paragraph in which to ease myself into the job.

The Chairman, of course, is as happy as a lark, and thinks the speaker must share his high spirits. Many public speakers have written peevishly about Chairmen; I tend to like them, and at the moment before they gesture me toward the reading-desk I envy them, because their task is done. But in nine cases out of ten the Chairman has, quite unwittingly, dished me; he has said things that provoke such gloomy reflections that I can hardly force myself to answer his call.

He has, you see, approached me by what may be called the biographical path. He wants to tell the audience who I am, and he begins by telling them that I was born, and when, and where. As soon as he mentions the date of my birth I can see the audience doing a little sum in their heads, after which they look at me with renewed interest, to see how I am carrying the burden of my years. Most of them look at me with the unmistakable satisfaction of people who were born in bigger centres of population than I. I experience an unworthy wish that I had been born in Rome, or perhaps in Byzantium. This is low geographical snobbery. Does it matter where one was born? Yes, to an audience it does, and I see them looking for straw in my hair.

The Chairman next rehearses the details of my education, endured in a variety of hells. Because I am a professor, and a writer, and am about to make a speech, the Chairman suggests that my education partook of the character of a Roman triumph. But I know better. I was that most tedious of educational subjects, a Lop-sided Boy, capable of learning anything that interested me in record time, but cretinous in my failure to comprehend whatever I did not like. In the Puritan schools of my youth this was worse—much worse—than being thoroughly stupid. It was assumed that I could not master mathematics and science because I was shiftless. And so, as the Chairman tells of my educational obstacle race I see before me the angry faces of those who were so determined to teach what I simply could not learn, would not learn, and passionately loathed.

But the Chairman is determined to present me as a Child Marvel. "At an unusually early age, he was appointed Literary Editor of *Saturday Night,*" he carols. True, but at that time *Saturday Night* had a total staff of six, of whom one was the Editor's secretary. The Editor dealt with politics and the higher reaches of Art; two men dealt with Finance, which was a very big factor in that paper, itself a long-standing money-loser; there was a woman who did Women's Affairs; and then there was the Literary Editor, who did anything else that turned up, including books. The financial officers of the publishing company that produced the paper harried us unmercifully because *Saturday Night* did not attract enough advertising. I remember one time the advertising manager demanded, as we went to press, that I remove a six-inch book review because Pussyfoot Closet Tanks had come in late with a six-inch ad, and wanted the space. I hastened to comply, for priorities were well understood on that paper; Literary Editor I might be, but money was money, and Pussyfoot must be served.

The Chairman is all kindness; as he romps through the public details of my life I am sadly aware of what lies behind them, but under the circumstances I cannot laugh or weep. I must keep my ears open for the moment when the Chairman looks indulgently in my direction and says, And now, ladies and gentlemen …

Then I rise and trudge to the lectern and place myself behind it, knowing well what I look like. When I was a boy it was thought a great joke to hide in a dark room with a flashlight; when somebody—one's mother, for preference—came in, one put the flashlight inside one's mouth and turned it on. The effect was that of an eerily illuminated Floating Head. And that is what the speaker looks like; the light on the lectern shines up at him from below; the Floating Head opens its mouth. It utters.

The panic terror and the conviction of unworthiness and depression I have described are the speaker's own; the audience does not share them. They are, as a general thing, friendly and on the whole optimistic about what is to come. And that is as it should be, for the speaker must keep his personal miseries from them and give them equal measure of tongue and heart.

Is it all misery, then? No, no. I am reminded of the story (was there ever a speaker who was not reminded of a story?) about the great Sir Henry Irving, when he visited the American tragedian Richard Mansfield in his dressing-room after Mansfield had played Richard III. Mansfield complained bitterly about the strain on his nerves of public performance; sometimes, he said, he wondered if he could sustain his powers until the curtain fell. Irving, himself a great Richard, eyed his colleague sardonically and said: "Well, Dick, m'boy, if you find it unwholesome, why do you do it?" If I find public speaking distasteful, why have I done it so often over several decades?

Because of the satisfactions of the tongue, when it is happily linked with heart....

Selected Works on the Art of Writing

Writing

1

The Conscience of the Writer

Many young people who want to write, or who have already begun to write, appeal to me for advice about what it is to be a writer, and what keeps a writer going through what may be a long life in a solitary profession. The writer's work, however prompt his publisher may be, does not reach his public until several months after he has finished it; before that time he has worked, necessarily in solitude, cheered by no one except perhaps a faithful and long-suffering wife. What makes him do it? How does he bear up during the long wait before some echo reaches him from his readers? How does he keep on into the latter part of his career? When in 1968 Glendon College in York University asked me to speak, I decided to try my best to put such advice as I had into a single utterance, and here it is.

My subject is "The Conscience of the Writer," and I accepted your invitation to speak not because I think I have anything new to say about it, but because I think that the familiar and basic things demand constant repetition, in an age when familiar and basic things are so often cast aside, as if we had outlived them. The writer's calling has been greatly romanticized—more so, I believe, than that of any other artistic creator. Painters, sculptors, and composers are regarded with a degree of awe by the public in general, but writers possess a special sort of magic, and I believe that in part it is the magic of what seems to be a familiar and attainable, yet somehow unrealized, element in the lives of many people who are not artists of any kind. Anybody can see that he is not going to paint like Picasso, or write music like Benjamin Britten; he is not so sure that he is not going to write like somebody whose writing he admires. He has learned the humblest techniques of the writer at school; he can put down words on a page; he has some idea of grammar, or he may have decided that grammar is an unworthy shackle on his inspiration; he is constantly meeting with experiences, or observing people, that seem to him to be the stuff of writing. But somehow he never writes.

He could do so, of course. Every writer is familiar with the person who buttonholes him and tells him about the book he would write—if he had the time. Or else they have fathers or uncles who are screamingly funny characters whose lives ought to be written at once. These people sometimes offer to collaborate with the author, providing the raw material if he will do the actual work of writing.

Such people are usually middle-aged. Younger people with the urge to write do not want to collaborate; they are, on the contrary, often suspicious that older writers will snatch their splendid inspirations and capitalize on them. These young people are often daring experimenters in technique, because their ideas can only be given adequate form in some wholly new way of writing—leaving out all the verbs, or perhaps writing nothing but verbs, but most often in the present day by describing, with gloating particularity, various sexual acts which they have just discovered, and of which they wish to make the innocent old world aware. But after a few months during which they burn with a hard, gem-like flame, these people cease to write.

The world is full of people who think they could write, or who have, at some time, written. But they do not stay with it. Why?

Is it because the real writer, the serious writer, who is a writer all his life, is a special kind of person? Yes, it is. And what kind of person is he? I do not pretend to be able to answer that question fully, for there are many kinds of writers, some of whom I do not understand at all, and some whom I understand but do not admire, although I am well aware of their talents. But they all have a characteristic—indeed a distinguishing trait in their psychological makeup—which makes them recognizable, and it is this that I have called the writer's conscience, although that is not a very satisfactory name for it. I use that phrase to describe the continuing struggle that goes on in the psyche of every writer of any importance. And by that expression "of any importance" I exclude the journalistic word-spinners, the ghost writers, the concocters of literary confectionery, although some of these are remarkable technicians. I am talking about the writers who try—perhaps not all the time but certainly during the greater part of their careers—to write the best they can about the themes that concern them most.

This is not a moral judgment and has nothing to do with the themes that writers choose. Perhaps I can make myself clear by instancing two books—Dostoevsky's *Crime and Punishment* and Max Beerbohm's *Zuleika Dobson.* One is an agonized exploration of the psychology of a criminal intellectual; the other is a charming joke about youth and love. One is clumsily written, with long passages of overheated and perversely sensitive emotion; the other is elegantly and exquisitely written, in a fashion so subtle that it yields up its secrets only after several careful readings. Both are great books, and I think it is foolish to say that one is greater than the other, as if one were marking an examination, and giving Dostoevsky higher marks because he tries harder. He didn't try harder. He just wrote the best book he could in the circumstances in which he found himself. So did Max Beerbohm. Both books appeal strongly to large numbers of readers, who encounter them at particularly fortunate moments in their lives. And I believe that it is because both writers wrote under the domination of conscience, and it is the subsequent revelation that gives the books their particular weight and value.

There are no absolutes in literature that can be applied without reference to personal taste and judgment. The great book for you is the book that has most to say to you at the moment when you are reading. I do not mean the book that is most instructive, but the book that feeds your spirit. And that depends on your age, your experience, your psychological and spiritual need. These days I find myself reading poetry rather a lot. But when I was ten what I liked to read best were bound volumes of a boys' paper called *Chums.* It had just what I needed, and it extended my world remarkably; however, when

I looked at some of that stuff recently I could not endure it. But I am sure I should not be reading what I read now if I had not read *Chums* then, and I am grateful. We do not read to make ourselves cultured, but to nourish our souls. Real culture is the evidence, not the reality, of the fully realized spirit.

This is one of my great quarrels with university courses in English; they require students to read lists of fine books, and to profess a knowledge of them that is usually superficial, though even this sort of knowledge is better than none at all. But for every masterpiece that is on the reading list, there are five that are not, and many students fall into the trap of thinking that anything that is not on the list is not Blue Brand Literature, and may be disregarded. This is not the intention of English courses, but it is what happens. The great difficulty is that the emphasis in universities is likely to be on criticism of literature, rather than on delighted discovery and surrender to it. Every student—B.A., M.A., or Ph.D.—knows what is wrong with Charles Dickens, though they have probably read nothing but *Great Expectations*, and read it once, when they were too young to understand it. The reason for this is perfectly clear: Criticism is comparatively easy in its showy but superficial aspect. Anybody can pick up its techniques and use them with a display of skill, just as anybody can make a spectacular cut with a surgeon's scalpel, simply because it is so sharp. But the vastly more difficult business of discovering literature, and giving oneself wholly into its embrace, and making some of it part of oneself, cannot be done in large classes, and not everybody can do it even in small classes. A surprising number of people can get Ph.D.s in criticism; to be a worthy reader of what writers of conscience have written is a very different matter.

Which brings us back to our theme—the writer and his conscience. Moral judgments based on the themes a writer chooses, I have said, are irrelevant. Evelyn Waugh was a writer of extraordinary conscience, and his novels, even when most serious, have a comic guise, and are spare and elegant in form. Tolstoy was similarly a writer of extraordinary conscience, but *Anna Karenina* and *War and Peace* are solemn and almost portentous in tone, and their greatest admirers will admit that they might have been the better for the cutting of large passages. It is of little use to say that *War and Peace* is a masterpiece because it tells us all there is to say about war; it tells us wonderful things, but Waugh's little novel *Scoop* tells us something that Tolstoy did not. This is not to say that the two books are equally "great" or "good" but only that every good book is good in its own way, and that comparisons are of extremely limited value. Unless, of course, you are a superficial critic, in which case you had better banish all humility in the face of genius and get on with your self-appointed task of awarding marks and establishing hierarchies. But if you want to know and feel what genius knows and feels, you must be a reader first, and a critic a very long way afterward.

Now—what is this conscience I have been talking about? It is the writer's inner struggle toward self-knowledge and self-recognition, which he makes manifest through his art. Writers, and artists generally, are notoriously resistant to psychoanalysis, and to put hundreds of thousands of words by both Freud and Jung into a nutshell it is because they are continuously psychoanalyzing themselves in their own way, which is through their work, and it is the only way to peace of mind, to integration, open to them. It is a life process, and in the work of a writer of great abilities who has been so fortunate as to live long it presents an awesome achievement. Consider the case of Thomas Mann; from *Little Herr Friedemann*, which he published when he was twenty-three, and *Buddenbrooks*, which appeared when he was twenty-five, the succession of his books reveals to us, beneath the themes, the fables, and the philosophical explorations, the development of an extraordinary spirit: *The Magic Mountain* (1924), the great *Joseph* tetralogy, which was sixteen years in the writing, *Lotte in Weimar* (1939), *Doctor Faustus* (1948), and that extraordinary book which appeared when the writer was eighty, *The Confessions of Felix Krull*—these are a few mountain peaks in a career of an artist's self-exploration. And what is revealed? A deep preoccupation with themes of death and disease, of sin and remorse and redemption, of myth and the irrationalities of life, of the wellsprings of the creative spirit, and at the last, in *Felix Krull*, a triumphant return and exploration of one of Mann's lifelong preoccupations, which was the link between the artistic and the criminal instinct, embodied in what I regard as quite the subtlest and most hair-raisingly erotic novel I have ever read. A concern, as you see, with some of the deep and continuing problems of human life.

Here we have what the great literary artist does; he explores his own spirit to the uttermost, and bodies forth what he finds in a form of art that is plain to anyone who can read it—though not necessarily to anyone who picks up his books.

The struggle is not easy and its results are sometimes disastrous, for reasons that we shall explore a little later. Psychoanalysis is notoriously demanding and disagreeable, when undertaken by a sympathetic and skilled physician: Consider what it means when it is a solitary venture, undertaken as a life sentence and carried out under the circumstances in which most authors live. Is it any wonder that the domestic lives of some of them are rumpled and unseemly? Or that many of them take to drink? Or that others escape into that attractive world of action where they can get so much easy acclaim by protesting or sitting in or freaking out or setting themselves up as great friends and patrons of youth, or whooping it up for the pill or LSD—doing anything, in fact, except getting on with the laborious task to which their gift and their temperament calls them?

Henrik Ibsen knew all about it, and he was one of the heroes who remained chained to his task until finally it broke him; for the last years of his life he toiled painstakingly every day over a copybook, trying to force his hand to learn, for the second time, the skill of making readable writing. Did you know that Ibsen was a poet? Here is a translation of one of his verses, full of meaning and of warning for writers:

> To live—is a battle with troll-folk
> In the crypts of heart and head;
> To write—is a man's self-judgement
>   As Doom shall judge the dead.

"A man's self-judgment"—that is the conscience of the writer. Whatever he writes, and whatever the summing up of that mysterious inner court may be, if it is carried through truthfully and manfully, we shall sense in it that quality that makes literature one of the greatest of the arts, and well worth the sacrifice and the frequent misery of a writer's life.

Sometimes I laugh when aspiring writers assure me that if they could get enough money—usually in the form of a grant from some handout agency subsidized by the government—they would go to Mexico, or the Mediterranean, or to Capri, and there they would be able to write—so readily, so fluently, so happily. Fools! "A man's self-judgment" will go with him anywhere, if he is really a writer, and he will not be able to command either inspiration or happiness or serenity. Of course if he is a mere scribbling tourist, or a work-shy flop, or both, it does not really matter much where he goes. But if he is a writer he will be wise to write wherever he finds himself. The history of literature is full of writers who have thought that the judgment of the inner court would be easier in some country outside his own.

This is not to say, of course, that a writer should not travel or gain experience. But if he is really a writer his task may be, not to seek experience, but to survive the experience that crowds upon him from every quarter. As Aldous Huxley has written, "experience is not a matter of having actually swum the Hellespont, or danced with the dervishes, or slept in a doss-house. It is a matter of sensibility and intuition, of seeing and hearing the significant things, of paying attention at the right moments, of understanding and co-ordinating. Experience is not what happens to a man: it is what a man does with what happens to him." Many years ago I read a book by the travelling journalist Richard Halliburton; he had climbed a very high mountain somewhere—I forget where because the book was not of the sort that sticks in the mind—and he recorded the reflection of his companion at the top. It was "Now I can spit a mile!" We are familiar with the reflections of Wordsworth, who climbed a few quite unremarkable hills in the Lake District. There is the contrast in what experience meant to a man of trivial mind, and to a poet.

Let us continue the theme of the writer's artistic experience considered in terms of psychoanalysis. To do so, I want to talk from the standpoint of C.G. Jung, rather than that of Sigmund Freud. Great as Freud was, and unassailable as his position is among the great liberators of the human mind, his actual technique seems more suited to the consulting room than to the university lecture room; his mind dealt more strikingly with problems of neurosis than with matters of aesthetics, and his cast of mind was powerfully reductive. After the Freudian treatment most things look a little shabby—needlessly so. Jung's depth psychology, on the other hand, is much more aesthetic and humanistic in its general tendency, and is not so Procrustean in its effect on artistic experience. The light it throws on matters of literature and on the temperament of the writer is extremely useful and revealing.

Jung is insistent on a particular type of development in the mind of anyone who meets the problems of life successfully; it is the change, the alteration of viewpoint, that transformation of aims and ambitions, that overtakes everybody somewhere in the middle of life. In women this change is physiological as well as mental, and consequently it has always been a matter of common observation. But in men the change is an intellectual and spiritual one of profound consequence, and this is something observable in the careers of virtually all writers of the kind we are talking about here—the committed writers, the servants of the writer's conscience.

Example is probably better than explanation at this point. The career of the late Aldous Huxley will be familiar to many of you. During the early part of his career his work was remarkable for its strongly satirical edge, for the brilliance of its wit, for its concern with matters of morality and especially morality as it relates to sex, which seemed to many people revolutionary and perhaps dangerous and destructive. He is rather out of fashion at present, but when the usual slump in reputation that follows a writer's death is over—it takes about ten or fifteen years—I think these novels will be prized for their stringent charm. But I well remember the surprise and excitement that was caused by the appearance of *Eyeless in Gaza* in 1936; it seemed to be a work by a new man, for its tone was inquiring, mystical, and tormented beyond anything we had found in him before. Of course the fashionable people chattered about his probable conversion to Roman Catholicism, and those who had chiefly valued the bitterness of the early books thought that he had "gone off" terribly, and lamented him as one lost. But the change in direction had been heralded for anybody with eyes to see it in his earlier book *Point Counter Point*, which was a tortured and questing book; the bitterness in it was born of revulsion rather than glee at the follies of mankind. And what was significant about *Eyeless in Gaza* was that it was written when Huxley was forty-two, and ripe for a change. If there had been no change, we should soon have tired of the old Huxley wearing the young Huxley's intellectual clothes. And from that time until the end of his life his exploration of mystical religion and his discussions of morality were at the root of everything he wrote.

Much the same sort of foolish hubbub broke out when Evelyn Waugh wrote *Brideshead Revisited* in 1945. Has our favourite jester gone serious on us, cried the people who admired his earlier books only because they were funny, and not because they were wise. But Waugh was forty-two, and his point of view had changed.

What is the nature of this change? It is part of intellectual and particularly spiritual growth. As Jung explains it, in the early part of life—roughly for the first half of it—man's chief aims are personal and social. He must grow up, he must find his work, he must find out what kind of sex life he is going to lead, he must achieve some place in the world and attempt to get security within it, or else decide that security is not important to him. But when he has achieved these ends, or come to some sort of understanding with this part of existence, his attention is turned to matters that are broader in scope, and sometimes disturbing to contemplate. His physical strength is waning rather than growing; he has found out what sex is, and though it may be very important to him it can do little to surprise him; he realizes that someday he is really going to die and that the way he approaches death is of importance to him; he finds that without God (using that name to comprehend all the great and inexplicable things and the redemptive or destructive powers that lie outside human command and understanding) his life lacks a factor that it greatly needs; he finds that in Jung's phrase, he is not the master of his fate except in a very modest degree and that he is in fact the object of a supraordinate subject. And he seeks wisdom rather than power—though the circumstances of his early life may continue to thrust power into his hands.

Now, the paradox of this change is that it does not make him an old man. What will make him an old man is a frightened clinging to the values of the first half of life. We have all seen these juvenile dotards whose boast is that they are just as young as their sons or their grandsons; they do not realize what a pitiful boast that is. They prate about their sympathy with youth, but they mean only the superficialities and ephemera of youth. Many of the sad smash-ups in marriages that we all see among middle-aged people have their origin in this attempt to dodge an inescapable fact. The values that are proper and all-absorbing during the first half of life will not sustain a man during the second half. If he has the courage and wisdom to advance courageously into the new realm of values and emotions he will age physically, of course, but his intellectual and spiritual growth will continue, and will give satisfaction to himself and to all those associated with him. And such courage and wisdom are by no means rare; they may show themselves among many people who have never thought along these lines at all but who have a knack for living life wisely; and they also are to be found among those who regard self-awareness as one of the primary duties of a good life. Paradoxically, such people are on better terms with youth than the shrivelled Peter Pans who dare not be their age.

How does this affect the writer, who is our chief concern here? It is important to him to manage this change in outlook with skill and humility, for a failure to do so can be his ruin. He may be one of those whose special gifts fit him for the kind of writing a man does before middle life. This has been the case with many poets, who appear to have lost everything but technical skill after the appearance of a number of fine—perhaps great—early works. One wonders what Byron would have been like after forty-five. One regrets that Keats did not live to give us the mature works of one of the greatest geniuses of youth. On the other hand, we recall that Cervantes, whose works written during his early life were capable, but not the sort of thing that it would occur to anybody to translate, astonished the world with *Don Quixote* when he was fifty-eight, and wrote the second part of it ten years later. We think of Goethe, who wrote the first part of *Faust* when he was fifty-six, and completed the mighty second part of that play between his seventy-fifth and his eighty-second year. I have already spoken of Thomas Mann, whose genius survived triumphantly until his death at the age of eighty, and I do not suppose it is necessary to point out that all the finest work of Bernard Shaw belongs to the second half of his life.

There are those who do not choose to make this necessary advance, or who repress evidence of it in their writing. It would be impertinent to speculate superficially on such a subject, but one may wonder if that is not what happened to Ernest Hemingway. And certainly if we examine the works of our own best-known writer, the late Stephen Leacock, with care, we wonder whether he was not trapped in the manner of his earliest writing. He did not set out on his career until he was in his early forties, but it was in the manner of his youth; his success was so great that he may have hesitated to introduce a new and deeper note into what was so gratefully accepted by his readers. The result is writing that is often thin and perfunctory. But in one of his last books—the short autobiographical sketch called *The Boy I Left Behind Me*—we are given a tantalizing sample of what he might have done if he had chosen.

There are exceptions to all rules, and you may be surprised to hear me name a writer who is one of the greatest technicians of the last fifty years, P.G. Wodehouse, who continues to produce novels—they have been discerningly called "musical comedies without music"—that are much like his earlier successes in tone, and are so brilliantly adapted to his aims that they continue to astonish us. He is in his eighty-seventh year and still writing. But he invented a highly artificial mode which no one has successfully imitated. Wodehouse, however, is no case of arrested development; if you think him immature, read his autobiographical volume called *Performing Flea*, which he wrote in 1951. Sean O'Casey, with characteristic spleen, had referred to Wodehouse as a performing flea, and in this book Wodehouse makes it plain that he is certainly no trivial entertainer, but a man of maturity, irony, and keen perception qualities not overwhelmingly demonstrated by O'Casey, whose best work was done by the time he was forty-four.

How does the real writer—the man with the writer's conscience, or temperament, or whatever label you choose—set about his work?

There are as many ways as there are writers, but there are a few well-worn paths, and of these I can only speak with certainty about the path I have chosen for myself. It would be more correct to say, the path my temperament has chosen for me. I combine writing with other sorts of work. For twenty-eight years I have been a journalist—not just a writer, but an editor, an employer, a man who had to make sure that his newspaper did not lose money, who had to worry about new machinery, new buildings, new contracts with unions, and continually to be concerned with an obligation to a community. When I had spent the day doing this I went home and wrote, altogether, works that fill eighteen volumes; I am at work on the nineteenth, and the twentieth exists in the form of extended notes. I am not counting four full-length plays that were produced but are not yet in print. I am not saying this to dazzle you with my industry, but to tell you how I do my work. I have always been grateful for my journalistic experience, which amounts to millions of words of writing, because it kept my technique in good muscular shape. I can write now without that humming and hawing and staring at the ceiling which plagues so many writers who have trouble getting started.

I have of late become a university professor and head of a college, and these tasks can hardly be regarded as a rest cure. My most difficult work in this realm is the correcting of student essays and marking examinations. Reading inexpert writing is deeply exhausting. It is like listening to bad music.

I have also had the ordinary family experiences. I am married and have three children, now all grown up, and I have spent countless happy hours in domestic pursuits—gardening, family music-making, getting together some modest but pleasant collections of things, amateur theatricals as well as some professional theatre work, and a kind of family life that seems perhaps to be more characteristic of the nineteenth century than of our streamlined era. I have sat on committees, and boards; I have made a great many speeches, and I have listened to what seem, in recollection, to be millions of speeches.

All of this I consider necessary to my life as a writer. It has kept me from too great a degree of that fruitless self-preoccupation which is one of the worst diseases of the literary life. It has provided me with the raw material for what I write. The raw material, you observe; before it becomes the finished product it must undergo a process of distillation and elimination. An author is a very different thing from a reporter, or an autobiographer. This way of living has confirmed a theory I formed many years ago, when I was at the age you have reached now, that myth and fairy tales are nothing less than the distilled truth about what we call "real life," and that we move through a throng of Sleeping Princesses, Belles Dames sans Merci, Cinderellas, Wicked Witches, Powerful Wizards, Frog Princes, Lucky Third Sons, Ogres, Dwarves, Sagacious Animal Helpers and Servers, yes and Heroes and Heroines, in a world that is nothing less than an enchanted landscape, and that life only seems dull and spiritless to those who live under a spell—too often a spell they have brought upon their own heads.

Do not misunderstand me. I am not being whimsical, and my world is not the cozy nursery retreat of Winnie-the-Pooh. It is a tough world, and it only seems irrational or unreal to those who have not grasped some hints of its remorseless, irreversible, and often cruel logic. It is a world in which God is not mocked, and in which a man reaps—only too obviously—what he has sown. I do not think I understand it all, but I think I am acquainted with a few corners of it. And I may as well tell you that I regard the writing I have done as little more than a preparation for the work I mean to do.

Although I have been telling you about what I have done that is not the primary work of a writer, I would not have you believe that I have merely fitted my writing into odd corners of my life. Writing has always been central to my life, and my real work. But I said that I was glad to have the ordinary occupations of a busy man to protect me against that self-preoccupation that is one of the worst diseases of the literary life. Let me explain: I do not write in my spare time, I write all the time; whatever I may be doing, the literary aspect of my mind is fully at work: It is not only the hours at the desk or the typewriter, but the hours spent in other kinds of work and in many kinds of diversion when I am busily observing, shaping, rejecting, and undergoing a wide variety of feelings that are the essential material of writing. Notice that I said feelings—not thoughts, but feelings. One of the burdensome parts of the writer's temperament, as I understand it, is that one feels quite strongly about all sorts of things that other people seem to be able to gloss over, and this can be wearisome and depleting. This is the famous "artistic sensitivity" that one sometimes hears people boasting about—very often people who show no other awareness of it. It is not a form of weakness. A writer is very rarely a wincing, delicate kind of man; in my experience he is often rather a tough creature, though given to hypochondria and sudden collapses of the spirit. I rely on a routine of daily work, and the necessities of a busy life, to keep me from succumbing too completely to the demands of a particular kind of temperament. My kind of writer—I can speak for no other—needs other work and a routine to keep him sane.

Let me return once again to the emphasis I laid on feeling, rather than thinking, in the writer's temperament. All sorts of people expect writers to be intellectuals. Sometimes they are, but it is not necessary to their work. Aldous Huxley was an intellectual, but he was not so good a novelist as E.M. Forster, who is not and does not like to be considered one. The writer is necessarily a man of feeling and intuition; he need not be a powerful original thinker. Shakespeare, Dickens, Dostoevsky—we do not think of them as intellectuals; Tolstoy's thinking was vastly inferior to his fiction; Keats was a finer poet than Arnold, though no one would deny Arnold the title of intellectual. I do not say that writers are childlike creatures of untutored genius; often they are very intelligent men: but the best part of their intelligence is of the feeling and intuitive order. Sometimes they are impatient and even rude with people who insist on treating them as intellectuals. It is not pleasant to be treated like a clock by some clever but essentially unsympathetic person who wants to take you apart to see what makes you tick. But the modern passion for this sort of thing has led to the establishment on many campuses of a man called the Writer in Residence, who is there, in part at any rate, for intellectuals to pester, take apart, and reassemble, under the impression that they are learning something about writing.

As I draw to a conclusion, I want to return to something I said at the beginning of this address, which is that the life of a writer may be likened to a long self-analysis. I suggested that the process was painful, and indeed it frequently is so. But it is something else—something that Freud never mentioned, because of his preoccupation with neurosis, but which Jung suggests: It is sometimes joyous, victorious, and beautiful. It is not fashionable nowadays to say that one's life has moments of piercing beauty, or that it brings hours which are not merely recompense, but ample and bounteous reward for all the anxieties and dark moments. But I am not a fashionable person, and I am saying that now.

The degree of self-examination that is involved in being a writer, and the stringency of the writer's conscience, which holds you to a path that is often distasteful, necessarily takes you on some strange journeys, not only into the realm of the personal Unconscious, but into the level below that. It is assumed, by many people who have read Freud and Jung, that these descents must always be alarming experiences, because Freud and Jung were so much occupied with people who were very seriously disordered. But the writer is not necessarily disordered, and great rewards await him in this realm, if he approaches it with decent reverence. He will have serious struggles, but sometimes his struggles are like those of Jacob when he wrestled with the angel at Peniel, and cried in his extremity, "I will not let thee go, unless thou bless me." And he received the blessing, and bore it all his life. That realm of the Unconscious, which is the dwelling place of so many demons and monsters, is also the home of the Muses, the abode of the angels. The writer, in his traffic with that realm in which dream, and myth, and fairy tale become mingled with the most ordinary circumstances of life, does not lack for rewards and very great rewards. Self-examination is stern and often painful, as Ibsen tells us in the verse I quoted to you, but it is not all bitterness.

I have spoken to you seriously, because I presume that you are serious people. Certainly I am one, though such reputation as I have as a writer rests—rests perhaps a little too heavily—on my qualities as a humorist. Never be deceived by a humorist, for if he is any good he is a deeply serious man, moved by a quirk of temperament to speak a certain kind of truth in the form of jokes. Everybody can laugh at the jokes; the real trick is to understand them.

I have spoken of the conscience of the writer, trying to give you some insight into what it is that distinguishes the writer by temperament, the writer who cannot help being a writer, from someone who may write very well, but who writes for a different purpose—to instruct, to explain, to criticize—and for whom therefore writing is a necessary technique rather than an all-absorbing art. If I have discouraged anyone, I am sorry, but honesty comes before even courtesy in such matters as this. And if I have made anybody look searchingly into himself, to determine whether or not he has the kind of artistic conscience I have described, I shall think myself greatly rewarded.

2

How I Write a Book

Many admirers of Davies's work wrote and asked him how he imagined, developed, and wrote a novel. He had the opportunity to answer these questions in an article for the *Toronto Star*, which was published on September 19, 1987. On a very hot August 18, he went to Massey College, which has no air conditioning, to begin his task. His daily diary entry provides a somewhat untypical picture of Robertson Davies at work:

Walk to the College in intense heat and arrive drenched, so I hang up my shirt and sit topless for the A.M. *Outside the CNE* [Canadian National Exhibition] *procession is marshalling, so there is much noise from bad, out-of-tune bands and shouting from organizers. I set to work and write my* Star *article.*

I suppose there must be as many ways of writing novels as there are authors, and in our time, when literacy is supposed to be in danger, there are hundreds of thousands of authors. Industry, though praiseworthy, will not produce a good book, and an author who drinks, drugs, womanizes, and gambles, will not, for those reasons, produce a bad one. If you really mean to write a book you will find your own way of doing it.

Nevertheless countless people, many of whom wish to become authors, want to know how an author works. The *Star* has asked me to tell you how I work, I wish the answer were more interesting.

Very briefly, what I do is this: I yield to a theme, I ponder over it, I make a mass of notes, then I begin writing and write every morning from 9:30 until 12:30, Sunday included, until the book is done; I have it professionally typed, I revise the text rigorously, then I have it retyped and send it to my agent, who sends it to the publishers and takes care of all the business arrangements. All told it takes about three years.

Sounds simple and clear, doesn't it? But let us look a little more closely.

I said I "yielded" to a theme. Like all writers, I get great numbers of letters and many of them are from students who ask, bluntly, "Where do you get your ideas from?" The answer, which they are reluctant to believe, is that I do not "get" ideas; ideas get me. I do not invent plots; they arise in my mind, beginning usually with some mental picture that will not go away. It demands to be examined and thought about. And as I think about it something like a plot emerges. It is not always a plot that I particularly like, but it likes me and won't go away.

That is why I have written to countless aspiring writers that if they do not have any ideas that demand to be written about, perhaps they should consider seriously whether writing is the life for them. In the words of my old friend, Nicholas Goldschmidt, "In the world of art, if you haven't got it, you've had it."

Did I say I "pondered"? Yes, I did, and I know it sounds pretentious, as if "think about" would not be grand enough for what I do. But "pondered" is the right word, because I do not *think* coherently about my theme. I let it present itself in a variety of shapes, and offer me characters and situations I know I cannot use. Then, as the pondering becomes more and more insistent, I begin to make notes, and that is often the longest part of the work of writing a novel. I try to be tidy about the notes, numbering and indexing them in a special book, and sometimes the notes fill 150 or 200 closely written pages. As the notes swell in number I read them over, and wonder what I can make of them. Because, somehow or other, a way must be found of telling the story.

This presents real difficulties and sometimes several methods will have to be explored before the right one declares itself. Shall it be first-person narration, and if so, shall there be more than one narrator? If this method is chosen, how do I deal with the problem that there are things in the story that no single person can know? Sometimes, as in *What's Bred in the Bone*, there are things no human being can know, but which the reader must be told, and then I have to call on spirits who have special knowledge. I have been sharply criticized for this, but if the critics can do it any other way, they are at liberty to try.

The method of narration is profoundly characteristic of the author, and no two authors have precisely the same character. Henry James is leisurely and profuse; Graham Greene is so compact as sometimes to be telegraphic. Who would wish either man to be other than what he is? Dickens whoops and guffaws and weeps in print; Thackeray is coolly ironic, and both are right. Tolstoy seems not to know when to shut up; Stendahl measures out his narrative like an apothecary. Flaubert agonizes over every word and Trollope writes his daily stint without, apparently, crossing out a line. Both have their immense virtues. Balzac intrudes his personality on every page, and E.M. Forster hides himself behind a veil, but a single, unattributed paragraph would enable us to identify either man. Only critics, those great and good men, would wish any author to write in a way other than his own. As the Welsh proverb has it, we must sing with the voices God gave us.

My own way of writing has been called, in a very complimentary phrase, magic realism—a mingling of realism based on close observation with elements which most people find quite out of this world, though not out of the world as it appears to me. I write of life as I perceive it to be, and luckily for me quite a large number of readers, in several languages, want to hear about it.

Then comes the actual writing. If I have suggested above that I am a pattern of industry, I only wish it were so. I try to write every day, but now and then I am tired, or written out, or even ill. I have never written a book in my life without having to pause for some wretched illness to take its course. This happens, I think, to everybody. Even Bernard Shaw, who presented himself to the world as a man without weaknesses and a monster of assiduity, reveals in his diaries (which we now have) that often he sat idle at his desk, utterly used up, eating boiled sweets, for which he had a childlike passion.

Then of course there is the Black Dog, the horrible, depleting depression to which Byron gave that name; when the Black Dog is on me, I look upon myself and curse my fate, and trouble deaf Heaven with my bootless cries. I have never known or heard of an author who was a stranger to the Black Dog.

Somehow, however, the book gets itself written, and now and then the passages written when the Black Dog was at his most malignant may be the best.

The book, once written, must cool off. That is while my secretary is at work. It takes quite a while for a typescript of five or six hundred pages to be transcribed in that neat, elegant, enviable professional form, in which every flaw is pitilessly revealed.

This is where the real fun begins. Revision! Cutting off some of the fat, but not all. Tightening and tidying. Making sure that the heroine does not have red hair on page 100 and raven locks on page 300. Catching shameful, pretentious mistakes, misquotations, and follies so stupid that the author blushes at them. Above all, shining up the vocabulary.

This does not mean substituting fancy words for common ones. More often it means substituting plain but strong words for flabby ones. It means giving every line of dialogue, so far as possible, the right flavour for whoever is speaking, and making the words spoken give the clue to how they are spoken, so that it is not necessary to fall back on nonsense like, "'Do you love me?' she wailed, clenching her hands till the nails drew blood from the flesh."

I try to write, so far as I can, dialogue in Standard English. Slang may be outdated by the time the book is in print, and attempting to write dialogue that suggests the speech of an uneducated person very quickly becomes patronizing. A word or two should be sufficient to show the level of literacy to which a character belongs. If the reader is attentive, a too-elegant expression, or a snatch of professional jargon, tells all that need be told.

Revision could go on indefinitely, and the author must know when to call a halt. Too much revision can ruin a book, just as too much kneading may spoil a loaf of bread.

After that, the fate of the book rests with its readers, and the author reflects that, if he is lucky, some of those readers have not yet been born.

What might keep it alive? Not being a bestseller, certainly. Try reading a few bestsellers of days gone by and see for yourself. Read *The Rosary* by Florence Barclay, or *If Winter Comes* by A.S.M. Hutchinson; bestsellers once, but who reads them now? What keeps a book alive is what Nabokov calls "the more or less irrational *shamanstvo* of a book"; the Russian word means enchanter quality. It is not essential in a bestseller, which is a commercial product, but a book must possess it if it is to live.

Writers, unless they have very bad habits, tend to live long lives, and go on writing so long as they can drag themselves to the—oh yes, the typewriter. I write on a machine, a simple affair; I don't want a word processor. I process my own words. Helpful people assure me that a word processor would save me a great deal of time. But I don't want to save time. I want to write the best book I can, and I have whatever time it takes to make that attempt.

I am old-fashioned enough to think that a book is a work of art. That is to say, the unique result of a unique temperament. Many are not, but that is what a real writer wishes to produce.

Art, as somebody—I think it was a Roman—has said, is long.

3

Jung and the Writer

Carl Gustav Jung, and his influence on Davies's work, was frequently acknowledged by Davies. Here, however, is one of the clearest tributes he was to make to Jung, and, since it was originally made in Sweden, it has not been widely disseminated.

Although Davies always maintained that he disliked travel, he managed to see a great deal of the world. For this 1989 lecture he went to the Gothenburg Book Fair in Sweden, where his publishers were promoting his latest novel, *The Lyre of Orpheus*. On the way back to Canada he gave the same lecture in London to The Society of Analytical Psychology on October 10, 1989, whose members may have been struck by his confession of mischief in the matter of defending his title *Fifth Business*.

On July 24, 1989, Davies wrote to a Swedish friend: *A very important reason why I have been so busy is that I am to visit Sweden in September to speak at the Gothenburg Book Fair (or should it be spelled Göteborg? Nobody will tell me). I gather that it is a very big fair and they have a great many speakers. My publishers are bringing me and Brenda from Canada for three days, I believe it is, and I am to speak on Torsdag 7 September, the program tells me, and my subject is "Jung and the Writer," which sounds very solemn, though I shall try not to be too heavy. But it is not exactly what could be called a humorous subject, and the program I hove received is full of funny pictures, so I hope the audience is not expecting a funny speech. But there will only be a few people present, I fear, because there are so many other things to attract the crowd. The star of the Fair, I gather, is to be a writer called Jackie Collins, of whom I have never heard. Do you know anything about her? But my publishers seem anxious to work me off my feet, and have sent me a long list of things I am to do, besides the speech.*

In his travel diary, Davies described the day of the lecture in Sweden, which was September 7, 1989: *Then at 4:00, my address on "Jung and the Writer" to a full attentive house. Chairman, Heidi von Born, a great enthusiast and a good speaker. She told me that, as a child, she had actually seen a flea circus: fleas pulled carts, duelled, etc. Says public health legislation put an end to this sort of show. My speech is listened to with extraordinary attention and seems to be a great success. All the Wahlström & Widstrand people very pleased and Mrs. Danielsson listened as the audience left and said the comment was remarkable. One woman said, "No I won't go home by tram: I want to walk and think about it." What could be better. Several children present me with scraps of paper for autographs: obviously don't know who I am and don't care. I sign "Jackie Collins" and they go away quite content. They presented me with flowers and a heavy wrought-iron candlestick: How do I get that home?—A rest and then dinner at an excellent restaurant: aquavit, caviar, and blinis; sole, Chablis, an ice, cognac, all of the best.*

You have been told that I am going to talk about "Jung and the Writer," and that is what I shall certainly do. But let me assure you that I do not mean to talk about C.G. Jung's psychology in detail and at length. Indeed, I am unqualified to do so, for, although I have read extensively in Jung's works, I have made no systematized study of them, and I am wholly lacking in that scientific quality of mind that would enable me to make them any clearer to you than would be the case if you read them for yourself. Indeed, a beautiful clarity and regularity is not characteristic of Jung's thought; he possessed an abundant, bountiful mind and a compelling curiosity which led him in a number of directions which dismayed his scientific colleagues and disgusted his master, Sigmund Freud, and was one of the reasons for the break between those two great men.

When I was a young man, I read extensively in Freud, and was captured and delighted by the elegance and apparent inevitability with which he reached his conclusions. But when I approached middle life I began to read Jung, and came under his spell, and have remained there ever since.

To explain why this was so, I must be perfectly honest with you. Indeed, I have resolved to be as honest as possible in everything I say to you, even when I have to speak of some very personal matters. The longer I studied Freud, the more I was repelled by his pessimism and the powerfully reductive trend of his thinking. I simply could not swallow the idea that sex was the dominating factor in human survival and in the human mind. As I looked about me I saw all kinds of people who appeared to live effective and even admirable lives without any discernible sexual concern, but I never met anyone who could go for a day without food without becoming deeply concerned with getting something to eat. To me it was obvious that self-preservation was the dominating force.

Perhaps this was a more personal reflection than I supposed. Critics have observed that my books are full of descriptions of meals, and people eating and drinking. But be that as it may, I thought Dr. Freud was stretching things farther than was justifiable by life as I saw it.

Also I was struck by the fact that all the commentators on Freud, all his disciples, could not deny themselves the satisfaction of saying nasty things about Carl Gustav Jung, and I determined to find out why this was so.

It did not take me long to make my discovery. Jung, though not as good a writer as Freud, possessed a far-ranging and, I must say, a poetical mind, and I found this deeply congenial to me as a writer. A psychological approach to the human mind and the human spirit which was generous toward the creative faculty suited me admirably, and in a humble way I became a Jungian. I should say at once that I have never been analyzed, either in the Jungian or the Freudian manner. I have not lost my high regard for Freud, whom I still think of as one of the greatest liberators of the human spirit in the history of our culture. But the cast of his mind—and every mind, great or modest in its scope, must have some broad determining attitude—was reductive, and when it came to the consideration of the creative faculty as it shows itself in art of all kinds, he simply said that he had to throw up his hands and declare himself vanquished. Not so Gustav Jung; he attacked the creative faculty and brought to bear upon it a mind that was primarily that of a scientist, but also that of a great humanist, and that was what I wanted.

I never thought that Jung was right and Freud was wrong, though I did think that Freud was most concerned with the sick mind, whereas Jung appeared to assume that the human mind, in its infinite variety, tended toward health and wholeness.

I must also tell you, because as I have said already I am anxious to be frank with you, that Jung appealed to me because he was, like me, brought up a Protestant—he a Lutheran and I a Calvinist—and Jung was a man who had in childhood lived in rural surroundings where there were all kinds of people and all kinds of animals; fields and trees and all the marvels of nature were everywhere about him, whereas Freud, despite his passion for mountain holidays, was a city man, and an overwhelming number of his patients seemed to be unhappy Viennese of the wealthy class. To a country-bred Calvinist of Celtic background, like myself, Jung's appeal was irresistible.

Nothing that has happened to me in the years since I was thirty-five or so, has shaken this loyalty. Indeed, since I began to approach the world as a writer, and to achieve some modest acceptance as a writer, everything has strengthened my fidelity to the Jungian approach.

This has been a source of strength to me, but it has also caused me a great deal of annoyance, because once it had become known that I was a student of Jung, large numbers of people have been quick to assume that I am nothing else. Studies of my writings have been published—a few of them even swollen to the length of books—that have demonstrated to the satisfaction of the authors that nothing I have written is not to be traced to that influence.

Many of the critics who think they know a great deal about me appear to know very little—certainly not enough—about Jung. Some of them have read extensively in Jung, but they have brought an unswervingly academic cast of mind to their reading. They are eager for certainties, and one of the things Jung makes very clear is that there are no certainties that are not personal certainties. These critics are looking for a system, and Jung is quick to insist that he is not a systematizer, but a man who in a large, general way, invites you to make up your own mind.

The learned critics have been by no means the worst of my trials. Education in North America has developed a deplorable tendency to invite very young and inexperienced schoolboys and girls to form opinions about aspects of life of which they have no personal experience. I have in my files—because I am one of those people who cannot bear to throw anything away—discussions of my books by children of sixteen and seventeen, in which they explain my books, and me, in terms of a Jungian system foisted on them by their teachers, who are not—I speak with the greatest moderation—people who know much about Jung. I receive, every year, a number of letters from schoolchildren who send me questions set down in lists—and ask me to answer them briefly and cleanly. To what Jungian type do I think that I belong? By what means do I apply the teachings of Jung to my writing? Are my characters constructed according to his typology? Some characters in my books seem to be hostile toward their mothers—what was wrong between me and my mother, and why? But this sort of interrogation does not end with letters. I receive telephone calls from students of all sorts wanting answers to questions their teachers have asked of them. (I should explain that in Canada, at least, teachers often tell their pupils that they will award specially high marks to anyone who has made direct contact with me and, so to speak, put me on the spot.) The most dismaying call of this kind came one night at nine o'clock from a youth of sixteen who said: "I've got to have this essay ready to hand in tomorrow morning, and I'm stuck. Can you give me some help with these-here Jungian archeotypes?" It was impossible to explain to him that no telephone conversation could help him; indeed, in his agony, I do not know what would have helped him except sudden and merciful death.

I assure you that I am not hostile to these children, but I refuse to strip myself naked and dance while they make films of the performance to show in their classrooms. As for the adult critics, I am totally floored by them. They have such marvellous certainty! Many of them appear to regard an author as an *idiot savant*—a wretch gifted in one realm, but wholly incapable of understanding what he does. But I know that writers understand very well what they do.

To put it briefly, in Jungian terms, a writer has unusual access to his Unconscious, and he has encouraged and developed that ability because it is in that way his best work is done.

That is the simple statement, and of course it calls for development. First of all, what is the Unconscious?

As the name implies, it is that area of the mind which is perpetually alive, which never sleeps, but is not directly involved in logical thought. It is the well in which memory of every kind, be it of experiences, feelings, fleeting impressions, things heard and said and, of course, of things read, is stored, not according to any logical plan, but in an *õlla podrída* in which things unknown and unrelated may come to the top, usually unexpectedly.

We all know what this is. It is the matter which floats across our consciousness when we are not thinking in a determined fashion about a particular subject. It can be embarrassingly trivial, or sentimental, or obscene; it can seize upon us unexpectedly, thrusting upward some idea, or criticism, or ill-timed joke. It is the thing that makes us laugh when our outward circumstances say that we should weep. It is the source of desires, or disloyalties, or bursts of anger or tenderness of which we have not previously been aware. Most of us thrust such fleeting wisps of thought back down into the Unconscious, with impatience or shame, because they seem to have nothing to do with the matter at hand. But they do—O, indeed they do—if we seize upon them and track them down, and ask them to yield up their secret. Which is what writers do.

J.B. Priestley once wrote that he was always amazed, and surprised, when he read that some writers—Dickens, for example—developed their plots, or were visited by their finest inspirations, when they were walking. He confessed that when he was walking he never thought in any coherent way, at all. His mind was like a cinema screen across which all sorts of odds and ends of irrelevant, unconnected trivialities passed in a perpetual foolish picture show. I know exactly what he meant. But I also know—and I think he knew as well—that some of a writer's best fishing in the Unconscious is done when that foolish picture show seems to be in command of his mind.

Coherent thought is not the only kind of thought, and perhaps it is not the most productive thought. It was Bertrand Russell, who certainly ought to have known what he was talking about, who said, "Intellect, except at white heat, is apt to be trivial."

If we hope to know someone well, we must have some access to his mind that goes beyond his intellectual approach to life. The characters in fiction who are most real to us are those whose thoughts as they related to his Unconscious mind are imparted to us. Hamlet's soliloquies tell us more about him than his conversations with his friends and enemies. Indeed, Hamlet's father's Ghost tells us more about Hamlet than about the Ghost. And in his extraordinary novel *Ulysses* James Joyce takes us into the character of Leopold Bloom by admitting us to some—not all, for that would be unendurably boring—but some of what Bloom allows to rise from his Unconscious as he walks about Dublin. And when Joyce permits us to overhear, so to speak, the mind of that simple, foolish, unhappy girl Gertie MacDowell, in the Nausicaa chapter, we learn how greatly the colour and the quality of her mind differs from that of Mr. Bloom, and a sense of the variety and complexity of human experience is made manifest to us in a manner that is truly wonderful. But the greatest marvel of all is the insight we are granted into the life of Mrs. Bloom, the former Marion Tweedie, in the final books of *Ulysses*, the Penelope chapter, which has been called one of the most extraordinary revelations of feminine psychology in all literature.

Certainly no one could pretend that James Joyce's command of such material came from a study of Jung. He did not, I believe, ever read a word of Jung, and his only contact with Jung was when he asked Jung to examine his greatly troubled daughter Lucia; in a later talk with Joyce, Jung said that in his opinion Lucia's grave illness was associated with her father's neurotic dependence on her. Joyce was furious, and never afterward ceased to speak ill of Jung. Obviously, no influence there. No, Joyce's insight into the workings of the Unconscious was a part of his gift as a writer, and all through the history of literature we come upon examples of writers with insight of this kind, centuries before depth psychology as a scientific study came into being.

There are writers other than Joyce who were contemptuous of all depth psychology, either Freudian or Jungian. The names of Evelyn Waugh and Vladimir Nabokov come instantly to mind. Were they fearful that their artistic gift was being "explained" and therefore diminished? They need not have feared. Both Freud and Jung were deeply respectful of the writer, and declared that the secret of artistic creation was beyond their power to explain.

But this chaos of memories and feelings and impressions we call the Unconscious is not all; it is merely the personal element in this Unconscious realm where creative work has its beginning. There is another and far deeper Unconsciousness which is not personal in the sense that it belongs to any single man or woman, but is the foundation of our common humanity. Jung has given it the name of the Collective Unconscious, and in it lies the memory and the instinct and the emotional structure of mankind, which exists in forms he calls archetypes. The word *archetype* has been dreadfully abused by people who think that it means, simply, a pattern. They do not distinguish between an archetype and a stereotype. An archetype is a pattern, certainly, but not in any simple sense; it is part of the inherited psychological structure of man and it is linked with instinct; the thing about it which is most difficult to grasp is that it cannot be identified in any single form and is evident only through its manifestations. You cannot nail it down but you can see what it does.

Archetypes were not original with Jung and he never pretended that they were. Plato was aware of them and wrote most eloquently about them, and they are recognized by his followers as Platonic Ideas. They are by no means simply literary or artistic in their nature and manifestation; they lie at the root of all that makes us human beings, rather than animals, though archetypal ideas are present in animals, as well.

For instance, I am told that day-old chicks will run to their mother for protection if you pass a hawk-shaped piece of cardboard over their pen, and cast the shadow of a hawk upon them. But if you pass the same shadow over them, but backwards, they are not interested. The hawk-shadow constellates in these not-very-intelligent little creatures an Archetype of Danger; and they respond at once. The archetypes that affect human beings are, understandably, vastly more complex.

Albert Einstein, the great mathematical physicist, was very much aware of the archetypal elements in his own work, and he called them "universal elementary laws." But for our purpose today, we shall speak of archetypes as they apply to the creative life of the writer. Access to these archetypes, which must necessarily be interpreted personally, is to be found in all literary production of the highest kind, which we define as classical.

The writings of Homer, of Virgil, of Dante, are full of archetypal apprehensions of the Hero-Struggle, of the Heroic Journey, of the Divine Woman. We find them everywhere in the plays of Shakespeare. In *Romeo and Juliet* and *Antony and Cleopatra* we find the archetype of—no, not of Romantic Love, for that seems to be a fairly new idea in the human psyche—but of Obsession, of Thralldom to another human creature. Doubtless we could find examples of that archetype in this room, if we chose to do so. The archetype of Ambition lies at the heart of *Macbeth*, and the archetype of Pride is fundamental to *Coriolanus* and *King Lear*. It is needless to multiply examples in Shakespeare. His access to the archetypal world is without equal.

A writer whose access to the world of Archetypes seems also to have been extraordinary, and whose work may be more familiar to such an audience as this, was Goethe. Put aside his poetry and his novels for the moment and think only of *Faust*, for it offers a superb example of both the personal and the collective realms of the Unconscious. In the first part of *Faust*, written when Goethe was at the beginning of his long life, it is the Personal Unconscious that dominates, but in the second part, which was the product of his maturity, we meet with a wealth of archetypal material from the Collective Unconscious which leaves us stunned, and often baffled by whatever we can grasp of its significance.

If there are Goethe scholars among you, I ask your forgiveness for this blunt approach to one of the supremely great works of Western literature. I am not sufficiently skilled in German to do more than stumble though the play in its original, but I have, of course, read many translations and I assure you that their value is directly concerned with the degree of understanding the translators have of the archetypal roots of what the poet has to say. Translators must be poets themselves, and fine poets, to make head or tail of that astonishing work. It has often been said that the second part of *Faust* cannot be successfully presented on the stage. I can only say that I have seen it brilliantly and lovingly acted, and it was one of the two or three supreme theatre experiences of my life.

Of modern exemplars of such access to the Collective Unconscious of mankind I shall not attempt to speak, but the name of James Joyce has already turned up, as it must, in this discussion, and perhaps some of you may recall a passage in Thomas Mann's *Memoirs of an Unpolitical Man*, which expresses with admirable brevity the characteristic attitude of the literary artist.

> The look that one directs at things [says Mann] both outward and inward, as an artist, is not the same as that with which one would regard the same as a man, but at once colder and more passionate. As a man, you might be well-disposed, patient, loving, positive, and have a wholly uncritical inclination to look upon everything as all right; but as an artist, your daemon constrains you to "observe"; to take note, of every detail that is characteristic, distinctive, significant, providing insights that are useful and relevant. You see these things as though you had no human relationship to the observed object whatever—coolly and deliberately—and in your work then, everything comes to light....

I invite you to take special heed of that phrase "coolly and deliberately." It is this apparent want of ordinary human charity and forgiveness, allied to intensity of feeling, that has won for many writers a reputation for being somewhat remote people; they see too deeply to be at all times agreeable companions, sharing the feelings of those around them. Unless they can learn to keep their mouths shut, and to reserve what they see for what they write, instead of letting it spill out in conversation, they can be ugly customers indeed, and when they are in the company of other writers they may sometimes be quarrelsome. They are too sensitive to be ordinary social beings, and unless they learn to wear a mask—such a mask as Thomas Mann wore, and which earned him a reputation as an extremely formal and reserved man—they can be difficult friends and uncomfortable companions. They are sometimes the prey of bad habits, of which heavy drinking is one of the commonest. The wives of authors—poor souls—know all about this.

Perhaps you are wondering, is he never going to tell us anything we did not know? This is like an introductory lecture on Jungian psychology. Do not be uneasy; I am going to tell you a few things now which are drawn from my personal experience, and which may give you an insight into how at least one writer goes about his business and the way in which these Jungian ideas relate to him. I assure you that I do not really wish to do so, I dislike personal confession, and as I have already told you, it sometimes leads overconfident people to think that they know me better than they do. But I said I would be honest with you; so here goes.

I shall talk for a while about my own work, and the way in which the processes I have spoken about manifest themselves in my writing.

I am very often asked, where do your writings originate? Schoolchildren phrase it more directly. They say: Where do you get your ideas? The answer, which is the most honest answer I can give, usually stops them in their tracks. I do not "get" my ideas—they "get" me. Let me offer an example.

In 1970 I published a novel called *Fifth Business*; it is still in print. People seem to like it very much, and some people study it in schools and universities. It had its beginning at least as early as 1960, and it did not appear as the germ of a novel or as a story of any sort. It came as a haunting image, which floated to the surface of my mind when I was idle, or sleepy, or bored, and it was always the same.

It was, as I say, an image or picture, and it was simple and clear. I saw a village street at night, in which two boys were fighting with snowballs; one boy threw a snowball which I knew had a stone concealed in it. He wanted to hurt his companion. He was devoured by spite and ill will. The loaded snowball was thrown, but it did not hit the boy at whom it was aimed; it hit a woman, who was severely hurt and who fell to the ground.

I did not pay much attention to this unexplained and idle fancy, but it kept reappearing until, after perhaps two years, I thought that I had better take a closer look at this image, and discover what it meant, and why it was so insistent. And that is what I did. I called up the image and invited it to tell me what it had to say. In a very short time the early part of the novel had taken shape in my mind. But it was not the story which eventually was written; as I first saw it, the story was about the husband of the woman who was hit by the loaded snowball, and whose child was born prematurely because of it, and who lost her reason because of the shock. This man was a parson, of a not very highly regarded Protestant sect, who was driven by this misfortune to devote his life to revenge on the boy who had destroyed his happiness. Revenge did not destroy his enemy, the boy, it destroyed the man himself.

But when I began to plan the story, it did not want to go in that direction at all. The emphasis was different. It wanted to be about the two boys who were fighting; it wanted to be about the child who was born prematurely because of their quarrel. It wanted to be about one of the boys whose whole life was dominated by his Calvinist feeling of guilt; the snowball which was meant for him had struck another, innocent person, and changed her life, and the life of her husband, the life of her child, so drastically that no such consequence could have been foreseen. And at last it influenced the life of the boy who had thrown the loaded snowball so that all his worldly success suddenly seemed valueless, and he died, whether by suicide or murder, in a characteristically spectacular way. As for the premature child, it made him a very unusual and special person.

It was a story of vengeance, but it was not the simple vengeance that I had at first foreseen, where the wronged parson sought the death of his child's enemy, and eventually brought about his own death. No: This was the vengeance of Fate, of Destiny, and it took more than fifty years to complete its spiderweb of events.

Vengeance, however, does not occur without some agency to bring it about. Who was the agency? It was the first boy, at whom the snowball had been thrown. Without doing anything directly about the matter, it was nonetheless his undying remembrance of that wicked action, and his weight of guilt because he thought that he was directly responsible for the misery of the mother and her unfortunate child, that eventually brought about the death of the evildoer. Or did it? He never knew, and nobody could even say with certainty quite what had happened, but somehow vengeance was demanded and achieved for the spiteful act of a thoughtless child.

Thus it became obvious to me that the boy acted the role of Fifth Business in the drama of my story.

What is Fifth Business? To explain that, let me pause for a moment and tell you a story which will throw some light on the psychology of at least one author, and also on the psychology of publishers, who are a very special class of people, as everybody at the Gothenburg Book Fair knows very well.

To me *Fifth Business* was the only possible title for the book, but it troubled the publishers who thought nobody would understand it. It is a theatrical and operatic term, used to describe the role in a play or an opera which is not the leading role—not the hero or heroine, the villain or the villainess—but is that of the man who explains the plot, and helps the plot along but who is not himself a leading figure in the plot; such a person used to be called the *raisonneur* in the French theatre. My book was about a man who played the part of Fifth Business in the plot, and I wanted to show what a very interesting person Fifth Business might be, if you examined him closely. But the publishers shook their heads.

The English publisher was especially troubled. "If only you could provide some satisfactory definition, right at the beginning of the book," he said, "something that would help the reader. Indeed," he said, "I must insist that you do that or I really do not think I can agree to publish the book."

So there I was. I had to have an authoritative definition and, as it happened, I had to have it within twenty-four hours. Was I stumped? Did I fail? I did not. The next morning I handed him this definition, which has appeared in every subsequent edition and translation of the book:

> Those roles which, being neither those of Hero, Heroine, Confidante, or Villain, but which were nonetheless essential to bring about the Recognition or denouement, were called the Fifth Business in drama and opera companies

organized according to the old style; the player who acted these parts was often referred to as Fifth Business.

The quotation was attributed to the Danish theatre historian Thomas Overskou, in his valuable work *Den Danske Skueplads*.

The publisher was overjoyed. He did not know that *Den Danske Skueplads* had never been translated into English, and that I knew no Danish. He did not know that in the succeeding twenty years a number of toilsome scholars would seek for that quotation in Overskou's many volumes, without ever being able to find it. He did not know that a considerable number of other scholars would accept the quotation as something Overskou might very well have written if he had thought of it. Nor did he, in spite of his great experience, appear to understand that writers are children of the god Mercurius or, as Thomas Mann has explained at length, that they have a strong element of the Trickster in them, and that if you ask them for a quotation they are very likely to provide you with one, and it will be just what you want. He did not understand that a novelist is a writer of fiction, and that not all the fiction may be confined to his books. The writer's mind is ambiguous in its deepest nature, and it is this quality of ambiguity which makes him a writer.

Ambiguitas is the adjective which Ovid applies to Proteus, whose gift it was to assume different shapes, in order to avoid being questioned. Never ask an author too many questions or you may get answers that you cannot wholly trust.

Why is that? Is it because the author is, to put it bluntly, a crook? No, I think it is because the author's access to his Unconscious makes him constantly aware of how deceptive even the world of seeming fact may be. If you doubt me, ask any honest judge how much of the evidence he hears in court is contradictory, even when the witnesses believe every word they are saying.

Now let us return to the writing of that novel *Fifth Business*, the origin of which I have explained. Did the story appear to me complete in form and detail? I have already explained that when I began to write the book the emphasis of the plot proved to be different from what I had expected when I wrote out a rough plan of the first few chapters. Nor did the plot come to me complete. It developed as I wrote, and I assure you that at the beginning I did not know how it would end. Of course I knew that by the end of the book the villain—if you want to call him that—would receive what is called in English, Poetic Justice—which means that he would have to pay for his evil act, though it had taken place fifty years earlier.

The foundation of the book, you see, is the belief I have long held, and which was impressed on me in my Calvinist childhood, that no good action is ever lost—and that no evil action is ever lost, either. Because I believe a work of fiction must be drama, the stone which so powerfully influenced so many lives when it was wrapped in that snowball, appeared at last to play a part in the death of the man who had thrown it. When I began the book I did not know how that would happen, but I trusted that I would find out. And so I did.

It is this sort of explanation, I know, which persuades some critics that an author is indeed an *idiot savant*, who does not know what he is doing. But that is a misunderstanding of the creative process. The author may not know consciously every detail of his story when he begins it, but his Unconscious knows, and it is from the Unconscious that he works. And if he is writing *Fifth Business* he must be aware that the Archetype of Retribution—of the Scales of Justice—is at work in the depths of his being. I say "being" rather than mind, because I believe that a writer's work is the product of the totality of his being, which invents far more effectively than the logical surface of his thought.

As I talk to you in this way, I fear that some of you may be saying to yourselves: "Ah, yes, it is just as we thought; these Jungians are mystics." I assure you that is not so. Gustav Jung was no mystic; indeed, he often spoke of himself as an empirical scientist, and if you read some of his case histories you will understand why. I am certainly no mystic, but because I am a writer, and have given my best energies to that form of art, I have learned to trust some of my mental processes, to approach them with confidence. I assure you that I do not warm myself at fantastic fires and dance in the light of glow-worms. I do nothing that great numbers of people do not do, but I pay attention to what my Unconscious says to me. Let me give you another example.

When I was writing *Fifth Business* and was about halfway through the book, I became aware that I knew a great deal more about my characters than could be suitably included in the novel which was in progress. I realized that I was writing about three men—the one who was called Fifth Business and whose life had been utterly changed by the accident with the snowball, but also about the boy who threw the snowball, and who had lived what he considered an enviable and successful life, until he came to the end of the road; and there was also the third man, the child who had been born prematurely as a result of the unlucky snowball, and whose life took a course that nobody could have predicted, because he became world-famous in an unusual profession. I must tell their stories, I decided, as those stories were already lying around in my mind, in bits and pieces, waiting to be put together.

But when I began the second book, I found myself in a difficulty. That rich successful man could never tell his own story, for he knew too little about himself to have any genuine insight; therefore I decided to tell about his life as it affected the life of his son, who was a victim of his unreflecting admiration for his father. But who was this son? He was a lawyer, and a brilliant one; a true gladiator of the court-room. He was also a drunkard, and did not know why. What indeed was he?

The answer came to me in what, for want of a more accurate word, I must call a vision. Yet I dislike using the word *vision*, for it plays into the hands of those people who do not have visions, and think that those who do are not quite rational. But there it was—one summer's day, I was sitting looking out over the valley which lies below my house, when a strange creature appeared, quite close to me. It was an animal of some sort, for it had a lion's body and mane, but it had a long tail with a forked end like a scorpion, dragon's claws, and—the face of a man. The man, moreover, whom I knew at once to be the hero of my story. This was a manticore, a fabulous beast to which I had never given any particular thought. This extraordinary creature was being led on a golden chain by a beautiful woman, in classical dress. These are not precisely the visitors one expects in the middle of a Canadian landscape. They remained with me for perhaps two or three minutes, and when they vanished I had my story and my character complete. My hero was not wholly a man, for he was as fierce as a lion, as venomous as a scorpion, as incalculable as a dragon—and yet he had the face of a deeply unhappy man. The beautiful woman, I knew, was leading him to his salvation, where the animal and mythical elements in his nature would be integrated into a whole and true human being. And so it was. I wrote the book, and called it *The Manticore.* Once again the publishers were not sure what to do with such a strange title, but this time they did not ask me for a quotation to explain it; they could look up "manticore" in any good dictionary, and discover that it was a fabulous beast.

These creative adventures of mine are not, I assure you, improved upon or touched up to make a good story. I tell them to you exactly as they happened. Is this what happens to all writers? Certainly not in the same way, but I am certain that all writers worthy of the name have flashes and intuitions from the Unconscious which are basic to their work. We have all read books which are purely invented—by which I mean that the writer has determined to write a story and has made one up by logical processes. Sometimes they work beautifully, like a good watch; detective stories, at their best, belong to this sort of writing. But they do not grip the reader, and give him flashes of insight about his own life; they do not enlarge his imagination or his sense of the astonishments and splendours that rise from the Unconscious to meet those who welcome them. Jung called these logically constructed works of literature "psychological" and he distinguished them from what he called "visionary writing."

Jung had some extremely interesting things to say about visionary writing, and the unseen current that seems to sweep the writer along when he is working at his best. He spoke of the social significance of literature, constantly at work educating the spirit of the age, conjuring up forms in which the age is most lacking. And indeed this applies to all the arts; much of the mystery of modern painting rises from the determination of the painter to show the world something that the world is deeply reluctant to see. And Jung says, "art"—he was speaking of literature but it applies to all arts—"art represents a process of self-regulation in the life of nations and epochs."

This process, however, should not be pushed to absurd and simple-minded extremes. At present there is a great vogue for the sort of writer who is described as *engagé*, which too often means that he writes a kind of superior journalism about the troubles of his times. Certainly admirable books have been written from inside knowledge of a world situation, or from a burning indignation at some contemporary injustice. But when the world situation has changed or the injustice been dispelled, or given a different form, these books seem to dwindle in their effect. It was Jorge Luis Borges who said, very truly, that of all the obligations that an author can impose upon himself, the most common and doubtlessly most harmful is that of being "modern." To write in the very latest style, about the most impressive contemporary theme, sounds convincing indeed, but unless the writing rises from the only true fountain of inspiration—and the Unconscious has shown itself to be not timely, but timeless—it will not be first-rate.

Once again I quote James Joyce to you. He said, "The supreme question about a work of art is out of how deep a life does it spring?" He did not mean how philosophically trained a life, or how extensively educated a life, but a life that was deep in self-knowledge and heedful of what that painfully acquired self-knowledge had to tell the writer who had fought for it. You remember that Ibsen said that life was a struggle with trolls, but the trolls may be persuaded to yield deep secrets. They may, to some heroes of the inner struggle, yield what Jung spoke of as "primordial experiences"—secrets from the depths of human spirit.

I spoke earlier of the questions that schoolchildren ask me. I return to these questions often because they are innocent; they are not cloaked in layers of literary theory. They often ask me: Are you religious? When I talk to them, and try to get to the bottom of their question, I find that they meet with things in my books which they cannot account for except as being associated with religion. But when I ask them, "Are *you* religious?" they often deny it, because they have the modern notion that to be religious means that one believes a lot of things that are plainly untrue. I explain to them that I must certainly call myself religious, but that the things I believe are indeed true, and I have seen them at work during what I must now agree has been a long life.

What does the word *religious* really mean? It comes from a Latin word which means to take care, to pay heed, to give thought to something. That is the word *religere*, which is the opposite of *neglegere*, from which our word *neglect* comes—to ignore, to close one's eyes to things, to live on the surface of life. Therefore I tell my inquirers that to be religious—at least as I interpret the word—is to be attentive, concerned, careful, and to look at life through eyes that are as clear as one can make them, and to bring conscientious scruple and a measure of intuition to whatever life presents to one's experience. Of course the word now means to give heed to godly matters, but I stick with the older meaning, and I am encouraged once again by Albert Einstein, who said that in our day the scientist is the truly religious man, because he has trained himself to neglect nothing, to set nothing aside as trivial, because the truth may lie hidden under a mass of triviality. But the artist, and as you know from what I have been saying, I consider the writer, if he takes his work seriously, to be very much an artist, is also religious in his attention to everything, and his willingness to see everything as a manifestation of the human spirit, which is itself a manifestation of God and God's will. This is tough chewing for very young people, to whom the very word *God* is irrelevant to what they think they know. They suppose that to be religious is to live under a yoke of codified beliefs which exclude or reject many things they think important. But the truth is very far from anything of that sort. The religious man is the man who tries, insofar as he can, to see everything as clearly as he can, even when what he is observing is shrouded in ambiguities. He understands that he cannot expect to understand everything, but he dare not ignore anything that lies within the scope of his vision, or that rises from the realm of the Unconscious.

When he has looked as clearly and as deeply as he dares, does he then slap down everything he has discerned on paper, and offer it to the world? No: Indeed he does not. He must present his vision of life in terms of his art, with all the skill in language, all the tact, all the special quality that marks it as his own. He may choose to write in the tragic mode, if that is where his gift lies. Or he may write in the humorous mode, which will certainly expose him to misunderstanding and probably to accusations of triviality. But he must go in the direction to which his gift guides him.

You see, I have now come to the point where I must use the word *gift*, which means no more in this context than that some people are born to be writers and some are not. We live in an age when many universities and schools offer instruction in what they call "Creative Writing." I cannot, however hard I try, convince myself that any teacher can show somebody else how to be creative, though of course he may uncover and encourage a creative gift if it already exists. Anybody who wishes to do so may enter into a friendly association with his Unconscious, but that will not make him a writer. Dredging up stuff from the Unconscious may put some ingredients on the kitchen table, but without a gifted cook it will never be turned into a meal that anybody wants to eat.

So, at the end, we find ourselves where Freud and Jung found themselves when they confessed that they had no explanation for the creative gift. We know a little more about it, perhaps, but we have not trapped its secret and we cannot give the secret to anybody else.

A modern writer who is much admired—though I confess that my own enthusiasm for him is well-controlled—used a Russian word to speak of the writer's gift. That was Vladimir Nabokov, and the word he used was *shamanstvo.* A Russian friend tells me that it means the quality of the enchanter, the magician, the worker of wonders. It does not mean the stage conjuror, who has a repertoire of clever tricks. It means the *shaman* who by gift and training is the source through which important things are imparted to his tribe.

The writer, if he is a serious writer, man or woman, tragedian or comedian, writer on epic themes like Tolstoy or on apparently slight themes, like Jane Austen, is one who brings great and important things for the consideration of his tribe. And he speaks to those of the tribe who are disposed to share his vision.

My theme, you remember, was "Jung and the Writer." Gustav Jung brought some very important things for the consideration of the whole world, but it does not lie in his power to make anyone a writer. But he may help you to a better understanding of your work, if you are a writer to begin with.

4

The Novelist and Magic

The University of Toronto, where Davies taught for twenty years, is the setting for several of his novels, most notably *The Rebel Angels* and *The Lyre of Orpheus*. Beginning with a reference to Michael Bliss, a solidly non-fictitious History Professor, and to a parallel lecture by the home-grown novelist Margaret Atwood, this particular lecture was very much a University of Toronto event, given as part of the Wiegand Lecture series there. Yet from that local base Davies takes the listener (and now the reader) on an astonishingly far-ranging tour. Few now remember a 1953 film (set on "a campus not unlike our own") entitled *Monster on the Campus*. Yet that film is engagingly described, along with *Faust*, *Hamlet*, *The Old Curiosity Shop*, *War and Peace*, Huxley and Joyce, not to mention the beliefs of Freud and Jung, as Davies's imagination takes wing, clearly inspired by the theme of magic.

Equally fascinating is his revelation of his own encounter with magic. Few of his readers will be aware of the vision that gave the central image, and indeed the title, to his novel *The Manticore*.

His diary records his pleasure at the success of the speech on November 8, 1989, when he was introduced by the former President of the University, Claude Bissell. It also reveals—amazingly—his shy belief that, at the age of seventy-six, he has finally mastered the art of public speaking: *To the auditorium of the Medical Building, which is crammed to the doors and people sitting on the stage. Give my Wiegand Lecture to great applause; Brenda says I have never been better, and*

Claude Bissell, who introduced me, said he had never heard me better. Worked like a Percheron, and got very hot, but the material was good and every point told. At last I feel that I have passed my test as a public speaker.

When I was invited to give this lecture Professor Bliss told me that you were to hear Miss Margaret Atwood talk about the novelist and science, and that you would like me to talk about the novelist and magic. Miss Atwood's task, though not an easy one, was clear; many novelists have written about science, including Miss Atwood herself. As well she may do, for she has a family background in science, as did Aldous Huxley, who introduced scientific material into almost every novel he wrote. I remember from my school days the interest that was caused by Sinclair Lewis's novel *Arrowsmith* (1925) which described in detail the temptations and travails of a young scientist; a great many medical students saw themselves in Martin Arrowsmith, for scientists, in their tenderer moments, are by no means immune from the soft solicitations of fiction. But I know virtually nothing of science, and have only once introduced a scientist into the cast of characters in a novel of mine. That was Professor Ozias Froats, who appears in *The Rebel Angels*; his special interest was in human faeces, which he hoped to prove was a much more important diagnostic element than had been previously considered. I know that my portrait of Ozy Froats caused some laughter among scientists, and some indignation, as well. Yet I had a good source for my idea—no less than a statement of Sir William Osler, about his use of this despised substance in the diagnosis of tuberculosis, and his intuition that it might yield much greater information to a determined researcher. And to my delight, just after that book had appeared, a friend of mine who is a medical man told me that some work on this very subject had recently attracted attention. But I know why my scientific readers laughed: My description of Professor Froats's experiments was not scientific, but novelistic; it was written to be comprehensible to readers who might have no scientific knowledge whatever, but who must be persuaded by me that Professor Froats was a great man, with a great idea. It was written also to illustrate one of the themes of the novel, which was that value and beauty are often found in places that people ignorantly despise. I needed an unrecognized great man in my story, and I had to make him great in my own way.

That was certainly the method of the novelist. But had it anything to do with magic? I suppose that is what I am to talk about now.

As I presume that a great many of you are scientists, you will expect me to define my terms. What is science? I put the question last summer to an old friend of mine who is a distinguished gastroenterologist. I expected that it might take him some time to answer, but nothing of the sort. He replied at once. "Science is the systematic study of nature," said he. Admirable. What, then, is magic? A possible definition is that magic is an attempt to control nature. When the witch of olden days put her evil spell on the beautiful princess, she attempted to control nature and destiny, and in the story she succeeded. When Macbeth sought out the Weird Sisters to discover what the future held for him, there was much mumbo-jumbo with "fillet of a fenny snake … eye of newt and toe of frog" which was perfectly justified, psychologically, because it helped to focus the occult powers of the witches and to deepen the credulity of Macbeth. Here again was the theme of value concealed in what seemed to be disgusting. The Witches were trying to control nature, and in the drama they did so very effectively. An Indian Rain Dance is an attempt to control nature, and I am told that it sometimes brings rain. Prayer of any sort is an attempt to control nature, and he would be a bold man indeed who declared that prayer was at all times ineffectual. But I must beware, if I can, of getting into the misty ground where magic and religion mingle, for that belongs to another lecture and I have no intention of giving it.

Does the novelist seek to control nature? Sometimes he does, for the novelist feels himself free to use anything that is needed by his story. Why he makes this grandiose claim is something that I shall talk about later. For the moment, let us look at a few instances in which a novelist has asserted something as a fact which is demonstrably untrue from a scientific point of view. But the novelist has made his point, which is not precisely scientific, unless you are prepared to regard psychology as a science. I shall address that subject later, as well.

Let us make a start with a novel which may not be familiar to everyone here, but which was enormously popular for at least fifty years after it appeared in 1894. It is *Trilby*, by Georges du Maurier. It sold innumerable copies, it became an extremely successful play, and it has been made into at least two movies. It is the story of a beautiful artist's model in Paris, named Trilby O'Farrell, who has a splendid voice but nobody can bear to hear her sing because she has no ear. Trilby's singing is a joke until she falls under the influence of an evil German-Polish musician named Svengali who demonstrates that when he has hypnotized Trilby she can be made to sing not merely in tune, but with the most exquisite musical taste—which is, of course, Svengali's. Between them they make an immense musical sensation, and have all musical Europe at their feet, until at a concert Svengali dies of a heart attack while conducting the orchestra, and at once Trilby begins to sing in her old, off-key, stupid manner, and is hooted from the stage.

This is the ever-popular story of the charismatic genius who achieves his fulfillment through another person, and of the woman who is incomplete without the man who evokes her finest qualities. The public eats it up, and very properly so because although it is not science it is magic, and people—I venture to say even some scientists—have a great appetite for magic.

Georges du Maurier wrote another very popular story called *Peter Ibbetson* (1891) in which a pair of lovers, who are separated by an unhappy fate, are able to meet and express their love in their dreams. The public was enchanted by it, and it became the theme of an opera.

Why were these books so popular? Because they gave convincing expression not to what was demonstrably true, but to *what the public wished were true.* People love to attribute demonic powers to hypnotists, who know how limited, though medically useful, their powers are. It could even be said that *Peter Ibbetson* was prophetic, for it is a commonplace of our day that people who have been widely separated may converse and, I suppose, make love, by means of the telephone. Nobody calls that magic nowadays, because once a magical wish, or a miracle, has been made available to everyone, it is no longer magical.

Another story in this category, still popular and known to every literate person, is R.L. Stevenson's *Dr. Jekyll and Mr. Hyde*, which appeared in 1896, before Sigmund Freud had demonstrated by psychoanalysis the extraordinary duality of man's nature. You remember it. The admired medical man, Dr. Henry Jekyll, discovers a potion which turns him into a creature wholly evil, who acts out, as we now believe, the submerged and inadmissible side of the perfect doctor's nature. It is a Freudian tale, and it is also a Calvinist tale, for, as I hope to mention later, there is nothing in depth psychology which was not known to theologians and literary artists for centuries before Dr. Freud gave it a scientific ground.

The popularity of Stevenson's tale is not hard to explain. Most of us are aware of, and frightened by, the figure of Mr. Hyde in ourselves. We keep Mr. Hyde safely in the cellar-dungeon, but from time to time we hear his murmuring, and now and then he escapes. Every day in the pages of the newspapers, we read of the exploits of somebody's Mr. Hyde. As readers of Stevenson's great story, we like to play somewhat dangerously with the terrible insight it contains.

We are all aware of the modern literary genre of Science Fiction, though we may not read it. It had its beginnings long ago, but it came into extraordinarily sharp focus with some novels at the beginning of this century written by H.G. Wells. When we read them now, we are astonished at their amazing prophetic quality. *The War of the Worlds* (1898) is about an invasion from Outer Space, which is a favourite bugaboo of millions of newspaper readers today. *The Time Machine* (1895) tells of travel through time, which is still unachieved, but who is to say when it will become a fact? *The Food of the Gods* (1904) tells of a biological catastrophe, and every day we are warned of just such horrors that will come if we do not immediately mend our ways and check our wholesale pollution. *The War in the Air* (1908) is very much a horror of our time.

Let us permit ourselves a brief digression, which is, however, not wholly without relevance to our subject of the novel and magic. I do not know much about Science Fiction, but I am told by those who do that some of its products are admirably written and rooted in science which does not outrage the spirit of genuine scientists. But there is a vast amount of Science Fiction on a lower level, which dribbles off into Science Fiction films and has an active life in SciFi Comics and Horror Comics, and these things number their audience in millions. What they exploit is not science, but the fears and the dreams which are only partly admissible of people whom I must call illiterate, although I know that in doing so I offend those people who are devoted to the principle that all people are created equal, and that what I call literacy is just a kind of academic snobbery. But these people of whom I speak are the very people who, in an earlier day, found food for their dreams in a crass form of religion. They were the people who invented and embraced tales of miracles worked by holy images, of visions vouchsafed to simple folk who were assured by a saint or even some more elevated religious figure that they would be cured of their ills, or that some extraordinary disaster would happen if there were not a widespread repentance among the faithful. Let me assure you at once that I am not deriding miracles or cures produced by faith, but I am expressing my incredulity about the frequency and the mechanical nature of their operation.

Only last year I visited a church in the Southern United States, which contained the mummified body of the bishop who had built the church. The body was covered with pieces of paper on which the people who made up the church's congregation had written their prayers for restored health. According to your ailment, you pinned your supplication to the relevant part of the body—for migraine, the head, for rheumatism, the hip, for weak heart, the breast, and so forth. I was assured that countless cures were achieved in this way, if the messages to the saint were accompanied by an appropriate gift of money.

Did I leave that church with my nose in the air, despising the simple folk and their wonder-working image? No, I most certainly did not. Those people had faith, and they knew what to do with their faith. The people I pitied, without despising them, were their innumerable fellow citizens who have no focus for their faith, but in whom the roots of faith are still alive, and who seek hungrily and foolishly for something to do with the power they feel, but do not—even in the vaguest and most superstitious sense—understand.

These are the people who, in New York, visit a sort of supernatural supermart, not far from Wall Street, where there is a collection of astrologers, numerologists, occultists, and other wonder-workers who will, for fifteen dollars for fifteen minutes, give you a "reading" and advice about your love life and your career and your most intimate problems. Who visits them—because the place is crowded every noon hour? I have it on the authority of *The New Yorker* magazine that a great part of their clientele is drawn from young workers in Wall Street, who say that it is as good as a visit to your analyst, and very much cheaper.

I speak of New York, but of course this sort of thing is found everywhere. Not long ago on Bay Street a small boy, whom I judged to be of Hispanic origin, pressed upon me a handbill advertising the services of a lady who would tell me my most intimate secrets and rearrange my life on very favourable terms. And the Personal columns of our newspapers contain advertisements promising everything the world of irresponsible magic can afford.

What is it these faithless, deprived people want? You do not have to read hard volumes of philosophers to find out. Read the comic strips; go to the cheaper sort of movies, and you will find out at once. They want marvels. They want magic, and they have put behind them the faith of their fathers which offered them marvels and magic, as much as they could absorb, linked to a firm ethical teaching.

I am a keen moviegoer. Sometimes I go for art, sometimes for well-planned narrative or adventure, and sometimes to find out what my fellow creatures desire in their heart of hearts.

In this latter category I have long remembered a film, made in 1953, called *Monster on the Campus*. The scene was a campus not unlike our own, and one of its admired figures was a brilliant young biologist. There may be some of his kind in this audience. His future was glorious, not only in his profession, but in the realm of love, for he loved and was loved in return by the President's daughter. Their love was pure. That is to say, it went no further than the mauling and face-chewing which Hollywood considers pure but interesting. Need

I say she was a blonde? Indeed, her blondness may have been more authentically scientific than any other element in the film. It was the good fortune of the young biologist to receive from the East Indies a specimen of extraordinary scientific interest; it was a coelacanth, which we were told was a fish long thought to be extinct, and therefore a relic of primeval times. When the crate containing this monster was unloaded at the laboratory, some nasty-looking juice leaked out of it, and a passing dog lapped it up. Later that day the dog became uncontrollable—a ravening monster—and had to be shot. Nobody except the audience put two and two together, but we in the audience shrewdly caught the inference. We were not astonished, therefore, when the young professor, opening the crate, accidentally caught his arm in the coelacanth's jaws, and received a tiny bite; like a good scientist he put a Band-Aid on it and thought no more of the matter. But oh!—brace yourselves for this—when next the moon was at the full the campus was invaded by a primitive creature, not to be described as human, who terrified everybody. The police could not catch him, for he had a great turn for tree climbing and jumping on the roofs of buildings. This monster, it appeared, had an unappeasable appetite for blondes, and it was not long before the President's daughter found herself in his loathsome embrace. The police had no alternative but to shoot him. As he lay on the ground, seemingly dead, he underwent a transformation. Slowly the caveman gave place to the handsome young biologist. The President's daughter, looking as bereft as it is given to a Hollywood blonde to look, hung over him as an elderly scientist explained that the evil juices of the coelacanth must have infected him and, at the full of the moon, returned him to an era unimaginably older than our own, when the appetite for blondes was less perfectly under control.

The audience in whose company I encountered this piece seemed well pleased with it. They had had a dose of science, and they had also been given a strong shot of magic.

I may say that this appetite for blondes among primitives is powerfully evinced in the popular film *King Kong*. Are we to assume from this indirect evidence that it is not really gentlemen who prefer blondes?

Even so absurd a work of science fiction as the film I have just described to you includes a few scientific trappings and exploits the modern notion that the world of wonders is now to be approached by priests in white coats, rather than magicians in conical hats and robes embroidered with signs of the zodiac. But in all of these tales, good and bad, the marvels are likely to happen to a single person or to a small group of persons. That is what seems to me to be unscientific about them. Surely a scientific fact must be authenticated by scores, by hundreds, of experiments which all yield, if not precisely the same result, results which are near to being identical? But when the Blessed Virgin appears to a group of children at Lourdes, we cannot demand that she reappear to people of all sorts until the scientific world is satisfied. The unscientific man or woman wants some marvel which applies to him alone; he does not concern himself with what his neighbours feel about it. And it is here, I think, that the magic of the novel, or the play, or the poem, satisfies a deep longing in the human breast. It is wholly personal.

When the Ancient Mariner suffers his long misery after the slaughter of the albatross, we do not demand that at least eighty percent of the personnel of the British Navy suffer a similar anguish of the soul before we believe in it. When, in the second part of *Faust*—I mean Goethe's *Faust* and not the popular opera—Dr. Faust encounters a whole world of archetypal figures who carry him into realms of experience to which only a supremely great poet holds the key, we do not require that every doctoral student in science undergo the same revelations. When Hamlet encounters his father's ghost we do not call for a Gallup poll to discern how many men have seen the ghost of their respective fathers. These marvellous revelations, which come deep from the soul of man, are embodied in literature as the experiences of single people, and we are ready to share their enlightenment without demanding what would be called scientific truth to back them up. We, as single readers or playgoers, share these experiences willingly, and regard them as valid insofar as they strike some responsive chord in ourselves. Why are we willing to do this?

Now we are getting into deep water, and not everybody is willing or able to swim in it without a lifebelt. In the early days of the

Christian church, one of the church fathers asserted that the soul of man was naturally Christian. I cannot agree with him, but I am convinced that the soul of man is naturally religious. And very properly you will require me to say what I mean by that.

Let us begin with the word *religion*. What does it mean? There are two popular derivations. One is from the Latin verb *religare*, which means to tie, to fasten, to assume a yoke. People who accept that derivation think of religion as adherence to a creed, a system of belief which dictates conduct and man's approach to the unseen world. But there is another derivation, which cannot be dismissed, from the verb *relegere*, which means to consider, to ponder, to examine and this is the derivation I myself prefer, because it implies a freedom to examine, and reflect upon every sort of experience in a personal way. It implies that fullness of life which is both illuminating and consuming, as it is implied in that saying of Christ's which is not in the Gospels but which is quoted by one of the earliest of the church fathers—Origen—and which is: "*Qui iuxta me est iuxta ignem est qui longe est a me, longe est a regno*"—and if my Latin is not of the sort you are used to, that means "Whoever is near to me is near to the fire, whoever is far from me is far from the kingdom." That fire is surely the consuming splendour of life which, from time to time, we may experience if we strive to do so. It is not something which we could endure all the time. It is the *striving* which demands our best energies and our uttermost intuitive powers. That striving is familiar both to scientists and to writers, if they accept their work with full seriousness. We remember Einstein's comment that the physicist is the truly religious man of our time. But what the scientist is able to reveal to us of that splendid fire is concerned with the world of nature and of fact. The writer strives to communicate as much of the fire as he can apprehend in terms which speak personally to individuals in his audience. One voice speaks to one hearer. When the writer succeeds, the means he uses to communicate what he has apprehended may seem to many readers to partake of magic.

This is not, of course, the magic of which I spoke earlier, by which ambitious people sought to control life, but it is the magic which is necessary to the writer if he hopes, even in the slightest degree, to describe and reveal life.

We are the inheritors of what may be called the Freudian Revolution. It began in 1900 when Sigmund Freud published his revolutionary book, *The Interpretation of Dreams.* For several years the book was neglected; the intervention of the First World War kept it from reaching the English-speaking world until the twenties, though it was translated in 1913. Acceptance of what Freud had to say was understandably slow. The interpretation of dreams had for centuries been the province of people who had no scientific standing, although they were eagerly sought out and patronized as they have been at all times in history. People of a religious turn of mind—the wearers of the yoke of which I spoke a few minutes ago—were quite ready to accept Joseph's interpretations of the dreams of Pharaoh, but they were certain that their own dreams were the result of indigestion or garbled memories or simply of the irrationality which they assumed was the whole world of sleep. At least, that was what they pretended. Many of them were credulous about dreams, as people have always been. But what Freud said, and what has now become accepted by great numbers of people, even when they do not really comprehend it, is that the human mind is vastly greater than the portion of it that asserts itself in consciousness, and that we all live a life of immense psychological complexity which influences us in ways that can only be approached with caution and a wary pragmatism. Dreams are messages from that otherwise inaccessible part of the psyche. Since 1900 Freud and his followers have heard and interpreted millions of dreams, and still there is no simple key to the dream world. Every dream is the creation of an individual psyche, and no general agreement about symbolism can be reached, for everybody's symbolism is personal.

Although Freud's approach to the human psyche—and I remind you that, the word means "soul"—was as scientific as such pioneering work can be, there were plenty of people who insisted that he was reverting to magic and occultism, and one of the great battles of his life was to establish his findings on a scientific basis. So much so, indeed, that he refused to pay attention to things which asserted themselves in his clinical experience which he thought would drag him toward the occult of which he had a horror. It remained for his rebellious colleague and pupil, C.G. Jung, to take a brave step into the world of what was called the occult, which simply means hidden from view, and therefore mysterious.

Jung was a man who was, if I may say so, much less hag-ridden than Freud. He did not have to brave the anti-Semitism of the Viennese scientific world, and because he claimed descent from Goethe he was inclined to examine the world of art and literature in a spirit which Freud thought unscientific. Jung didn't care. He plunged into the science of the past, not because he believed it, but because he wanted to see why people in the past—people no less serious and intelligent than himself and Freud—had agreed to believe in it. Alchemy? What made so many highly intelligent people devote their lives to a study which was on the face of it irrational? He took the plunge and it may be said that he redeemed alchemy from the discard into which it had been thrown, revealing its psychological rather than its physical importance. Astrology? Well, was it not an ancestor of astronomy, devised by people without telescopes and with a cultural background that led them to describe what they could apprehend about the stars in terms which do not agree with modern science? But Jung devoted quite a lot of experimentation to astrology, and came up with the finding that, while it was about fifty percent nonsense, it was also about fifty percent worthy of consideration. (This was not, I hasten to assure you, the sort of astrology that you find nowadays in newspaper columns and fashion magazines which never, never, never predict an evil fate for anyone.) He gave a great deal of study to religious beliefs—to Gnosticism in particular—which the Church had long ago condemned as damnable, and he discovered that the Gnostics were no more damnable than any other group who sought to live according to a strict creed, and that they had possessed some psychological insights which were only damnable to a Church that would not tolerate psychological speculation except on its own terms.

These, however, were by-works in the immense amount of speculation and psychological exploration that Jung was able to cram into a busy life as a practising psychiatrist, a life that extended to eighty-six years. For the purpose of our discussion today—a purpose which I assure you I have not forgotten, however far I seem to be ranging from it—I think that his most important assertion as a psychologist was that Evil is a reality, and not just a departure from Good, which is the norm.

Like so many apparent novelties in human thought, this is really a re-assertion of something that used to be assumed as part of everybody's belief. But strict Church doctrine for many centuries had insisted that Evil was simply a *privatio boni*, a temporary falling away or lapse from Good. The writers and chroniclers of the Bible believed no such thing. "Be not deceived; God is not mocked: for whatsoever a man soweth, that shall he also reap." "The imagination of man's heart is evil from his youth." "God will not do wickedly, neither will the Almighty pervert judgment." "The wages of sin is death." But sin has fallen out of fashion and many people who have never heard of the doctrine of the *privatio boni*—sins as a simple and temporary lapse of Good—are nonetheless loud in asserting it. The murderer, the rapist, the mass-killer, the torturer, the terrorist, are not evil people; they are sick, and we must try to cure them, and if that means keeping them at the public expense for several decades, so be it. There is no such thing as Evil, and if something that looks uncommonly like it asserts itself, it is part of the burden of our humanistic philosophy to rebuke it as mildly as we know how.

Don't be alarmed. I am not calling for a revival of capital punishment or the lash. I am saying that Jung, from his very large clinical experience and his observation of the world about him, believed in an element of Evil which was separate and autonomous, and which was at work in human life, and—to return to our original theme—this is a belief which many writers of the highest attainment have believed also, and the struggle between Good and Evil has been the substance of much of their most powerful work.

The century which is coming to an end has experienced Evil as have few previous ages in human history. Three of the most extensive and murderous tyrannies known to mankind—those of Stalin and Hitler and Pol Pot—have flourished in our time. War has lost any chivalric glamour it may have possessed and has become a horror involving whole populations, and extermination on a scale unparalleled. Creeds which we thought belonged to the Middle Ages have shown themselves to be alive and more fearfully powerful than ever before. But do we talk of Evil as a force in the world? No, we prattle about economics and historical inevitability and all sorts of things which avoid the root of the problem. God and the Devil as contenders in the human drama have been banished from the stage, and that is profoundly irreligious. Irreligious in the sense of the word that I presented to you; it is failure to consider, to ponder, and to examine the world of man as it is. Certainly our politicians never do anything of the kind.

Our artists, however, make the attempt whenever they are people of sufficient stature to undertake such work. It is frequently complained that their work—their paintings, their music, their books—are chaotic either in form or content. This is an entirely just criticism; their work may be chaotic—though it is not always so—because it reflects the chaos of the world about them. They feel that they should do this, and in that feeling lurks a temptation to which many artists—writers in particular—fall victim.

The temptation is to become the artist *engagé*, the writer who addresses himself to the problems of his time, describing them, and thereby trying to persuade the world to come to terms with them. It sounds splendid, doesn't it? The writer as the possessor of a specially acute perception, of a particularly rich compassion, of a heart aflame with disgust and revulsion at the wickedness of mankind—is that not his duty, his highest calling? And certainly it is true that many fine books have been written under this impulsion. But the temptation is to think that these huge themes are the only important themes, the truest themes, for literary art. The temptation for the technically capable but intellectually second-rate writer is to say to himself: "Where is there trouble? Where is there misery? Where is the action? Where can I find a cause to support my next book? How can I show myself a person of overflowing compassion? Where can I drop a rain of tears?" This is the temptation of the Devil himself, and for one Solzhenitsyn there are a dozen fakers who are indignant and compassionate because indignation and compassion pay very well, and such books are considered to be "serious" by people who enjoy vicarious compassion. You do not find much magic in these books of the *engagé* writers, and although they may enjoy an immediate success they do not last very long, for new miseries arise to require the compassion that was expended on the old ones. Being sorry for mankind has nothing much to do with attempting to understand mankind.

I mentioned Solzhenitsyn a moment ago. He is not as much in the public eye as once he was. There are many people who regard him as an outstanding example of the writer *engagé*, because he deals with huge themes. Yes, but how does he deal with them? Always in terms of individuals upon whose lives the great themes have overwhelming influence. His books are stories about people, not primarily about history or politics. Tolstoy's extraordinary novel *War and Peace* does the same thing; the fates of individuals give the book its fascinating power. It is only at the end, when Tolstoy cannot control his passion for theorizing and philosophizing and nagging that the book goes off the rails, and we bog down in an explanation of what Napoleon might have done if he had been Leo Tolstoy. But when he is at the top of his form as an artist, and keeps the philosopher in check, he talks about people. And that is what the best novels do, and it is in relation to people that they exercise their magical power by reshaping observable fact to suit their own ends.

They must do so if they hope to make the effect on their readers which the readers desire. Let me offer an extreme example. How long is it since you read Dickens's novel *The Old Curiosity Shop*? If you have read it at all you surely remember the death of Little Nell, which is described at length and with a great deal of pathos and—it must be said—quite a lot of sentimental unction. Critics have made cruel fun of it. But if you read it with an open mind, you understand and feel what Dickens means by it. The pathos of a life cut short in youth, the fragility of life itself, the sadness which we feel when virtue and goodness of heart in a single life are lost to the world, arise palpably from the page and we are moved, unless we are suffering from an excess of rationality. We may not be drowned in tears as we read it, for that is not the fashion of our time; but we understand why Dickens wept as he wrote it. This is the writer's art on a high level.

I ask you to contrast the death of Little Nell with the death of another child in a novel much closer to our own time. It is Aldous

Huxley's *Point Counter Point*, in which he describes with a good deal of clinical detail the death of a little boy who has meningitis. Huxley was a man who had a strong scientific bias, and he spares us nothing of the child's agony, and we are glad when it is over. But are we touched in our innermost feeling? I don't think so, because the child's death is a gratuitous horror. It seems to be lugged in to make our flesh creep. Little Nell dies of something that is not identified; meningitis is a dreadful reality. What we remember from Huxley's book is likely to be the fear which that death inspires in the child's grandfather, who realizes that his own death must be approaching, and he dreads it with all the power of a pitifully egotistical nature. He seems almost to think that the child's death postpones his own. Huxley, in some of his critical work, makes cruel fun of the death of Little Nell, and we may perhaps think that he wrote of the child's death in his own novel in order to show us how a clear-eyed, unsentimental, unweeping, remorselessly modern spirit faces such an event. But the effect of Little Nell's death is unforgettable, however we may regard it, and for the life of me I cannot even remember the name of Huxley's unhappy little boy.

What is the difference? Is it simply modernity contrasted with nineteenth-century sentimentality? Not at all. If we read *The Old Curiosity Shop* with real critical feeling we know that the death of Little Nell is a contrasting passage with the death of the wholly evil, terrifying monster Mr. Quilp. Not long before Nell's death we read of the shocking end of Quilp, whose evil deeds are coming to a culmination where escape is his only recourse, and in seeking to get away from his pursuers he takes a false step, tumbles into the filthy waters of the river, and drowns horribly. It is not in the single death of the child, but in the two deaths in which Good and Evil meet with their reward, that the power of the end of the novel resides. It is in such passages that the genius of Dickens is manifested, leaving Aldous Huxley as a brilliant novelist of vastly lesser powers.

Dickens has dealt with the great theme of Good and Evil, in both of which he had unbounded faith because—if we believe some of his most recent and most perceptive critics—he knew both those elements in his own nature. Huxley nowhere in his work shows much concern with Good, and he seems to regard Evil as a thing of chance, an unmotivated horror in a world without direction.

James Joyce once said that the measure of a book was the quality of the mind from which it sprang. That seems to be a truism, but like many truisms it is often overlooked. The great literary artist concerns himself, in a thousand contrasting ways, with problems of Good and Evil, both of which are realities in his own vision of the world and of mankind. Oh, but you may say, look at Jane Austen: Where do you find such elements in her work, which is seriously, and often extravagantly, admired? Well, look at Jane Austen again, and see what you find. She did not write of Good and Evil as did her contemporary and admirer, Sir Walter Scott, but she knew what the score was, if I may be permitted a wholly uncritical term. Speaking of Jane Austen, Scott himself said: "The Big Bow-Wow strain I can do myself like any now going; but the exquisite touch, which renders ordinary commonplace things and characters interesting, from the truth of description and sentiment, is denied me." Scott spoke with the generosity that was characteristic of him but his point is a valid one. Not everything a novelist may wish to say needs to be said in the Big Bow-Wow strain, and the comic genius of Jane Austen is incontestable. But God preserve us from a literature written wholly by Jane Austen and her kind. The Big Bow-Wow strain is a necessity of literary art, and fine-honed social comedy will not reach the full span of human concern.

Fine-honed social comedy, in the Jane Austen sense, is not, however, the only kind of comedy, or the greatest kind. There is a tendency among readers generally, and even among many academic critics, to consider Tragedy a literary mode very much superior to Comedy. I don't agree. Comedy does not mean simply making people laugh. It is not the art of the stand-up comedian, the wise-cracker. It is a way of looking at life which explores some of the noblest aspects of the human spirit. The greatest comic writer in our language was Shakespeare. Oh I do not mean those often-painful scenes in which clowns crack jokes that have lost their point. I mean the totality of those wonderful comedies that made us feel, when we have seen them well presented on the stage, that life is great, and that the human spirit is unconquerable. Shakespeare's most splendid scenes of comedy are often those in which nobody makes a joke. I have long cherished a remark by G.K. Chesterton, when he said that *A Midsummer Night's Dream* was one of our greatest explorations of the mysticism of happiness. It is a happiness that is remote from obvious fun, although *The Dream* has some fine examples of that sort of comedy. But it is not the wild humour of the Athenian workmen who decide to act a tragedy, but that wonderful moment when the bewitched weaver, Bottom, awakes from his enchantment and tries to recover the marvels that he has experienced that presents us with Shakespearean comedy at its peak, emanating from what Chesterton once again calls "the god-like and inexhaustible carelessness of a happy man." We do not laugh, or laugh very hard, at that scene, but when it is well acted we are enveloped in tenderness, and wonderment, and rich fulfillment—in the truth of Comedy, in fact.

Both Comedy and Tragedy can be faked. There are people who think they have experienced Tragedy when they have simply been made to feel miserable. And there are people who think that they have encountered Comedy when they have been made to laugh, without much regard for what they are laughing at, or where their laughter comes from. But in our impressible world, I think it is easier to fake Tragedy than Comedy, and what some critics call "the tragic sense of life" may often mean no more than a sense of the disappointment of one's personal life. Tragedy and Comedy, in their finest flights, are elevating, enlarging, and produce a quality of serenity and courage.

Are Tragedy and Comedy everlasting? Are they part of the spirit of man, archetypal in their grasp on our concept of life, on the very matrix of existence? I wonder if this is so. Tragedy and Comedy, as we know them, extend only from the fifth century B.C., and that is not a long time in the story of man's mind. How long is it since anyone wrote an unmistakable tragedy? I should put it at 1896, when Ibsen wrote *John Gabriel Borkman*. And what do you find in that? Is it the fall of a great king or a hero? No, it is the long dissolution of a financial genius which I suppose is the modern equivalent. Perhaps some of you are eager to tell me that *Death of a Salesman* is a tragedy, but I cannot agree; as Sidney says, "Tragedy concerneth a high fellow," and Willy Loman is not a high fellow; he is a duplicitous Bagman.

But it is of interest that in presenting the fall of Borkman and also of Willy, both authors have to resort to the kind of magic which—I assure you I have not forgotten it—this speech was intended to discuss. But allow me one further excursion into a bypath which is not really a bypath.

Why is Comedy tending more and more to become mixed with pathos? Why is Tragedy no longer stark in its approach to the fall of a great man? It is surely part of the Freudian Revolution, and I need not remind you that Freud was a great admirer of the genius of Henrik Ibsen. But it is not to Freud, but to Jung, that we must turn for an answer to the question I have asked, for Jung reminded us of the curious Neoplatonic theory that the history of mankind proceeds in eons, each measuring about two thousand years, and which are equivalent to the Houses of the Zodiac. We are now in the last few years of the Eon of Pisces—the Eon of the Warring Brothers—and as we have been somewhat tiresomely reminded by popular music, we are drawing near to the Eon of Aquarius the Water Carrier, which is regarded as the sign of *the union or reconciliation of opposites.* According to some calculations we shall enter that eon decisively in the year 1997, but there are other astronomers—not astrologers, I may say—who put the date somewhere around the year 2154. But these changes do not come about suddenly, and there will be no unmistakable bump when the Age of Aquarius finally arrives.

What will it bring? We already have some hints of a reconciliation of the Warring Brothers in the move toward the blending of Tragedy and Comedy that I have mentioned. We no longer see life quoted so much in terms of black and white, of Evil as opposed to Good, of God as wholly divorced from the Devil. The sentimentality of which I spoke earlier is a shallow evidence of this evening-up; the sentimentality that insists on seeing the good in every man, however apparently evil his actions are, is balanced by the determination of the media—who dictate so many of our accepted ideas—to belittle and diminish people whom we might once have imagined to be great. Thus we have biographies of statesmen and philosophers which are eager to show their worst side, revealing every petty vanity and sexual peccadillo, and biographies of criminals, like Gênet to speak of one, which declare them to have been unrecognized saints. There will be a lot of sentimental nonsense to be waded through before we reach the truth of the Age of Aquarius, but already there are evidences of a mature acceptance of what the future may bring.

Many of these are to be found in literature. In poetry, certainly, and in drama, but I think most insistently in the novel, which is the foremost literary genre of our time.

It would be tedious to go into this question at length, and anyhow it would call for a series of talks, and not one, to make any detailed exploration of the theme. Let me confine myself, therefore, to the work of James Joyce, an extraordinary and not in every way a pleasing genius, who is known to us chiefly through two extraordinary novels: *Ulysses*, published in 1922 and very slowly accepted as a masterpiece above the prejudices of censors and people whose only eyes were in the back of their heads; the other great novel was *Finnegans Wake*, which appeared in 1939.

If you have read them, or one of them, nothing that I can say will enlarge your understanding of them. But many people have not read either, for they are difficult books, written by an egotist who could not imagine how better mankind might spend its time than in poring over his works. Therefore allow me to give a hint or two at what they contain.

Ulysses, as the title suggests, is about a man who undertakes a great voyage, and in this case the traveller is a Jewish advertising salesman called Leopold Bloom, and his journey is through the city of Dublin, from morn to midnight. The likeness between Bloom as Ulysses, Stephen Dedalus, the young schoolmaster, as Ulysses' son Telemachus who seeks and finds his father, and Molly Bloom as Penelope, the wife of the hero, is clear and detailed, but it is done with such subtlety that we must nudge ourselves to see the Heroic tale in the bourgeois doings of these Dubliners. But the hero tale is there.

Finnegans Wake is a much more difficult book, and in some places seems to be impenetrable. Ulysses makes extensive use of the "stream of consciousness" technique, and of parody, and in places it takes off into high realms of fantasy, without ever losing its grip on the reality of Dublin life. But *Finnegans Wake* begins in the middle of a dream, and continues in that dream for 628 pages of the most demanding, exasperating, dense, incomprehensible exploration of the consciousness of the dreamer that you can imagine, expressed in language that mingles portmanteau words, words in several foreign languages, arcane words from past literature, quotations, passages of lyric beauty, and outrageous puns. Reading it is like nothing so much as wrestling with the Giant Briareus with his hundred arms and his fifty heads, all of them shouting and laughing.

Yes, laughing. Even the most penetrating of critics sometimes miss the point that these two extraordinary novels are huge comedies, in which the depths of experience and the fantasy life of man are explored with the torch of the Comic Spirit. The history of mankind, and the human and mythical elements in what goes to make up that history, are all shown in the dream life of an unremarkable Dublin pub-keeper, and at least we can discern that Joyce is saying that every man and woman contains the truth of every man and woman who has ever lived, and that truth is cloaked in the muddy vesture of everyday life.

This, I put it to you, is the magic of the novel. I suppose we must embark on the question of where it comes from.

I do this, I assure you, with reluctance, because I do not really want to talk about the way I write my own novels, nor do I wish to seem to liken my own novels to the very great works of which I have already made mention. But what alternative have I? I have already said that the novel is wholly personal in its appeal; one reader, with one book, encounters the mind of one author. Not all the science in the world can explain or chart the different ways in which the book reaches its reader, and I, as one author, cannot speak with any knowledge or authority about the way other authors work. Of course there are similarities in the broad method, but every writer works in his own way and I cannot effectively embrace any other. So I have no alternative but to talk about myself as a writer of novels.

When I first began to write novels I was often criticized for elements in the plots which seemed to the critics to be inadmissible in any serious work of fiction. This was the first mistake of the critics; being Canadians, they could not conceive that any right-minded fellow Canadian would write novels that were not meant to be taken in the spirit of serious realism. They knew about Humour, of course; they recognized it; and they gave it cautious acceptance, but it was a genre by itself, a thing for which one was awarded the Leacock Medal; humour ought not to spill over into serious work—for there was still hope that somebody was going to write The Great Canadian Novel, and the critics were damned sure it wouldn't be funny. But in my early novels they were presented with works that were formal, funny, and appeared to lack that higgledy-piggledy quality which the critics thought was characteristic of serious life. They objected to my use of coincidence, because they never noticed any coincidences in their own lives, although I—being religious in the careful, observant psychologically alert sense of that word—found plenty of coincidences in mine. They objected to my style, which they thought needlessly formal. What they did not see, or did not choose to admit, was that I was writing comedies, and comedies freed from that necessity to simulate the humdrum quality of ordinary life which was at that time thought to be the mark of a good novel.

What most annoyed them, however, was my way of introducing things into my novels which hinted at what they called the supernatural—at a life existing at the same time as ours, and influencing ours in a variety of great and small ways, and sometimes intervening in our lives decisively. But I did not mean these things to be supernatural because that is a stupid term. No, my novels were simply psychological, and for a variety of reasons I was strongly aware of these psychological elements, was heedful of them, and could not keep them out of any story I thought worth telling. I was not interested in realism in the ordinary acceptance of the word; my realism was psychological realism and the way in which it manifested itself in my stories could not be accommodated to a narrower conception of reality. "Mr. Davies, as usual, makes his obeisance to the Dark Powers," wrote one critic. And indeed I did so, because to me those powers were inseparable from my vision of life, comic though it was. And to me they were not dark, but numinous. I was not a photographer, catching in black and white what the lens of the camera could see; I was a painter in oils, including what I, as an author, could see.

Why? It is here that I have to tell you one or two things which I have not spoken of in public, because I thought they would be misunderstood. But I have now come to a time of life when I really don't care very much whether people understand me, because I have spent my life trying with my best efforts to understand myself. I am one of those creatures—by no means uncommon—who were called by Bernard Shaw, in his discussion of the character of Joan of Arc, Galtonic Visualizers. It is not a very good term but it strives for scientific accuracy and therefore I offer it to this scientific audience. Things of importance come to me not in philosophical reflections, but in flashes, in sudden perceptions of the unseen, indeed I suppose I must say in visions. It is not, I assure you, because I have a screw loose, but because my arrangement of screws is wholly personal. As a child I had these perceptions, and I did not talk about them even to my mother, because they seemed odd, and private. I once, as quite a young boy, saw something in the sky which was so astonishing that I treasured it without knowing in the least what it was. I could take you now to the very place in the street where, on my way home from school, I saw it. It was not for another thirty years that I learned from my study of Jung that it was a vision of the Unus Mundus, the One World, the Totality and interdependence of all things. Don't ask why a schoolboy should see such a thing. I saw it, and that's all there is about it, and later on it crept into my novels and plays.

Once, as a child, I was frightened very powerfully by a witch, a figure of evil—of evil transcending anything I had ever knowingly encountered in my life. It was in the attic of our family house, where I was playing, when suddenly I knew that the witch was there, in a cupboard; I could see her through the cupboard door. For a very long time—it might have been half an hour but probably it was less—I was frozen, not daring to move a muscle while the evil creature stared at me with a chilling smile. She knew me, and her knowledge was not benign. When at last I escaped I dared not speak of it, and thought I should never get over it.

I did so, however. I was nearer sixty than fifty when I met that witch again, in a dream. She fixed me with her glare and her smile, and as I dreamt I thought I should once again be frozen by that spell. Not so. I roused myself, and walked toward her, holding out my hands. "Can't we be friends?" I said. And believe it or do not believe it as you will, the witch became a benevolent figure, took my hand, and was terrifying no longer. I did not need an analyst to tell me what that meant. It meant a measure of self-conquest.

All my life I have met from time to time strange figures, sometimes witches, sometimes ghosts, and I have learned not to fear them. They are the way in which I encounter truth or whatever of truth it is given to me to understand. And it is this painfully gleaned truth that I seek to impart in my novels, and I have a great many letters from readers that make it plain that many people have responded to my truths, for which I make no extraordinary claim, but for whose validity, limited as it may be, I have no doubt at all.

One of the assertions of C.G. Jung, whose work has served to explain to me many things which would otherwise have remained dark, is that people may encounter in dreams or visions things of which they have no previous knowledge. One of his favourite examples was of an illiterate Negro prisoner in an American jail, who had a vision that was explicable only in terms of a very old and somewhat obscure Egyptian legend. The man could not possibly have read about it, or heard about it, and he was not a man of uncommon intellectual powers. What he saw, said Jung, was something that exists in the Collective Unconscious of mankind. It exists, and apparently from time to time some part of it makes its way to the surface of the mind of some living person.

I have had an experience of that kind. Some years ago I was at work on a novel, the central character of which was a man of complex but ill-comprehended character, and his personal problems had driven him to drink. I don't like the word *alcoholic*. It has a Nice Nelly sound that troubles me. My character was, to put it grossly, a boozer. As I wrote about him, I knew quite a bit about him, but it wasn't in focus; I did not know quite what I intended for him. Novelists have these problems.

One day, after lunch, as I was sitting in the open air, in that condition of abated consciousness which often follows lunch—no, I wasn't asleep, and I do not suggest that lunch is a key to the visionary world—I saw two figures approaching me. One was a beautiful young woman, dressed in classical garb, with flowing hair and an air of confidence about her which was immediately arresting. On a golden chain she was leading an animal; it had the body and head of a lion, the clawed feet of a dragon, a tail which was barbed as the tails of scorpions are barbed in ancient art, and it had the anguished face of a man. What on earth was it? As the vision faded I scraped about in my mind for a name for that curious creature, and after consulting a dictionary of mythology I had it. The creature was a manticore, a thing composed of a man helplessly trapped in the attributes of beings that were less than human. When I came to myself I knew that I had the clue to my book and my character. I called the book *The Manticore* against the advice of my publisher—publishers are not often visionaries—and rather a large number of people have liked it, if I may judge by its continuing popularity and the letters from readers it has inspired.

There you are. You asked me to talk about the novelist and magic, and I have done so, and as you see, the magic isn't magic at all, when once you know how it comes about. It resides in a realm that has always existed and from which such works as *A Midsummer Night's Dream* and *The Ancient Mariner* have arisen as well as many such humbler literary creations as my own. I am not, as you see, a writer *engagé* in the usual sense of the term, but I am a writer deeply immersed in the only world of which he can hope to have any indisputable knowledge—the world of himself. Unless the writer is prepared to write unsparingly and sometimes painfully of himself, he hasn't much to say that has the ring of truth. He may cloak what he has to say in a formal style, as I do, and in a comic mode, as I do, but the source from which his writing comes is neither formal nor comic in essence, but is turbulent, pressing, and vital, and it is a world where Tragedy and Comedy have mingled.

I have described the writer to you in terms that mark him as the religious man—religious in the sense in which I defined the word earlier. Not as the expounder of a creed, or the zealous supporter of a cause, but as one who approaches life with care, and indeed with reverence; who examines everything he can as carefully as he can; he is not afraid of a paradox or an outright contradiction in what he finds, and in some cases is one who points the way to the thoughts and preoccupations of the future.

In our century extraordinary efforts have been made toward the exploration of the universe about us, and the culmination of that work has been the landing of man on the Moon. In spite of all the fuss, that didn't amount to much. There were people who said that it was merely to show technological superiority to Russian science, and that may be so in part. There were those who said that it achieved nothing much except to leave an utterly irrelevant flag and some rubbish on a hitherto unviolated planet, but that is not the whole truth. What that venture did do was to mark the beginning of an exploration that will in time take man deep into a world now unknown, which may contain secrets of which we cannot even dream. Space travel is one of the most enlarging adventures to come in the Age of Aquarius.

You notice that I said "*one* of the enlarging adventures." There is another fully as important and perhaps more important without which space travel will mean little. For what is the point of sending men and women into space whose personal lives are lived on the surface of the mind, whose perceptions are clouded by ignorance of themselves, whose understanding of what mankind is does nothing to fit them for great adventures. Bravery is not enough. Technology is not enough. Psychologically unevolved men and women may be both brave and fine technologists. The other great adventure of the future is the exploration of the coming to terms with the innermost self, the wellsprings of humanity, the linking of the demonic and the civilized, the joining of hands between Apollo, the Giver of Light, and Dionysius, the Lord of the Dark Forces, the recognition that God and the Devil between them unite to make a third power which must be encountered and so far as possible comprehended.

Has that anything to do with the novel, which you pick up, put down at will, use to beguile an idle hour, and perhaps think of as a modest contribution to the ever-changing culture of the time?

Well, yes, it has, if you will permit me to be shameless in asserting the essence of the art of which I am a humble but careful practitioner.

For the novelist, indirectly perhaps but persuasively, he hopes, is pointing you in the direction of the new discovery, the new conquest, the great new adventure. That is, if you want to call it by an ambiguous name, his magic, his enchanter quality.

And if you do not believe a word I have said, I have at least done what you asked: I have talked about the novelist and magic.

5

Fiction of the Future

In the autumn of 1994 in Canada and the winter and spring of 1995 elsewhere, Davies and his wife were engaged in the "Dog and Pony Show"—the tour arranged by the publishers to promote *The Cunning Man*. When a special full-dress lecture was called for, this was the one he chose to give, first as the Duthie Lecture in Vancouver and later in several other cities.

This, the latest of his full-length lectures, was also one of the most sombre. As it ranges back and forth in time—from Heracleitus to Professor Francis Crick, who helped discover DNA and now suggests that there may be a religion gene—this look at the future is clearly the work of a man who has lived a long and thoughtful life, before returning to the comforting thought that Ecclesiastes was right: "there is no new thing under the sun": *Visit the theatre with Sherry to check lights; seats 2,500 and sold out! Lecture at 7:30: very warm reception and score heavily answering questions, which I did as honestly as I can: they are presented to me written on slips and I choose which to answer, weeding out sillies. Sign a lot or books though I was promised I need not …*

I have chosen to talk to you about the Fiction of the Future, and when you hear such a title you have every right to question my capacity to talk of what is still unknown. Am I a clairvoyant or an astrologer? By no means. But I have seen quite a bit of what is now the past, and during my years as a journalist it was my daily job to record it and comment on it; long ago I came to the conclusion that "the thing that hath been, it is that which shall be; and that which is done is that which shall be done; and there is no new thing under the sun." (Ecclesiastes 1:9) But of course the thing that hath been is always presenting itself in new garments, and is always being experienced freshly by new generations, so there is an illusion—a very strong and exciting illusion—of novelty. And that is a good thing, for otherwise we might think that we were all on a treadmill of endless repetition and that life was not worth having. Which of course it is. Life is an ever-renewing pleasure for most of us, and if we are not too spoiled with that pleasure, we recognize it and are grateful for it. If we think about it seriously, just living from moment to moment is an adventure, involving a co-operative effort between our infinitely complex physical and psychological selves and the multifarious universe in which we exist. And although there may be nothing new under the sun, what is old is new to us and so rich and astonishing that we never tire of it. If we do tire of it, if we lose our curiosity, we have lost something of infinite value, because to a high degree it is curiosity that gives meaning and savour to life.

Already, in my introductory words, I have told you two things that underlie everything else that I shall say. I have quoted from the Bible and have told you that I used to be a newspaperman. Why are those two things important, and how are they linked? Many years ago I was reading a biography of one of my literary heroes, the great Norwegian dramatist Henrik Ibsen, and I learned that when he was asked by an admirer—I think it was Edmund Gosse—what he read that underlay his extraordinary perception of life, he replied that he read nothing but the Bible and the newspapers. Gosse saw a well-worn Bible in the great man's workroom, and it was known that every day of his life in Oslo (it was then called Christienia) Ibsen dressed himself impeccably, walked to his favourite restaurant, and sat at his favourite table in a corner; and there all the day's newspapers were brought to him (because in those days restaurants provided newspapers for their customers) and he sat for two hours, drinking aquavit, and reading, and peeping over his paper at the other diners. He read all the papers from end to end, including the advertisements, and he read not only the serious dailies but also the comic papers.

It was here that he gained his profound and wide-ranging insight into human life, it was here that he found his plots, and when he went home he identified what he had read in the daily news with what had been written so long ago by those Hebrew chroniclers, and found the same stories about the three great subjects of all literature—Love, War, and Death.

(As a footnote, I might mention that when Ibsen walked into his restaurant, everyone stood up until he was seated. They knew how to treat authors in those days.)

When I read that, and thought about it, my attitude toward my newspaper work was transformed; I had known that I was a chronicler of my times, and that although the appearance of human experience was perpetually changing its form, the material remained the same. The impress of today was printed in the wax of the ages; the imprint varied, but never the wax.

I was especially interested that Ibsen read the *comic* papers, because all my life I have been a great reader of "the funnies" as they are still called—though God knows they rarely make me laugh—because they give an insight into what people who never philosophize, and who would be astonished if you called them thinkers, imagine the truth of life to be. In *Dagwood and Blondie* a clever woman who seems to be a featherbrain dominates her husband, who really is a featherbrain and who toils under the domination of Mr. Dithers, an unappeasable boss. In *Peanuts* a thoughtful and logical little boy is dominated by a determined, truculent little girl, though he knows that his vision of life is truer than hers. In *Sally Forth* a wife and mother who is also a businesswoman bears her burdens with stoicism and supplies stability for her husband, who seems to know no care, and her obnoxious child whose demands and criticism are unending. She is the heroine of our time, for millions of readers.

How different these seem to be from the funnies of my youth, when Mutt settled all his arguments with Jeff by hitting him on the head with a spittoon; when the *Katzenjammer Kids* reduced daily life to chaos, and made fierce fun of newcomers to this continent in a way that would outrage the proponents of Political Correctness. And indeed what would Political Correctness make of *Happy Hooligan* who was a cheerful mental defective; or of *Count Screwloose of Toulouse* who was an achrondoplastic dwarf; or of *Barney Google* who was in love with a horse? In the transformation of the funnies we see plainly the change from the comparatively carefree anarchy of feeling during the twenties to the guilt-ridden, apprehensive, Politically Correct spirit of our time, when virtually nothing can be laughed at, when the West is expected to bear all the troubles of the East, and when the retributive justice of the past appears to be giving place to a world where the psychological wounds of the criminal class take precedence over the wrongs of those who suffer from their criminality.

Newspapers have changed their character during my lifetime. They used to be the principal carriers of the world's news, but television holds that position now. Television, however, has serious limitations; it is a visual medium, and it is dominated by the principle that nothing is news unless you can take a picture of it. It is here that the newspapers still hold their own; so much of what goes on in the political world cannot be effectively photographed; statesmen, in their expensive but uninteresting clothes, make very poor TV and their prolonged deliberations are dull when we see them on the box. Politics must be interpreted, and newspapers have become their untiring interpreters. Even MacNeil and Lehrer cannot hold you for too long with a description of what is happening in the world, but at your leisure you can read half a dozen interpretations written by newspaper columnists and draw your own conclusions. That doesn't happen on television; it draws your conclusions for you, and the conclusions it draws are those of people whose primary job it is to see that you do not change your channel. Thus catastrophic wars are seen in terms of starving children, or weary troops of refugees; the reasons for the wars, even when they can be discovered, are too complex for the picture box. If we knew the reasons, our sympathy might cool. The TV journalists cannot permit your sympathy to cool, for emotion, not intelligence, is what holds you to the small screen.

Intelligence, not perhaps on its highest level but far beyond the sheer emotionalism of TV, has found its refuge in the newspapers. There is discussion there, for even the most modest paper has a few columnists, who may not be profound thinkers or deep students of affairs, but at least you can read what they have to say, and reread it if you wish, and draw conclusions of your own. You can write to the paper and dispute with a columnist, but you most certainly cannot dispute with television. It is significant, is it not, that television now offers printed versions of its educational programs, but not of its programs of opinion.

Another great strength of the newspaper is that you can keep it, or some part of it, for so long as you please. Television cannot be recalled. When I was a very young man I read an excellent book by a French scholar in which he recommended that everybody should keep a dossier of newspaper clippings related to their principal subjects of interest; it was a way, he said, to become a modest expert on any subject you pleased, and also to observe how quickly fashions in ideas changed. I began a personal newspaper file then, and I have it still. It is now very bulky, and from time to time I dip into it to remind myself of the past.

Do you want to know what sort of things I file? Some of the headings are Crime, Psychiatry, Religion, Pornography, Medicine, Art, Music, and other more personal concerns like Grotesqueries and Strange Manifestations of the Holy Ghost. Most of the clippings are serious. Indeed, they were all meant seriously and if I take them somewhat lightly, that is my preference. For instance, I am delighted with the news that in February 1984, Muhammed Aloo, aged 100, married a fourteen-year-old girl in a Muslim ceremony; his best man was eighty-six. I have quite a lot of information about the family of Pierre Plantard de Saint-Clair who claims direct descent from the marriage of Jesus Christ and Mary Magdalen. On a somewhat lower social level I am interested in the murder in which a man killed his brother because he used two rolls of toilet paper in a single day. And of course I cherish the account of a suit brought by a U.S. Marine against three tough girls who ambushed him and at gunpoint required him to have sexual intercourse with them until he was utterly drained; very properly he sued for rape and the court upheld his suit.

But, you may ask, what has this to do with the fiction of the future? Do you suppose the fiction of the future will radically differ from the fiction of the past? It will seem to do so, because fiction does evolve in manner, if not in matter. Quite often young writers come to me to talk about writing, and many of them are greatly puzzled about how they can keep up with the times. My advice is always to forget about the times, because we all belong to our own time, and there is nothing whatever that we can do to escape from it. Whatever we write will be contemporary, even if we attempt a novel set in a past age, and put on fancy dress, so to speak, in our prose. You can always tell when a novel was written, however the author may toil to place it in an historic past. *Henry Esmond* is unmistakably a Victorian novel, and a fine one, though Thackeray has done his best to clothe it in the prose of Queen Anne. Robert Graves's splendid *I, Claudius* and *Claudius the God* have been given a wonderful Latin clarity of prose, but they cannot disguise the fact that they are post-Freudian novels. So we need not worry about being modern; we cannot escape it.

That is why I tell the young people who want to talk to me about writing that they might profitably cast their minds back to the vendors of fiction in the past. Indeed, to those storytellers many hundreds of years ago who spread a mat in the marketplace, sat on it, placed their collection bowl well forward, and cried: "Give me a copper coin, and I will tell you a golden tale." We have some of those tales still—*The Arabian Nights* was composed entirely of them—and they are golden indeed, as are also the folk tales recorded by the Brothers Grimm. So golden are they, that we can trace their features in many novels that have just fallen from the press. What is astonishing about these old stories is how modern they are in feeling, if not in superficialities.

So we need not worry about modernity. But we do. Oh yes, we do. We are strongly conscious that we stand on the brink of what looks like a great leap in time. It isn't. It is simply one tick of the clock, but it will carry us from the twentieth century into the twenty-first, and for many people this has an almost magical quality.

Indeed, such progressions of time had a deeply magical quality in the past, when many learned people were concerned with the World Astrological Clock, which measured time in Eons of two thousand years each, every Eon supposedly being under the domination of one of the signs of the Zodiac. The Eon we are just winding up is the Eon of

Pisces, the fishes who are seen swimming in opposite directions. And who can dispute that the past two thousand years have been marked by contrarieties which seem wholly inexplicable but which nevertheless have been historical facts? By the reckoning of the World Clock we are moving into the Eon of Aquarius, and have been doing so for something like two hundred years. The great astrologers foretell an era of flux, of change, of liquid uncertainties. If you wish to pursue this sort of thinking, you will remember that the age now passing—the Age of Pisces—saw the rise and dominance of Christianity as one of the great world religions, but as the Age of Flux draws nearer, Christianity appears to be losing much of its strength, though it is wholly improbable that its message will be completely lost. But the Age of Flux will require that Christianity and other religions be regarded in a new light, and already we have seen flashes of what that new light may be. A new world for women—because the great religions of the past have never been considerate of women—and a new attitude toward sex, which has not yet declared itself in the nervous shiftings and compromises of the present day. A world, it may be, in which the dominance of what a great poet has called "getting and spending" may be moderated, although we should not build any socialist-utopian dreams on what that moderation may bring. A world perhaps of greater interference in the life of the individual? That might well be, though inevitably in an age of flux such interference would meet with strong resistance. But these waves of change do not happen quickly and some long periods of what looks like certainty may have to be endured by our posterity before they are overthrown by something else. Flux, in world terms, does not mean rapid turbulence and turmoil. It is slow, and we can say with certainty that, although it is slow, it is also sure.

Our posterity will have to make its peace with great new religions. By a religion I mean some body of doctrine that demands acquiescence and conformity by virtually everyone, and which hunts down the nonconformists with righteous fury.

You will not be surprised when I say that one of these new religions, which is already rising to extraordinary power, is Science.

What is Science? The word simply means knowledge but now we use it to signify what experimenters can tell us about the universe in some aspect of its variety. Such knowledge is gained by experiments which confirm hypotheses, and stated very crudely it may be assumed that if an experiment can be carried through a hundred times with the same result, the hypothesis has been shown to be a fact. This of course is totally different from Art, in which nothing is ever precisely the same from one instance to another. The scientific approach to humanity is wholesale; the approach of art, and the art we are talking about here is fiction, is retail. Not masses, but individuals.

I speak of Science as a religion because of the priestlike authority it now assumes in its assertions about many things, and especially about public health. I use the word *priestlike* somewhat sardonically, because we know how brilliantly the priests of past times interpreted history, and especially the history of those who opposed them, to suit their own purposes and support their own doctrines. This was not calculated roguery; all priesthoods are certain that they know the truth and know that it is their duty to protect mankind from error. Instances of this sort of action in the world of Science abound. How weak the voices seem that oppose the evangelical fervour of the scientific opponents of smoking tobacco! We are now assured that not only smokers themselves, but those who are exposed to their exhaled smoke, are in mortal danger, and that unborn children may suffer irreparable damage if somehow tobacco smoke is transmitted to them by expectant mothers who associate with smokers. I am old enough to remember the fervour with which reformers in the past denounced all alcoholic drinks and could prove, with statistics, that a great number of human ills had their origin in the saloon. It is the statistics that bother me because I know a little about how they are achieved. Give a first-rate statistician a supposed fact to prove, and he is a traitor to his craft if he cannot prove it for you. The old saw is true: Figures cannot lie, but liars can figure. I do not question the sincerity of the scientists who assure us that tobacco is a deadly poison; but I have lived long enough to have seen how much sincerity can be aroused on behalf of things which in the end proved insubstantial. I often think of the remark of Havelock Ellis who said that the sophistication of a civilization might be measured in terms of its judicious use of poisons. The jocose question, "What's your poison?" is not quite as shallow as it at first seems. Is it coffee? Is it speed—however you interpret the word? Is it alcohol? Is it self-righteousness and determination to save your fellow man however he may protest that he does not wish to be saved? That last one is a terrible poison indeed, because it is not widely recognized. It was the mainspring of the Christian missionary movement.

Nevertheless, Science must have its day, and a very terrible day it may be because scientists, though superbly trained in their own great mystery, often carry into their work an ethical outlook which may be called primitive. They can do marvels, but they do not care where the marvels may lead. Perhaps that is unjust; many of them do care, but their voices are drowned out by the cries of those whose personal interest is served by something which may not be in the interest of mankind. We know now what doubts were felt by many of the greatest scientists about atomic fission, but they could not be heard above the enthusiastic approbation of lesser men, and many politicians, who saw an immediate advantage in what atomic fission might achieve. But it is fruitless to pursue this theme: The time for the discovery of atomic fission had come, and if it had not been achieved and used immediately as an instrument of power, it would certainly not have lingered much longer in the womb of time.

What has this to do with fiction, you may ask? Here I am on uneasy ground, because the whole world of Science Fiction is closed to me. I simply cannot interest myself in it. But I am aware that it has shown itself prophetic in many instances. The authors propose solutions to scientific problems at which real scientists laugh, but from time to time the laugh is turned against themselves. I think of a movie that was made in 1966, *The Fantastic Voyage*, in which some scientists shrank themselves, and a kind of submarine in which they could travel, to such dimensions that they could be introduced into the bloodstream of an ailing man, and travel through his body to his brain, there to operate on the blood clot that threatened his life. The film was very popular, but it was assumed to be fantasy.

Nevertheless, I read recently in the newspapers of the work of some Australian engineers who are concerned in what is called nanotechnology, which is the construction of tiny machines. Already motors less than a millimetre long have been made and Japanese researchers are designing microrobots small enough to travel through blood vessels and deliver drugs to precisely the right organ in the body; they are powered by a battery a hundredth of the size of the red blood cell and capable of generating twenty millivolts for about forty-five minutes. When we applaud the achievements of these men, I think we should not forget Otto Klement, who wrote the story of *The Fantastic Voyage*, and drape him in a modest prophetic mantle. Scientists are very clever men, but they have no monopoly on imagination.

The great scientific enthusiasm of our time is, of course, the investigation of the genetic code, which has been described as "the greatest discovery of all time" because it is expected to reveal, as one enthusiastic journalist puts it, "the secret of life." You must excuse me from explaining it to you in detail. It is rather complex and would take up a lot of your time, and I suppose that many of you are fully familiar with it already. All I know about it is what I read in the newspapers, and the best I can do for you is to offer a very quick rundown on what a gene is. Now attend very carefully, please, or you may miss something vital. Each of the body's one hundred trillion cells has a nucleus: Inside the nucleus are forty-six chromosomes, arranged in twenty-three pairs: each chromosome contains genes, which are white areas: each gene is made of the double helix of DNA, which, as I do not need to tell you, is deoxyribonucleic acid, which is the complex molecule that constitutes the genetic material of living organisms: the cross-links between the helices are the bases that form the genetic code. This genetic code is identified by three billion letters, and by the year 2005 the scientists expect to have it all sorted out and after that presumably everything is plain sailing. Are you with me? Good. The secret of life has been unveiled and what will happen next is anybody's guess.

The greatest part of the work on this extraordinary leap forward in the understanding of life has been done, and is still being done, at Cambridge in the Cavendish Laboratory by James Watson and Francis Crick. Of course work is being done in every advanced country under the aegis of something called the Human Genome Organization, popularly known as HUGO. Overwrought journalists say that this work compares in scale with the Apollo moon landing and the Manhattan Project to build the atomic bomb. By scale I suppose they mean the number of people involved and the money spent, because the moon landing has not told us much we didn't know before. A celebrated modern historian, A.J.P. Taylor, described it as "the biggest non-event of my life" and there are many who agree. The atomic venture has certainly not proved, in ordinary use, the great boon that was promised, though it is still a terror when threatened for use in war. In peace it has proved to be dangerous, in spite of great precautions.

When the three billion letters that make up the genetic code have at last been arranged in the right order it will apparently be possible to identify in the foetus of the unborn child the gene which disposes toward breast cancer, heart disease, diabetes, and a number of other serious human ills. Then what do you do? Abort the foetus or take a chance? A nice theme for fictional treatment, that one. What if the genetic prediction shows the unborn child to be prone to accumulation of cholesterol, or of becoming a psychotic, or being gay? The opportunity to develop a humanity free from all its ills, perfect in health, with no leaning toward crime and no ethical problems, is a great temptation to a certain type of mind. It would be extraordinary if, under such circumstances, governments did not decide to take a hand in the decision. And we all know how clever governments are about ethical problems. Genetic engineering is said to be the coming thing. And tinkering on behalf of some idea of human betterment would be an irresistible temptation.

Professor Francis Crick has even suggested that there is a religion gene, which determines whether its carrier will become a believer. Now *there* is a chance to rid the world of what Sigmund Freud described as an illusion, and have a human race with no sense of awe or obedience to inherited moral codes. If God is not already dead, as many people insist He is, the chance is coming to kill Him.

Who would take God's place? God—the Christian and Hebrew God, and the gods of Olympus and of the past, were open to appeals for mercy. The Gene is implacable. The discovery that so many of our activities are the result of our genetic makeup ushers in a new fatalism.

God—you understand that I use the word very generally and not with special reference to the Jehovah of the Old Testament—allows you to discover and experience your destiny slowly, as it happens. But when your genetic code can be read by your doctor, you and he, and your government, can know a great deal about yourself long before it happens. This is the new astrology. The old astrology is notoriously open to error and misunderstanding. But the genetic forecast cannot go wrong. What kind of life does that promise? Let me read you something in which two modern writers foresee the future of a family.

"Hugo wakes and checks his bedside clock. It is 8 A.M., May 2 in the year 2044 and he has 306,600 hours, or 35 years, to enjoy before he can expect the onset of Alzheimer's disease his genetic profile predicts. Above the bed hangs a colourful computer-generated chart that baldly presents the stuff of his life: his genetic strengths and weaknesses and their implications for his health, finances and his fitness to be a parent. The morning begins with a breakfast of hi-bran cereal and soya milk to which Hugo must limit himself in the sombre knowledge that he has an inherited predisposition to heart disease. Into the kitchen runs his three-year-old daughter Anna. She is proving more precocious than he and his wife Jean had been led to expect during their sessions with a counsellor in the genetic planning clinic. But will her parents regret the choice of bright red hair, green eyes and a dusky complexion which turns out to be more arresting than attractive in the child? … Though a natural City type, Jean works from home as a consultant. Her genetic profile, for which she was first tested ten years ago, recommended a swift departure from the frenetic world of the dealing room after an extra copy of chromosome 8 was detected and indicated a risk of leukemia. Her session with a Harley Street cell-formation expert was definitely worth the investment, although it doubled the family's annual insurance premium … In spite of strict legislation governing the use of such personal information, Hugo and his wife are concerned by press stories that employers are paying shadowy agencies to provide black-market genetic profiles of prospective employees. Lobby groups representing the 'genetically challenged' claim that a single hair is enough to ruin a person's career. But such legitimate anxieties are out-weighed by the control Hugo and Jean feel they exercise over their lives."

I think that Hugo and Jean are dreamers if they believe that in their world they will have control over their lives for long. In a civilization where the genetic code may be determined at birth what government is going to waste time and money educating the genetically inferior? They will become a slave group, inexorably directed toward the kind of work they are best fitted to do. The genetically superior will at birth have passed the examination that directs them toward the ruling caste. When we think how many of the world's geniuses have come from disastrous genetic backgrounds, endowed, we know not how, with gifts that have built and extended our civilization, we wonder what genetic engineering will be able to do that works better than chance? Why did Beethoven emerge from physical and moral squalor? Why did Goethe emerge from a long line of intellectual nobodies? Can genetic engineers tell us? Can they, by their art, replicate genius? And who are the genetic engineers? Persons of high intellect, perfect physique, and numbing normality, one presumes; persons heavily weighted on the scientific side and thus, while not hostile to arts and learning, have the attitude toward such things that is dictated by their highly logical minds. Such a world has many advantages.

Oh, has it, you say; but you have been painting a bleak picture of what it might bring. Oh yes, there are advantages in a genetically managed world. Better therapies for such diseases as cannot be stamped out. And of course commercial benefit, to which the world of the geneticists is not unheeding. The Centre for the Exploitation of Science and Technology has estimated that drugs derived from genome research will be worth sixty billion dollars a year by the year 2010. And won't that be delightful for those who provide the drugs? And those who invest in them, getting in on the ground floor.

Improved health screening is a decided benefit, warning those who are likely to develop certain ailments to go on diets or do other appropriate things, to keep heart disease or cancer at bay. And think what a blessing it would be to employers, banks, and insurance companies to estimate whether or not they should become involved with people whose genetic pattern was likely to cause trouble.

Beneath a benevolent front, banks and insurance companies are, to put it as kindly as possible, very canny.

Genetic engineering could improve food plants, making them resistant to drought, or plant diseases. This is already in progress, and has already discovered that there are problems, unsuspected, in feeding such plants to animals who respond unexpectedly—having, of course, no understanding of the marvel that is being tested on them.

(Or have they, and being without speech, are unable to tell us about it? The geneticists assure us that the genetic makeup of a human being is 98.4 percent the same as that of a chimpanzee. What a pity that our brother the chimp is unable to share his thoughts with us. What a lot that difference of 1.6 percent appears to make! Almost as great, may we say, as the difference between Einstein and—I had better not say?)

And we are assured that under genetic engineering, animals could produce organs that could be transplanted into humans without being rejected. Surely this will greatly increase the number of neighbourhood zoos, to which appeal can be made whenever somebody is seriously injured in a motor accident. How close we shall grow to Nature in the coming world! And of course psychoanalysts will have to cope not only with the inner child, but also the inner dog, monkey, or perhaps hen. There's a theme for fiction!

There are of course things—not organs but entities which in the past we were assumed to have—with which we shall no longer have to bother. Dr. Francis Crick thinks that what we have been accustomed to call the soul is simply grey matter and of little consequence. Dr. Crick is a Nobel Laureate. So are they all, these mighty scientists—all Nobel Laureates, and not to be cheeked by the likes of you and me.

When am I going to begin talking about the Fiction of the Future? But I have been talking all the time of the rich soil in which it will grow. Genetic engineering—what could open up a greater prospect to the writer of bestsellers? The Great Gene Scandal in Big Business, when it is discovered that the Chairman of the Board is genetically inferior, and that the jealous mockery of those who have always said that he was no better than a chimp has proved to be dreadful truth? There's a plot for you! And here's another: Hugo and Jean marry, or decide to cohabit, and have a child. They put in their order with the gene scientist and in due course their ideal child is born, genetically suited to the parents and they to it. But something goes wrong: Hugo has, somewhere in his makeup, a recessive gene which leads him to have an affair with a girl at the office, who has a particularly strong combination of sexually attractive genes. Do Hugo and Jean fight? Of course not. They agree to part amicably. But what about the tailor-made child? What happens to it? Which of the new unions will it fit? There's a *New Yorker* story for you. And of course all stories written on such themes must have happy endings. Nobody may blaspheme against the gene world, any more than in Queen Victoria's reign they could hope for popular success if they blasphemed against the Christian God.

Of course there will be darker tales, written by authors who value their inner vision above popular success. It requires no great feat of imagination to see what desolation of the spirit—if an author is still so courageous as to suggest the existence of such a thing—could arise in a world where so much can be controlled and scientifically determined. Can we suppose that in the future there will no longer be that group—call it ten percent of society—which cannot accommodate to the civilization of their time, because they seem to be living in a different time? Their fate in a world where so much could be controlled by a variety of agencies and by governments composed of genetically sound people, and under the domination of Presidents and other rulers whose election had depended on the widest possible dissemination and public study of their genetic pattern—their fate, I fear, would not be as endurable as it is even now. And a wretched fate has always made good material for fiction.

There will be fiction of a finer sort, warning against the horrors that await a world which has gone—in the Biblical phrase—whoring after unbridled science. We have already had some examples of this. So long ago as 1932 Aldous Huxley published *Brave New World*, about a future in which everything is controlled, and everybody happy—or as happy as people can be who have never known any other mental state. It is not perhaps a very good novel, for in it rather more than in most of Huxley's fiction, his ideas are vastly more interesting than his characters, and fiction at its best is an art devoted to the exploration of character. It is a world where no art exists, because people with no gamut of feeling need no art, and art may be disruptive. I reread it last summer, and in the heat of July it chilled my bones.

But did it fill me with fear? No, it did not. Nor do the newspaper reports of new triumphs in genetic study make me tremble for a future in which all of mankind will be guided and conditioned by what scientists believe is good for it. It certainly did not make me fearful of the end of all art, and fiction among the rest. As an experienced and careful newspaper reader I know better than that, and I have seen too many scientific marvels subside quietly into something less than was foreseen for them by the Henny-Pennys of the media who rush as often as possible to tell the King that the sky is falling.

Genes may explain much, but I do not think they can explain the inveterate hatred between the Serbs and the Croats, or the destructive ill will of the Hutus and the Tutsis. They cannot repeat Nature's splendid jokes, like Mozart and Shakespeare. They can do much for mankind, just as Pasteur's germ theory has done, but like Pasteur's germ theory they will become accepted as one of the miracles of science which the greater part of mankind is aware of, does not understand, and benefits from without quite knowing how. But the great gods of Chance and of Necessity, which the Greeks called *Anángke*, will continue to rule mankind as they always have, and in their cruel compulsions and sly jokes the writers of fiction—the real writers and not simply the followers of fashion—will find their themes.

Perhaps at this point I should interject that a new universal language is in the womb of time, but will not come to birth right away. It is the language of mathematics. My authority is the great philosopher, Alfred North Whitehead, who predicted, in 1941:

> Mathematics is the most powerful technique for the understanding of pattern, and for the analysis of the relation of patterns … Having regard to the immensity of its subject matter, mathematics, even modern mathematics, is a science in its babyhood. If civilization continues to advance in the next two thousand years, the overwhelming novelty in human thought will be the dominance of mathematical understanding.

What might that mean to fiction? I cannot tell, but unless the entire structure of the human mind and spirit changes, I think that fiction will have a continuance for those who are impatient of the insistence of mathematics on certainties as opposed to probabilities, and even if mathematics develops to encompass the ambiguities of human experience, one wonders if it will ever have anything whatever to do with one of the greatest developments of the human spirit. I mean humour, the true deep humour, and not simply the humour of jokes. Not wisecracks among mathematicians about the Reciprocal of Pi.

One of the very great sages of the past, to whom I have always paid particular attention, was called Heracleitus; he lived about 2,500 years ago, and his ideas still seem to me to be fresh and widely applicable. He thought that the first principle of the universe was flux, a sequence of becoming and perishing. The world neglects him, and he is called The Weeping Philosopher, because people of sunny nature cannot bear his notion of the eternal ebb and flow; they think it pessimistic, because they are wedded to the idea that the history of mankind is unquestioningly progressive, and that every day in every way things are getting better and better. This notion of serial progress is particularly popular in the New World. But in spite of our nervous optimism, we seem always to need a bugbear ruler somewhere upon which we can fasten the fears without which civilized man seems unable to live. The bugbear used to be God; now it seems to be Science.

Heracleitus is not gloomy; he is just long-sighted. His most famous principle was that of regulating opposites; that is, in a terribly tight nutshell, the principle that positive and negative, struggling for supremacy, bring about equilibrium, or harmony. The grand name for this idea is dynamic monism, and we can catch glimpses of it out of the corner of an eye, though we cannot command the whole scheme unless we make an intensive study of history.

These warring opposites, like the fishes going different ways which are the symbol of the astrological sign of Pisces—can we see anything of them in the modern world? Well, as a determined newspaper reader I can inform myself every day about the latest developments in tolerance, political correctitude, and scientific advance and I can contrast them, sometimes on the same page, with the news that in the rural districts of South Africa, where a new freedom has just asserted itself, there is also a sharp rise in the number of witch burnings; by midsummer of 1994 there were records of seventy-one such burnings, which is greater than the total for all of the previous year. And where freedom of speech is loudly proclaimed in our part of the world, Muslim fundamentalists have now declared the death of two authors to be imperative, because they have contradicted the Koran. Can these opposites run together and form a balance? Heracleitus would probably say that as they exist side by side in what we triumphantly proclaim to be a global village, they are already doing so. The witch burners are our neighbours.

I assure you that I am not straying from my theme, which was the Future of Fiction. The field for fictional exploration is broader perhaps than it has ever been, because the world reads more. Nothing that concerns mankind is alien to the teller of tales, whether he is the one who unfolds a mat in the marketplace, or the one who works in her solitary room with her word processor. The writer looks with satisfaction toward our official entry into the Era of Flux, because if he pays heed to his daily paper, he has daily and almost hourly assurances that flux and the compensating dynamism of opposites is boldly at work.

He does not imagine—unless he writes Science Fiction and wants to make your flesh creep—that genetic engineering is going to reduce mankind's variety. Nor does he believe that good genes alone will produce a good human creature with a good destiny. If he should momentarily be tempted to think any such thing he has but to turn to his Bible for the ancient assurance that *Anángke* is still the ruler of all. He reads: "I returned, and saw under the sun, that the race is not to the swift, nor the battle to the strong, neither yet bread to the wise, nor yet riches to men of understanding, nor yet favour to men of skill; *but time and chance happeneth to them all.*" (Ecclesiastes 9:11)

In those words he knows that whether its form is the film or television, or simply the unfailing, reliable printed book, the Future of Fiction is safe. It is a necessity of life. For as Socrates assured us so long ago, the unexamined life is not worth living.

Theatre

6

How to Design a Haunted House

If one makes a lot of speeches one is sure to be seized at some point by the desire to stop posturing as an authority, and to borrow the motley of the clown. I yielded to this impulse when the Ontario Association of Architects asked me to speak in 1960. All artists like jokes about their work, but many people forget that architects are artists, and treat them rather as if they were monumental masons—dealers in heavy, indestructible wares of awesome solemnity. From their reception I knew that my speech was a rest for the architects and it was also a rest for me. Of course one should not attempt too often to be funny in public, and one should certainly never strive to be one's funniest, because in such circumstances the psychological sanction known as the Law of Reversed Effort comes into play, and the funnyman is left diminished and covered with shame.

You are kind indeed to ask me to be with you on this occasion, and I appreciate the honour you do me. You have completed three days of addresses, of boards, of panels, and yet here you are—only slightly tranquilized—to subject yourselves to yet another speech. I am not unaware that some of you, at any rate, expect me to make an *amusing* speech, and I truly wish that I could assure you that I am about to do so. But it is not in mortals to command success—especially funny success. Furthermore I have all my life suffered from the fact that I am a deeply—I might almost say a neurotically—impressionable person, and for the past month or so the thought of the professional eminence and personal distinction of this audience has weighed so heavily upon me that I now feel that it would be impertinent to offer you anything less than the most profound and solemn reflections of which I am capable. Further, as *you* so well know, every man cherishes in his heart the belief that, if fate had been kinder, he would himself have been a very great architect. So, if I should chance, however fleetingly, to be amusing, I assure you that it is entirely inadvertent, and has only happened because I can't help it, and I apologize for it in advance.

My subject, as you know, is "Architecture, What Else…?" Who would pass up the chance to talk to a captive audience of architects about their own profession? To this topic, after some thought, I added the rider, "Literature, of Course" because I lost courage and thought I might not be able to talk long enough about architecture to fill up the necessary time.

You are, I hope, breathless with excitement, wondering how I can possibly bring these two great arts together in a single after-dinner speech. It has been easier than you might suppose. I am going to talk for a little while about *the Drama and the Novel, and the influence of architecture on both*. And, as plays and novels are really distilments of life itself, I shall inevitably talk about the influence of architecture on life.

Of course I am going to find fault. You know that without telling. Nobody speaks to an architect except to find fault. It is an occupational hazard you share with newspaper editors.

Let us begin with the Drama. You people have just about killed it because of the revolution you have brought about in theatre design. There was a happy age when we had wonderful playhouses, with terrible scenery: Now you have given us terrible playhouses with wonderful scenery.

When people went to the theatre in the eighteenth and early nineteenth centuries, they bought an uplifting sense of personal splendour for the price of admission. Yesterday you listened to a discussion of "The New Sensualism"; those old theatres were packed to the doors with the Old Sensualism. To the doors? Yes, and outside the doors, as well. The playhouses looked like temples, and the audience approached them in a spirit they brought to no other building. Indoors, the playhouses were modelled on palaces, and every playgoer became a nobleman, or at least an associate of noblemen, when he took his seat. Many of those old buildings are still in existence in Canada, because even the most malignant and bloody-minded City Council cannot pull them all down at once, and when we visit them we are immediately impressed with their *remarkable sensuous plasticity of surface.* (You didn't know I could talk Architectese, did you? I have always been a good linguist and can pick up a smattering of any language, quite quickly.) In those old theatres there is ornament everywhere. In the meanest of them there is a frieze, or perhaps a statuary group, of the Nine Muses, and Apollo is usually somewhere to be found. There is nothing puts an audience in the right mood for a trivial farce about adultery so quickly as a good preliminary stare at the Nine Muses.

But it would be quite wrong to suppose that the baroque opulence of the old theatres meant that they were designed without taste. They were not, as foolish people suppose, all tawdry gold and garnet plush. There is a newly decorated theatre in New York—the Billy Rose—which has been refurbished on that principle, and it is a horror. I don't ask for barbaric colour, but especially in a climate like ours, colour, inside and out, is of the uttermost importance. The theatres I speak of were not garish or vulgar. No, those old theatre interiors were decorated in the most elegant combinations of fawn, brown, and gold, and in many of them a subtle use was made of a colour which modern decorators seem to shy away from—a wonderful olive green. Everywhere you saw combinations of richness and elegance of which the secret seems to be lost, for of late years there has been a widespread notion that the secret of elegance is austerity. Of course, in our saner moments we all know that the secret of elegance is taste. Austerity is what happens when people dare not trust their taste.

If you doubt what I say, visit the best remaining examples of theatre I speak of. Go to that beauty at Drottningholm, in Sweden. Go to the Old Vic, in London, or the Theatre Royal at Bristol. In this latter playhouse, even in the footmen's gallery, the elegance and excitement of the building is palpable, and I say, quite seriously, that it is easier to enjoy a play in such a theatre than it is in the modern theatres I shall speak of in a moment. The reason is that the building was designed with enjoyment—public pleasure—foremost in the architect's mind.

One of the charms of these theatres, which cannot be recaptured because of the change in our social structure, is the comfort and convenience of the boxes. People sat in boxes for privacy—and of course we all know that to desire privacy today is to show oneself unfriendly, and probably fascistic. But in those boxes one could see without having to be seen; the chairs were movable, which is a great comfort, because democracy has not yet reached the point where we are all born of one size; it was possible to flirt in them, which was a great addition to the entertainment, and if you had no taste for flirting, there was nothing to prevent you from taking a servant with a picnic basket, and having a light meal as you watched the play. Show me the theatre today when you can flirt and eat, either consecutively or at once!

Don't let us talk about the movies. I know what goes on there, and I don't think it can be described as either eating or flirting—unless you use those terms very loosely.

These were exquisite playhouses, designed to flatter and accommodate the audience in the greatest possible comfort. But on the stage—! The scenic art was in its infancy—and a very peevish, rickety infancy, too. The scenery showed rooms with no windows, and frequently with no doors. When people wanted to enter or leave, they walked through open wings at the sides of the scene—apparently right through the wall. The royal palace and the swineherd's hut were both of precisely the same size. The effect of this scenic poverty on playwrights is of course familiar to you all; they couldn't depend on really handsome scenery, so they had to fall back on substitutes—like poetry. It was out of the question for them to write a play which depended on any circumstance of architecture. One of the great revolutionary plays of our time was *A Doll's House*, written by Ibsen in 1879; the climax of the action comes when the oppressed wife, Nora, leaves her husband's house and *slams the door*. With that play, Ibsen brought architecture and modern scenic design into the theatre: If anybody could have found a door on a stage before that time, and had been so foolhardy as to slam it, everything behind the proscenium would have fallen down.

When Nora slammed the door, the modern theatre was born. And what a house you have provided for it! Where's the sensuous plasticity now? Where's the stimulating visual sensuous delight you hypocrites were talking about yesterday? Do you see it in our modern playhouses? You were in the O'Keefe Centre earlier today for what your program calls, with admirable restraint, a "pre-lunch aperitif." I was not with you, and I am curious about your experiences. Did you happen to notice Apollo anywhere? How many Muses were there after you had finished your aperitif—nine, or thirteen? I don't know. I wasn't there. I'm only asking for information.

I know nothing about the O'Keefe Centre, but I have been in a lot of other new theatre buildings in Canada. I call them that, because I was in them on theatre business, but they were really high schools or hockey arenas, or multi-purpose auditoriums which had, clinging about them, the fetid stench of secondary education and economical community planning. They were not temples. They were not dedicated to any of the gods, and they certainly had nothing to do with any of the rowdy, jolly demigods, like Folly or Pleasure. Maybe they had Stereo-Structural Sensualism; there seemed to be an awful lot of naked steel showing in some of them. I am so old-fashioned that it still makes me ashamed when I can see what holds a building up. It is honest, I know, but where is its charm? Such painfully honest architecture might perhaps be called the New Immodesty.

But on the stage of these places! What elegance of design! What breathtaking splendour! And what practicality! Windows that open and shut at the touch of a finger; doors that never stick; taps that squirt water without fail—all the things, in fact, that you can't get in your new $170,000 house. There is always, and necessarily, an air of fantasy, of a splendour beyond ordinary life, about the stage. Nowadays it reveals itself, strange to relate, in the perfection of the carpentry and plumbing. And as for design—those of you who saw the Comédie Française when it last came to Toronto will remember the setting for *Le Bourgeois Gentilhomme*, which was the work of

Susanne Lalique. Which of us would not have a house like that, if it could be built anywhere except in a theatre?

You will notice that I have said nothing about accommodation for the actors. Of course it is always terrible, but even here there has been a change. In the old theatres they had smelly kennels in which to change their clothes. But nowadays, after the School Board has cut the estimates and changed the plans, they have nothing at all. Have you ever tried to transform yourself into a great character of drama in a schoolroom? The ghosts of dead mathematics teachers clutch at your costume and smear your makeup. Actors of an earlier day dressed in bad conditions too, even in barns. But the barns were unmistakably associated with Life; those schoolroom dressing accommodations speak of education, of repression, of being kept in after four, and their air vents whisper of lingering and chalky death. Humour is put to silence, Passion is rebuked, and Imagination is made to dance in chains.

Gentlemen, I appeal to you with all the force of which I am capable: Give us back a theatre which it is a pleasure to be in! Give us colour, give us Muses, give us Joy! Oh, I know how much trouble you take to get the right seats, but you are caressing us at the wrong end. The *spirit* also demands its satisfactions, and man cannot live by foam rubber alone. Give us a whisper of grandeur, of excitement. Without it the theatre perishes. And that means that you must feel something of the spirit of the theatre in your own breasts. When you design an auditorium or a theatre, I beg you to banish the puritanism which seems to be the fashion in modern architecture, and invoke a vastly more appropriate spirit. I mean the spirit of one of the great ornaments of your profession, Sir John Vanbrugh.

Now let us turn to Architecture and the Novel. Modern novelists have turned their backs on architecture—except in detective stories, where it is absolutely essential to prove that nobody could have entered the room where the beautiful blonde was murdered. But the great novelists of the past leaned very heavily on architectural devices, usually of a kind not found in modern building. You know the kind of thing I mean. In countless novels written fifty years ago the heroine, having discovered that her husband was deceiving her with the beautiful brunette, crept away to the *nursery* to weep over her beloved children.

How is she expected to do that in a house which hasn't any nursery? No woman of ordinary sensibility can creep away to weep in the *rumpus room*. The thing is a psychological absurdity, and by making it so you have contributed to the breakup of the modern home.

And the *study*—how many modern houses have a study? Yet every man needs a study. Not to study in, of course, but to retire to when the pressure of domestic life is too great. He summons the other members of the family to meet him there. "George, I should like to see you in my study," he says to his son, when he wants to tell him to stop spending so much money. "Mary, come to my study," he says when he wants to tell his daughter to break off her affair with that beatnik she has been meeting on the sly. "My dear, will you come into my study," he says, when he wants to tell his wife that he knows what she has been up to with that handsome Mexican dentist. But most of all he needs his study to *sulk* in. Every man must have a private sulking-place, and as his wife always wants the bedroom for that purpose, he must have a study, or bottle up his sulks. And if he bottles his sulks, it won't be long before he has to be taken away in a straitjacket. How can he sulk in the living area, which his children are using as the play area, while his wife is right beside him in the kitchen area, without so much as a screen to divide them? By forgetting the study you have struck an underhand blow at the mental health of the nation.

His wife, as I have said, sulks in the bedroom. I wish I could call it a *boudoir* but those wretched little boxes in modern houses cannot rise to the dignity of such a term. You know what a boudoir is. It's a bedroom that you can pace in. Consider this passage, from a very fine novel, written not quite a century ago by Mrs. Henry Wood:

> Scarce able to see through the mist of tears that clouded her violet eyes, Lady Maude sought her boudoir. There, among the treasures she had brought from her childhood home, she paced the floor, lost in sombre reverie. Had I but known, she mused as she walked toward the window, had I but known when I gave my trust, my hand—yea, all that a woman holds in store of love and

tenderness—to Cyril, that a day might come when I should wish, nay, implore Almighty God, for the power to recall every gift, I should have ended my life rather than yield to his suit. Yes, all of this, these broad acres, this stately mansion, yes, and—O God, be merciful!—even my children, I should have wished undone.... She turned at the window and continued her weary pacing.

Do you see what I am getting at? She said all of that while making one trip from the door to the window. The book tells us that Lady Maude was tall—say five foot eight—and therefore one of her paces might be estimated at twenty-five inches. Everybody knows that when you are pacing and regretting at the same time, you take a step to every word. Therefore Lady Maude took 85 paces of 25 inches apiece, which is 2,125 inches or 177 feet from door to window. Assuming that the room was a double cube, and that she was walking the long way of it, that means that the dimensions of her boudoir were 177 by 88, giving her a floor space of 15,576 square feet. No wonder she was able to keep the treasures of her old home in it. If they had included a couple of race-horses she could have kept them in it, without serious inconvenience.

But the important point is that she was able to pace in her boudoir, and the novel has a happy ending. I put it to you, gentlemen, would it have had a happy ending if Lady Maude had been cooped up in one of the bedrooms of which the Canadian Council of Women have been complaining to Mr. John C. Parkin?

If we are to believe the evidence of literature, the houses in which people have lived greatly, and sinned nobly, were all big. Evidence in support of what I say crowds into the mind. What were the words of King Duncan as he greeted Lady Macbeth at the entry to Glamis?

> This castle hath a pleasant seat. The air
> Nimbly and sweetly recommends itself
> Unto our gentle senses.

However, that is getting into the realm of public health and town planning, and I won't press it.

However, I would like to urge upon you the convenience and charm of an amenity which was to be found in virtually every house described by Sir Walter Scott. I refer, of course, to the Secret Passage.

Time and again in Scott's novels somebody reveals that a secret passage leads from the castle to the shepherd's hut, and as it inevitably led also from the shepherd's hut to the castle, it meant that both the shepherd and the lord of the manor had the good of it. It made life much simpler at all kinds of junctures when simplicity was needed. You could escape from the castle in a hurry, and you could also get into the castle unseen. In cases of murder or abduction this was invaluable. In ordinary domestic crises it meant that somebody could slip down to the hut and borrow a bottle of whisky if guests came unexpectedly. Still more often, it meant that the shepherd could sneak up to the castle and steal a bottle of whisky when he wanted one. It provided that element of surprise, of the unexpected, which modern domestic architecture so noticeably lacks.

How long is it since any of you included a Secret Passage in a new house? Of course I realize the difficulties you work under. Modern contractors don't know how to keep a secret. The union would certainly object to the old custom of cutting out the tongues of all the men who had worked on the job. The building inspector—they never have any imagination—would insist that it be equipped with electric light, drainage, and an air-changing system, because he would not realize that the essence of a secret passage is darkness, dampness, and a seepage of natural gas.

If you want to know what happens when somebody tries to build a secret passage today, just look at the mess on University Avenue at Bloor. The only secret is when it will be finished.

Yet another household convenience made familiar to us in historical novels is the *oubliette.* The works of Dumas are full of oubliettes. In its simplest terms, an oubliette is a very deep, dry well, or perhaps a disused privy, down which you can push people. Because the oubliette is deep and made of stone, they reach the bottom in a damaged condition, and there is no way out. A well-used oubliette can become rather objectionable, and ought to be located as far as possible from the boudoir. Among other things, the screams can be very trying to delicate nerves.

Please do not suppose that I am encouraging crime. The oubliette was not an instrument for settling family quarrels, or dismissing unwelcome guests. And—this is very important—no oubliette was ever built simply to be an oubliette. It became one when you threw really bad people—criminal, depraved people—into it. This circumstance, of course, has given rise to the proverbial saying that *you can't make an oubliette without breaking yeggs.*

I could continue in this strain for some time. There are countless amenities which every house needs, for literary uses, and which have been allowed to disappear from modern domestic design. The attic, for instance—invaluable for nostalgia; it is a proven psychological fact that you can't be nostalgic on the ground floor. And the cellar—admirable for murders, for knife fights in the dark, for the walling up of wives who have not worn well. Your objection, I know, is that a house equipped with all these handsome comforts would be rather large. True, but when the owners have finished with it, no ingenuity at all is needed to convert it into a first-class Funeral Home. The boudoir is of ample size for a chapel, you can garage the hearse in the Secret Passage, and the oubliette provides ample, cool accommodation for Unfinished Business.

I have spoken of Drama and Fiction as they relate to architecture, and I hope that I have reminded you of the fact that you, gentlemen, are the designers of the scenery against which we act out the drama of our personal lives. What our personal lives are you know only too well, and I really think that you must bear some measure of blame. If we are dull, who knows what a livelier setting might not do to improve our performances? If we lack splendour, is it because we live in circumstances where a single splendid gesture might knock the place down? Don't suppose that I blame you entirely. You are what we have made you, fully as much as we are what you have made us. But would it not be possible for some of us—a few of you architects, and a handful of us ordinary people—to conspire to bring a whisper of magnificence, a shade of lightheartedness, and a savour of drama into the settings of our daily lives? I think it would. Anyhow, I think we should try.

7

Lines Written in Dejection After Seeing a Performance of Hair on Epiphany, 1970

Like most writers, I produced some verse when I was young, but it was of such an unfashionable sort nobody wanted it. I liked strict forms, and rhymes, and showed what was considered an unpoetic tendency to be cheerful. Even now I write poetry on the sly, so to speak, when it seems to be the obvious form for what I have to say. Here is an example.

"Aquarius! Aquarius!" the hoarse young voices sang,
Heralding a new era in the world's horoscope
As Pisces wanes and the ambiguous sign rises.

So what, Aquarius, do *you* bring?
New Ice Age?
New Spring?
Anything for us
Born at the end of Pisces?
Any new virtue,
Or the sour stench of old vices?
(We haste to the theatre
As the Magi sought the Star,

Seeking an epiphany in HAIR:
Finding that most of the cast
Depressingly pronounce it HA'R.)

"A cold coming we had of it
Just the worst time of the year
For a journey, and such a journey;
The ways deep and the weather sharp,
The very dead of winter."

But we hoped for a dawning of youth
In the fine old playhouse;
Such renewal as the Magi found,
Or Simeon, in the Temple.
But alas, not a Babe, but babes were on view
(Some, very recently, sucklings)
And the whole possessed crew
Shouting F U C K!
(Had they, we wondered, known Love.)
Shouting S H I T!
(Whatever that word may have meant
To those who seemed never to have heard that
"Love has pitched his mansion
in the place of excrement.")

They offered us two great revelations:
First—THAT NAKEDNESS IS INNOCENCE.
(There they stood, for us to see,
With drooping breasts and pubic hair like
Highlanders' sporrans;
Or else with narrow chests, shrivelled privates,
And incipient varicose veins.
Gothic was this nakedness, not Greek.)
Thus was innocence manifested nightly and twice on
Wednesdays and Saturdays, for a figure not lower
than the Equity minimum.

Second—THAT WAR IS A HORRIBLE BUSINESS.
(Which we, who had been born into one war
And worn through another,
Already knew with the thoroughness of those
Who have chewed and gagged down bitter herbs.)

These were their revelations.

Of course there were many false epiphanies;
The Magi made many fruitless journeys ere they died.

So, Aquarius, what else is new?

8

Jung and the Theatre

When I am asked why I have spent so much time, over the past twenty-five years, in the study of the work and thought of Dr. C.G. Jung, I reply that it is because Jung's discoveries and speculations throw so much light on my work as a student and teacher of literature. Jung always insisted that he was a scientist, and unquestionably that was true; but he was also a great humanist, and although I deplore partial and facile application of Jungian ideas to literary criticism, I know that a serious study of Jungian thought is one fruitful path of literary study. What follows is a suggestion, necessarily brief and incomplete, of what a Jungian approach reveals about some plays of the nineteenth century whose literary value is not of the first order, but whose appeal to large audiences over a long period is explicable on grounds of their relevance to some matters of deep human concern. This speech, somewhat varied in form, has been given to the Analytical Psychology Society of Ontario in 1973, to the Analytical Psychology Club of Chicago, and to the C.G. Jung Foundation of New York in 1977.

During the past fifty years we have grown accustomed to the use of Sigmund Freud's attitude toward life, or some version of it, as an instrument of artistic criticism. But criticism of the arts springing from the thought of C.G. Jung has been much less familiar. Jung was drawn toward literary criticism himself: It creeps into his scientific writing repeatedly and we may ask ourselves how much he may have repressed in order that the ideal of science might be served. Herbert Read has written interestingly about painting and sculpture from a Jungian point of view; there has been some useful and stimulating criticism of the sculpture of Henry Moore—who seems very often to be seeking to give archetypes a shape—along Jungian lines. Of late years a renewed interest in the painting of some of the Romantics has brought forth Jungian explications; I am thinking especially of some books written about the Swiss-English painter Henry Fuseli. Jungian comment on literature has come from a somewhat unsuspected source, for one would not immediately have thought of J.B. Priestley as a Jungian; but he acknowledges a great debt to Jung, and some of the best passages in his much underrated book *Literature and Western Man* are Jungian in inspiration and method. Indeed, I have sometimes thought that the sheer weight of common sense in that book, and its Jungian bias, are what have put conventional critics so much against it. For Jungian thought, although it looks at common sense through a prism that splits it into many facets, leaves it common sense still, and much of the reluctance of conventional people to recognize it as such is no more than the ordinary disposition of the intellectual to prefer the complex to the simple, and the distant vision to what is directly under his nose. In Jungian terms it might be described as an over-valuation of the Thinking Faculty.

In attempting to talk to you about Jung and the Theatre I must at once admit to having bitten off far more than I can chew. There is enough material in the subject to engross the attention of a year-long weekly seminar, and anything that I can do tonight must be confined to a hop-skip-and-jump. Was Jung interested in the theatre? It seems that he was not, and in all the *Collected Works* I can find only two references in the Indexes to either Theatre or Drama. These references are, however, strongly suggestive. It goes without saying that they are the comments of a writer who seems to regard the theatre, as so many people do, as primarily a branch of literature. I disagree with that point of view, for the theatre was already old when what we generally call literature was still unheard of. The theatre is as old as Prophecy and the Epic, and to look upon it as the bastard sibling of such johnny-come-latelies in the arts as the Novel or Lyric Poetry is to do it a grave injustice. The appeal of the Theatre is primal, and it continues to be so even in its most modern forms. The more it partakes of primal quality in feeling, the more effective it is as theatrical art.

Jung gives me courage. He writes: "One might describe the theatre, somewhat unaesthetically, as an institution for working out private complexes in public." I may as well jump in with both feet and mark out my ground at once: In my opinion the theatre is a house of dreams, in which audiences gather to share a dream that is presented to them by a group of artists who are particularly skilled in bodying forth dreams. The script of the play is at best no more than the plan from which they work; it may be a plan of unique literary value, but it is not and cannot be the whole of the dream which is presented on the stage, because many other artists may bring their contributions to that completed artistic whole. There are the actors, who are skilled in the crafts of making themselves vivid and attractive in roles which present characters often at variance with their private personalities; in great plays these actors must also be highly skilled speakers, who give point and cogency to the words they say which cannot be rivalled by the person who reads a play to himself. And there is the designer, who offers a splendid *milieu* for the dream, aided by a designer of lighting who may claim to be an artist in his own right. And there is the composer, whose music supports the play and intensifies the feeling it evokes. And there is the audience itself, which provides each of its members with a sense of sharing the experience of the play, which also heightens the effect of that experience. A fine performance of a great play is one of the most compelling and rewarding experiences our culture provides, and it is also a highly sophisticated version of that experience of which anthropologists have written, where members of the tribe gather together to be told a great dream which is of importance to the tribe.

Do you think I am making extreme claims for the theatre? Certainly I am talking about the theatre at its best. I am thinking of certain performances of great plays I have seen during my lifetime, such as a thrilling performance of Goethe's *Faust*—the whole of it—presented on two successive nights at the Salzburg Festival. I am thinking of a magnificent performance of *The Magic Flute* which I once saw at Covent Garden—because I include opera under my general heading of theatre. I am thinking of certain performances of Greek plays, of Shakespeare, of Ibsen, of Chekov, and certainly of some splendidly life-enhancing performances of superb comedies, such as *The Way of the World*, *The Country Wife*, *The School for Scandal*—performances which were great experiences of what G.K. Chesterton so finely called the "mysticism of happiness."

I am not talking only about television serials, or B-movies, but television serials and B-movies have their place, as well, because those who claim to experience and value art only on the highest level know nothing whatever about art; television serials and B-movies body forth the dreams of a large number of people, or else money-greedy entrepreneurs would not continue to manufacture them. Art is not democratic; it is aristocratic, and to suggest that everybody will love the highest when they see it is demonstrably rubbish. They won't. But they will love what reaches them, and the human need which is satisfied by television serials and B-movies is nearer to the human need which feeds on *Hamlet* and *Oedipus* than either of them is to the psyche of the person who cannot dream, or does not dare to dream, and who is bored by the theatre.

What we expect to find in a dream, of course, are dream figures and archetypal involvements. It is for this reason, I believe, that Realism in the theatre is a dead end. When I was a very young man a play visited Toronto that was, at that time, the very pinnacle of Realist drama. It was Elmer Rice's *Street Scene*. The stage setting was of a group of houses in a New York slum. The windows opened, and could be shut. Garbage cans containing real garbage stood at the front doors. Some of the garbage had fallen on the pavement, and occasionally people slipped on it. A woman was having a baby in one of the upstairs flats, and her groans and occasional piercing shrieks punctuated the play. A policeman passed up and down the street, and children jeered at him. Morning gave place to midday, which in its turn gave place to dusk; one marvelled at the cleverness of the man on the switchboard. It was all quite wonderful. You could almost smell it. But to save my life I cannot remember what the play was about, and I have not since cared to read it to find out.

In that same autumn, however, I saw *A Midsummer Night's Dream* for the first time. The company had little money, but they had a good deal of talent and they acted the play in a setting which was simply curtains. The magical flower which figures in the action was obviously a paper flower, and when Bottom appeared in the ass's head it was plain that it was a head made of *papier mâché.* This was the very opposite of Realism. But it was a great dream, and nobody in the audience cared a damn about Realism after the first ten minutes. I have seen that play, I suppose, at least a dozen times since, sometimes sparely set on the stage, and sometimes very lavishly and beautifully mounted. Every time I respond in the same way: I am the Duke, I am both the male lovers, I am all the clowns, I am Bottom the Weaver making a glorious ass of himself in the enchanted wood. Because, you see, this is one of the very greatest dreams of the tribe, and whenever I see it I feel both immeasurably enriched in myself and also very much more a member of the tribe. Here, in the present, the past has spoken to me, as I know that it will speak to the future when I am no more. And this is not Realism which is an imitation of surfaces; it is the vast, complex panorama of life itself, of which I am a part, and which the great dream permits me to experience, for the duration of the play, at the very centre.

I feel, however, that it would be unfair if I spoke to you now solely in terms of Shakespeare and Goethe and the mighty Greeks, because supreme works of art are themselves convincing arguments in favour of any theory to which they can be attached, however frail the attachment may be. So in order to demonstrate my ideas about the Jungian content of effective drama I am going to confine my examples to the popular drama of the nineteenth century—to what is called—usually with an undertone of contempt—melodrama. Nobody can then say that I am marshalling an army of great writers on my side in order to cloud my argument. Melodrama has, until quite recently, been considered beneath serious criticism, because its literary content is not arresting. Its theatrical—or, if you think the word more impressive, its dramatic—content is, however, indisputable. Melodrama was a theatrical mode which filled the theatres of the nineteenth century, and if we despise it, we would do well to remember that there were people in those audiences whose taste we admire in matters of the novel, of poetry, of all the arts, of statesmanship, and of philosophy; if they were not fools in these things, why should we assume that they were fools when they went to the theatre?

When people speak of melodrama, however, they are often referring to the worst examples of the *genre,* and surprisingly often they are referring to plays they have never seen seriously and well presented. One of the greatest and most successful writers of melodrama, Douglas Jerrold, described it in a government report as a type of play having a great many telling situations, with a physical rather than a mental appeal. Well, it depends on what you mean by "mental"; certainly we do not go to the theatre in order to hear philosophers debate, but neither do we go to see nothing but physical action. We go, most of the time, for emotional experience; the theatre is a temple of art, and that means a temple of feeling.

If we are to talk about melodrama, I must describe a few examples to you. I should like to begin with a play which I regard as a very great melodrama, and which has had considerable success on the stage. The name of its author is not wholly unknown, either. I speak of Lord Byron's play *Manfred.*

Byron himself described *Manfred* as "very wild, metaphysical and inexplicable." Briefly described, it is about a nobleman who is in despair because he has, in some manner which is not specified, destroyed the woman he loved. It is made abundantly clear that this woman who is given the name of Astarte was his spiritual likeness, his feminine self—as we should say in our Jungian vocabulary, she was his Anima. Listen to the words in which he describes her:

> She was like me in lineaments; her eyes.
> Her hair, her features, all to the very tone
> Even of her voice, they said were like to mine;
> But soften'd all, and tempered into beauty:
> She had the same lone thoughts and wanderings,
> The quest of hidden knowledge, and a mind
> To comprehend the universe: nor these
> Alone, but with them gentler power than mine,

Pity, and smiles and tears—which I had not;
And tenderness—but that I had for her;
Humility—and that I never had.
Her faults were mine—her virtues were her own—
I loved her, and destroyed her!

WITCH: With thy hand?

MANFRED: Not with my hand, but heart, which broke her heart;
It gazed on mine, and wither'd. I have shed
Blood, but not hers—and yet her blood was shed;
I saw—and could not stanch it.

Separation from her is intolerable, and Manfred seeks the aid of magic to recall her spirit. He is confronted by terrifying apparitions of many kinds, and at last he is confronted by Rhadamanthus himself, the great Judge of the Underworld; in answer to the emotional power of his demand the Phantom of Astarte appears, and though he begs in agony for her forgiveness, she speaks only to predict his death. And, at the end of the play he does indeed die, refusing spiritual comfort and unrepentant of his pride and his sins, defying the evil spirits that seek to possess him, and hopeful that the mercy of Astarte will lead him to bliss—which means reunion with her.

Byron told a friend in a letter that the germs of *Manfred* were to be found in a journal which he had sent to his half-sister, Augusta Leigh. This was the sister whom it was pretty generally asserted that he had loved incestuously, and who bore what was believed to be his child. The mainspring of the plot of the play is incest. It does not much matter that Augusta Leigh was rather a silly little woman, and that her fate was not that of the heroine of the play. What matters is that Byron has written a very fine play about a man who is divided from his soul, who seeks reunion with it, and gains it at a terrible cost.

The Jungian elements in this play are easily identified. Manfred is the Fatal Man, the incubus-devil who destroys what he loves but who seeks Redemption; the consulting rooms of analysts are crowded with such people, though they do not describe their plight in Byronic verse. The Phantom of Astarte is the lost Anima, "whose voice was like the voice of his own soul, heard in the calm of thought." There is also a Wise Old Man in the play, the Abbot of St. Maurice, whose advice Manfred scorns; there is an archetypal Friend, who saves Manfred from self-destruction before he receives Astarte's promise of redemption. And there is the Witch of the Alps, a figure of the dark side of the Anima, whom one is sometimes inclined to think might have been a better match for Manfred than the beautiful Astarte. There they all are, the Jungian Theatre Company of the Archetypes, acting out their accustomed roles, and speaking in Byronic verse of a high order. In *Manfred*, the date of which is 1816, we have a drama which deals with a splendid, passionate grappling with the dark side of man's nature, in a dramatic *milieu* where only death may be accepted as the settlement of all debts.

Not every writer of melodrama was a Byron, of course, and during the nineteenth century we often see this great theme degenerate in lesser hands into the struggle of Virtue against Vice, where both Virtue and Vice have been reduced from aristocratic, heaven-storming dimensions to merely *bourgeois* conflicts. But let us not be superior, for the *bourgeoisie* has its soul struggle as well as the poets and the aristocrats, and things must be described in terms which are congruous and comprehensible to those who wish to understand them.

The drama of the Redeemed Man is common enough in the nineteenth century. There were several versions of *The Flying Dutchman*, condemned to sail the seas until he is freed by the love of a pure woman. We know it still, and respond to it still, in Wagner's powerful opera of that name. The man who kills his soul appears again and again. In Victor Hugo's play *Le Roi s'amuse* it is the savage jester who, in his desire to avenge himself on an enemy, kills his own daughter—the only creature he loves. That story persists, too, in Verdi's *Rigoletto*. And there is the drama of the Lost Lady, the woman who seems to be of doubtful virtue, but whose nobility of soul is far above the understanding of the lover who turns against her. It has had many versions, of which the most famous was the younger Dumas's *La Dame aux Camélias*, once again preserved for us—and still doing sell-out business—in Verdi's *La Traviata*.

Why do we continue to respond to these figures and the dramas in which they appear? Because they are of archetypal power. It is beside the point to say that they are not "like life." Which life are you talking about? The life of the daily papers, or the inner life of the psyche? Indeed, does it matter, for it is unusual to read the daily papers without finding at least one news report in which, beneath the surface, we detect an archetypal strain in some crime of vengeance, or wounded pride, or despair because a spiritual treasure has been lost. In the theatre, understandably, such stories are presented in a heightened form, in which all the tedium and apparent irrelevance of everyday reality has been set aside. But if you strip tedium and irrelevance away from many painful and arresting human predicaments you arrive at an essence which we may call melodrama, and its simplified form is dreamlike.

Consider, for instance, the most commonplace of plots, which was used for a thousand melodramas, and which occurs to many people whenever the word *melodrama* is used. I mean the plot where an Innocent Village Maiden is loved by a Worthy Young Man, but whose virtue is menaced by the Villainous Squire. Eventually there is a showdown, in which the Squire is worsted, but before that happens both the young people have felt the weight of his oppression. The plot became a melodramatic cliché simply because it was also a cliché of human experience. In a highly stratified society a man of wealth and position can, if he wishes, rob a girl of inferior station of her virtue, and social historians have made it plain that in the nineteenth century it was by no means usual for a humble girl to reach the age of sixteen with her virginity intact.

It is no use saying that in such cases the girl may have been a wholly or partly willing party to her seduction, and that her humble lover accepted the situation as he found it. Whatever the facts of her own special case might have been, a humble female playgoer liked to think that she had been wronged; to present before her eyes the case of a girl who was an idealized version of herself, who struggled to maintain her virtue, and did so, was acceptable drama to her. It was as though she were living through her own drama again, in a greatly improved version. It was a dream of virtue, and who would be so hard-hearted as to deny her the satisfaction of that dream? Those to whom virtue is a luxury, dream of virtue. The aspirations of the psyche, and daily reality, are not identical.

In this century there have been several extremely popular plays which are based on the notion that love, and goodwill—but especially Love—will overcome all difficulties, and bridge all chasms of social or cultural difference. Such a play was the immensely successful *Abie's Irish Rose*, in which Love overcame the gulf between Catholicism and Judaism. A more recent example was the play called *A Majority of One*, in which a Jewish lady of no particular culture but a rich folk wisdom discovered that she and a Japanese gentleman of substantial wealth and rather advanced culture were soulmates. These plays succeed because people wish that the ideas they put forward were true. They are wish fulfillments. They are, in fact, dreams which millions of by no means simple people cherish in their inmost hearts.

But to return to nineteenth-century melodrama, and the archetypal figures it presents, is there anyone here who knows Dion Boucicault's famous play *The Colleen Bawn*? Probably not, but it had a successful stage life of more than fifty years, beginning in 1860. Very briefly, the story is about a young Irishman of aristocratic birth, Hardress Cregan, who loves a girl who is distinguished by her beauty and goodness, Eily O'Connor, known as the Colleen Bawn, which means the Beautiful Maiden. But Eily is of humble birth, and Cregan soon finds that his family look down on her, and he thinks he cannot accept her as his wife. The plot is subtle and complex, but in a few words, he conspires at her murder, although it is his mother who actually sets the machinery of the murder in motion. What is interesting to us is that the murderer, who fails in his attempt, is a hunchbacked servant named Danny Mann, who loves Hardress like a brother; in fact, they are foster brothers. Precisely what he is we are told in the first few lines of the play. A friend says to Cregan:

Hardress, who is that with you?
HARDRESS: Only Danny Mann, my boatman.
KYRLE: That fellow is like your shadow.

DANNY: Is it a cripple like me, that would be the shadow of an elegant gentleman like Mr. Hardress Cregan?

The author of *The Colleen Bawn* was no Jungian. but he was a very able playwright, and in the characters of Hardress and Danny Mann he gives us a Hero and his Shadow, and it is the task of the Shadow to do the evil deed which the Hero desires but does not like to contemplate. When Danny has been killed, Hardress is redeemed, and we are led to believe that he is wholly reconciled to his humble sweetheart.

But there is more to concern us in this deeply interesting play. Who kills Danny Mann, sparing the heroine from death and redeeming the hero? He is a delightful rogue called Myles-na-Coppaleen, who is a horse breaker, a poacher, a distiller of illegal whisky, and unquestionably the largest spirit and most able man in the play. He is, indeed, its Hero in a very special sense, for he loves Eily O'Connor deeply—though not silently, for he is eloquent and witty—but knowing she loves Hardress and knowing himself to be something of a scoundrel, he gives her up at the end to the man she loves.

In Myles-na-Coppaleen we have a figure who is easily recognizable in Jungian terms as the Mercurius, the rogue who is sometimes benevolent and sometimes a trickster, an enemy to the law and the revenue officers, but a great friend to people of noble spirit, and to lovers. This Mercurius figure is by no means confined to this play alone; it is part of the apparatus of melodrama. Not infrequently the part was represented as being an Irishman, and much of the character that Irishmen have in popular opinion for being witty and irresponsible is the result of these stage representations. Boucicault created several of them, though they occurred before him, and after he had ceased to write.

But there is another element in Myles's character to which I call your attention. He loves the girl, but he does not get her. She goes to another man whom he believes to be more worthy of her love than himself. This situation is a common one in melodrama. It is the theme of Renunciation. Perhaps you are familiar with it in one of the most celebrated of all melodramas, *The Only Way*. It is adapted from Charles Dickens's *A Tale of Two Cities*. The drunken, dissolute, but noble-hearted lawyer Sydney Carton, loves Lucie Manette, but he knows himself to be unworthy of her: He contrives to die by the guillotine in the place of the man she truly loves, and who loves her, the French aristocrat Charles Darnay. His final words have become a melodramatic cliché: "It is a far far better thing that I do than I have ever done; it is a far, far better rest that I go to than I have ever known." But I assure you stage speeches do not pass into the common speech because they are contemptible; they become clichés because they contain a truth. And what is the truth in this case? Is it, perhaps, that Sydney Carton loves Charles Darnay at least as much as he loves Lucie Manette? If so, I suppose we must call the emotion homosexuality, but it is certainly not homosexuality as it is presented by the Gay Liberation Movement. We must remember that the circumstance which made it possible for Sydney Carton to pass himself off as Charles Darnay was that they were uncommonly alike in appearance. Was Carton perhaps the Shadow of Darnay? Was he, in dying that Darnay might live, preserving whatever was best in himself? I do not want to push these Jungian explanations too far; they are too obvious to need feverish and insubstantial support. Let us suppose, therefore, that what lies behind the theme of Renunciation may sometimes be homosexual feeling. Surely we may admit that homosexuality, like heterosexual love, may lead to acts of nobility when it is associated with a noble spirit. And let us remember that a redeemed Shadow contains much that is of worth.

No discussion of this sort would be possible without some reference to the archetype of the Wise Old Man. He is a commonplace of melodrama, and sometimes he is presented with extraordinary power. A very popular play of the nineteenth century was *The Hunchback*, written by Sheridan Knowles, and first performed in 1832. Briefly, it is the story of a beautiful and accomplished girl named Julia, who has been brought up by the hunchbacked agent of the Earl of Rochdale. This strange, testy, but wise and good man brings to her Sir Thomas Clifford, who is noble and honourable, and they are betrothed. But when Julia discovers that Clifford has lost his fortune she rejects him, and accepts in his place a man who is obviously a fool. The plot is complex and interesting, but when at last it is resolved, we learn that

Master Walter, the Hunchback, is the rightful Earl of Rochdale and also Julia's father; he had concealed his identity in order to spare her the ignominy of having to acknowledge a cripple. But he is able to make her rich and marry her to Clifford, and has the coolness to describe the agony of the young people, which he himself has brought about, as "wholesome, though severe."

The plot is manifestly absurd on the surface, but its appeal goes far below the surface. The theme of the proud girl who rejects the worthy but penniless suitor is a good one, and in another nineteenth-century favourite, *The Lady of Lyons*, by Bulwer-Lytton, it is exploited even more successfully than in *The Hunchback*. There is a special satisfaction for audiences—women as well as men—in seeing a beautiful and proud girl humiliated. But what interests us at the moment is the character of Master Walter; he is unquestionably one of those ambiguous monsters from fairy tale——wise, uncanny, seemingly unkind, unpredictable, and extremely powerful—who puts the hero and the heroine through the fire of his trials so that they may prove themselves worthy of his eventual bounty.

This is the stuff of myth and fairy tale, and certainly of archetype. I call your attention to the frequency with which disguise and concealed identity occur in these old plays. It is assumed that a great and wealthy man may conceal himself—and his very obvious humped back—for twenty years, without anybody spotting him. The only explanation for this absurdity is that people wish it were so. It is extraordinarily difficult to disguise oneself thoroughly, but much drama—some of the greatest drama—rests on the assumption that it can be done. And of course fairy tale is full of it. And do we not all wish that it were so—that we might mix among our friends unknown, and live another life unsuspected? Part of the task of the theatre is to make wishes come true, and this is an instance of it.

Another and better play in which the archetype of the Wise Old Man is the mainspring of the plot is *Richelieu*, by Bulwer-Lytton, which was first seen in 1839, and held the stage for ninety years. The plot is about an attempt on the part of some French courtiers to lure the ward of the great Cardinal Richelieu into a compromising situation, when she will become the mistress of the King, Louis XIII; there is also some political intrigue. But the play depends on the display of the many facets of the principal character, Richelieu himself. He is sometimes a worldly statesman, he has been a great lover and a warrior; in moments of moral fervour he remembers that he is still a priest.

I want to quote some lines of this play to you because they are characteristically melodramatic. It would not do to speak of Richelieu without mentioning the scene which was most admired by audiences, and which very happily illustrates one aspect of the archetype of the Wise Old Man—the Wizard, the possessor of supernatural powers.

BARADAS: My lord the King cannot believe Your Eminence
　　So far forgets your duty and his greatness
　　As to resist his mandate. Pray you, Madam,
　　Obey the King—no cause for fear!
JULIE: My father!
RICH: She shall not stir!
BARADAS: You are not of her kindred—
　　An orphan—
RICH: And her country is her mother!
BARADAS: The country is the King!
RICH: Ay, is it so;
　　Then wakes the power which in the age of iron
　　Burst forth to curb the great, and raise the low.
　　Mark where she stands, around her form I draw
　　The awful circle of our solemn church!
　　Set but a foot within that holy ground,
　　And on his head—yea, though it wore a crown—
　　I launch the curse of Rome!
BARADAS: I dare not brave you!

The whole play is written in that sort of blank verse, and it is by no means bad. Indeed, it is immensely effective on the stage. And its secret, I think, is that it has the true archetypal ring. Do you remember that in *Memories, Dreams, Reflections* Jung writes: "Archetypes speak the language of high rhetoric, even of bombast"? When he wrote that he was somewhat over-modestly trying to excuse the high tone which he himself had taken in the composition of the *Seven Sermons to the Dead*. Now the language of the *Seven Sermons* may be embarrassing if you are presenting yourself to the world, or even to yourself alone, as a man of science. But it would not come amiss in melodrama. What Jung says is quite true; elevated feeling expresses itself in elevated language, and if the writer does not happen to be a great poet—and they are few—the language of high rhetoric may serve him well and he may acquire a fine mastery of it. Repeatedly in melodrama the characters break into highly rhetorical language under emotional stress, and the audiences of the nineteenth century saw nothing wrong with it. In some unsophisticated plays very unlikely characters, soldiers or sailors, defend themselves against unjust reproach in language that shows extraordinary literary complexity. It was assumed by simple audiences that nothing but the best was good enough for the hero, and this inflated language was the best they knew. Similarly it is by no means uncommon in melodrama to find a young man or woman of humble birth, whose parents speak in a rural or lower-class dialect, expressing themselves in entirely correct, and even somewhat pretentious, upper-class English. One of the problems of the modern dramatist is that his characters are not permitted to be eloquent. We are at the moment in the grip of a resolute belief that nobody of any moral worth is able to express himself literately at all, and this shows itself not only in modern theatre dialogue, but in the public utterances of our politicians.

Other instances of the use of archetypal material in nineteenth-century plays could be brought forward, but I do not seek to weary you. I feel, however, that what I have to say would be incomplete even in this sketchy form if I did not make allusion to the figure of the Friend, the helper and server, who assists the Hero in time of need, but who does not seek to usurp the central role of the Hero. In melodrama it was by no means unusual for both the Hero and the Heroine to have a Friend of this sort, and it was an accepted convention that these friends should be comic characters. They were not strong in intellect, but they had mighty hearts; they said foolish things and worked themselves into foolish situations, but in the hour of crisis they could be counted on to do marvels. Not surprisingly, these

Friends often served their employers as Valet and Lady's Maid. At the end of the play, when the Hero and Heroine were romantically united, or reunited, the Friends were comically united to the delight of the audience. Because audiences for melodrama were very fond of symmetry, and had also a splendid Jungian feeling for quaternities, two marriages, uniting four people, was a conclusion to their taste.

The other archetypal figure I must mention, however briefly, is the Miraculous Child. Two examples, from very famous and popular plays, will suffice. They are Little Willie in *East Lynne* and Little Eva in *Uncle Tom's Cabin.* When Little Willie dies we know—and we feel a chill at the knowledge—that the fortunes of his mother, Lady Isobel, have now reached a point of desolation from which they will never recover. And when Little Eva dies we recognize that the fate of the St. Clair family is sealed, and also that Uncle Tom's luck has gone into eclipse. It was my good fortune to see *Uncle Tom's Cabin* twice in childhood, and as I was a child myself, and a member of an unsophisticated audience, I felt the emotion without any interference from a superior critical faculty. When Little Eva died I knew that bad times were coming, and the light had gone out of the Hero's life. And when, in the final tableau, Little Eva appeared as an angel, and Uncle Tom's chains fell from his hands as he mounted into Heaven at her behest, I felt a great uplifting of the spirit, because I knew that his luck, or whatever you want to call it, had been restored to him, and that his salvation was assured. This was certainly primitive drama, but it was drama about a very big theme, presented in wholehearted imagery; it was crude, but it was very much nearer to *Hamlet,* who also had flights of angels singing him to his rest, than it was to some trivial comedy about adultery or worldly ambition.

I began by saying that the theatre could be, and often is at its best, a place where an audience meets to experience one of the great dreams of the tribe. I have chosen my examples from an era of drama which I do not suppose is familiar to most of you, because it is not composed of plays which are read except by specialists in the history of the theatre. I did this purposely, so that you would not think that I was trying to support my case by references to masterpieces which carry great prestige. And I have talked about plays which all had great popular appeal, reaching not only playgoers of high cultivation, but also very simple people who went to the theatre for a night out, and a big value in emotional experience. They are not realistic plays, and it would not be far wide of the mark to call them dreams or fantasies.

Let me repeat what Jung said about his own encounter with by no means dissimilar experiences: "I wrote down the fantasies as well as I could, and made an earnest effort to analyse the psychic conditions under which they had arisen. But I was able to do this only in clumsy language. First I formulated the things as I had observed them, usually in 'high-flown' language, for that corresponds to the style of the archetypes. Archetypes speak the language of high rhetoric, even of bombast. It is a style I find embarrassing; it grates on my nerves, as when someone draws his nails down a plaster wall, or scrapes his knife against a plate. I had no choice but to write down everything in the style selected by the Unconscious itself.... Below the threshold of consciousness everything was seething with life."

It is from the source thus explored by Jung that much of the literature of Romance comes, but the melodramatic playwrights, many of them men of humble gifts and limited sensibility, seem often to have transferred the bombast of their inspiration directly to the stage without any of the alchemy observable, for instance, in the drama of Byron. But even at its worst, melodrama continued to draw on that realm where "*everything was seething with life*," and to transfer as much as possible of that extraordinary psychic vitality to the stage. The plays, so neglectful of the externals of reality, were psychologically convincing because they spoke from these depths to corresponding depths in their audiences. However crude the effect might sometimes be, melodrama did not shrink from that battle with troll folk, in the crypts of heart and head, which Ibsen said was the essence of life. So far as the conventions of the nineteenth century allowed, they tried to deal with much that was personal, subjective, and psychologically daring, and for the first eighty years of that century they made the essence of the Romantic Movement available to sections of the public that would be unlikely to encounter it in any other form.

Because I have drawn my examples from the nineteenth century I would not wish you to think that archetypal and dream material has no part in the drama of our time. Theatre, film, and television abound in it, but to trace its influence there would take more time than we have tonight. Permit me, instead, to point out that much of this melodrama of which I have been speaking, and the Jungian, archetypal material with which it deals, is still vital and popular in the opera houses and ballet theatres of the world, and that as opera and ballet they engage the deeply serious attention of some of the foremost theatre artists of our time, drawing large and by no means simple-minded audiences. It is only the emphasis that has changed; music has replaced language as the primary means of expression, and language supports music. A fine performance of *Rigoletto*, or *The Magic Flute*, or *Giselle*, or *Le Lac des Cygnes* is an experience in which we discern, and by no means dimly, the melodrama of the earlier day, and the mighty archetypal world from which it drew its themes. Nor is it irrelevant that opera and ballet are international in appeal.

If we seek the supreme genius in making the Jungian archetypal world manifest in the theatre of our time we shall find him in no playwright of the nineteenth century, but in Giuseppe Verdi, and in the works of Verdi we are transported immediately into that realm of phantasmagoria and dream grotto where only the greatest artists are at home, and to which C.G. Jung, for a different purpose, has carried the illumination of his very different genius.

9

Children of the Moon

An Operetta for Young People

In the introduction to *Children of the Moon* in *Happy Alchemy,* I wrote:

> Robertson Davies had an idea for this libretto at the time of the production of *Dr. Canon's Cure.* He began writing it in December 1982 and finished in early 1983 because Ruby Mercer of the Canadian Children's Opera Chorus had requested another libretto to follow the success of *Dr. Canon's Cure.* The project was never completed; the music to date remains unwritten.

I am delighted to report that the music has now been written. In 2005 I got a call from Dean Burry, a young Canadian composer with experience in writing children's operas, saying how thrilled he was by the libretto published in *Happy Alchemy,* and asking if he could write the music. At this writing, the music is ready, and we are working on having a production mounted in the near future.

Dean has been very kind in allowing me to include two songs from the first draft for piano at the end of the libretto.

Characters

MISS ROSE PRIMM, a beautiful teacher
BARNEY O'GRADY, a handsome farmer
ZADKIEL, a Gypsy

A GOOD GIRL
A RICH BOY
TWO ORPHANS (m. & f.)
BABY GENIUS
FILLPAIL A COW (two singers)
SECOND-SIGHTED SAMMY
VENTRILOQUIST BOY

CHORUS of the Children of the
Pumpkin Centre Public School

(The stage is empty save for a large banner overhead which reads PUMPKIN CENTRE COUNTY FAIR 1901. At the back on the horizon is a cut-out of tents, and a Ferris Wheel; it should be possible when night falls at the end of the Opera for the Fair to be seen in silhouette, and show a few coloured lights, and for the Ferris Wheel to revolve.)

(WHEN THE OPERA BEGINS the Chorus of Children and all the Young Principals march onstage, singing heartily F.H. Torrington's patriotic song "Canada, the Gem in the Crown"; they carry small flags, some the Union Jack and some the Canadian Red Ensign, and as they march and countermarch in wonderful patterns they wave their flags, directed by their teacher Miss Rose Primm, who is young and beautiful, but consumed by her desire to seem efficient, disciplinary, and wholly absorbed in her office as an instructor in learning and morals. She is soberly dressed but cannot help looking delightful and desirable.)

CHORUS: Canada, the Star and Dominion,
That shines in the beautiful west,

Where the Sun in a robe of vermilion
    Sinks softly and sweetly to rest;
The land of a great federation,
    Which time will never untie,
Till it swells to a glorious nation,
    With a charter that nothing can buy.

Then cheer, cheer, for Canada,
    For her sing loud and long
We will defend dear Canada
    In battle and in song.

The Gem in the crown of Britain
    The fairest it ever shall be;
A cross in the glorious banner
    That floats upon ev'ry sea;
The pride of our fathers we'll ever
    Defend and claim as our own,
And we know that old England will never,
    Her Canadian daughter disown.

Then cheer, cheer for Canada,
    For her sing loud and long;
We will defend dear Canada
    In battle and in song!

MISS PRIMM: Class!—at attention:
Grades four to ten—Right turn!
    Now, stand at ease!
    All of P.C.P.S.
You, Pumpkin Centre Public School, are here
To enjoy our Pumpkin Centre County Fair.

CHORUS: O, the Fair! Our Fall Fair!
We are here for the fun of the fair!

MISS PRIMM: No! Who said fun?
I will not hear that word said:
Put the idea of fun out of your head!
The only true enjoyment
Is in the mind's employment.
So—concentrate instead
On rural culture, and what follows suit—
The Bottled Fruit,
The tender Squash,
The succulent Beet Root:
Home Cooking Arts
The jellying and the potting,
The pickles, chutneys, jams,
The knitting, and the knotting;
The subtle crochet, and the skills that lurk
Behind the lovely brow of Fancy Work!

CHORUS: How daedal the needle!
O macramé, O matting!
O multi-beaded bags,
O many-splendoured tatting!

MISS PRIMM: Then turn your wondering eyes
Upon the great surprise;
Our glorious Provincial Government—

CHORUS: O bounteous friend! O force benevolent!

MISS PRIMM: Well may you say so—
Our Provincial Government
Turns us from kitchen-culture
To serious agriculture;
And in a special darkened tent
The Inmost secret of the Egg betrays
(Using electric rays
Without the egg's consent);

(O revelation ne'er to be forgotten!)
And shows us in a trice
  If an egg's fresh or rotten!
Class—on your toes!
What is this called?
  Who knows?

GOOD GIRL: Such miracles of handling
  Bear a simple name—
    Egg candling.

CHORUS: O wonderful! Egg candling!

MISS PRIMM: First lesson of the Fair
    Is the lesson of thrift;
  Class, I urge you, beware
  Of wastefulness and drift;
  Though your parents may choose
    To use any bank,
  Your School Board offers you
    The Penny Bank!

GOOD GIRL AND RICH BOY:
    O the Penny Bank
    Is the children's friend;
    Put a dollar in the Penny Bank
    And at the year's end,
  Your interest is immense—
    You've a dollar and three cents!

CHORUS: Shun every urge to spend,
  Never, never, never lend—
    Your reward will be immense!
    Three cents for nothing!
      Three free cents!

THE ORPHANS: The path of the investor
Is forever closed to me:
I'm an orphan, a pore orphan,
And never will I be
A storekeeper, a farmer
Or a landlord with rents,
'Cause I haven't got a penny
So I can't dream of three cents.
If the Penny Bank is Heaven
I am Lazarus at the door,
And the Penny Bank is closed to me—
Pity the wretched Pore!

BABY GENIUS: If the Penny Bank is Heaven
Salvation's path is stony;
I've a very superior intellect
But I can't hang on to money!

CHORUS: But money, money, money,
Is the children's friend;
Put a dollar in the Penny Bank
And at the year's end
Your reward will be immense—
You've a dollar and three cents!
It's money for nothing!
Three—
Absolutely free—
Cents!

MISS PRIMM: No, don't say free,
Say the reward of Prudence.
Prudence, sister of Providence,
Brings assured success:
Wasteful, uncharted living
Spells poverty and distress.
Egg candling, household arts, the Penny Bank,

These are the agencies good people thank
For making life wise, and thus long, and healthy;
Certainly solvent, and—it could be—
WEALTHY!

BABY GENIUS: Is wealth the goal?
Is Wealth the Vision Splendid?

CHORUS: Yes, for wealth feeds the soul,
Wealth is what Fate intended!

(Enter BARNEY O'GRADY, *a handsome young farmer.)*

BARNEY: Good day, good day, good day to you all,
Pupils of Pumpkin Centre!
And a special good day to you, Miss Primm,
Sure, and this is a happy encounter!
For today is the day of my mightiest venture—
I offer my finest cow
To the searching gaze of the judges' eye,
Ah, what will they make of her, now?
Fillpail the Queen, my butterfat queen,
My glorious champion cow!

CHORUS: Hail, hail to Fillpail!
Fillpail, the champion cow!

(Enter FILLPAIL, *obviously a very superior cow, but modest.)*

BARNEY: Fillpail, mavourneen, I see thee before me,
Decked for the Fair, and as fresh as the dew;
Master, you call me, and yet I adore thee,
Sweet as your butter, as cream good and true.
What will the night bring of triumph or sorrow,
Love's Dream for me, and blue ribbon for you?
Butterfat champion, Queen of my dairy
Fillpail mavourneen, my hopes rest on you!

GOOD GIRL: A song of love!
My heart goes out to him!
Fillpail, he sings,
But, oh, he means Miss Primm!

MISS PRIMM: *(aside as the others caress Fillpail)*
If Fillpail wins the prize,
I know he'll pop the question!
I see the lovelight in his eyes
As he hints at the soft suggestion!
O Love, you hang on Fillpail's horns
And swell in her splendid udder!
Triumph, O Fillpail, win today,
The alternative makes me shudder!
Fillpail, dear Fillpail,
Yours be the victory!
Love rides upon your horns
And love is all to me!

CHORUS: If Fillpail wins the prize,
He'll surely pop the question;
We see the lovelight in his eyes
As he hints at the soft suggestion!
Oh, how we love Miss Primm!
We dote on Barney O'Grady!
If you do not win,
Their future is grim—
Triumph, O Butterfat Lady!

BARNEY: Now, if you please, I'll take Miss Primm with me;
And you, you rogues, get on with your holiday!

MISS PRIMM: Oh, no—
Oh, yes—
What do I mean to say?
I should remain,

But long to be away!
Torn between Love and Duty, as you see—
O Love, O Duty, can't you two agree?
Pupils, I go—I must—
O heart, be brave!
You, class, be still,
Be quiet,
Above all—
Behave!

(She goes with BARNEY: *Immediately the children change their demeanour, becoming much more at ease.)*

GOOD GIRL: Oh how I love Miss Primm's severity,
Her affectation of extreme austerity;
Her lightest word gives me a shameful thrill:
I love Miss Primm till I am nearly ill!

ORPHAN GIRL: That's all salt taffy,
Rose Primm is daffy
About Farmer Barney
And his Irish blarney!

CHORUS: Here's a fine thing!
Our teacher's in love!
She flushes, she blushes,
O Heavens above!
Here's a fine thing!
Our teacher's in love!

RICH BOY: Aw nuts! Miss Primm is not like that;
She's straight as a cedar stick!
Would she kiss and cuddle
And get in a muddle
With a simple country hick?
Aw no! Miss Primm will hold right out

For a rich man with a castle
'Cause her head's screwed on,
And her brains are plumb,
And she'll give old Cupid a rassle!

ORPHAN BOY: She pretends to be tough,
But she's sappy enough;
She's dawny and faddy
For that cow-happy Paddy!

CHORUS: Here's a fine thing!
Our teacher's heart soars,
She flushes, she blushes,
Sews lace on her drawers;
And that's a sure sign
That teacher's in love!

Second-Sighted Sammy
Tell us true—
What's our teacher
Going to do?

SECOND-SIGHTED SAMMY:
Just gimme a minute—
Oh boy, I feel the Power!
Come on, let's go the limit!

(Some strong boys hold him upside down, and shake him; he prophesies while standing on his head.)

Upend me, somebody,
Put me in my trance—
I see a pair of overalls—
Yep, blue denim pants!
And sewed all over 'em
Are lovely posies—

Wait—now I've got it—
They are—yes—Primroses!

CHORUS: Primroses!
Oh, Rose Primm!
Primroses!

SECOND-SIGHTED SAMMY:
And wait—above 'em
Floating in the air,
Is a Mystical Presence,
A Being Rare!
O Gee, it's smiling!
O Gee, it's smiling!
Wait a minute—Wow!
I see it clear, and Hokies—
It's a Cow!

GOOD GIRL: Fillpail for sure!

RICH BOY: Has it a giant udder?

SECOND-SIGHTED SAMMY:
Yep, it's a whopper!

CHORUS: Oh, with joy we shudder!
Cupid, embark your ship of love
And Fillpail, guide the rudder!
Sail on, sail on, Rose Primm,
To a land of milk and honey,
Where dwells a tender Irish heart
And a farm and lots of money!

CHORUS OF GIRLS:
Lucky, O lucky Rose,
Headed for wedded bliss!

Say Fortune, do you hold for me
  Such a romance as this?
We know that telling fortunes
  Is very, very wrong,
But where is the girl
  Who finds no hint
In this innocent old song?

Monday's child is fair of face
Tuesday's child is full of grace,
Wednesday's child is full of woe,
Thursday's child has far to go,
Friday's child is loving and giving,
Saturday's child works hard for a living,
And the child that is born on the Sabbath Day
Is blithe and bonny and good and gay!

ALL GIRLS: Monday's child is fair of face—

SOME GIRLS: And that's me! That's me!

BOYS: No, you're not, you're ugly and freckled!

ALL GIRLS: Tuesday's child is full of grace—

SOME GIRLS: And that's me! That's me!

BOYS: No you're not, you're nasty and cranky!

ALL GIRLS: Wednesday's child is full of woe—

SOME GIRLS: And that's me! Poor me!

BOYS: Always crying! Use your hanky!

ALL GIRLS: Thursday's child has far to go—

SOME GIRLS: And that's me! Wayfaring me!

BOYS: The farther the better, through rain and snow!

ALL GIRLS: Friday's child is loving and giving—

SOME GIRLS: And that's me! Generous me!

BOYS: Boo! You're as tight as the bark to a tree!

ALL GIRLS: Saturday's child works hard for a living—

ORPHANS: And that's me! Orphans are we!

GIRLS AND BOYS:
You've only your rotten parents to thank,
You know you were born
The wrong side of the blanket!

ORPHANS: Picking on orphans! picking on orphans!
You can't go to Heaven
If you pick on orphans!

GIRLS: And the child that is born on the Sabbath Day—

GOOD GIRL: I'm a child of the parsonage! That's me!

GIRLS: Is blithe and bonny and good and gay!

BOYS: You're a pain in the neck
Whatever you say!

GIRLS: Hateful, nasty dirty boys!
Shut up your horrible
Ignorant noise!

BOYS: Girls are silly and girls are stupid!
Hurrah for the Penny Bank!
Down with Cupid!

Melodrame *(There is a fight; some very daring girls run at the boys and slap them. The boys slap back, whereupon the girls fall to the ground and weep as if they had been stabbed. There is some pulling of hair. The* ORPHANS *dodge about egging on the fighters and making whatever trouble they can ... Enter* ZADKIEL, *A Gypsy Peddler, fantastically dressed, with a plumed hat and all the toys and souvenirs he sells hanging about him.)*

ZADKIEL: Souvenirs, souvenirs—
The best in the Fair!
Buy my souvenirs!

Here! what's amiss?
Boys and girls fighting?
What a way to behave
At a fairday outing!

Now my missies and masters,
Open your pockets;
Boys, buy my pony whips,
Girls, buy my lockets.
See my fine whistling-birds,
See my kaleidoscopes,
Rare Phenakistoscopes
Telescopes, gyroscopes!
Girls, see my rings,
Cut to a prism;
Boys who love magic,
Here's Ventriloquism:
Your name, young master?
John, do you say?
Look, with this in my mouth,

My voice flies away!
Listen—John! John! John!

VOICE FAR AWAY:
John, John, John!

BOY: It must be an echo!

VOICE FAR AWAY:
No, I'm calling for John!

ZADKIEL: It's a wonderful secret—
Now, take my advice
Here's the book that tells all
And includes the device
And it's wonderfully
Gloriously,
Cheap at the price!

(The Boy buys, as the children have been buying all through his song.)

ZADKIEL: Now here is a friend
You can always call on,
When money is short
And desires are many:
Fortunatus' Purse—
Someone lend me a penny—

(Several do so)

See—I drop it inside,
Turn the purse a few times,
Then—what have we here?
All the pennies are dimes!
Here's a fortune for sure,
And you'll have me to thank.

RICH BOY: That's a thousand percent.
Golly! Now where's your Penny Bank!

(He buys.)

ZADKIEL: Buy from Old Zadkiel
The Romany friend;
Here is good fortune
That knows no end!

CHORUS: Charley has a dollar!
He can buy for us all!
Come on, now, Charley,
Don't be stingy and small!
Take Charley's dollar,
He has plenty more;
Charley's made of money—
His father owns the store!

ORPHANS: Soak the rich! Soak the rich!

ZADKIEL: No, Charley's dollar
Pays for Charley only;
You all must pay for yourselves
If you've only a penny.

ORPHANS: Gimme a penny!
I haven't any!
Pity the wretched pore!

BABY GENIUS: Bang goes my dime!
Oh, ain't it a crime?

SECOND-SIGHTED SAMMY:
The cost of living,
Increases ever,

But it isn't a patch
On the cost of pleasure!

ZADKIEL: Empty your purses,
Buy my bargains rare!
Buy Zadkiel's treasures,
Finest in the Fair!

Lay out your money
For pleasure unending;
Learn the great lesson
That pleasure comes with spending!

BABY GENIUS: All my money's gone—
I'm skint, I'm broke;
Have I spent wisely,
Or sent it up in smoke?

GIRLS: Please, do you tell fortunes?
Please, do you tell fates?

ZADKIEL: Aye, that I do. I know
Where Destiny originates!
Tell me your hour of birth,
The month, the day,
And from my Zodiacal Chart
I'll prophesy, I'll say,
All that will come your way!
But first—
You must pay!

(Now the CHILDREN *disclose their secret stores of money—inside pockets, the tops of stockings, in the heels of boots, braided in hair: this is their most secret, long-hoarded treasure. Meanwhile Zadkiel sets up a large brilliantly painted Wheel of the Zodiac, which he can spin easily to each sign as he names it.*

He has grown even more mysterious, and has put on a many-coloured cloak.)

ZADKIEL: *(he speaks above evocative music)*
All creatures born are children of the Sun
Whose hour of birth shows how their fortunes run:
See here my Mazzaroth, my Zodiac,
My starry wonder, my Genethliac,
Melodrame My Fortune's Wheel, my Round of Life and Death,
That tells the infant from his earliest breath
What Span of Years,
  What meed of Gold is his:
    His Loves, his Kindred, Opportunities,
    His bounden Task, his Mate, his Enemy,
    Death's Hour,
  And what Inheritance may be;
His God, his Soul, his Ruler and his Friends
What be his Ills, Betrayals, Shameful Ends:
  All are revealed,
  Don't miss your lucky chance—
    Old Zadkiel speaks—
    Your silver—
    Now … The Dance!

ZADKIEL: *(sings now)*
For this is the Dance
  The old, old Dance,
The Dance of the Children of the Sun!

See, the Ram begins the year,
  Adventurer and Pioneer:
First of the Children of the Sun.

CHORUS: And the Wheel goes around and around!
  Adventurer and Pioneer—
And the Wheel goes around and around.

ZADKIEL: Next the Bull, with patient tread,
Gold and silver deck his bed:
Second of the Children of the Sun.

CHORUS: And the Wheel goes around and around!
Gold and silver all the year,
Adventurer and Pioneer:
And the Wheel goes around and around!

ZADKIEL: Now the Twins, clever and fickle,
Cold in love, tongue sharp as sickle:
Third of the Children of the Sun.

CHORUS: And the Wheel goes around and around—
Quick of wit and cold in love,
Gold and silver all the year,
Adventurer and Pioneer:
And the Wheel goes around and around!

ZADKIEL: Now the Crab, the Moon's dear daughter,
Born to bathe in spirit water
Fourth of the Children of the Sun.

CHORUS: And the Wheel goes around and around—
Bathed in waters of the Moon above,
Quick of wit and cold in love,
Gold and silver all the year,
Adventurer and Pioneer:
And the Wheel goes around and around!

ZADKIEL: Now the Lion, molten-gold,
King of all, the young and old:
Fifth of the Children of the Sun.

CHORUS: And the Wheel goes around and around—
Molten gold and born to reign,

Bathed in waters of the Moon above,
Quick of wit and cold in love,
Gold and silver all the year,
Adventurer and Pioneer:
And the Wheel goes around and around!

ZADKIEL: See the Maid amid the grain,
Golden harvest, silver rain:
Sixth of the Children of the Sun.

CHORUS: And the Wheel goes around and around:
Lo, the Maiden of the Grain,
Molten gold and born to reign,
Bathed in Waters of the Moon above,
Quick of wit and cold in love,
Gold and silver all the year,
Adventurer and Pioneer:
And the Wheel goes around and around.

ZADKIEL: See the Scales of Harmony,
Justice, Reason, Courtesy,
Seventh of the Children of the Sun.

CHORUS: And the Wheel goes around and around:
Justice, Reason, Harmony,
Lo, the Maiden of the Grain,
Molten gold and born to reign,
Bathed in Waters of the Moon above,
Quick of wit and cold in love,
Gold and silver all the year,
Adventurer and Pioneer;
And the Wheel goes around and around.

ZADKIEL: Now the Scorpion, rashly bold
Draws his power from Pluto's hold;
Eighth of the Children of the Sun.

CHORUS: And the Wheel goes around and around:
Born a Pirate Bold to be,
Justice, Reason, Harmony,
Lo, the Maiden of the Grain,
Molten gold and born to reign,
Bathed in Waters of the Moon above,
Quick of wit and cold in love,
Gold and silver all the year,
Adventurer and Pioneer:
And the Wheel goes around and around!

ZADKIEL: Now the Archer, sure of aim,
Strikes to the hottest of the flame,
Ninth of the Children of the Sun.

CHORUS: And the Wheel goes around and around:
Marksman hits the fiery mark,
Born a pirate bold to be,
Justice, Reason, Harmony,
Lo, the Maiden of the Grain,
Molten gold and born to reign,
Bathed in Waters of the Moon above,
Quick of wit and cold in love,
Gold and silver all the year,
Adventurer and pioneer;
And the Wheel goes around and around!

ZADKIEL: Now the Goat, the witty, subtle—
Spirit sad, but quick rebuttal:
Tenth of the Children of the Sun.

CHORUS: And the Wheel goes around and around!
Sonsy face but spirit dark,
Marksman hits the fiery mark,
Born a pirate bold to be,
Justice, Reason, Harmony,

Lo, the Maiden of the Grain,
Molten gold and born to reign,
Bathed in Waters of the Moon above,
Quick of wit but cold in love,
Gold and silver all the year,
Adventurer and pioneer:
And the Wheel goes around and around!

ZADKIEL: Next the careful Water Carrier,
Thinker, Scientist, and Inventor:
Eleventh of the Children of the Sun.

CHORUS: And the Wheel goes around and around—
Maker, doer, and inventor,
Sonsy face but spirit dark,
Marksman hits the fiery mark,
Born a pirate bold to be,
Justice, Reason, Harmony,
Lo, the Maiden of the Grain,
Molten gold and born to reign,
Bathed in Waters of the Moon above,
Quick of wit and cold in love,
Gold and silver all the year,
Adventurer and Pioneer:
And the Wheel goes around and around.

ZADKIEL: Last the Fishes, going nowhere,
Facing both ways, sworn to Jupiter,
Are the twelfth of the Children of the Sun.

CHORUS: And the Wheel goes around and around!
Facing both ways, holds to centre,
Maker, doer, and inventor,
Sonsy face, but spirit dark,
Marksman hits the fiery mark,
Born a pirate bold to be,

Justice, Reason, Harmony,
Lo, the Maiden of the Grain,
Molten gold and born to reign,
Bathed in Waters of the Moon above,
Quick in wit and cold in love,
Gold and silver all the year,
Adventurer and pioneer,
And the Wheel goes around and around—
For this is the Dance—
The oldest Dance—
The Dance of the Children of the Sun!

(The Children dance in a round.)

*(*MISS PRIMM *returns and is horrified—or perhaps it is truer to say she is terrified—to find the Children liberated, happy, and, as it certainly appears to her, "out of hand.")*

MISS PRIMM: What's this? What's going on here?
Who is this stranger?

ZADKIEL: Old Zadkiel, pretty lady,
Fear no danger;
A humble Gypsy, and a starry messenger—

MISS PRIMM: A fortune teller?

ZADKIEL: Please, no anger!
I only read
What's written in the sky:
I did not write it there—
Innocent am I
Of any harm
I speak but what I know
That which is written above
Shall be below!

'Twas from on high
  The word was given—
"Be it on earth,
  As 'tis in Heaven."

MISS PRIMM: Blasphemy! Superstition!
Children, come away!

CHORUS: Oh, please, Miss Primm,
Hear what he has to say!

ZADKIEL: Hear me, pretty miss—
Hear me, Miss Primm,
Who shall be Rose O'Grady!

CHORUS: She's to be Rose O'Grady!

*(*MISS PRIMM *faints dead away, into the arms of the Children.)*

BOYS: Rub her hands!
Loosen her stays!
Burn feathers under her nose!

GIRLS: Boys, stand back!
This isn't for you—
Off with these awful tight clothes!

(They strip off MISS PRIMM*'s tight outer garments, so that she is in her white shift: They let down her hair, which flows over her shoulders; she now looks her real age, and her real self.)*

GIRLS: See, in her shift,
She looks like a bride!
O glorious, lovely white Rose.

ZADKIEL: What is above,
Must be below—

(BARNEY O'GRADY enters, and is transported at the sight of Rose, who has now recovered and stretches out her arms to him.)

BARNEY: ZOE MOU, SAS AGAPO!*
—Now, what have I said?
Sure, I'm speaking in tongues!

ZADKIEL: Greek, sir, is the language of love!
In victory's hour, sir,
Greet your bride, sir,
And praised be the Heavens above!

CHORUS: Praised be the heavens above!

BARNEY: Rose Primm, mavourneen,
I see thee before me,
Decked for a bridal
And fresh as the dew!

MISS PRIMM: Barney, my own one,
Oh, what has befallen me?
Barney—oh, dare I
Surrender? I do!

BOTH: Blest be the day
That brings triumph and gladness
True love requited,
And Blue Ribbon, too
Fillpail's the triumph
And ours the dear madness,
Oh, what a Fair Day that leads me to you!
Triumphant Fair Day, that leads me to you!

---

*A classical Greek endearment: O my Life, I love thee!

(Enter FILLPAIL*, modest but conscious of triumph, wearing a splendid blue rosette and a ribbon saying* FIRST IN CLASS*. She now reveals that there are two voices concealed inside her, and she sings a duet with herself, in delightful harmony.)*

FILLPAIL: Though but a cow I be,
Rich thoughts arise in me,
And when they do—
O-le-O-lahee-hoo!
I yodel.

The Cow Cabaletta

Yodelling's a bovine art,
That sets us cows apart,
And as a yodeller,
I'm a model.
So, on this lucky day,
Join me boys and girls, I pray,
Bliss, on this happy day,
Be total!
So—
Let's yodel!

(The CHORUS *and all* PRINCIPALS *join with* FILLPAIL *in a Tyrolienne Yodelling Chorus, at the discretion of the Composer. Night has fallen, the lights on the distant fair begin to twinkle, and the Ferris Wheel begins to turn.)*

BARNEY: See, darkness brings in
Its own rich treasure,
The secret delights
Unbefitting the day;
Then off to the Midway,
You children, and measure
Its joys to the bottom,
For Barney will pay!

CHORUS: *(girls)* O, the pink candy floss,
O the dolls, O the ribbons,
The rings green and red,
The brooches, the scarves!

CHORUS: *(boys)* The monkeys, the Fat Woman,
The Human Skeleton,
The perilous rides,
O, the giants, and dwarves!

CHORUS: *(both)* The weight guesser's chair,
The games and the prizes,
The whispers in darkness,
The merry-go-round,
The hot, thrilling blisses
Of hasty, snatched kisses,
The fun of the fair,
And Calliope's sound!

ZADKIEL: As above, so below,
There is wisdom in nighttime
When the bright stars above
Urge us on to delight;
Let the wisdom of day
Be confined to its right time,
But now, let the heart
Learn the wisdom of night!

When the full blaze of day
Into darkness has run
It has great words to say
To the Child of the Sun;
For here is the dance—
The Nighttime Dance—
That is danced by the Children of the Moon!

VENTRILOQUIST BOY:
Are we also the Children of the Moon?

(Voice in reply): Of the Moon—
Yes, Children of the Moon!

VENTRILOQUIST BOY:
So the Wheel really does go around?

(Voice in reply): Yes, the Wheel goes around, and around!

CHORUS: The Wheel goes around and around

(The Moon rises in the Sky.)

BABY GENIUS: Daytime thinker, nighttime dreamer,

SECOND-SIGHTED SAMMY:
Light-time prophet, dark-time schemer!

GOOD GIRL: Tame to woo, but wild to marry!

RICH BOY: Fortune haste, and sorrow tarry!

ORPHANS: Bad beginning brings great ending—
Woe betide the condescending!

FILLPAIL: Daily be the bucket brimming,
Nightly work the stripping, skimming!

MISS PRIMM: Chalk and ruler, long farewell,
Music is the wedding bell!

BARNEY: Richest land and fairest wife,
Children be the crown of life!

ZADKIEL: Fates to read, and fates be sold,
There's the Gypsy's fortune told!
From on high
The word was given,
Be on earth
As 'tis in Heaven
The word is given none may unsay—
ZOE MOU SAS AGAPÓUME!*

CHORUS: ZOE MOU SAS AGAPÓUME!
And the Wheel of the Night goes around and around
For the Children of the Moon!

For this is the Dance,
The oldest Dance—
Of the CHILDREN OF THE MOON!

(Round dance in which all join except ZADKIEL *who waves to them and steals away.)*

The End of the Opera

---

*Greek: O Life, we love thee!

Music from *Children of the Moon*
Libretto by Robertson Davies
Music by Dean Burry

Fillpail, Mavoureen

from *Children of the Moon*

Text by Robertson Davies
Music by Dean Burry

B.
Pu - pils of Pump - kin Cen - tre! And a spec - ial good day to you, Miss Primm,
Sure, and this is a hap - py en - coun - ter! For to -
mp cresc.
day is the day of my might - i - est ven - ture, I
f
of - fer my fin - est cow to the search - ing gaze of the jud - ges' eye. Ah,
mf mp mf mp

B.
what will they make of her now?
Fill - pail, the Queen, my
STUDENTS:
I.
Hail, hail to Fill - pail!
II.
Hail, hail to Fill - pail!
B.
but ter fat queen, my glor - i - ous cham - pion cow.
piu rit.
I.
Fill - pail, the cham - pion. Fill - pail the cham - pion. Fill - pail the champ - ion
II.
Fill - pail, the cham - pion. Fill - pail the cham - pion. Fill - pail the champ - i - on
cresc.

Tenderly
43
I.
cow!
Oo.
Oo.
II.
cow!
Oo.
Oo.
BARNEY:
B.
Fill-pail, ma - vour-een, I see thee be - fore me, Decked for the
Tenderly
sub. mf
50
I.
Ah
II.
Ah
B.
Fair and as fresh as the dew. Mas - ter you call me, and yet I a -

cresc.
f
mf
I.
II.
B.
ah.
Oo
dore thee.
Sweet is your but - ter, as cream, good and true.
f piu mosso
What will the night bring of tri - umph or sor - row, Love's Dream for me, and blue rib - bon for
you?
But - ter - fat cham - pi - on, Queen of my dair - y.
Ah

(♩= 100) GOOD GIRL:
mp
A song of love, my heart goes out to him.
Oo
Oo
Fill - pail ma - vour - een, my hopes rest on you!
(♩= 100)
mp
Slightly faster
rit.
mf
Fill - pail, he sings, but oh, he means Miss Primm.
ROSE:
mf
If Fill - pail wins the
Slightly faster
rit.
mf
sim.
(pop!)
(pop!)
prize, I know he'll pop the ques-tion! I see the love-light in his eyes as he hints at the soft sug-
sim.

R.
legato
ges - tion! O Love, you hang on Fill-pail's horns and swell in her splen-did ud - der!
legato
Tri - umph, Fill - pail win to - day, the al - ter - na - tive makes me shud - der! ugh.
f
Fill - pail, dear Fill - pail, Yours be the vic - tor - y! Love rides u - pon your horns, and
marcato

103 STUDENTS:
mf
I.
If Fill - pail wins the prize, I know he'll pop the ques - tion. We see the love-light
II.
If Fill - pail wins the prize, I know he'll pop the ques - tion. We see the love-light
R.
love is all to me.
3

109
I.
in his eyes as he hints at the soft sug - ges - tion! Oh, how we love Miss Primm, we dote on Bar - ney O'
II.
in his eyes as he hints at the soft sug - ges - tion! Oh, how we love Miss Primm and we dote on
3

115
I. Grad - y. If she does-'nt win their fu-ture is grim. But if Fill - pail wins the prize, I know he'll pop the
II. Barn-ey O'-Grad-y. If she does-'nt win their fu-ture is grim. But if Fill - pail wins the prize, I know he'll pop the
R. Love you
B. Fill-pail, ma - vour - een, I see thee be -
121
I. ques - tion. We see the love-light in his eyes as he hints at the soft sug - ges - tion! Oh,
II. ques - tion. We see the love-light in his eyes as he hints at the soft sug - ges - tion! Oh,
R. hang u - pon horns! And then
B. - fore me, Decked for the Fair and as fresh as the dew.

Lilting (♩. = 88)
I.
how welove Miss Primm, we dote on Bar - ney O' Grad - y. If you don't win, the fu-ture's grimm. O
II.
how we love Miss Primm and we dote on Barn-ey O'-Grad-y. If you don't win, the fu-ture's grimm. O
R.
swell in her ud - der. If you don't win, the fu-ture's grimm. O
B.
Mas - ter you call me, and yet I a - dore thee. If you don't win, the fu-ture's grimm. O
tri - umph But - ter - fat Lad - y!
tri - umph But - ter - fat Lad - y!
tri - umph But - ter - fat Lad - y!
tri - umph But - ter - fat Lad - y!
Lilting (♩. = 88)
mf

BARNEY: mf
Now, if you please, I'll take Miss Primm with me; And you, you rogues, get on with your hol - i - day!
Agitated (♩=132)
ROSE: f
Oh, no! Oh, yes!
mp (aside)
What do I mean to say?
Agitated (♩=132)
mp sim.
I should re-main but long to be a - way! Torn be-tween Love and Du - ty,

R.
as you see. O Love, O Du-ty, can't you two a-gree? Pu-pils, I go. O
heart, be brave! You class, be still, be qui-et. A-bove all BE-HAVE!
sim.
sub. f
sub. f sim.
(♩. = 88)

The Cow Cabaletta

from *Children of the Moon*

Text by Robertson Davies
Music By Dean Burry

(♩=104)
F.
ay - hee - hoo! I yo - - - - - - del!
(♩=104)
F.
Yo - del-ling's a bo-vine art, that sets us cows a - part. And as a yod - 'ller I'm a
F.
mod - el. So on this luck-y day, join me boys and girls, I pray. Bliss on this hap-py day be

F.
to-tal! So let's yo-del!
STUDENTS:
I.
O-dl ay hee o dl
II.
O-dl ay hee o dl

I.
o ee tee, o dl ay ee o dl o O dl-ay-hee o dl-o-dl-ay-hee lay hee o dl-
II.
o ee tee, o dl ay ee o dl o O dl-ay-hee o dl-o-dl-ay-hee lay hee o dl-

I.
II.
1.
2.
mf
o! O-dl o! Lay hee tee o dl - ay hee tee o dl - ay dee o dl-li dl - o dl - ay hee tee. O dl-
o! O-dl - lo! Lay hee tee o dl - ay hee tee o dl - ay dee o dl-li dl - o dl - ay hee tee. O dl-
rit.
(𝅗𝅥 = 116)
ay - hee tee o dl - ay dee ho. Ay ee o dl - o - dee o hee hee. O dl - ay - hee o dl - o ee tee, o dl-
ay - hee tee o dl - ay dee ho. Ay ee o dl - o - dee o hee hee. O dl - ay - hee o dl - o ee tee, o dl-
ay ee o dl - o. O dl - ay - hee o dl - o - dl - ay hee lay hee o dl - o! O-dl-
ay ee o dl - lo - de - lo. O-de - ay - hee o dl - o - dl - ay hee lay hee o dl - o! O-dl-

58 2.
(𝅗𝅥 = 126)
mp
cresc.
f
I.
o!
O - ho-dl-ay - hee.
O - do-dl - o!
O - ho-dl - ay - ee - hee!
O - dl - ay
II.
o!
O ho-dl - ay - hee o - do-dl - o - hee!
ay
64
o
ay
O-dl - i - dl - ee. O-dl lay - ee
o ay - O-dl - o - dl - lo O -
o ay - O-dl - i - dee.
ay - ee
o - ay - ee O-dl - o - dl - o O
70 FILLPAIL (+OTHERS):
F.
accel.
O-dl - ay-dee o-dl - o lay-dee - o - dl - o, Lay-dee - o - dl-ay-dee - o - dl - o!
lay - ee tee. O-dl - ay o ay O-dl - i - dl - ee. O-dl -
lay ee tee. ay o ay - O-dl - i-dee.

F.
Ay___ O - hee, Ay - - - o - - - lo lay - hee
I.
lay - ee o___ ay - - O - dl - o - dl - ay - hee o - ay -
II.
Ay___ o - ay___ ee___ o - dl - o - dl - ay - hee o - ay -
F.
o - - - - ay___ Lay - - o - - lay!___
I.
o - - - - ay___ Lay - - o - - lay!___
II.
o - - - - ay___ Lay - - o - - lay!___

10

Opera and Humour

This lecture was given as the Prince of Hesse Memorial Lecture at the Aldeburgh Festival, Aldeburgh, England, on June 11, 1991. The Festival was founded in 1948 by the composer Benjamin Britten and the singer Peter Pears. Aldeburgh is a small fishing town on the east coast of England, made famous largely because Britten lived there for many years and because of the existence of the Festival. The lecture series was started in memory of Prince Ludwig of Hesse and the Rhine, and his widow was, at this time, the President of the Aldeburgh Foundation.

Davies noted in his travel diary: *Give the Hesse Lecture in the Town Hall; a decided success and indeed I think I stunned them, but delighted the Princess who said that many previous lectures had been short-weight—"wanting in content," she put it. Jokes went well and eased them painlessly into the Jungian-Heraclitean part. So that is done, and well done. Lunch after with the Princess; a party of thirty and a large and luxurious luncheon beginning with chilled vodka. The Princess is a Scot, eighty and determined, charming and very much on the beam: liked her immensely.*

In the lecture that follows Davies draws on the Strauss opera *Ariadne auf Naxos* for examples of humour in opera. He wrote in his travel diary of a production he saw on October 3, 1995: *The Canadian Opera Company* Ariadne auf Naxos *very well done under Bradshaw; sensitivity but not to the point of degeneracy. Fine cast: Isabelle Vernet as Ariadne, partnered by David Rampy as Bacchus; they both sang admirably and intelligently: Zerbinetta was Tracy Dahl who sang brilliantly but was cruelly costumed. Kristine Jepson as the Composer sang splendidly and made the Composer's yielding to Zerbinetta touching and beautiful. So—a great evening for the ear and one forgave what one saw. The Nymphs were very personable and sang finely. Only the comedians were under par, and their roles are impossible: acrobats and great mimes do not sing: their costumes were messy. Produced by Tom Diamond, tactful and funny in the right places, and noble when nobility was called for. Monty Wood played the Prima Donna's pet: twenty seconds of glory. David William was the Major Domo: a fine actor but failed here: inaudible. What happened.—This opera is one of my great favourites: a great and daring theme of Tragedy and Comedy mingled, superbly worked out. A theme very dear to me for I value Tragedy less than Comedy, for it exalts in so many cases a noble stupidity. Not, of course, in Shakespeare except in* Othello.

Let me begin by dispelling any impression you may have received that this is going to be a funny lecture. As soon as I had imparted my title—"Opera and Humour"—to Miss Sheila Colvin, I began to regret it, but the word had been given, and there was no way in which I could recall it. You know why: The programs and brochures for such a festival as this must be printed early in the season, and once they have been given to the printer, there is no room for second thoughts. So—"Opera and Humour" it must be, and if anyone has come this morning expecting one of those side-splitting talks about the performance of *Lohengrin* when the swan made its entrance backward, or the time when Tosca could not find the knife and had to murder Scarpia with a candlestick, I beg that person to feel free to leave at once. I shall not take offence. I intend to be serious about my subject, and as you know, when someone undertakes to be serious about humour, the result is certain to be of the uttermost gravity.

Having thus warned you, let us talk for a while about humour. I assume that we shall get to opera in good time, but not at once.

Humour is extraordinarily hard to define, and even the meaning of the word is in dispute. Everybody claims to have a sense of humour;

at least, I have never met anyone who would admit to having no sense of humour. But when this "sense of humour" is examined, it usually proves to be sharply limited and often—though not invariably—it is conditioned by considerations of class, of education, and of nationality. The theatre audience which is convulsed by *No Sex Please, We're British* is certainly not that which is delighted with *The Way of the World*; the man who reads and rereads the romances of P.G. Wodehouse is not the man who is enthralled with the complex humour of *Finnegans Wake*; the fun of Martin Amis is certainly not that of Jane Austen. Yet all of these works may claim to be humour of one sort or another. There are people who wince at a pun, and people who cannot resist a pun. There are people who confine humour to funny stories and do not acknowledge it in any other form. A Russian friend of mine once told me that the Russians had no sense of humour, apart from an elaborate facetiousness. A French friend assured me that the French have the most acute perception of humour of any nation in the world about everything but themselves. As for the English sense of humour, it is widely celebrated. I wish I had time to offer you some examples of Canadian humour, which tends to be ironic, but I do not wish to dispel the widely held notion that Canadians have no sense of humour. I once had a dispute with a group of Swedish professors at the University of Uppsala as to which country, Sweden or Canada, was the dullest in the world. It was a draw; they claimed superiority because of their long history, and I claimed it because of Canada's immense land mass, which gives us space for tremendous expansion, even of such things as dullness.

Humour has been pursued by many distinguished scholars, who have attempted, with the uttermost seriousness, to say what it is. I have the chief works in this field, and I can say of them, as the schoolboy said of the Complete Works of Matthew Arnold, that they are no place to go for a laugh. One of the most famous is *Le Rire, Essai sur la signification du comique*, by the philosopher Henri Bergson; Bergson's proposal, very roughly, is that comedy arises from the rigidity, the failure to adapt to circumstances, which makes a person behave like a mechanism, and society seeks to correct this defect by its laughter. But unquestionably the most famous book on the subject is *Wit and Its*

Relation to the Unconscious by Sigmund Freud; it is a brilliant book and not an easy book to master, and its psychoanalytical discussion of what is funny, and why, is illuminating without being, to me at least, wholly persuasive. Incongruity, relief of tension, and resolution of conflict are all observable in humour, but something prevents me from accepting Freud's explanation as a wholly satisfactory one. The reason is that, like virtually all of Freud's thinking, it is reductive in tendency, and his ideas about humour support his deeply pessimistic view of life. I have never been convinced that pessimism is the only possible philosophical attitude for a thinking person; it is notable in some of its aspects, but it is not all-inclusive. I had a friend, a deeply learned man, who used to assure me from time to time that what he called The Tragic Attitude was the only one possible for anyone who was not foolishly deluded about the nature of life. I cannot accept that because it exalts the mind of man as the measure of all things. In the great tragedies of the Greeks it is the suffering of an individual which is supposed to darken the sun for everybody who is aware of it. That is an egotism I cannot admire. The mind of man, though perhaps the most splendid achievement of evolution, is not, surely, the answer to every problem of the universe. Hamlet suffers, but the Gravediggers go right on with their silly quibbles. Hamlet is great but he is not the only creature under the sun.

So, brilliant as Freud is, I would hesitate to apply his theory of humour to opera, or indeed to any manifestation of the creative spirit. He was not at his best when he approached the world of creative art. To his credit it must be said that he admitted as much.

Of course the academic critics have had their say about the nature of humour, though not about its origins. Indeed, in my own country the University of Ottawa publishes twice yearly a compilation called *Thalia; Studies in Literary Humour*, and in it you may read carefully thought-out studies called "William Cowper as Mock Epideictic Elegist," and "Social Myth as Parody in Jack London's Northern Tales." These discussions are in themselves interesting, but the light they shed on the nature and origin of humour is not blinding.

Not only the philosophers and the psychoanalysts have presented us with theories of humour, of course; the scientists have been at work as well. Their experiments are often fine examples of unintentional humour. We cannot go into this subject at length, but I should like to present you with the finding of some scientists who claim to have discovered that women find jokes funniest when they hear them with the left ear, because this ear relates to the right hemisphere of the brain, which processes information more holistically than the left hemisphere, which is analytical.

Think of the work that must have gone into this discovery! Call up in your minds the silent laboratory, in which the white-coated experimenters are gathered around a steel chair, in which a woman sits; she wears a hospital gown and electrodes are attached to her wrists, ankles, and diaphragm, which in turn lead to a device that measures her responses. Her left ear is filled with a medicated wax, and is covered by an earmuff, which has a lead plate inside it, to exclude all sound. A total hush prevails. The most important of the investigators approaches her, and leaning forward speaks slowly and clearly into her right ear. He reads very distinctly from a book, and we can see that the title is *Joe Miller's Jests*. "Why does the chicken cross the road?" he reads. An interval of a full minute passes before he reads the answer, "To get to the other side." The woman's eyes cloud over; her response, if anything, is an expression of disgust. But now there is a half hour's break, while the subject is given a cup of tea, and her right ear is blocked, while the left ear is syringed out and restored to full usefulness. When silence has been restored, the chief investigator approaches her once again. "Why do firemen wear red braces?" he asks. A minute passes and he gives the answer, "To hold up their pants." Eureka! The woman is immediately convulsed, slaps her thigh, tumbles out of the chair, and rolls upon the floor, helpless with laughter. The attendants give her a tranquilizer and she is wheeled back to bed, to recover. It is thus, you see, that science enlarges our lives and expands the boundaries of human knowledge.

You may well protest that it is easy work to make fun of these deeply serious people who have tried to explain something of the nature of humour, and you may well ask me if I can do better. I do not know, but I can try. I have no unshakeable confidence that I shall succeed wholly, but perhaps I may open another approach to this elusive subject, and someone following me may smooth the path that I have hacked through the undergrowth.

Let me begin by brushing aside all simple jokes, wisecracks, and journalistic or television drolleries. They are well enough in their way but they are poor substitutes for what I take humour to be. *The Oxford English Dictionary,* defining humour, calls it "that quality of action, speech, or writing which excites amusement; oddity, jocularity, facetiousness, comicality, fun. The faculty of perceiving what is ludicrous or amusing, or of expressing it in speech, writing, or other composition; jocose imagination or treatment of a subject." Of course a dictionary must record educated usage, not opinions, and I think that indeed educated usage banishes humour with such grandsire terms as jocular, facetious, comical, jocose. But all these words suggest something that is done to us by a determined funnyman, to which we lend ourselves with a sense of having for the moment set aside our accustomed gravity; in such circumstances humour is imposed upon us; it is not something that is evoked from within us. I think that we all have, in some measure, a quality within us that may be termed humour, which asserts itself independently of the determined work of the clown, the gagman, or the sophisticated wit. After all, the word *humour* used to mean something that was characteristic of a human creature, and I think that indeed it is so still.

To explain what I mean, you must bear with me during a brief venture into the psychology of the late Carl Gustav Jung. Not that Jung wrote about humour; so far as I know, no speculative thinker in the psychoanalytical world save Freud ever did so. You will search in vain in the indexes of works of philosophy or psychology for any references to humour. For centuries it was considered an unworthy, undignified quality. My guess is that because humour always suggests uncertainty, or ambiguity, the wise men feared it. But Jung gives us hints as to where to look for humour. Indeed, the search for it recalls those medieval legends, where we set out to find a sacred spring in a tangled wood. We meet with many dragons and misdirections on the way, but we hope to get the better of them, because we know that the water of the spring brings magical transformation. I do not exaggerate in my use of the metaphor of the magical spring. Schopenhauer was unusual among philosophers because he declared a sense of humour to be a "divine" characteristic, because it made it possible for a man to maintain his soul in freedom and to seek that ultimate joy in life which lies in the creation or cherishing of what is beautiful. *Possible for a man to maintain his soul in freedom*. Freedom from what? What puts him in chains? This is where our Jungian exploration leads us into a very dark wood indeed.

Jung was a deeply learned man, and one of the bases of his thinking derives from the writings of Heracleitus, a Greek philosopher who lived long before Plato, and of whom we know little. But he said some things of enduring worth, and chief among them is a declaration that there is unity in the world, but it is unity formed by the combination of opposites. From this comes his most famous declaration that "Everything flows; nothing stands still." And with this goes the belief that anything, if pursued to its farthest extent, turns into its opposite. In our world, where so many things are pursued without moderation we see this principle at work: Charity, driven as hard as it can go, becomes a vast organization which seems to exist to support itself; so it is with research, which demands vast funds to support the research, creating a structure which would fall to the ground if the aim of the research were ever achieved. (A friend of mine, an ironical scientist, says that if a cure for cancer were ever found, it would create disastrous unemployment.) We see this principle in the pursuit of pleasure, which eager, craving, tormented people pursue to a point where it becomes a weariness. Moderation, the Golden Mean, the Aristonmetron, is the secret of wisdom and of happiness. But it does not mean embracing an unadventurous mediocrity: Rather it is an elaborate balancing act, a feat of intellectual skill demanding constant vigilance. Its aim is a reconciliation of opposites.

Nowhere, I think, is this task more difficult than in preserving a balance between the contrasted attitudes toward man's fate, the Comic and the Tragic. The Comic, pursued without discretion, runs into a shallowness which brings in its wake a triviality of mind and spirit which produces results that may be tragic; the Tragic, as with my friend who declared it to be the only endurable intellectual stance for an intelligent man, produces in its farthest reaches a gloomy egotism which impresses the onlooker as comic. But in seeking the Golden Mean we cannot be content with a bland rejection of both the Tragic and the Comic until life becomes a kind of vanilla custard, fit only for spiritual and intellectual invalids. No, the Golden Mean is not a sunny, untroubled nullity, but a deep awareness of possibilities, with one eye cocked toward Comedy and the other eye skewed toward Tragedy, and out of this feat of balanced observation emerges Humour, not as a foolish amusement or an escape from reality, but as a breadth of perception, and what Heracleitus called "an attunement of opposite tensions, like that of the bow and the lyre." A reconciliation of opposites, indeed.

Such a duality of vision may make us sad at the great party which is given to a colleague who is about to retire, his usefulness having expired; in the midst of the jollification we are aware of the eyes of his younger colleagues, fixed on his professorial chair, or his seat at the head of the boardroom table; this is the duality of perception which made Bernard Shaw laugh uncontrollably at his mother's funeral, as he thought of what she would have said about the obsequies. A sense of humour, in the true sense, is not always a comfortable possession.

What I have been saying, of course, offers only examples and instances—very commonplace and simple ones—of the way in which the sense of humour may work. But examples do not say anything about the nature of the sense of humour itself, and here I must return again to the thought of Dr. Jung. It is my belief that humour is, in fact, an archetype, and one about which very little, if indeed anything, has been said. You will understand my diffidence as I pursue my argument; I make no claim to being a deeply learned Jungian, and in what I am going to say I may go wrong, but I do not think I shall be wholly wrong.

I have used that tricky word *archetype,* which has gained a good deal of popularity and is used loosely to describe any complex of ideas, or any situation that may come up in discussion. But an archetype, in the sense that Jung used it, and in which he inherited it from the thought of Plato, is not so easily defined. It has been called "a hypothetical entity irrepresentable in itself and evident only through its manifestations." In other words, you know it by its effects, but cannot grasp its cause. A familiar archetype is that of First Love, of which most people have some knowledge. It seizes upon its subject, bringing about changes both mental and physical and provoking actions which seem inevitable to the subject, but which may be inexplicable to the lookers-on. Not all archetypes work so obviously or, as a usual thing, so briefly. Any of us, at any time, may fall under the spell of an archetype, for good or evil.

Why do I suppose that humour is archetypal in its manifestations? (Because, as I hope I have made clear, an archetype may be known only by its manifestations; its essence cannot be pinned down.) I think so because humour seeks a balance in what is perceived—a balance that lies between the comic and the tragic, aware of both but not wholly committed to either. It is an archetype that seems to face both ways, and therefore we might call it the Janus Archetype, after the Roman god *Janus Bifrons*—Janus with Two Faces. Janus who looks both East and West; Janus, who is thus constantly aware of possibilities. Janus, who might therefore be taken as the God of Humour.

You may well be wondering when I am going to get to opera, and how do I propose to associate this theory of humour that I have been talking about with music. Simply by telling you how compellingly such humour seems to me to assert itself in some of the greatest operatic works, and in some which are not usually thought of as great but which cannot be ignored in any such talk as this.

Virtually all operas, including many that seek tragic stature, contain some humorous element, and during the nineteenth century the inclusion of some comedy was thought to be obligatory in the melodramatic plots that served as the basis for opera libretti. Such operas abound with comic labourers, or absurd notaries, or elderly widows who give an opportunity for *buffo* singers to appear briefly and amuse the kind of people who thought them funny. We think of the Sacristan in *Tosca,* for instance, or that remorselessly funny monk in *La Forza del Destino* who appears when Leonora seeks sanctuary in a monastery. Anyone who ever saw the late Salvatore Baccaloni in any of these roles knows the kind of funny-walking, eye-popping, funny makeup performance I mean—unlike anything on earth, or in the heavens above, or in the waters under the earth. As we survey these characters—and they are numberless—we form a poor opinion of the comic invention of nineteenth-century librettists. Of course they were working in the atmosphere of a melodramatic theatre where comedy had to be shoved into the action with a shoehorn, because it did not arise naturally from the plot; in melodrama there are the really important people, whose high seriousness and splendour of character never waver, and there are lesser folk—comic servants in many cases—who are allowed to make jokes and do absurd things. There are really two worlds; the world of drama and the world of comedy, and they mingle uneasily. The notion that the two might ever unite in one person is unthinkable; in *Rigoletto*, for instance, the jester is a tragic figure and, although his profession is that of a clown, we never hear him crack a single joke; when he jeers cruelly at Monterone we know that irony is intended and that the evil at which he jeers will recoil on his own head. If we permit ourselves such irreverence, we wonder how on earth *Rigoletto* ever got, and held, his job as a funnyman.

Even Mozart, who had comic genius of a high order, never permitted it to appear in any of his avowed tragedies. When lesser composers were at work, they were inhibited by the lack of comic perception in their librettists, and one suspects also in themselves.

Consider as an example Donizetti's *Lucia di Lammermoor*; I choose it because it has held the stage for 150 years and never fails to draw an audience when a great soprano plays the title role. To compare the libretto by Salvatore Cammarano with the novel by Sir Walter Scott is a depressing business. I do not speak of Cammarano's determination to make the plot comprehensible to an Italian audience by throwing aside Scott's careful descriptions of Scottish degrees of social standing; nothing is made of the fact that Edgar of Ravenswood is vastly superior to the common Lucy Ashton; Cammarano cannot define religious sympathy within the Scottish Church; it is nothing to him that Edgar is an Episcopalian and a ritualist, whereas Lucy is a stark Presbyterian. What would that mean in Roman Catholic Italy? (I have seen a production in which so many crucifixes adorned the ancient Presbyterian home of Lucy Ashton that Walter Scott would have died either from rage or laughter.) But I do think that Cammarano, if he had more than a schoolboy's command of English, might have made use of some of Scott's fine humorous characterizations, such as the splendid Caleb Balderstone, and not have changed the chaplain Bide-the-Bent into the characterless Raimondo, a sort of half-priest half-secretary whose principal duty seems to be to provide a fine bass in the celebrated Sextet. There is room in a novel for humour, but not in an opera, it appears. If it were possible for us to question Cammarano about what he thought he was doing, he would certainly reply that he was providing a simple dramatic scaffold on which the composer might hang some melodious upholstery, and that subtlety of character had nothing to do with it. As for humour, such dramas as *Lucia* and *Il Trovatore* afford no place for such triviality.

It is the concept of life, you see. Tragedy and comedy can never meet. Not, that is to say, in opera. Not in the classical theatre of France. Why, we may ask? Quite simply because to introduce tragedy into comedy and vice versa is work for a great master, and great masters are few.

The supreme master in this line, of course, is William Shakespeare. None of his great tragedies is without its comic relief. Hamlet meets the Gravediggers at Ophelia's funeral; when the tension of the knocking at the gate in *Macbeth* is at its height, in comes the Porter, full of drink and dirty jokes. The examples could be multiplied but I do not wish to bore you by telling you what you already know. And what is the result of these comic intrusions? It reminds us that the world is wide, and that although Hamlet is in deep distress, there is another world just over the castle wall; Macbeth is deep in evil, but to at least one of his servants life is a thing of lewd merriment. The tragedy is made more poignant by being made more personal. The city of Thebes was ravaged by plague when Oedipus was King, but Prince Hamlet suffers alone. This is a recognition of the wholeness, the infinite variety, of life, and of the dominance of Janus, who faces two ways.

Does Shakespeare bring tragedy into comedy? Again and again he does so, and the comedy is more effective for it. An example I particularly cherish comes in *Henry IV, Part II*, when Falstaff is jesting with the harlot, Doll Tearsheet, and she bids him to begin to patch up his old body for Heaven. Falstaff replies: "Peace, good Doll! do not speak like a death's-head, do not bid me remember mine end"—and it is as if a shadow fell suddenly over the whole rowdy, scabrous scene.

Can this happen in opera? Perhaps, but I do not know of any powerful instance of it. One of the most tragic operas of our century is Berg's *Wozzeck*, in which the misery of a wretched man is presented, frequently in farcical terms; but a whole scene is needed to achieve each example. The shot-silk, Shakespearean effect of comedy or tragedy intervening to deepen a dramatic effect is not part of the genius of music.

Here I may tread on some toes. All my life I have been devoted to music and have taken enormous pleasure in opera. But my principal love is the theatre, and it is impossible to spend a great deal of time with both without being aware that music is a comparatively slow means of expression. Spoken dialogue makes a joke in three words. Music must take its time.

Consider again the entrance of Falstaff in any of the Shakespeare plays in which he appears—the two parts of *Henry IV*, and *The Merry Wives of Windsor*; as soon as Falstaff steps on the stage we know him to be a great comic creation because of what he says. But compare the entrance of another notable comic, Baron Ochs in *Der Rosenkavalier*. How many bars it takes to get him onstage, and establish him as who he is! Music, however rapid the tempo, is deliberate in offering its message. And when the Baron is to be reduced in self-esteem by a series of practical jokes, what a time it takes and what a deal of shrieking and scampering about! With Falstaff the Prince has but to say, "I know thee not, old man," for us to feel the chill. Drama rises like an eagle; it sometimes seems that music has to do a great deal of flapping its wings before it gets off the ground.

My task, however, is not to talk about what opera cannot do, or does unwillingly, but to offer examples of humour of the profound, archetypal sort that I have described that appear in opera and which, in my opinion, lift such operas as have it into a special category of masterworks. They are not in every case operas that serious musical critics put high on their lists. Let me begin with one that rarely meets with serious discussion, but which has held the stage since 1728, and after the First Great War achieved an extraordinary London run of 1,463 consecutive performances. I refer, of course, to *The Beggar's Opera.*

Why do I introduce this featherlight ballad opera into a supposedly serious discussion of operatic art? Because I think it has never been given quite the sort of recognition it deserves, and which goes far to explain its unfailing freshness and popularity. It demonstrates in the clearest terms the combination of comic and tragic elements into a work that produces the particular sort of pleasure, what perhaps I may call "the glory in the breast," which is humour.

We all know that *The Beggar's Opera* had its beginning in a suggestion made to John Gay by Jonathan Swift that a Newgate pastoral "would make an odd, pretty sort of thing." And how right the Dean was! The combination of a plot which is a tapestry of villainy, betrayal, and infidelity with tunes—many of them folk songs—of the uttermost charm and delicacy has produced a work of unique quality; every roguery, every cynicism and bitterness of heart is turned to innocence and simple beauty by the music. When we see it well done, in the true spirit of its origin, we come out of the theatre delighted, not forgetting the harshness of the story, or the duplicity of the politicians it originally caricatured, but possessed by that deep serenity which I take to be the ultimate effect of the truest humour.

I have said "when we see it well done," and I mean done as Gay intended it—simply and prettily, allowing its darker themes to assert themselves without emphasis. But many musicians of high attainment have been unwilling to permit that, and Arthur Bliss, and Benjamin Britten, and Kurt Weill in his German version, have been determined to rub our noses in the dirt of the plot, as if we had not wit enough to see it and judge it for ourselves. They have utterly missed the point of the work which is a splendidly ironic juxtaposition of the prison filth of plot with the hedgerow sweetness of the music. Serious musicians, unable to understand the magic of Gay's simplicity, have striven mightily, with huge orchestras, crying, "Look! Look! This is the tragedy of life! Macheath is a scoundrel and Polly is a sad slut; look on their works, spectators, and despair!" But we don't want to despair; we want to relish the irony, the absurdity of the thing, and be enlarged by its true humour. The best version of the original is still that of Frederick Austin, who never wrote a bar that a hundred other accomplished orchestrators might not have written, but who nevertheless never put a foot wrong, because he had seen the true nature of his material. He had simply seen what makes *The Beggar's Opera* a masterpiece of music and theatrical humour, and took care not to spoil it.

Let us turn now to a very different acknowledged masterpiece of operatic comedy, Verdi's *Falstaff*. I confess that it is not a favourite work of mine, and that as a treatment of Shakespeare's *The Merry Wives of Windsor* Ralph Vaughan Williams's *Sir John in Love* is far superior. It is the libretto that I cannot like. *The Merry Wives* is the one play of Shakespeare's in which he has given us a comedy of contemporary life; this is the bourgeois England in the reign of the first Elizabeth, and the real hero of the play is not Sir John Falstaff, but the town of Windsor with its merchants, its spirited women, parson, physician, innkeeper, busybodies and gossips, roustabouts and children, all linked in a community. Vaughan Williams has given us all of that in a work of great lyric beauty and happiness, but for these very reasons his opera lacks the powerful impact of Verdi's. Verdi demanded of his librettist, Boito, a strong plot about a single character and a single joke—the favourite joke of the Mediterranean world—which is cuckoldry. Boito delivered the goods, and Shakespeare went into the dustbin. Verdi's opera, wholly Mediterranean and Catholic, has no hint of England about it. It contains some splendid music and a star part for a great *buffo*, but Vaughan Williams's opera has made a brave attempt to convey something of the spirit of Shakespeare in music, and has come admirably close to doing it. In his music we sense much of the tragedy and depth of feeling that lie behind the comedy. I do not feel any of that in Verdi, where Falstaff's reflections on his increasing age seem lacking in shadow. Perhaps we should remind ourselves how much the *commedia del arte* had contributed to the theatre, and remember that it came from Italy; Falstaff becomes a splendid *commedia* figure, but much of the buffoonery still clings. The *commedia* was fun without shadows, and I hope I am making clear my point that the deepest humour never lacks for shadow.

How admirably this is shown in the operas of Mozart. It is easy to lose one's balance in talking about Mozart, as it is about Shakespeare, but I do not think anyone will contradict me when I speak of the shadowy quality, the bittersweetness, which is so often an element in his comedy. *The Marriage of Figaro* is full of it. We are not so strongly aware now as were its first audiences, of the impropriety of suggesting that a servant may be a cleverer man than his master, but most decidedly when this opera first appeared that was looked upon as questionable humour. Perhaps this is the place to say that much of the finest humour *is* questionable. The people who fear humour—and they are many—are suspicious of its power to present things in unexpected lights, to question received opinions and to suggest unforeseen possibilities. They are people whose world is, they think, founded upon rock. Such people think of humour as an emollient, a balm for sore feelings, an oil for troubled waters; and indeed it may be all of these things, and it may also be their precise opposite. And of the deepest humour a reconciliation of opposites is the strongest quality.

It is in this area that Mozart moves with masterly assurance. It is not astonishing that in our century, when psychoanalysis has wakened us to the ambiguity of so many human emotions and actions, Mozart has taken so prominent a place in the world of art. In *The Marriage of Figaro*, when the Count, an inveterate philanderer, is moved to ask pardon of his Countess, we find, in a musical phrase, what it would take a psychoanalytical writer an essay to express—the complexity of feeling of a man whose self-doubt drives him to empty infidelity, while his innate moral sense makes him ashamed of himself. Time and again in this opera we find musical comment that illuminates and deepens Da Ponte's by no means trivial libretto, and this musical comment is made with a sure but light touch—something which cannot be said for every genius, as, for instance, Wagner. In passing, I may say how frequently composers do not seem to credit their audiences with ordinary common sense and agility of perception. Music, like all arts, readily becomes tediously didactic.

No comment of this sort about Mozart could avoid some reference to his metaphysical masterpiece, *The Magic Flute*. When I was a boy, receiving my first instruction in music, I was assured that *The*

Magic Flute was an incomprehensible muddle, in which the divine composer had wasted his time with a cretinous librettist whose playlet was a botched Christmas pantomime. We know better now. Schikaneder was a thoroughly competent librettist when we understand what he is doing, but when I was a lad people were not so familiar with the concept of the Hero-Struggle in life, or the significance of initiations and rites of passage in establishing a human creature as an individual in the true sense of the word—a complete and unified human being. Schikaneder and Mozart work within a Masonic frame, which derives from the initiation ceremonies and rites of ancient times, and doubtless the adventures of Tamino have resonances for Masons that escape the rest of us. But we do not need Masonry now to tell us that for a young man to come face to face with life, and win his soul—personified by the heroine Pamina—he must undergo trials that will prove or disprove his worthiness. We are aware also that lesser trials await the less psychologically developed Papageno. This is offensive to some modern democratic thinking, which would like to believe that all souls are the same size and develop in the same way. Fortunately we have no time at present to discuss this fascinating theme.

In *The Magic Flute* the conflicting opposites are the Queen of the Night, who is all evil, and the sage Sarastro, who is all good, and the tension between them gives its energy to the opera. But we must remember Heracleitus and his theory of the regulatory function of opposites. The Queen is the shadow of Sarastro, and thus there is a link between them. We are assured that the Queen is evil, but we may think that the evil that sings like that is so attractive that we might very well mistake it for good. Nor are we wholly won by the nobility of Sarastro; we may disloyally think that after a few years of his company one might have had enough of unremitting wisdom and goodness. In the opera we happily enjoy the best of both worlds. That is one of the most splendid gifts of art, where we are enabled to have our cake and eat it, too. When the curtain falls and we have enjoyed the splendid balance between Good and Evil, where the Janus god is casting an eye in both directions and we are wrapped in the serenity of a glorious, and probably precarious, balance. This is humour at its pinnacle. It is here that we are aware of what G.K. Chesterton finely called "the mysticism of happiness."

It is out of the question, of course, in so brief a survey as this, to go deeply into the question of which operas may be said to achieve this highest form of humour and which do not. But there is one that tackles the problem head-on and, in my opinion, achieves a splendid balance; it is Richard Strauss's *Ariadne auf Naxos.*

You recall the circumstances of that work. It was originally meant to serve as an afterpiece for Molière's *Le Bourgeois Gentilhomme.* The richest man in Vienna is giving an entertainment for his friends, which is to include the performance of an opera, a show by a troupe of Italian comedians, and—much the best of all—a great show of fireworks. The young composer of the opera is outraged that his deeply serious work in which, he declares, "the mystery of life is revealed," is to be followed by some comic trash called *Fickle Zerbinetta and Her Four Lovers*—"a merry comedy with dancing, light, tuneful music and a plot as clear as daylight." But worse is to come. The order goes out, from the great rich host himself, that in order not to delay the fireworks the harlequinade must be performed simultaneously with the tragedy. And in spite of extraordinary displays of temperament, that is what happens, because, although art is art and must be served without thought of self, artists must live, and if the opera singers and the comedians are to have their fees, they must obey the command of their employer.

What follows is a masterwork of profound psychological penetration, as well as a splendid piece of music. Strauss had as his librettist Hugo von Hofmannsthal, who was extraordinary among librettists in being a fine poet and literary man apart from his work with the composer. And so he intertwines the tragic tale of Ariadne, the maiden who saved Theseus when he sought out the Minotaur in the labyrinth by giving him a guiding thread; Theseus, ungrateful wretch, abandoned her on the island of Naxos, and it is there, in the company of three nymphs, that we see her, grieving for her lost love and longing for Death.

The circumstances of the rich patron's entertainment, however, mean that she has to do this under the observation of the Italian comedians—the fickle Zerbinetta and four comic, lively, ebullient suitors. Zerbinetta is astonished that Ariadne is taking things so hard:

To be thrown over by a lover is certainly disagreeable, but another and perhaps a better one will come along soon. And anyhow, is a girl who really exerts herself to charm ever short of lovers? Zerbinetta cannot understand it at all.

Ariadne is resolute for Death, and begs him to appear and be her last and longest lover. Zerbinetta determines to give her some sound woman-to-woman advice, which she does, in an aria of astonishing brilliance. Men, she says, are faithless, but irresistible. Women are not faithless but often, when she believes she belongs to one man and to him alone, a new love steals into her heart, and she finds herself both true and false at once. She deceives one man—and yet she loves him truly; it is never a matter of caprice, but of compulsion, and is it not marvellous that the heart should have so little understanding of itself? But every lover comes like a new god, and she surrenders without a word.

Zerbinetta and her lovers find that Ariadne cannot comprehend what the charmer from the comedy is telling her. But Zerbinetta has hope; in time Ariadne may come to speak the language of love she has been so eloquently expounding.

And indeed it is so, for in the distance are heard cries of triumph which Ariadne interprets as the approach of Death. But it is nothing of the kind; it is Bacchus, who has escaped from the love of Circe, and who is immediately enthralled by Ariadne. He is not the captain of the sable ship that sails a dark course; he is the lord of Life, and in rapturous music he declares his love; Ariadne yields to him, so that we last see them entering the enchanted cave on the island which she thought was to be her grave.

So Zerbinetta's prophecy that one lover succeeds another has come true, but not precisely in the terms of Zerbinetta's own delightful and essentially comic understanding.

The effect of this opera when it is no more than adequately performed—and I have seen it under circumstances that were not of the best—is to make manifest humour in the form that I have been attempting to describe in this talk. It would be absurd to describe the means used by Strauss and Hofmannsthal as obvious, but certainly it is crystal clear. The comic approach to life and love is directly opposed to the tragic approach, on the same stage and simultaneously, for we are aware of both the comedians and the creature of mythic nobility at the same time. The comedians are sprawled out on the beach of Ariadne's island, watching her every move, and listening without comprehension to her tragic utterance. The effect is magical. Here we have that bringing together of the opposites of which I spoke earlier; here we have the union of comedy and tragedy to produce a splendid synthesis, with a very strong hint that everything depends on the way you look at it—which is the wisdom of the street, but not for that reason contemptible. If you must have it in a handsomer package, remember Hamlet's observation that there is nothing either good or bad, but thinking makes it so. And what is the effect on the audience?

It is enlarging, delighting, contenting. It sends us out into the world more deeply aware, not of simply the opposites of comedy and tragedy, but of the fluidity that brings them together. It moves us not precisely to optimism, because that word has been abused and suggests a shallow refusal to see and take heed of the dark side of life. Perhaps the word for the feeling I mean is serenity, a high acceptance, a recognition that Heracleitus's doctrine of eternal flow is a great truth, and while we may not, in ourselves, find the moment when the one element changes into the other, that moment will come and the consciousness of its inevitability may give us courage in adversity, and balance in good fortune.

That, I suggest, is humour in its highest form. In our century we have known dreadful tyrannies and fearful inhumanities, and of these by no means the least have been the sufferings of prisoners, confined in circumstances of degrading cruelty. From the stories that have come out of those prison camps we know that the survivors were those who had a faith, or a philosophy, that gave them a vision of life that rose above their fearful sufferings. Nor, we learn, were such people grimly pious, or wrangling philosophers. Rather, they were possessed of a serenity at the root of being, which sustained them. In the extremity of adversity they did not lose sight of the Golden Mean.

It would be remarkable if this serenity, this extraordinary human possession, did not manifest itself in art. In the highest art it does so, and as I hope I have persuaded you, we sometimes meet with it in the opera.

11

Melodrama: The Silver King

Davies always had a great affection for melodrama ("not a form of drama that appeals only to simple people") and so was pleased to have an opportunity to speak about it at the Shaw Festival at Niagara-on-the-Lake. The lecture was part of the July Seminar of 1993 and took place on July 17. The play under discussion was *The Silver King*, which he had seen a few days before. As always, he recorded it in his Theatre Diary.

On June 11 he wrote: *Set to work on the Shaw piece on* The Silver King; *it moves trudgingly, but I have begun so early I will have time to tart it up—want to stress melodrama music.* On June 12: *On with my melodrama piece and do somewhat better, but I am conscious of having said it all many times before, and having nothing much that is fresh to add.* July 17: *My lecture goes very well and Ron* [Bryden] *is very pleased. Lots of laughs and prolonged applause.*

July 14, evening: *At the Festival Theatre,* The Silver King, *done well and imaginatively with no trace of tedious guying of its deeply melodramatic substance. As Denver, Stuart Hughes acted well, but lacks the splendid presence the part calls for: But as Nelly, Sherry Flett was true and moving. Barry MacGregor a fine Spider and as Mrs. Spider Jan Alexandra Smith was unexpectedly powerful. Robert Benson a fine Coombes, rather like Perkins Bull—a sinister Santa. Splendid setting and exemplary production by Christopher Newton. The audience (full house) received it with enthusiasm. As Jaikes, Jack Medley very nearly stole the show and topped the applause in the call—How splendid to see a play with substance.*

My task this morning is to talk to you about *The Silver King*, the play by Henry Arthur Jones that is offered to you in this Festival as an example of the drama of the nineteenth century. We are very lucky that this Festival offers, every year, something from the nineteenth century, because it gives us an opportunity to enjoy play-going as our great-grandparents knew it, and thus we are able to peep into the past and discover, in the pleasantest way, that the past has much to be said for it. It is impossible to talk about this year's play without revealing a great deal about the story, and I am sorry for that, because it would be much better if you could simply attend the play and let its thrills and its moments of high emotion come to you freshly. Such plays as *The Silver King* were never meant to be lectured about; they belonged to the theatre and to a world of romance which a great many people suppose is now dead—I mean the world of melodrama. But I hope I may persuade you that melodrama is by no means dead and that it is not a form of drama that appeals only to simple people. I am certain that all of you here have been experiencing melodrama during the past few weeks, but it never occurred to you to give it that name. And you are not simple people, are you? No, of course not. You are the kind of people who attend drama festivals, and seminars; you are sophisticates, and nobody could pull the wool over your eyes. I don't know what you expect from *The Silver King*, but it is my job to talk about a few of the things you are going to get.

Let us look at the story, to begin. The chief character is a young man named Wilfred Denver; he is a good fellow at heart, a thoroughly decent sort, with a country background—and for some reason a great many people believe that country people are more moral and upright than city people. But Denver drinks heavily and he gambles recklessly, and he is in a bad way when first we meet him. That is in a skittle alley; which is also a betting shop and a place where liquor is sold. Denver has had heavy losses at the races, and he is drunk; he meets a man named Ware, who hates him, because Denver has won the love of the girl whom Ware wanted for himself. Ware taunts Denver with having dragged his wife down by his dissolute habits, and Denver unwisely allows himself to be heard saying that he will kill Ware. A drunken extravagance of speech, but dangerous talk. Denver rushes after Ware, in spite of Nelly's attempts to dissuade him.

Now we meet the second most important character in the play, the villain. He is a very smooth villain, who moves in very respectable circles under the name of Captain Herbert Skinner, but to the underworld he is known as The Spider, and he is planning a big jewel robbery, in which Ware's clerk is implicated, because he is going to make it possible for the thieves to get into the vault where the diamonds are. By ill luck Ware returns to his flat, finds The Spider and his accomplices at work, and in a moment of bad judgment The Spider shoots him. Denver arrives, drunk and furious. The Spider arranges that the drunken Denver should be chloroformed and left on the scene while the robbers escape. When Denver recovers consciousness he finds that his revolver is in his hand, and one shot has been fired—the shot that has killed Ware, whose body lies before him. Denver is horrified, naturally enough, and determines to escape if he can.

Now we meet a vital character in the drama, Denver's wife, Nelly. She is everything a wife should be—faithful, true, noble of spirit, and ready to stick to her man through thick and thin. She lives with their two delightful children, Cissy and Ned, and another very important character indeed; this is Daniel Jaikes, an old servant who has remained with the family from better days, and who is noble and self-sacrificing as only a stage servant can be; he keeps the Denver family going with his savings, and never dreams of being paid. Denver comes home to his wife, confesses to the murder he has not committed, and she helps him to escape. He takes a train to a distant place and then seeks to cover his tracks by jumping from the train as it speeds north. But he learns very shortly after that the train has been wrecked, and several passengers destroyed in the resulting fire.

In his anguish, Denver has prayed in words that became famous: "Oh God! put back Thy Universe and give me yesterday! Too late! Too late!" But it is not too late; he realizes that his prayer has been answered in a very subtle way. The Wilfred Denver who is being pursued as a murderer has, so far as the world knows, been killed and burned in the railway accident. God has, in His own fashion, given Denver the yesterday, and the second chance, he craved.

Now there is an interim of three years and six months. Nelly Denver is in deep trouble, for her cruel landlord, who is The Spider under his respectable guise, is determined to evict her and her children. They are nuisances on his property. Even the faithful Jaikes has no solution; because of his age he is unable to get even the odd jobs that might have brought in a little money. The children are ostracized at school, because it is known that their father was a murderer. The boy is seriously ill, and if the family are evicted he will surely die. Things could hardly be blacker.

But then little Cissy comes home with a purse full of money which has been given to her by a mysterious stranger, a man with silver hair. Of course this stranger is Will Denver, who has returned from Nevada, where he has made an enormous fortune in the silver mines, winning the name of the Silver King. But although he can get money to his family, and reveal his identity to Jaikes, he dare not be too bold, for as Will Denver he is still wanted for murder. He must clear his name before he approaches his wife and children. He manages to intrude himself into the riverside warehouse where The Spider's gang congregates, disguised as a simpleton called Deaf Dicky, and there he learns the truth about the murder, and his own innocence. The Spider is brought to justice, the exile is at last free to disclose himself to his wife and children, and after desperate trials all is well; at last we see the Denver family kneeling in their now-luxurious home, to give thanks for God's mercies.

I have done my best to put the story before you without making fun of it, and when you see it I think you will admit that the playwright has given it a seriousness that convinces, and has used language which is for most of the time acceptable as ordinary speech. Of course it is not ordinary speech; the stage has no use for ordinary speech. All stage speech is heightened and distilled and given a certain sort of suitable eloquence. Even the supposedly allusive, cryptic speech of Harold Pinter is very carefully constructed. We could not bear to listen to a play which was in the speech of ordinary life because it is too loose, too repetitive, too uninteresting to hold our attention. But what you hear in *The Silver King* passed very well as ordinary speech when the play first appeared at the Princess's Theatre in London, on November 16, 1882. The speech of The Spider's gang deserves particular attention; they are criminals, hardly literate and of limited intelligence, and that is how they sound, but there is no exaggeration. The Spider and his wife speak like people in any one of a hundred plays about good society in the latter part of the nineteenth century. It is when we come to the Denver family that we hear speech that is not precisely that of every day. Theirs is often of heightened speech.

This is owing to the skill of the playwright, Henry Arthur Jones, who was an innovator in his time. After his early melodramas he wrote a number of plays about society and upper-class life which were very successful in their own sphere and which put forward some ideas that were advanced in their time. But we may perhaps reflect that Jones had bad luck, of a kind that happens to playwrights and indeed all writers. If there had been no Shakespeare, we should now think of Ben Jonson more generously as the very great dramatist he undoubtedly was. But throughout history Jonson has had to play second fiddle to the greater man. Henry Arthur Jones might appear to us as a more important innovator in drama if he had not been at his peak contemporaneously with two formidable rivals—Oscar Wilde who was wittier, and Bernard Shaw who was cleverer.

Jones was a figure familiar in many areas of nineteenth-century life—the serious-minded, intelligent, industrious man who rose above humble beginnings and made the world pay attention to him. He was born in 1851, the son of a small farmer and his wife who were both deep-dyed Nonconformists. It is difficult to convey to a modern audience what that means, and some of you who are from the United States may not even know what a Nonconformist is. To what did these people refuse to conform? To the doctrines of the Church of England, which dominated the religious life of England in the nineteenth century as it had done since the Reformation. And if any of you are so remote from the history of thought that you do not know what the Reformation was, I shall see you in the vestry after the service. To be a Nonconformist was not simply to go to a place of worship other than the parish church; it was a social class, a climate of thought, and a political colour that encouraged rebellion against the seeming laws of society; the Nonconformist did not believe that he had to live out his life in the station in life in which it apparently pleased God to call him. If he had what it took he could rise in the world, and thousands of ambitious people did precisely that. One of them was Henry Arthur Jones.

Nonconformity, however, is something which appears to be bred in the bone. It imposes a seriousness about life which very few people are able to shake off; it also, unfortunately, gives an impression of Knowing Best to those who adhere to it. Their philosophy is: I have succeeded in the world and made circumstances bow to me, and this is evidence not only of my own ability but also of God's favour toward me; therefore I am able to advise and rule people who come under my influence with the assurance that what I say is probably God's word and what I want is God's will. Sometimes this worked as a benevolent force, but very often it led to a kind of moral tyranny, and a harshness toward anybody who dared to disagree. To me, Nonconformity rose from the later plays of Henry Arthur Jones like the smell of burnt cabbage in a middle-class home.

An important aspect of Nonconformity was its cult of the Bible as the fount of all wisdom. But the Bible takes much of its colour from whoever is reading it, and it provides a text to support almost every shade of opinion, however preposterous. Jones was an enlightened Nonconformist, but a Nonconformist for all that.

All of Henry Arthur Jones's plays—and he wrote something like sixty plays altogether—have a strong moral foundation. This does not mean that they were goody-goody plays or simple-minded plays or that the morality stuck out of the fabric in an obvious and irritating fashion. When he hit his stride he wrote plays that appealed to fashionable audiences who took them seriously. He was, far more than Shaw, accepted as a leader of popular opinion. But the trouble was that he had not Shaw's intellectual scope, and his morality was that of the great majority of people who, without being stupid, rarely questioned anything that appeared to be an accepted fact of moral, or economic, or social life.

He was, for instance, contemptuous of Ibsen. He thought Ibsen a man of ability who simply didn't understand his job or the ways of the intelligent world. He wrote a play called *Breaking a Butterfly*, which was in fact an adaptation of Ibsen's *A Doll's House*, and in it he showed Ibsen how it should be done. Ibsen, thought Jones, didn't understand women, and he, Jones, most decidedly did. But Jones, like so many Nonconformists, seems to have known only two kinds of women—good ones and bad ones; the notion that a woman was a human being with an incalculable mixture of good and bad in her nature simply did not enter his head. He seems to flirt with such a dangerous idea in one of his successes, called *The Case of Rebellious Susan*, but Susan is not really very rebellious when compared with a Shavian heroine. Perhaps it was because Jones rose from humble beginnings into good society, and never quite ceased to take good society at its face value. But of course that was long after *The Silver King*.

The play we are discussing was highly praised in its day as a refinement and improvement on melodrama as it had previously existed. It won acclaim in no less influential a journal than the *Pall Mall Gazette*, and the critic was Matthew Arnold, who was by no means an easy man to please. And while we are talking of Arnold it may not be amiss to say that what we call melodrama was enjoyed and praised by people whose opinions we cannot lightly dismiss—writers such as George Eliot, Anthony Trollope, Charles Dickens, and Lewis Carroll. Arnold particularly praised the production of the play, by the popular star Wilson Barrett. He said, "Instead of a company with a single powerful and intelligent performer, with two or three middling ones, and the rest moping and mowing in what was not to be called English but rather stagese, here was a whole company of actors, able to speak English, playing intelligently and supporting one another effectively." The play had a long run, in terms of the nineteenth century, and after the hundredth performance the London *Times* said that Barrett had worked to raise "what for want of a better word is called melodrama into the region of literature and poetry, and natural tragedy." This is high praise from a most respected source and it must have made Barrett's heart glow. In the words of *The Times* we recognize the yearnings for refinement, for improvement, for lifting of public taste, which was characteristic of the nineteenth century. But enduring, living stage work has sources that might astonish and dismay such serious-minded souls as Matthew Arnold and writers for *The Times*; refinement is a surface quality, not the enduring substance, of theatre, which is an art that sinks under the burden of too much refinement and which must have a saving quality of coarseness in order to please and endure.

To begin, the play was a disputed collaboration; Jones worked not only with the star, Wilson Barrett, but with another playwright, Henry Herman, who, when *The Silver King* became a great success, complained that Jones had robbed him of his share of the credit. To this Jones replied that Herman had written only one line—"An angel from Heaven has sent it!"; he also said that Herman could not write correct or colloquial English, as he had not a drop of English blood in him and could hardly speak English correctly. Such disputes were not uncommon. When Henry Irving had an extraordinary success with *The Bells* in 1871 the translator and adapter, Leopold Lewis, complained that he had not been given enough credit, though Irving continued to pay him for the use of the play as long as Lewis lived. The complexities of writing for the stage in the nineteenth century were not resolved, and a proper royalty system established, until the century was almost at an end, by which time a playwright of Jones's stature could rely on a very reasonable return for successful work.

To return to the genesis of *The Silver King*, the story is told by Chance Newton, a much-respected critic and man of the theatre at the time, that Wilson Barrett approached Herman—who was his business manager—and Henry Arthur Jones, who was just beginning to make a name, saying, "Look here boys, the sort of play I want is *East Lynne* turned around. That is, with a man in the position of Isabel Carlyle; lost to the world for a while—reported to be killed, like her, in a railway accident, if you like—and returning secretly in disguise, well-off though totally unable for a time to see or succour his suffering wife and children." What Barrett wanted was a play in which he could exploit the popular theme of self-accusation and tortured conscience.

Why? Because that was very much to the taste of the last quarter of the nineteenth century. Self-accusation was "in." Did you enjoy meat?

The vegetarians were down on you as an eater of carrion who was coarsening and destroying his body. Did you smoke? You were poisoning yourself and everybody around you. Drink, of course, was old stuff, but still a strong form of reproach. Among the highbrows Swinburne and Ernest Dowson proclaimed the joy and anguish of sin in many of its forms but chiefly in its sexual aspect. Does any of this sound familiar? Is there something about the close of a century which provokes the perverse passion for guilt? Are we not at this moment in just such a situation where everybody, in some form or other, is a sinner, weighed down with guilt? It's enough to make one believe in astrology.

Barrett's reference to *East Lynne* is of great interest. It was one of the most popular of the nineteenth-century melodramas, rivalling even *Uncle Tom's Cabin*. The chief character, Lady Isabel Carlyle, is by any ordinary standards a dubious figure. She is an adulteress, and rather a sneak and eavesdropper, but the story is so loaded on her side that she provokes pity in everyone who sees the play or reads the book—if anyone still reads it. And how she repents! Her repentance and eventual death would draw tears from a grizzly bear. *East Lynne* is a very crudely written play, which Jones's play most decidedly is not. But beauty combined with penitence is a sure card in the theatre, and Wilson Barrett knew it.

Who was Wilson Barrett? To begin, he was a magnificently handsome man who thrilled both men and women with his splendid masculinity. I stress that, because the nineteenth century demanded of a leading actor either that he should be a male beauty, like Barrett and a score of others (of whom Johnston Forbes-Robertson was an especially gifted example, with looks that made him a Pre-Raphaelite saint on the stage) or else the actor must be a man of compelling magnetism and distinction, like Henry Irving. People went to the theatre to gape at these handsome figures, and probably to lust after them; that was certainly the case with Lewis Waller, a great male beauty whose performance in *Monsieur Beaucaire* marked the top of his career; he had a gigantic fan club of gallery girls, who called themselves the KOWS—Keen on Wallerites—and who came night after night to worship him. It must be said that he was a modest man; this sort of acclaim embarrassed him and he depended on his wife to defend him from other women. But I must emphasize that these actors were more than male beauties; they could really act, and good judges declared that their performances were thrilling.

The demand that actors should be handsome and dress well is very much a thing of an earlier day. It lent a romance and glamour to the theatre that has quite disappeared. If you met a member of the theatre company on the street in this town, would you recognize him? A hundred years ago you could have spotted him at a hundred yards. But nowadays the demand for fine looks has been transferred to the movies, which are the popular theatre of our time. I shall have something to say about this later.

To begin with, then, Wilson Barrett was very handsome and he had a magnificent, muscular physique which he delighted to expose on the stage. He particularly liked Roman parts, such as that of Marcus Superbus in his famous play—he wrote it himself—called *The Sign of the Cross*. Its success was triumphant, and in our own century a silent film and two talkies have been made from it. In it Barrett was able to exploit to the full one of his principal attractions. I refer to his breast. And I mean his breast, not his chest. The masculine bosom has not often surpassed in splendour its female counterpart, but in Barrett's case it decidedly did so, to the rapture of his female fans, and to the despair and derision of his male contemporaries. Not only had he a splendid bosom—or buzzem, as it was called in those days—but he had a magnificent neck, strong and pillar-like. How did he acquire these beauties? The answer is simple; as a boy he had been apprenticed to a blacksmith and he forged his figure, so to speak, at the anvil.

You see, I am giving you a considerable amount of anecdote about the nineteenth-century stage, not only because it gives me pleasure, but because I want to counteract a tendency in modern theatre historians to make the nineteenth century too solemn, too loaded with deep artistic significance. Of course it was artistic—splendidly so—but artistry is not a solemn, dead thing that flourishes in universities and seminars on solemn subjects. Art is alive, or it is nothing, and the people who create it are highly coloured. Even Henry Herman, of whom I spoke earlier and who has a peripheral place in the history of

The Silver King, was an interesting character; he had a glass eye, which replaced one he lost in the American Civil War. He was a great chaser of women, though he himself lacked attraction, being grotesquely fat. He had a pretty wit: Once he refused to pay a cab fare, accusing the cabby of having cut out his eye with a flourish of his whip—he held out the glass eye in proof before the astonished onlookers. He called himself a dramatic author, but he hated the labour of writing, and so he liked to confide his dramatic ideas to aspiring young men who didn't mind putting pen to paper, allowing him to take the larger share of the profits. He met his match in Henry Arthur Jones, whose Nonconformist outlook on life would have no truck with such double-dealing.

A theatre that contained figures like Wilson Barrett and Henry Herman was splendidly alive, but it liked to play dead when there was anything to be gained by it. When clergymen and serious-minded critics acclaimed *The Silver King* or *The Sign of the Cross* as a great force for good, Barrett was delighted, but he always kept his feet on the ground; moral values must arise from strong dramatic situations; the theatre might at times walk hand in hand with the church, but it must never make the mistake of following it.

Why, you may ask? You are probably thinking of modern clergy who have no dread of the theatre. In the nineteenth century the theatre was still regarded by millions of people and virtually all Nonconformists as a place of dubious moral standing. Lewis Carroll, the author of *Alice in Wonderland* and *Through the Looking Glass*, was a keen theatre-goer, and had many friends among the theatre folk, of whom Ellen Terry was the most eminent. But he refused to take a young lady who was a friend of his to meet Ellen Terry because no unspotted (unspoiled) girl should make the acquaintance of an actress, however eminent.

He was a clergyman, because if he had not been one he could not have held his position as a don at Christ Church in Oxford. Certainly the clergyman rather than the fantasist was on top when he wrote this: "Let me pause for a moment to say that I believe this thought, of the possibility of death—if calmly realized and steadily faced—would be one of the best possible tests as to our going to any scene of amusement being right or wrong. If the thought of sudden death acquires, for *you*, a special horror when imagined happening in a *theatre*, then be very sure the theatre is harmful for *you*, however harmless it may be for others; and that *you* are incurring a deadly peril by going. Be sure that the safest rule is that we should not dare to *live* in any scene in which we dare not *die*."

It was this attitude, among people of the intellectual station of Lewis Carroll, that impelled Henry Irving's long struggle to make the theatre respectable. Perhaps he overdid it; the theatre in our day has become a place of complete respectability allied to a numbing intellectuality, but consider the situation that Irving faced. We know now that for some time Ellen Terry was his mistress, but when they lived only a very few people knew it, and not all of them could be certain.

I have already spoken to you of Matthew Arnold's warm praise for *The Silver King*, and I have contrasted it with Wilson Barrett's insistence that the young Jones and the old Herman should concoct for him something founded on one of the most popular and artistically unchaste melodramas of the time—*East Lynne*. The contradiction is an interesting and fruitful one—apparent refinement and restraint balanced against coarse sensationalism and tear-jerking pathos. Melodrama was the drama of the people, and they loved it hot and strong; but the movement toward general education in the nineteenth century was having its effect, and there was a place for a kind of melodrama which did not produce pathos and sensation with such unrestrained vehemence and coarseness. But the elements which made melodrama what it was remained unchanged. A sensational plot, strongly drawn characters, and no time wasted on psychological explorations or emotional niceties—that was the recipe.

Was it as coarse and vulgar as the highbrows insisted, and as they still insist? Indeed it was, but it was something else; it went straight to the depths of feeling which are common to all mankind. If a play touches deep feeling, it need not worry too much about improbabilities of plot, far-fetched coincidence, and characters who seem to have but one dominating characteristic or emotion. The refinement of *The Silver King* is on the surface. If we look below we find the archetypal situations and characters that have served melodrama since the days of Shakespeare, who was a master melodramatist as well as being a psychologist and a poet of blazing genius. And though Shakespeare had his faults, extreme refinement was never one of them.

The characters—where shall we begin? With the hero, of course. Wilfred Denver has a touch of complexity in his character; when the play begins we see him as a man given to drink and gambling. But is he a weak man? No, at the slightest hint of a reflection on his wife he shows himself a true Hero, chivalrous and bold. He is tricked into a false situation; he thinks he has committed a murder, and immediately he comes to himself—to his true self—and he prays: "Oh God! put back Thy Universe and give me yesterday," he begs, and that is precisely what God seems to do. He is given that inestimable gift, a Second Chance. The grateful Denver is a reformed man, and he devotes the new life he has been granted to industry—and the nineteenth century, and particularly its Nonconformist element, had the deepest reverence for industry—and when he has made his great pile he becomes a benefactor of the poor, as well as restoring his family to respectability—another Nonconformist fetish—and affluence, without which respectability is somewhat restricted.

He is the Melodramatic Hero in a particularly fine aspect. Noble, chivalrous, a lover of children, and a man redeemed by trial, we see in the latter part of the play a man who has put behind him the booze and the gambling mania and become a spiritual and financial success. The Baptist Church, in which Henry Arthur Jones was raised and from whose maternal breast he never fully weaned himself, would have been proud of Wilfred Denver. The scene in which he listens to the children singing their simple hymn in the school, packages up and delivers to us the whole impact of the play;

What though my sins as mountains rise
    And reach and swell to Heaven,
Yet Mercy is above the skies
    I may still be forgiven.

You see? Denver, sinner and headed for ruin, has been forgiven and reclaimed by Divine Mercy.

Then let me stay in doubt no more
    Since there is sure release,
For ever open stands the door,
    Repentance, Pardon, Peace.

I have not been able to trace this hymn, and I wonder if Jones may not have written it himself; it fits the play so exactly. "Repentance, Pardon, Peace"—surely at some time or other most people have experienced the longing for cleansing and the bliss of a new life. You, ladies and gentlemen, does your mind never stray back to the old family farm, where your white-haired mother wept over your youthful misdemeanours, and you, joining your tears with hers, knelt in the dear old kitchen to pray for help in living a better life? It doesn't? Shame on you! But perhaps, as you have come away from your psychoanalyst's consulting room, having paid him almost a hundred dollars for—Repentance, Pardon, Peace?—you experienced the emotion that lies at the heart of *The Silver King*. Somewhere in most of us there is an image that looks very much like Wilfred Denver. It is the image of the Good Man Falsely Accused, and which of us has not at some time played that role?

The Good Man, yes, but what about the Good Woman? When we look at Denver's wife, Nelly, we see a figure common to a thousand melodramas, but do we recognize her as what she is? She looks rather a spiritless creature, unequal to the trials that life heaps upon her. But considered psychologically, she is something quite different. She is what some psychologists have called the External Image of the Soul of the Hero; she is his better nature, she is the Eternal Feminine that draws him upward; if you know the old play of *Everyman*, you recognize in Nelly Denver the character called Good Deeds, who at last assures the Hero of his salvation. As a part for an actress, it is pretty dull; but as a peg upon which the audience can hang its ideas of all that is good, faithful, and pure, and as an appurtenance to the Hero, she is invaluable.

What about the Villain? You can't have a melodrama without one, because he is the architect of the Hero's trials and misfortunes. Melodramatic villains are an interesting study; they are rich, they seem to wear evening dress more often than is normal, they are great rhetoricians and speak in a fancy lingo that nobody has ever heard from lips that were not villainous. Further, they are rotten to the core. Now here *The Silver King* breaks some new ground, and in The Spider we meet one of the earliest manifestations of the Gentleman Crook, who has been as popular a figure in our century as the Gentleman Detective. How we love those figures who bring gentility and a whiff of High Life to otherwise mundane occupations! The Spider wears evening clothes, but only in the evening; he lives a life of luxury but not of vulgar opulence; he has an assured place in society but he is not an ostentatious swell. He speaks politely to his wife, he seems to have no lustful interest in Nelly Denver, but he is hard-hearted; he will evict Nelly, not out of sheer malignance but she must be got rid of because she is a reminder of Denver. The Spider is the Villain of this melodrama sure enough, but he is not a vulgar waxwork of a Villain; there are lots of Spiders in every society.

Now we come to a figure vital to melodrama, and he is the Comic Man. Tragedy is not supposed to have Comic Men in it, and French critics have been very severe with Shakespeare because he wiggles a Comic Man into every one of his tragedies—and the tragedies are vastly helped by the contrast the Comic Man affords. He is an assurance that outside the world of misfortune in which the tragic figures live, there is another world, inhabited by simple people of good and simple nature, where tragedy has not blackened the skies. The Comic Man in *The Silver King* is Daniel Jaikes, the old family servant, who remembers Denver's father, "the Old Squire," and Denver as a daring, lovable boy, and Daniel is determined to stick with Denver and Denver's wife as long as there is breath in his body. His savings are all spent to help Nelly in her distress and he wants no payment; indeed, he does his feeble best to earn money for them by doing odd jobs. And he is full of jokes and happy inspirations. Indeed, in skilled hands he is almost the best part in the play.

Why is this sort of character so popular? Because melodramas at their best are fairy tales, and as I don't need to tell an audience of your degree of sophistication, fairy tales embody the dreams, the wishes, the traditions of mankind, and one of those wishes is for a Helper who can be relied upon to come to our aid when we seem almost to sink under the blows of Fate. In fairy tales this Helper is often an animal, a clever cat, or a donkey who can find the path when the Hero has lost it. In Melodrama the Helper is most often a Comic Servant, who possesses a sagacity that saves the day time and again. Of course he is not the social or spiritual equal of the Hero, or the External Soul of the Hero. No, no; he is happy in his humble station and asks nothing better than to be of service. Have you never longed for such a helper? We all live in a world where fairy tales are not so irrelevant as we might suppose.

So, there you have the principal ingredients of melodrama: the Hero, the Heroine, the Villain, and the Comic Servant. But *The Silver King* gives us a glimpse of another character who was soon to take the stage, and a whole genre of fiction; he is Samuel Baxter, the detective. As detectives go today, he isn't up to much. He does not dominate the action and has no great scene in which he unfolds the mystery and denounces the Villain. But he is remarkably like a *real* detective; he hangs around in the places where criminals meet, and he keeps his eyes and ears open. He knows who the crooks are, and he is waiting for a chance to catch one of them in the act. He is, in fact, believable.

But we don't want detectives to be believable; we want them to be omniscient and unnaturally clever. Jones was probably aiming at realism when he created Baxter, but the unrealistic and thrilling detective had already been seen on the stage nineteen years earlier in a play called *The Ticket-of-Leave Man*. That detective's name was Hawkshaw. I can still remember actors who, when they felt the impulse to do so in private conversation, would make motions—the left hand removing an imaginary cap, the right hand seeming to remove the wig, and the third is for the hand with the cap in it to remove an imaginary pair of false whiskers—while they spoke the magic words, "I am Hawkshaw, the Detective"—this having been the culminating line of the play. Samuel Baxter is no Hawkshaw; he has not given his name to a profession, as Hawkshaw has done.

Having talked thus far about *The Silver King*, it may be well to conclude with some general comments about melodrama. The Jones play was praised by people who did not generally concern themselves with the theatre, and won for the author, and for Wilson Barrett, reputations that grew with the years. Barrett was hailed as "a thoughtful, refined, and scholarly man," which was coming it rather strong, for although Barrett was undoubtedly a good fellow, he was a man of the theatre first, last, and all the time. Mr. Gladstone praised him and praised Jones and unless Queen Victoria had so far condescended as to offer a few words of encomium, there was no nineteenth-century praise that carried more conviction. Serious people wanted the theatre to appear on the side of whatever was serious, and as comedy could not be depended on, and tragedy did not appeal to a wide-enough public, melodrama was the theatrical form that carried the greatest intellectual and moral weight. And it was that burden which would have destroyed it, if melodrama had not been indestructible.

What is it, really? The name tells us all. At the beginning of the nineteenth century it was a romantic and sensational stage-play, with interspersed songs and a musical accompaniment which was either continuous or frequent. It was also expected to have a happy ending, but that did not necessarily mean the uniting of lovers. One of the most continuously successful of melodramas was *The Corsican Brothers*, which ends when the ghost of one of the brothers appears to the other, who has avenged his death, speaking the words: "Weep not, dear brother, we shall meet above." Indeed, death concludes many of the most popular melodramas, including the deathless *Camille*, where the great-hearted courtesan expires saying: "All the pain is gone! Is this Life? Now everything appears to change. Oh, how beautiful! Do not wake me—I am so sleepy," while her lover Armand cries, "Camille! Camille! Dead! Dead!"

It is of great interest, by the way, that death which was so common on the Victorian stage in this form of transfiguration and peace, is virtually never seen thus in modern drama, where death is violent and final. Are we more realistic than our forebears, or merely more afraid of death? But that is not a theme that can detain us now.

The musical content of melodrama was made necessary in the early part of the nineteenth century because the law still forbade the presentation of what were called "legitimate plays," meaning the classics and plays of serious literary worth, in any theatres except those which held royal patents, which were Covent Garden and Drury Lane.

This was the law until 1843, by which time a tradition of drama with music had gained acceptance for the best of reasons: The music supported the drama in a way that words alone could not do. The writers for the popular theatre were not gifted men of letters; they were hacks, and their hack dramas, written quickly and for poor pay, were not able to stir the emotions of a simple audience unaided, and were greatly strengthened by assistance from the orchestra.

As melodrama gained in stature, the writing became better, and the music became better, as well. Instead of being anything that the orchestra leader thought might fit a dramatic situation, music of good quality was especially written for specific plays.

Consider *The Bells*, which Henry Irving played over a thousand times during his career as unchallenged leader of the British stage. (Incidentally, Irving would not permit *The Bells* to be described as a melodrama, but it was unquestionably a drama with music.) I have Irving's own copy of the music for *The Bells* and it is a splendid example of the way in which music was used to heighten, without overwhelming, the action on the stage. The music was written by a French composer, Etienne Singla, for the first production of the play in 1869, and he was asked to London to conduct when the play opened in London at the Lyceum Theatre on November 25, 1871. The score is elaborate: Twenty-six players are required, including strings, woodwinds, brass, and drums. There is an Overture, and twenty-seven passages of music of varying lengths to accompany scenes of special dramatic importance, and to mark the entrance of crucial characters. The music, which relies heavily on Alsatian folk songs, to partner the setting of the play, is used in a fashion very much akin to the leitmotivs of Wagner. It is very respectable music, without being in any way obtrusive, which Irving would not have permitted. Indeed, the story is told that when Sir Arthur Sullivan wrote music for his production of *Macbeth*, Irving was unsatisfied with the music that accompanied one of his soliloquies, and at last demanded that the orchestra play it without the melody—and that proved to be exactly what he wanted. *He* was the melody, and no rivalry was permissible. It is worth adding that Sullivan concurred without complaint; he knew very well that music to accompany a play must not seek to dominate.

In passing, I must take note of a use of music to accompany melodrama which will be within the recollection of many of you who are here present. During the era of the silent films, they were accompanied in hundreds of the lesser movie houses by a piano, played by an artist of what we must now recognize as extraordinary versatility. Every feature film was accompanied by a thematic cue-sheet for the pianist, and it gave the cue for every scene in the film, the length of the scene, and the music that was to be played to support it. I am lucky in having a collection of these cue-sheets, and they are of the greatest interest. Consider that for the 1923 filming of *The Green Goddess*, in which George Arliss starred, every phase of the action has its musical accompaniment defined, with reference to the compilation of popular music in which it could be found; the music ranges from very popular airs, to what the film people called "classical"—as, for instance, Saint-Saëns' "Funeral March of a Marionette," which supports the scene where the wicked Rajah of Rukh pursues the dewy English maiden round and round a table, determined to plant his loathsome kiss upon her pure lips. There are thirty-six music cues, in all. As a boy I sat transfixed during dozens of such films, and always aware that Mr. Harrison, who played the piano, was adding immeasurably to the thrill of what I saw. From time to time in very serious films, like *The White Sister*, starring Lilian Gish, Mr. Harrison would slide almost imperceptibly from the piano stool to the bench of a parlour organ, upon which he played music suitable for religious scenes. These movie pianists were as adroit as cathedral organists in the way they could change ("segued" was the technical term) from key to key, from mood to mood, without unseemly breaks. They are a vanished race but memory holds them in respect and affection. In them the spirit of a thousand melodramas lived well into our century, not in the sophisticated form of such scores as that for *The Bells*, but as orchestra leaders in humble theatres glued them together for plays now forgotten. If you want to find out what those orchestras were like, and what sort of musicians played in them, I suggest that you read Balzac's splendid novel, *Cousin Pons*.

Melodrama is not dead. It lives in the movies, where every film has a score specially written for it, and sometimes of high quality. It lives in television: Next time you watch, observe how your response is being nudged in the desired direction by the music. Melodrama lives in our opera houses, for dozens of the most popular operas—*La Traviata*, *La Bohème*, *Madama Butterfly*, *Rigoletto*, *La Tosca*, one could go on for a long time—are musical versions, by acknowledged masters, of plays that were melodrama successes before they became operas. They create excitement and often draw tears, just as did the stage versions because, as E.T.A. Hoffmann so finely said, "the lyre of Orpheus opens the door of the underworld," and music touches us as only the finest words of the greatest poets can do. Music releases emotion directly, and it knows no barrier of language.

When I was a boy, living in a somewhat primitive community, it was my good luck to see *Uncle Tom's Cabin* twice, and I assure you when Little Eva died, while a choir of her loving slaves sang "Nearer, My God to Thee" at her bedside, an audience of lumberjacks and mill-hands wept unashamedly. Do we ever dash away a tear when Violetta in *La Traviata* dies to exquisite music? I know we do. The degree of sophistication and the level of art are far divided, but the effect is achieved, surely and firmly.

That is what melodrama means. It appeals not simply to the intellect, but to the heart, and even in our own seemingly harsh days audiences still have hearts to be touched. And I hope your hearts will be by *The Silver King*.

12

Alchemy in the Theatre

In 1994, Robertson Davies was asked to write an article for *The New Theater Review*, which is published by Lincoln Center Theater in New York. As always he wrote pieces like this well ahead of their due date, and on July 1 (defiantly avoiding the modern usage Canada Day) he noted in his diary: *Dominion Day: did not like what I wrote yesterday so buckle down and rewrite and finish the Lincoln Center piece. Am pleased with myself; the old journalistic skill has not deserted me.... P.M. help Brenda transplant some lily-of-the-valley to the upper garden, then dig part of a bed, and enjoy it.*

Davies refers here to a production of *Pericles* as an occasion for alchemy in the theatre. This is what he wrote in his Theatre Diary about the production in question, which he saw at The Stratford Festival, Stratford, Ontario, in 1973.

July 24, Tuesday: .... *At 7:30 the opening performance of* Pericles. *Very fine and we quickly abandoned any doubts which the preliminary stuff by* [the critic Herbert] *Whittaker, about bad play, necessity to hack, patch, rewrite, and smooth over, might have provoked. Jean* [Gasçon] *had treated it as fairy tale on a high level, with respectful care for the mythological and ceremonial elements in it; Leslie Hurry had designed it in accord, with all the splendour of barbaric colour which is his—except for the women's costumes, and Hurry does not understand women, for he had put them in tight peek-a-boo skirts and bosom-huggers, so that they lacked flow and mystery. Still, it was otherwise splendid. Notable performance by* [Nicholas] *Pennell as Pericles, noble, suffering under the gods, trusting—a true hero, indeed. We see the controversial Nachum Buchman as Antiochus, and he has as fine a voice as I have ever heard, and great command. Christine Forester, as his daughter, was a lump of bare Eve's flesh which seemed small incitement to incest; they needed some beautiful Jewess, tawny and mysterious. Martha Henry a fine, grave Thaisa but she was outshone by Pamela Brook as a first-rate Marina, playing in noble strain as Pennell did, and carrying full conviction in her virtue. Milly Hall strained rather as the Bawd and her girls were comic, as stage whores commonly are—healthy, pink kids with gleaming teeth, who had painted themselves hollow-eyed, and put fancy mormals on their hams, without achieving any effect save that of rude health and rather dull virtue. Powys Thomas a fine magician as Cerimon. Barry MacGregor played Boult: consulted his doctor about pox and wore a pox-rotted nose and a left contact lens which gave him an eerie bleared, greyish eye. Also held his pizzle much of the time to simulate priapism. But despite all this elaborate decay he continued to look like a hero trying to be a wreck. Nice chap. A notable evening.*

Alchemy is one of those useful words often employed by critics when they want to suggest that some good work has been done in the theatre with unlikely material. Why unlikely? Because, in general usage, alchemy means the transmutation of base metal into gold. But the word, like *glamour*, has been too freely and loosely employed; both words have magical implications, but their magic is not cheap. What was alchemy, and how has it come to its present condition as a drudge word for critics—who are, it must be said, often careless writers?

Alchemy was the chemistry of the Middle Ages, and it persisted into the sixteenth century. Indeed, it had few practitioners until comparatively modern times. Goethe was perhaps the most celebrated of these, and I am sure that there are a few alchemists in New York at this moment, if we knew where to look for them. It once had a secret significance which I shall touch on shortly, but to most people it meant elaborate processes by means of which it was hoped to turn base metals into gold. Of course it attracted crooks, and they gouged money out of gullible or greedy people, as we see in Ben Jonson's wonderful play *The Alchemist*. But beneath the primitive chemistry and mystification lay something deeper, the true alchemy, which had to be closely guarded because it was founded on a heresy—nothing less than that there was a way to salvation outside the Church. The alchemists pursued a path which was supposed to lead to spiritual perfection, or at least to point out the road to it. (If you are curious to know more, the subject has been thoroughly and fascinatingly explored in volumes 12 and 13 in *The Collected Works of C.G. Jung*.) They are deeply interesting once you accustom yourself to the oddity of the subject. Of course this sort of rivalry could not be countenanced by the Church, and alchemists stood in peril of persecution as heretics—very dangerous heretics—because most of them were, in terms of their time, learned men and women and advanced thinkers. (Learned women? Oh yes, for each alchemist had his *soror mystica* who shared in his work, and some of these, like the famed Maria Prophetissa— still remembered in the kitchen as the originator of the *bain-marie*—were among the most famous of the initiates.)

What alchemy really means is something which has attained to such excellence, such nearness to perfection, that it offers a glory, an expansion of life and understanding, to those who have been brought into contact with it.

What the critics mean, then, when they talk of alchemy in the theatre, is something so good that it seems to have gone beyond what may be explained in terms of talent.

Is such a usage justifiable? Judging from my own theatre experience I would say so, for I have encountered theatre alchemy several times in a life in which theatre-going has been the principal and most cherished experience of art.

I think of the Habima Players in *The Dybbuk*; of a performance on successive nights of both parts of Goethe's *Faust* at Salzburg. (The Second Part of that play, which has puzzled so many students, reveals itself in terms of alchemy, among other concepts.) I recall a performance by the Old Vic Company when it visited New York after the end of the Second World War, of *Uncle Vanya*, which seemed to explain so much about what that war was fought to defend. Heavy stuff, do you say? Theatre which has been touched by alchemy is never heavy. I have seen comedy which was in the alchemical vein too, and I could go on about it if I had limitless space. But I have never seen a theatre performance in which alchemy was at work in any play that lacked literary substance—the hand of the writer who is himself a true theatre artist. You cannot make gold out of garbage though, distressingly, there are theatre directors intent on some inner revelation of their own, who can make gold into garbage.

Sometimes unlikely substances may be transmuted, and I am thinking now of a production at the Shakespeare Festival in Stratford, Ontario, of Shakespeare's *Pericles, Prince of Tyre*. It has never been counted as one of Shakespeare's greatest, but as it appeared in that production it was a truly great and deeply moving drama of loss and reconciliation, and as we saw it we knew that under the dust of its chronicle form glowed the true theatre gold, which alchemy had revealed.

The alchemy begins with the playwright, just as great music begins with the composer but has no life until it is played by great musicians. Shakespeare is the mighty magician here. By means of a dropped handkerchief, as Coleridge says, he sets in motion the tragedy of *Othello*; out of lovers' quarrels and amateur actors and the often mauled and degraded notion of a fairy world he contrives the truly alchemical wonder of *A Midsummer Night's Dream*. But Shakespeare is *hors concours*. Must a playwright be a poet to bring about alchemy?

No, but he must be aware of what Thomas Mann, tongue in cheek, spoke of as the much more complex rhythms of prose, and he must have weeded and cultivated his vocabulary—not to produce exotics, but to root out faded blooms. As Synge says in his Preface to *The Playboy*, "In a good play every speech should be as fully flavoured as a nut or an apple and such speeches cannot be written by anyone who works among people who have shut their lips on poetry."

We think of playwrights who know nothing of poetry but who are deft hands with the wisecrack. The real delight of the theatre is not to rock from guffaw to guffaw until—as critics love to say and producers love to put in their advertisements—the audience is "rolling in the aisles." This is not comedy. Comedy may certainly deploy as splendid wit, but the greatest comedies are those which reveal character. Nor is simple gloom the stuff of tragedy and it is here that playwrights and theatre artists fall into the booby trap of "realism." Unrelieved realism—the photographic reconstruction of raw life—is impossible in the theatre, which is illusion.

I recall the hosannas that greeted Elmer Rice's *Street Scene* in 1929, because of its supposed unrelenting realism, but even as a very young playgoer I knew that the realism was another form of illusion; nobody who had ever lived on a street could believe that so much incident, however commonplace, could happen in the space of a day in so ordered a fashion. Realism is a form of Puritanism, a rejection of illusion as a cheat, unworthy of serious artists. In the great days of alchemy there were hopeful people who thought that heaps of old iron, fences and fire tongs, could be transmuted into gold. It is for this rubbish that the realists have sought alchemical transformation in the theatre. A few great playwrights, notably Henrik Ibsen, have pretended to realism, but nowadays the plays of Ibsen are given brilliant and revealing productions in which the clumsy trappings of realism have been set aside.

Perhaps the biggest booby trap of all those that lie in wait for the theatre artists of our day is the yearning for "relevance," for the treatment that will reveal some supposed "message" for our time in an acknowledged classic. Of course the play would not be a classic if its relevance did not extend to our time and its message was not plain. A recent production of *Othello* that I saw put the action in an American tropical army base, trashed the poetry and reduced the pride, pomp, and circumstance of glorious war to a political wrangle, and brought the tragedy of the great leader to something resembling the journalistic story of O.J. Simpson. It is true that the history of a commonplace soldier may be tragic; Wozzeck proves it, but Wozzeck's realism is entirely deceptive, a distillation of the misery of unhappy millions. It is a tragedy of mankind, not of an individual. It is a dangerous example for the unwary. "Tragedy concerneth a high fellow," said Sir Philip Sidney, and you reduce the high fellow to the ranks at your peril. You cannot reduce the Doge of Venice to, for instance, Richard Nixon, without losing something of dimension.

Great drama, drama that may reach the alchemical level, must have dimension and its relevance will take care of itself. Writing about

AIDS rather than the cocktail set, or possibly the fairy kingdom, will not guarantee importance. The problems and predicaments of mankind are unchanging; that is what Ibsen meant when he replied to a query about where he found his plots that he found them in the Bible and the newspapers. Classics are not given added relevance by putting them in modern dress, where the men are in bare feet and the ladies make devastating play with their revealed navels. The old comment that all periods of time are at an equal distance from eternity says much, and pondering on it will lead to alchemical theatre while relevance becomes old hat.

Stratford

13

A Letter from Friar Bacon & Friar Bungay

Robertson Davies loved a joke and was known to indulge in some elaborate pranks. When he noticed that the scene in *Macbeth* involving the three witches and their unappetizing cauldron had been omitted, he sensed an opportunity:

I wrote this letter to Tanya in 1962 when Macbeth *was first presented at Stratford directed by Peter Coe—and a sorry mess it was! I thought this spoof would cheer her and also the company, which it did as she posted it on the notice board in the Green Room.*

I tried a similar spoof on Tony Guthrie in 1955, when I wrote to him in the character of an historian, deeply learned in Scythian lore, offering to direct the makeup of Tamberlaine's warriors with special attention to ornamental painting which threw the male nipple into angry prominence. Tony was bewildered by it, and it was Tony Quayle—who played Tamberlaine—who smoked it as a hoax.

FRIAR BACON & FRIAR BUNGAY
Necromantic Suppliers and Supernatural Warehousemen
(Founded 1594)

Miss Tanya Moiseiwitsch,

Festival Theatre,
Stratford, Ont. Canada

Dear Miss Moiseiwitsch:

It has been brought to our attention that in the current production of Macbeth at Stratford, the first sixty-eight lines of Act Four, Scene One have been omitted, doubtless because of the difficulty of securing the properties necessary to its apt performance. As a very old-established firm, who had the honour of victualling this extremely effective scene for Mr. Shakespeare himself in 1606, may we quote you the following attractive bundle, which we can supply on receipt of a cable, our telegraphic address being Paddockanon.

"Toad, that under cold stone
Days and nights has thirty-one
Sweltered venom sleeping got …"

Immediately available in unlimited quantity from our own gardens. True Bufo vulgaris as supplied to Mr. Shakespeare. $3 per doz.

"Fillet of a fenny snake"

Blindworm, from the Norfolk Broads, $3 per doz., filleted and shipped in ice. We recommend, however, fillet of adder, as each order includes the "fork," thereby effecting a pleasing economy. Fillet of adder, $8 per doz. shipped in ice.

"Eye of newt and toe of frog"

Pleasing minor items, shipped dry; soak for two hours before curtain time. Our MERLIN'S MIXTURE $2.50 per lb.

"Wool of bat"

Per generous hank, unwashed, $6. Washed, $12.

"Tongue of dog"

Recent difficulties with the R.S.P.C.A. make this formerly reasonable item somewhat expensive. Mongrel: $1 per tongue. Pedigreed: $5. Shown at Crufft's: $8.

"Adder's fork"

See above. Separately $6 per doz., dried. Exercise care in handling.

"Blindworm's sting"

A very attractive dried bunch, comprising approximately fifty stings, $5.

"Lizard's leg"

Our South American special. Large: $1. Small: 25 cents.

"Howlet's wing"

Genuine English howlet, warranted from churchyard or belfry, "not a wing is sold till it is five years old." $12 per wing.

"Scale of dragon"

From Continental China, guaranteed, $18.50 per scale. From Formosa, no guarantee, $5 per scale.

"Tooth of wolf"

Best Canadian timberwolf, $9 per tooth.

"Witch's mummy"

Increasingly difficult to obtain, and we must limit orders to one pound per customer per month. Best quality, from the Carpathians, $250 per pound. SPECIAL—While she lasts!—Dracula's Aunt Sybilla! A steal at $750 per pound, packed in her own skin! Many personal hairs in each package! A MUST for the large operator!

"… maw and gulf
Of the ravined salt-sea shark"

Fresh daily from Newfoundland. $35 per set.

"Root of hemlock digged i' the dark"

Per root, $4. In powdered form, $3.50.

"Gall of goat"

From Wales, packed in "slips of yew." Open with care as the fumes have been known to overcome experienced Stage Managers. Per gall, $28.

"Finger of birth-strangled babe
Ditch-delivered by a drab."

From a Salvation Army home for Repentant Magdalens. Guaranteed ditch-delivered, as the Chief Obstetrician is Dr. Duncan Ditch, M.D., FRCP, per dozen, $4.

"Add thereto a tiger's chaudron …"

An item rarer than it was in the great days of the Empire, but still available. Royal Bengal Chaudrons, $80 each. A cheaper class of chaudron, from zoos and circuses, at $50 each. Delivered in ice, C.O.D.

"Cool it in a baboon's blood"

True baboon, per carafe (approx. 1 litre) of superior bouquet and body, $15. Canadian native baboon, bottled by a Canadian Winery (screw-top returnable bottle) $3.

We undertake contract work, supplying your Stage Management nightly for the duration of your run at an inclusive price of $38.50 each night. We have many letters on file attesting to the effectiveness of this service, and extraordinary manifestations are by no means uncommon in theatres where it is used.

Awaiting the favour of your esteemed order, madam,

for: Bacon and Bungay

14

Stratford Forty Years Ago

In November 1991, Davies was asked to write an article for the Stratford Festival Souvenir Program of the following season, the Festival's fortieth. The anniversary was a great cause for celebration and Davies was just the person to write the piece, having been involved with the Festival for many years as a Member of the Board of Governors, a lecturer, and an always-enthusiastic playgoer.

After the first year of the Festival in 1953, Robertson Davies and Sir Tyrone Guthrie wrote, and Grant Macdonald illustrated, *Renown at Stratford*, which was encouraged and published by W.H. Clarke of Clarke Irwin & Co. of Toronto. Davies had not yet begun keeping his Theatre Diary but in the book he wrote of the original 1953 production of *Richard III*:

On the first night, and at more than one subsequent performance, the audience rose to its feet and cheered when Alec Guinness appeared to acknowledge their applause at the end of the play. Had we seen a great Richard? Or was this a tribute to a player who had cast in his lot with an unproven venture, as a gesture of encouragement to the theatre in a new country?

There can never be any final judgment on this matter. Both emotions—gratitude for a fine performance, and gratitude for a fine gesture—were mingled in this applause, and there is no means of sorting them out. But it may be said that this production of Richard III *had a noble sweep and produced upon the audiences that completeness of effect which is possible only when the theatre has worked its truest magic; the crown of this production was Alec Guinness's performance as Richard. Experienced lovers of the theatre, and playgoers to whom Shakespeare came quite new, united to applaud him, and therefore we may say that his performance rose far above any accumulation of critical points. It was a fully rounded artistic creation, and auditors of every condition yielded to its enchantment. Let those who reserve the adjective "great" for performances which take place in capital cities describe this one by what term they please—we know what we saw and felt at Stratford.*

After another production of *Richard III*, Davies wrote in his diary, Wednesday, July 13, 1988: *Thirty-fifth anniversary of the opening of the Stratford Festival. "Survivors" are invited and Brenda and I go. Some of the survivors are that indeed. There are even pseudo-survivors, including one who reproaches me because he was not mentioned in* Renown at Stratford: *mad, perhaps? The play is of course* Richard III *and of the four Richards we have seen here—Alec Guinness, Alan Bates, Brian Bedford—Colm Feore is the dismal forty-fourth. No sense of aristocracy or even of command—simply an Italian bandit. One recalls Guinness's fine, reserved dignity, and the sense of class that pervaded Tony's* [Guthrie] *production* [Stratford, 1953]. *As Gielgud said, directing* Richard II *at Oxford: "Never forget, these are tremendous swells!" Feore did the deformity by adopting a paraplegic walk—knees together and legs straddling outward like a trivet. Astonishing to begin but a bore as the play progressed for it was grotesque rather than menacing and made the fight an absurdity as one good push would have put him on the ground. The production dull and slow and one heard—the words were clear—but no meaning came with them, for the actors too plainly did not care. Amateur faults: snowy hands on murderers and churls: the usual ecclesiastical boners—a bishop carrying his own cross! The children boisterous and bad. A dull evening and symptomatic of what is wrong with the Festival: needs shaking up from top to bottom. Alf Bell died July 12 and his name is affectionately heard everywhere.*

Stratford fifty years ago is easily described; what does the infallible Karl Baedeker have to say in his *Handbook for Travellers in Canada*? …

"a divisional point and important railway centre ... an agricultural and industrial city ... prettily situated on the Avon ... its schools include a Collegiate Institute and a Provincial Normal School." But in 1953 Stratford underwent a transformation which nobody had foreseen, not even Tom Patterson, who brought it about.

Stratford forty years ago suddenly became a theatre town, and saw the beginnings of what is now generally admitted to be the foremost centre of classical theatre in North America. Nobody forty years ago thought that would happen or had a clear idea of what it might mean. I well recall my own early visits to Stratford, for I was one of the few non-Stratfordians to be a member of its earliest Board of Governors. Why I was so honoured I cannot truly say, except that I was a friend of Tyrone Guthrie's, who knew that I liked long chances and would do anything to give the theatre in Canada a lift. My personal expectations for the infant Festival were high, because I had great faith in Guthrie, whose organizing ability and theatrical wizardry I knew well, but as I sat at those early Board meetings, I knew that I was an outsider and carried little of the real responsibility for what was happening; the Stratford citizens who sat there with me were undertaking a venture which could cost them dear in reputation and good hard cash. They hadn't much notion of what a theatre festival might be, but they knew that their town was no longer an important railway centre and something must be done if it were not to lose significance. They were prepared to take a very long chance—for chances don't come longer anywhere than in the theatre. So they listened with caution to Tom Patterson, and very soon they were listening in astonishment to Tyrone Guthrie.

His impact on Stratford was immediate and extraordinary; the town had never seen anything like him before. He was not like anybody's idea of a great theatrical director. With his height, air of command, and informal dress he was often described as looking like a policeman off duty. And indeed there was something of the policeman about him—his gimlet eye, which awoke a sense of guilt in the sluggard; his remarkable physical strength, which showed itself in immense endurance and an ability to absorb malt liquor without visible consequence; his sometimes rough and peremptory dismissal of arguments he did not choose to consider. This was his Scottish side. But he had an Irish side, which showed itself in a lighthearted approach to difficulties that looked insurmountable, a brilliant wit, and very often in a sort of inspired silliness, which confused people who had, a moment before, heard him uttering what sounded like the thunderings of Jove. Not an easy man for the sober citizens of an Ontario community to understand.

He was, however, irresistible, or almost so, for there were Stratfordians who resisted him and did so until they had reluctantly to admit the success of what he had done for the town. But everybody associated with the Festival venture was hypnotized by him. To be with him was to breathe a finer air, to be swept into a world where life was strenuous but entrancing.

So, the Festival came into being with Tony as its inspiring spirit. And how lucky that was for Stratford, because he was, in all things that related to the theatre, a man of unimpeachable probity, and he recommended nothing, insisted on nothing, that he was not prepared to support with every ounce of his remarkable energy.

Suddenly, there was the Festival, and that story has been told many times and need not be repeated here. Tony's enthusiasm spread through the town and the town responded in ways that were both characteristic and admirable. Actors had to be housed; people found houses and overcame the fears of those who thought actors must be fly-by-nights and fallen women. Visitors had to be housed, and people were found who threw open their homes, charging minimal prices for excellent beds, and breakfasts of astounding variety and quantity. Churches undertook to provide hot meals for the playgoers who could not squeeze into the town's few hotels and cafés. The Festival was a town festival and everybody with an ounce of daring wanted to get in on the action. It was thus that the town made the Festival its own, and not an exotic visitor.

As a dweller in Eastern Ontario I watched this development with astonishment, for, though Eastern Ontario has virtues of its own, enthusiasm and bounteous hospitality are not among them. Was it a matter of heritage? The people of Western Ontario tend to be descendants of English settlers, from the gentler parts of the Old

Land, and from Germany. The Scots and Irish of Eastern Ontario are a different breed.

Not everything went smoothly, of course. The press was not pleased that Guthrie would not admit its representatives to rehearsals. What could he be hiding? He was, of course, protecting artistic creation on a high level, which is something the press has never been quick to understand. But when the uttermost is being demanded of Canadian actors who have never been so stretched before, it is not fair to invite reporters to watch them. Nor, if reporters had been present, could Guthrie have spoken in the combination of extravagant rhetoric and quarterdeck profanity which was his rehearsal mode.

The actors were a puzzle to some Stratfordians. "What do you do in the daytime?" was a question often heard, from people who had never known what hard work make-believe can be.

There was turbulence. The local newspaper did not, at first, favour the Festival, and it had its following. *Maclean's* magazine, a national publication, carried an article which was somewhat jocose and patronizing about Stratford's presumption in attempting a Festival of the first rank, as big-city papers tend to be when writing about smaller places. The writer went so far as to say that Alec Guinness who was, with Irene Worth, at the head of the acting company, was cold and standoffish and kept the local people at a distance. This was trivial and untrue, but for some reason Guinness was deeply offended and wanted to sue the magazine for libel. He was not to be deflected from this determination, and because I knew something about the press, I was deputed by the Board to reason with him. It was not easy, but when I pointed out that such a suit would be a long time coming before the court, and would simply give further circulation to an inept article, he withdrew, without being wholly appeased.

The public could not peep at rehearsals, but it could, and did, take the keenest interest in the digging of the hole, and the pouring of the cement, for the amphitheatre. Most of all, it loved the huge tent. The master of the tent was Skip Manley, a circus man, gaudy in dress and richly beringed; he worked with his crew for sixty hours without a break to raise the poles, the guy wires, and the canvas. It was such a tent as sultans dream of, for inside the heavy canvas shell it was hung with cloth of royal blue, establishing an atmosphere of opulence and distinction which Canadians do not associate with tents. Manley slept in the tent, and managed it through winds and storms like the captain of a great galleon, for there was unceasing and unrelenting need to ease it here, tighten it there, and adjust the stress on the four huge cedar poles that bore the greatest strain.

All this was to be seen, and Stratford saw it. What could not be seen, but which hung like a storm cloud over the Board, was the terrible financial responsibility, for demands were daily—hourly—and there was never enough money. But great acts of faith were called forth, courage was demanded and shown, the people who had decided to back the venture bent—sometimes distressingly—but they did not break. This was municipal heroism, a virtue we seldom hear celebrated.

At last came July 13—not a date of happy omen—and the opening performance. A few minutes before *Richard III* began, my wife and I were standing with Tony and Judy Guthrie between the canvas and the blue inner tent, far down on the right side of the amphitheatre. It was the only time we had seen them a prey to nerves. They were deeply apprehensive, for they knew how much hung on what happened in the next three hours. They were not fearful for themselves, but for the troops of friends they had made in Stratford. Could this absurd adventure succeed?

If it had not done so, you would not be reading this recollection now.

15

World of Wonders

Davies was involved with the annual summer Shakespeare festival at Stratford, Ontario from the outset. He was a friend of the first director, Tyrone Guthrie, and an original member of the board from 1953 until 1971. In 1979 he and Brenda Davies were honoured by being made Permanent Members of the Festival.

Davies's influence at Stratford extended far beyond that of the usual board member. He wrote the three books that recorded the first years of the Festival, and even assisted in the adaptations of historical plays there. In his biographer Judith Skelton Grant's words: "At intervals Davies has also written half-a-dozen articles for the Festival's souvenir programs, given five papers at the Stratford seminars and three public lectures, and contributed to *The Stratford Scene 1958–1968*."

Perhaps none of these can have been as congenial as this lecture, which allows us to hear Robertson Davies, Man of the Theatre, discuss the play that has been made of the work by Robertson Davies, Novelist. This lecture was presented on June 14 and June 19, 1992, in the Avon Theatre during The Stratford Festival Celebrated Writers Series, when his own novel *World of Wonders* was adapted for the stage by Elliott Hayes, a young playwright tragically killed in a road accident not long after.

He wrote to a friend in August of that year: *The enclosed program offers an excuse for my delay in answering your last, splendid letter. To say that I have been busy with the play is not quite true for I have not taken a direct part in getting it on the stage. But its production involved me in a surprising amount of work, including two lectures that I gave about the problems involved in making a novel into a play; they were very well attended to my surprise, because I did not think people would be greatly interested in such a subject, but they were and the questions they asked afterward were searching and probing in a surprising and complimentary way. The man who did the stage version, Elliott Hayes, is an experienced playwright and did an excellent job in which I did not interfere at all. The audiences were large and very pleased with the play, and on the whole it has been a decided success.*

The production was elaborate and expensive. Because it is about a conjuror and illusionist it was necessary to show some of his illusions, and the audience loved them. Perhaps the most popular was at the very end of the play, when Eisengrim, the conjuror, took the notes that had been made by the man who wanted to make a television show of his life, and threw them out into the audience, where they flew up into the roof of the theatre and disappeared. A very good ending for a play about magic—the magic of the stage, and the magic of life.

I am going to talk to you about the novel called *World of Wonders,* and about the play, *World of Wonders,* that you are going to see this afternoon. I shall attempt to explain in what ways they are alike and in what ways they differ, and why. I do not really know why you want to hear about these things. Why don't you simply go to the play, and enjoy it as a play? But that would be against our national character. We Canadians are gluttons for instruction; we dote upon lectures. (I am like that myself: I would much rather listen to somebody lecture about—let us say—a cholera epidemic in Calcutta than go to Calcutta and take part in it personally.) A lecture is a peaceful experience, lulling to the senses and enlarging to the intellect without being too exciting. But when it comes to giving a lecture myself, about something that is very near to me, it is an entirely different matter; I am suddenly overcome with reluctance. I don't want to talk to you about what I do, how I do it, or why I do it. You have the completed product.

Do you care how it comes into being? Surely my job is to offer you the completed product, not to take you on a tour of the workshop.

Why do I feel like that? Because writing a novel, if you do it seriously, is an act of creation. It is not simply a matter of invention; you do not just make up a story and write it out. You live with the book that you are writing for many months, during which you have to dig it out of yourself, often with discomfort and even pain. You do it with every ounce of sincerity and devotion you possess. And when it is done you say "That's that" and dismiss it from your mind. It is finished, complete insofar as you can make it so, and you don't want to dig it up and examine it and go through all that act of creation again. Indeed, it can't be done.

There is more about the act of creation than what I have told you; when you have once finished your book, you have finished it for all time. You cannot go back and redo it or alter it, because you wrote it in the first instance as your instinct told you it should be. If you tinker with it afterward, the chances are very great that you will make a mess of it, because second thoughts in these matters are rarely best.

A famous instance concerns one of the greatest of playwrights, Henrik Ibsen. Many of you will be familiar with his play *A Doll's House.* It ends, you will recall, when the wife Nora tells her uncomprehending husband why she must leave him to save her soul. It is one of the most powerful scenes in all drama. It is the considered work of a master. But it gave such great offence that when it was to be performed in Germany, and the demand for an altered ending was so insistent, Ibsen was forced to yield, and wrote a happy ending for the play. The German critics, you see, who had read the play said it was psychologically impossible that Nora should leave not only her husband but her three small children. (Critics are all great psychologists, and understand life much better than authors.) So Ibsen wrote a syrupy conclusion in which the pull of motherhood was too much for Nora, and she sank to the ground, crying, "Oh, this is a sin against myself, but I cannot leave them." You can imagine the joy and relief in the audience. Ibsen himself described this change as "a barbaric outrage," and so it was. It serves us today as an example of what tinkering with an already completed work of literature can do.

At various times in my life I have been asked to prepare plays or film scripts based on my novels, and I have had enough experience to know that for me it is a hopeless task. What I have written once, in a particular form, I cannot change into something else.

This is not to say that it cannot be done. Somebody else may do it and do it very well. That is what has happened with *World of Wonders*. Elliott Hayes has prepared a dramatized version of the book and in my opinion he has done it admirably. The evidence of his success is that what has emerged in his stage version is a radical reworking of the material of the novel *in dramatic terms*. That is something quite different from preparing a stage version of the novel as it exists. Many of you, I dare say, have sat, as I have, through dreary plays which have been gouged out of the novels of Dickens. They stick too closely to the original, novelistic form. They are not Dickens and they are not plays. Of course, in later years some fine films have been made from Dickens, like the imaginative and deservedly successful *Nicholas Nickleby*. The serial effect of a novel—the narration of one incident after another for a reader who carries the whole of what he has read in his mind—is quite a different thing from dramatic action. The play, *World of Wonders*, gives you as much of the novel as the stage can absorb in about two hours. That is because the actors and the other stage artists concerned in the production of the play can give you instantaneously and through the eye and ear a vast amount of what the author has to express in prose, and in prose that does not bore you with too much tedious instruction. A playwright may rely heavily on his actors to push the action forward, and very often a nod or a glance from an accomplished actor will do what the author has to do in a careful paragraph of writing.

The author is, in his own way, a playwright or a film director, but he has to be the scene painter, the orchestra, and a whole cast of actors in order to make his effect. What he does is a solitary act of creation. What the playwright and his colleagues do is a complex work of collaboration. The final effect of the novel or the play may be just the same; but the method of reaching the audience or the reader is wholly different.

Did I say that the author's work was a solitary act of creation? That is not quite true. He is a collaborator every time somebody reads his book. The reader must join with the author in bringing the book to life. In the theatre of his mind the reader must put the characters onstage, hear their voices, take pleasure in their individuality. Certainly that is what the author hopes. But is that the way we invariably read books? Do we not read at too fast a pace? Do we not sometimes skip parts that may be very necessary to the totality of the book, but which do not happen to please us at the moment? Do we really exert ourselves to bring the book to life? You cannot imagine how passionately the author hopes for good readers, who will exert themselves to find the energy and the colour in his book which he has worked so hard to put there. Real reading—the reading that brings the book fully to the understanding of the reader—is hard work of a special kind, and not everybody is equally gifted as a reader.

Thus, you see, the playwright or the adapter has advantages that the author may envy. But the author has his advantages, too. The actors in the play can convey all the action, and quite a lot of the psychological complexity of the novel upon which the play is based, but there are some things that elude them.

When you are watching a play you must catch it on the fly; and if it is a complex structure, and if the ideas it contains are touched on lightly, you may miss a part of what is being offered. One of the themes of *World of Wonders* as a play is that growing up, sharpening your wits, and indeed becoming yourself is a lifetime pursuit; you do not achieve all the maturity that can be yours on your twenty-first birthday. The play illustrates this, but it is put into words only once, when Liesl says: "You gain your mastery of your art at the cost of your innocence." The line may slip by without catching your attention and understanding. But it is important, and if you were reading the book you might wish to stop and think about it. Is it true? Has it been so in your own life? Is innocence too high a price to pay for mastery of something important? What is innocence and how do you distinguish it from stupidity? This is the advantage of the printed page; you may squeeze your orange of all its juice before you go on to the next thing. Not only do you read: You may reread, but you cannot ask actors to go back and repeat themselves, or give you a few minutes in which to think.

In *World of Wonders* there are basic truths that underlie the novel, which the novel can insist upon without arousing the hostility of the reader. Let me try one or two of them on you.

> Be not deceived; God is not mocked: for whatsoever a man soweth, that shall he also reap.
>
> As a dog returneth to his vomit, so a fool returneth to his folly.
>
> Vengeance is mine; I will repay, saith the Lord.
>
> A merry heart doeth good like a medicine: but a broken spirit drieth the bones.
>
> A fool's mouth is his destruction, and his lips are the snare of his soul.

In a novel it is possible to demonstrate these truths without preaching too strenuously at the reader; they are very much more difficult to show on the stage, for each one is the subject for a play in itself. A novel is a much more complex structure than a play can dare to be. A play has one or two themes, but a novel may have many.

In other words, a novel may deal extensively in ideas, but a play which is too much concerned with abstractions will be at serious risk of alienating its audience, which comes to the theatre to see something happen, not to hear about what might happen.

Let us talk for a while about the novel which underlies the play called by the same name. What is a novel, anyhow?

It has been said with, I think, great truth, that a good novel is a tale to the simple, a parable to the wise, and a direct revelation of reality to a man who has made it a part of his being. What is the tale of *World of Wonders*?

The book is the third volume of a trilogy, which is now called *The Deptford Trilogy,* because it is about the lives of three men all of whom were born in the little village of Deptford, in southern Ontario. These three achieve fame, in three wholly different ways: One becomes an important financier and entrepreneur, whose career is crowned by his appointment as Lieutenant-Governor of Ontario. One becomes a schoolmaster and teaches for forty-five years at a famous boys' school in Toronto, but his fame rests on his books about saints, and he gains a reputation as a hagiologist. The third endures a hard fate for many years, but at last achieves a curious fame as the world's foremost magician, conjuror, illusionist. The great financier is not wholly surprising as one who came from a very small place; the historian and hagiologist is more surprising because his enthusiasm is a strange one for a man raised in a Presbyterian family in a Canadian village; the third, the magician, is very surprising, for we do not expect anyone like that from a background wholly innocent about the world of theatre and sophisticated showmanship. The really surprising thing is that the lives and fates of all three men are linked by a single happening, which might be described as an accident—if you do not happen to agree with Dr. Freud that there are really no accidents, and that in this life what happens to us is determined by what we are. That is a hard doctrine, but it deserves attention.

What was this accident? It happened at 5:58 o'clock P.M. on the 27th of December, 1908. Two of the boys, Dunstan Ramsay and Boy Staunton, both ten years old, had been playing, and had quarrelled. Staunton threw a snowball at Ramsay, and Ramsay, sensing that it was coming, stepped out of its path, and the snowball hit a woman on the head. The shock to her was great, for concealed in the snowball was a stone; she collapsed, was taken home, and a few hours later gave premature birth to her son Paul, the third man in the trio.

I called it an accident: But what sort of accident was it? Certainly it was not an inexplicable or unmotivated happening. Ramsay dodged to avoid the snowball, but just how did he dodge? Did he dodge in front of the woman who was hit, and if he did so was he not guilty of her injury, and its consequence? How much did he understand of what he was doing? Certainly he understood the consequence, suffered pangs of guilt for it all his life. Indeed, it may be said that the guilt of this incident was the most powerful force in shaping his life.

As for young Staunton, who threw the snowball, what do we make of him? A stone concealed in a snowball is a dirty trick, and as it happened, an evil deed. But to what extent is a child capable of evil, and to what degree is it exonerated from the consequences of its actions? This is a point on which I have opinions that are not the usual ones, for I think children are much more aware of what they do than we are inclined to think, and that they are capable of evil behaviour, and that the evil is intentional. Nowadays we are very sentimental about children, but I do not think we understand them as thoroughly as we imagine we do. Anybody who truly remembers what it was like to be a child remembers also the gigantic egotism and self-will of the child, which is controlled only by physical weakness and to some extent by fear. After the snowball found its mark, and the supposed accident became a village scandal, young Staunton denied all knowledge of it, and threatened young Ramsay with dire reprisal if he ever told what he knew. Staunton refused to face the truth, and denied his guilt, and it appeared that he had wiped it from the record of history.

And what about the third man, little Paul Dempster, who was hurried into the world untimely and thus, as he says later, robbed of eighty days of Paradise—the Paradise of the womb where all is love and protection? What happened to him would kill anyone who was not a born survivor. He suffers many external degradations and miseries, but his worst trial is that for many years he has to live the life of Nobody; he is the secret mechanism that works a sideshow trick—a card-playing automaton—and no one is supposed to know that he exists; he has been robbed totally, it appears, of humanity and personality. But he overcomes it and he borrows a personality from a man he idolizes, a great romantic actor, whose double it is his job to be in plays where a double is required. But he does not gain a personality of his own until his idol is dead, and then it is a personality so burnished, so splendid that it persuades huge audiences to regard him as a truly great man. It is only his closest friends who know his secret, which is that he is the deprived child who was robbed of eighty days in Paradise, and is determined to make the world pay for it.

That is what he does. How he does it I shall not tell you, because you are going to the play to find that out, and I would be a spoilsport if I let it out now. But in the end Paul Dempster, who has become Magnus Eisengrim, is a great man, and one of his two best friends is Dunstan Ramsay, who has been haunted all his life by two things: that he brought about Paul's premature birth by a failure of decency on his own part, and that Paul's mother, even in her madness, was a saint of heroic virtue. As for the third man, Boy Staunton, he dies mysteriously.

Ever since the first of these three books, *Fifth Business*, appeared I have been plagued by people who demand of me, "Who killed Boy Staunton?" Why they ask I cannot tell, because it is as plain as a pikestaff who killed him. The explanation that is given in one of Magnus Eisengrim's magic illusions says: "He was killed by the usual cabal: by himself, first of all; by the woman he knew; by the woman he did not know; by the man who granted his inmost wish; and by the inevitable fifth, who was keeper of his conscience and keeper of the stone." Nobody dies of a single cause, but of a complexity of events. The doctor who signs the necessary certificate may write "Cancer"—but what led to the cancer? A man may die, as Boy Staunton did, in part, by achieving a life's ambition, and finding out how much it is worth. And often there is, as the Brazen Head says in the illusion in the play, a fifth figure, whose involvement in the plot is necessary but not immediately observable.

Who killed Boy Staunton? "Vengeance is mine; I will repay, saith the Lord." But the Lord may use one, or several human agents to work out his design and manifest his judgment. And it may prove, if you wish to read the book on which this play is based, that the death of Boy Staunton was not the death of a criminal, and it may even be regarded as a mercy, considering the point which had been reached in his life.

It is not simple, you see. Life is not simple. Art is not simple. Perhaps only television is simple. I have been a writer now for over fifty years, and during that time critics have had a great deal to say about me, some of it good and some of it bad. But one of the things that has been said, and said often, is that as a writer I am a moralist, and I think that that is true and perceptive criticism.

What is a moralist? It is not, of course, somebody who preaches some system of morality which is supposed to make good people and a good world. A moralist is not an exponent of a creed. A moralist is somebody who observes life as carefully as he can, and draws conclusions from what he sees. He sees that fashionable enthusiasms about behaviour are short-lived, and that some things appear to be so self-evident that it is no exaggeration to call them truths. They are not new. Truth does not deal in novelty but in age-long endurance. Because some of the truths the moralist observes have been given unforgettable expression in the Bible, there are people who think that the moralist is an enthusiast for Biblical morality. Not at all; there are portions of the Bible that make any sensitive person's flesh creep, they are so cruel and unforgiving. The moralist is not a cheapjack follower of the Old Testament—or of the New Testament, for that matter. He sees what he sees and he records it. And what does he see?

> Whatsoever a man soweth, that shall he also reap.
>
> As a dog returneth to his vomit, so a fool returneth to his folly.
>
> A merry heart doeth good like a medicine: but a broken spirit
> drieth the bones.
>
> A fool's mouth is his destruction, and his lips are the snare of
> his soul.

And a very great deal more, along the same lines. And if the moralist happens to be a writer, that is what he bases his writing on—the observation of the way life appears to work by very old rules.

I wonder how many of you are familiar with Rudyard Kipling's poem, called "The Gods of the Copybook Headings"? I bring it up now to show that authors of recent time are just as powerfully aware of the way in which basic morality works as were the wind-and-sand-blown prophets of the Old Testament. Listen to this:

> As it will be in the future, it was at the birth of Man—
> There are only four things certain since Social progress began:—
> That the Dog returns to his Vomit and the Sow returns to her Mire,
> And the burnt fool's bandaged finger goes wabbling back to
> the Fire;
> And that after this is accomplished, and the brave new world
> begins
> When all men are paid for existing and no man must pay for
> his sins,

As surely as Water will wet us, as surely as Fire will burn,
The Gods of the Copybook Headings with terror and slaughter return!

That is tough talk, but morality *is* tough talk, which is why silly people try to brush it aside as old-fashioned and irrelevant to life as we—our wonderful, wonderful selves, toward whose perfection mankind has been striving ever since the Big Bang—as we understand, or misunderstand it.

I said some time ago that a novel of any weight is a tale to some readers, a parable to others. Is *World of Wonders* a parable? A parable is a story which points out a truth in terms of physical action. Does *World of Wonders* point out a truth? Oh yes, lots of truths. One might be summed up in the popular saying You Never Can Tell. You never can tell where something quite extraordinary and unexpected will come about. In a little Ontario village three men may be born so closely together that their lives run parallel courses, who may influence the world in quite different ways. Boy Staunton, after all, did do a remarkable job of distributing and assembling materials during the Second World War: Dunstan Ramsay made a lot of people aware of saints who were by no means disposed by nature or training to pay any attention to saints: Paul Dempster, when he became Magnus Eisengrim, brought wonder and marvel into the lives of countless people whose lives were very short of those elements. And all of these three men were linked by a single action that needed only a few seconds to take place—the throwing of a loaded snowball.

Part of the parable element in my story is that every action brings its reaction, and that you cannot always foresee what the reaction may be. If you throw a stone into a pool, the ripples will spread and spread until they reach the shores and continue as an impulse long after the ripples have ceased to be visible. After all, we are now assured that the Big Bang which occurred such an incalculably long time ago, set in action impulses that have resulted in such astonishing creatures as you and me and the complex world in which we live. The throwing of that snowball at 5:58 o'clock P.M. on the 27th of December, 1908, set up ripples which continued long after the death of Boy Staunton, sixty years later, when he was discovered in Toronto Harbour, locked in his expensive car, with a stone clenched in his mouth. The ripples included Paul Dempster's wretchedness as a boy and his triumph as a man, and Dunstan Ramsay's long expiation of his guilt toward Paul's mother, and his preoccupation with saints.

Another element of parable in the novel is its demonstration of the truth—not a moralist's truth but a scientific truth—that nothing exists without its contrary. There is in all things a positive and a negative, and this is as true of human lives as it is of everything else. The three men who are the principal figures in the story are examples of this principle.

Consider the case of Boy Staunton. He seemed to the world around him an enviable and admirable fellow—handsome, rich, attractive to women, able to discharge big responsibilities with ease and perhaps a touch of genius. Yes—but always in his life there was a hint of that stone-in-the-snowball philosophy, the determination to impose his will upon others which leads so often to overdoing things which could be achieved more gently. Handsome, yes, but male beauty fails as quickly as its female counterpart. Rich, yes, but the failure of riches to buy anybody his heart's desire is proverbial, and Boy's heart's desire was to shine in the eyes of the world as gloriously as his ideal, Edward, Prince of Wales, and he ends up as the Lieutenant-Governor elect of Ontario, which is a very honourable position, unless you happen to see yourself as a Prince. Attractive to women, yes; but does the man who is attractive to women ever take the trouble to know women as human beings, and not as extensions of his own egotism? Every gift that was showered on Boy Staunton had its opposite, and in the end it was the opposites that were his undoing.

What about Dunstan Ramsay? An excellent schoolteacher, and those who saw him on the job saw no more than that, and thought him a useful but dull fellow. But in the world of true scholarship his opposite was found, and he gained fame in a very special scholarly world—a fame quite unknown to his colleagues in Colborne College, for what has hagiography to do with a school for boys? But Ramsay's was a crippled life; the Calvinist, Presbyterian morality in which he had been brought up, and which forced him to think that he was responsible for the madness of Mary Dempster and the premature birth of Paul, made him a suffering, haunted man, who thought too much about God, and did not give enough heed to the Devil until the Devil confronted him and laughed at him.

And Paul Dempster, *alias* Cass Fletcher, *alias* Faustus LeGrand, *alias* Mungo Fetch, *alias* Magnus Eisengrim—surely his life was all tilted toward the negative side? No, not quite, for he attained fame and made everybody around him subservient to him. He dominated large audiences of people who paid handsomely for him to deceive them with his illusions. But for his splendour he paid, because it was a life without love, though at the end he achieved something which, if not love as it is generally understood, was a wonderful substitute and much more exciting than love often is.

There are other elements of parable in the book, but I will not trouble you with them now. If you haven't read the book it would be presumptuous of me to suggest that you do so, but if you want to sort out all the elements of parable that are in it, you cannot expect to get them from the play, which by its very nature passes you by so quickly that you cannot take in everything. That is not a failure of the play, of course. It is part of the delight of plays that we leave them feeling that we have not quite encompassed all that was said and done. If you ever feel that you have got everything out of a play at a single sitting, you may be sure that the play was, in theatrical parlance, a turkey.

I have spoken of a novel as a tale—a simple story for those who do not want to look beyond that. And I have spoken of it as a parable, which is to say a story that illustrates certain truths. But there was a third dimension to the novel, was there not? The critic spoke of it as being perhaps a revelation of reality. Does *World of Wonders* reveal anything of that kind? I hope it does. An important part of the revelation lies in the character of Liesl. If you have read the book you remember who she was: Fräulein Dr. Liselotte Naegeli, a very rich Swiss woman who is the business partner of Magnus Eisengrim, and the financier who enables him to mount his Soirée of Illusions so handsomely that all other magic shows look tawdry in comparison. She is also a woman of unusual cultivation and taste, and it is she who gives the Soirée of Illusions its quality that appeals to people who would not ordinarily be attracted by a magic show; it is she who provides the distinction which Eisengrim, who never had any education or much experience of the world of culture, could not provide. She is described on the theatre program as "Autocrat," and some of you will remember that Diaghilev used the same title in his relation to the Ballets Russes, and the name she used for stage purposes is Liesl Vitzlipützli. The name has made a lot of people ask questions; it is the name of one of the devils who served that great magician, Doctor Faustus, and it was Liesl's joke that she took this servant's name when she was, in fact, the final boss, the top dog, of the show of which Eisengrim was the star.

Liesl is a great deal more than that, however. She is hideous. She has been deformed by a disease which attacks a few unfortunate people when they are adolescent, and which makes their growth extraordinary, so that they may have huge hands, or feet, or a grotesquely deformed skull. You might expect a woman so deformed to live a life of seclusion, but Liesl has fallen under the spell of Eisengrim, who has himself made something extraordinary out of a wretchedly deprived beginning, and whose influence on Liesl is such that she adopts the manner of a supremely beautiful woman and—Gorgon though she is—she has many lovers—of both sexes. Eisengrim owes much to Liesl; she made him a gentleman and rather better than that word usually implies. But Liesl also owes much to him because he sets her free from the physical prison in which misfortune has locked her.

You do not achieve victories like that and remain a nice, well-bred Swiss lady with an interest in the theatre. Gaining a victory over life brings wisdom of one sort or another, and it has brought Liesl a wisdom that has made her a mischief maker when she meets someone as tightly bound up in his psychological makeup as Dunstan Ramsay. Ramsay has never been in love. He has thought he was in love, but his extreme wariness of women, which came about because of his experience with his possessive, dominating mother, has meant that his love was always cautious; he always had a way of escape if things became too demanding. In love affairs he always swam with water-wings. It is Liesl who decides that it is not too late for Ramsay, in middle age, to find out about the real thing, and she sets about to seduce him. Not, I assure you, by playing coy games; she simply invades his bedroom in her pyjamas and goes straight to the point. The effect is magical. Ramsay is never the same again.—By the way, I should perhaps utter a warning to any ladies among you who think of trying Liesl's methods that it is not quite as plain sailing as it looks, and you had better stick to the methods you know.—The result is, that when they are all considerably older, we meet Liesl and Eisengrim and Ramsay all living together in her luxurious Swiss retreat. They are as happy as larks, all in love with one another and with themselves, and face old age with joy.

People have asked me if Liesl is the Devil. It is extraordinary what questions people ask authors about things that are very plain in the book. What is the Devil? Who is the Devil? Like God, one of whose sons he is—and if you don't believe me check with your Bible—it is uncommonly hard to define, and you are hopelessly lost if you attempt to define him simply in human terms. But of course, like God, he has his human side, and sometimes he has been called the Spirit of Perversity, or Contrary Destiny. I am not a theologian and I make no attempt to define the Devil. But I know that there is one thing he undoubtedly is: He is a personal element in everybody's nature, and he may be defined as everything that a man or woman condemns, detests, and is certain that he or she is not. Consider the characters in the novel, and in the play. Ramsay has never thrown off his Presbyterian upbringing, great expert though he may be in the remarkable world of saints. Ramsay does not believe that he can be the slave of passion, a violent lover, a man swept utterly off his feet by sexual fury. He does not believe that he can be a liar, a deceiver, a concocter of false history—in fact a thorough-going academic crook. But it is Liesl who shows him that he can be all these things, and what is more, glory in what formerly filled him with detestation. She sets him free. Not free to go to the dogs and become a villain, but free to know that villainy has a place in his makeup, and that the dogs are never very far away. This is the knowledge that brings on his heart attack, when he realizes that by keeping the stone that Boy Staunton hid in the snowball when both boys were ten years old, he was acting, perhaps creditably, as a keeper of evidence, but he was acting in a very different spirit as well; he had vengeance and bitterness in his heart; he was an agent of an evil impulse—fully as evil as the impulse that led Staunton to conceal the stone in the snowball.

There is a character in the story who does not make it into the play. He is an old priest who says to Ramsay: "If you would know yourself, however slightly, you must meet and shake hands with your personal Devil; you will probably find that he is not at all a bad fellow." The old priest is wickedly delighted to find that Ramsay's personal Devil appears as a woman.

Liesl is, you see, the feminine element in the novel. That village simpleton that Ramsay loved and Staunton married, and that charming English girl whom Ramsay was almost inveigled into marrying, are not very deep studies of femininity. But I think Liesl is. She teaches two men vital things about themselves and thus she completes their nature just as her nature is completed by them and I think that is what women do, when they are at their best. But certainly it is as his personal Devil that Liesl first appears to Ramsay.

Because I have been talking about God and the Devil as I so often do, many people assume that I must be very religious. I am always surprised when people tell me that they are not at all religious. It seems to me that to live without religion is to condemn oneself to a world which is the psychological equivalent of decaf coffee, non-alcoholic wines, fatless butter-substitutes, paper made out of reconstituted garbage, language dominated by "political correctness," and all that rubbish which is supposed to make life safe and inoffensive and hardly distinguishable from death. Only of course we never talk about death and hope to read in the paper some morning that science has found a cure for it.

But what is religion? The dictionaries tell us that the origin of the word is obscure. It may come from a Latin word that means associating oneself with something in the past, and wearing it as a yoke, or it may come from another word that means to go over things again, to think matters through, to remember, to correct. It is in this second sense that I would describe myself as a religious man. To give the most serious consideration of which one is capable to the elements in life which confront one seems to me to be following a path which is not content with simplicities, and which cannot reject or set aside the innumerable things in life which suggest purposes and powers of which we have only the most fleeting perceptions. The intervention in life of what must be called Fate, the purpose which is achieved by happenings that appear to have no explicable reason (or which may even fly in the face of reason), the sense which is familiar to everyone that he or she is not guiding his life, but is being impelled by something unknown and perhaps not in any ordinary sense benevolent—these are the things that make it impossible for me to accept any of the arguments advanced by people who feel that religion has exhausted its part in the life of man and is exposed, as Sigmund Freud argued, as an illusion.

But has what I have been saying any connection with my earlier talk about God and the Devil? Those words are a convenient shorthand for vast elements in the fate of mankind, in the fate of the world and the universe, and in the fate of every human creature which we cannot hope to pin down with definitions or scientific formulae and which we have to accept as vast realities far outsoaring the portion of reality which is perceptible to us. We have to reject the egotistical human notion that we can, or should, discover and explain everything.

What do we mean by religion? Many people cannot separate the words from orthodoxy—some code of belief that has been laid down and to which the religious person tries to adhere as best he may. The most influential orthodoxy in our part of the world is Christianity, and Christianity asks its followers to strive for human perfection, thereby bringing nearer that Kingdom of God which will bring peace and perfection to our world. It is here that I must disagree, respectfully but firmly. I think perfection an inhuman and impossible ideal, because it ignores elements in human experience and history which cannot be wished away. These are the things which we sweep together under the heading of Evil, or to use the shorthand terms I spoke of earlier, the Devil. You cannot banish the Devil by being so good, or merely goody-goody, that he shrinks away from your presence, ashamed of himself. You must meet him eye to eye and hear what he has to say. You may even learn from him, as do all the chief characters in *World of Wonders,* for every one of them has met the Devil and come away slightly scorched but immensely wiser—even Roland Ingestree, the man who wants no truck with anything that he would call supernatural, which is a word silly people apply to anything they do not want to include in nature. Ingestree belongs to that very large class of people—often highly educated and influential people—who truly believe that Man is the centre and measure of all things, the highest development of life, and that when the individual consciousness is closed by death, that is the end of the matter. They are not interested in Man as the instrument of some vastly greater Will than they can comprehend, and they do not see their refusal as a limitation of their understanding. As for the Devil, they laugh. And laughing at the Devil amuses the Devil a great deal more than it amuses the laugher, because he knows how easy such people are to bring wholly under his rule.

Many of you, no doubt, will have understood from what I have said that I am a student and follower of Dr. C.G. Jung. But Jung asked for no orthodoxy among his followers, and no missionary spirit. I am not trying to convert you to my beliefs, but only to explain a very little about what lies beneath the surface of my writing. The aim is not, "Be ye therefore perfect, even as your Father which is in heaven is perfect"; the aim is Know Thyself.

And what has this to do with my novel *World of Wonders,* and this play that has been derived from it? I assure you, it has everything to do with it. The book attempts to demonstrate in really quite a humble way that many things we regard as certainties are not certain at all, and that two and two only make four in arithmetic and cannot be counted on to do so in life. Neat certainties have a very limited truth. But there are some things which, in a very large and general way, do seem to work themselves out in the widest possible variety of ways, but with consequences which are almost—notice that I say almost—predictable.

When I spoke earlier about a definition of a novel, there were three elements, were there not? A tale: Yes, we have talked about the story of *World of Wonders.* And a parable: Yes, we have talked about the demonstration, through the story, of some old truth. What was the third? It was "a direct revelation of reality to the man who has made it a part of his being." Surely that is rather a tall order? A direct revelation of reality? Is not the novelist taking himself rather too seriously when he talks of revealing reality? Yes, indeed that may be, but unless a novelist regards himself simply as an entertainer, that is what he hopes for. Of course he does not expect to succeed with every reader, but he tries. And in what ways does he try?

Now we are getting into deep water, because we are going to talk about Style, and under that heading monstrous quantities of nonsense have been talked and will be talked in the future. I shall try not to talk nonsense.

There is a Style for every serious writer. It is the evidence, shown in his writing of what he himself is. He may be an immensely serious man, like Tolstoy or Thomas Mann, and they seize us, and hold us by the weight of their determination to see life steadily, and in terms of almost photographic realism. Or he may be someone like Graham Greene or Evelyn Waugh, who appear to superficial readers to be concocters of adventure stories or funny stories, but whose moral weight is evident in every line they write and whose seriousness of outlook is beyond question. Or the writer may be a Dickens or a Balzac whose books illuminate our world so brilliantly that we never see life again in the same terms. The styles exemplified by these writers and hundreds more whom we cannot mention are of the uttermost variety, but there are labels, if you like labels, that may be attached to certain groups among them.

I said that some critics had labelled me as a moralist, and although I do not quarrel with that description it makes me rather uncomfortable. If I had to choose a label, I suppose I should be driven to the world of art criticism to find one; I think that if I am anything, I am a Mannerist. In saying that I am putting my head into the lion's mouth, for to many critics Mannerist is a dirty word. It implies an artificiality or frivolity, a lack of artistic weight, which repels critics who are themselves utterly solemn—notice that I say solemn and not serious, which is quite a different thing—in their outlook.

If your idea of a truly great picture is Van Gogh's *Irises,* which has commanded the highest price ever paid for a picture, you will not like the Mannerist pictures of such triflers as Michelangelo, Raphael, El Greco, and others of the kind. My own favourite Mannerist picture is in the National Gallery in London, and it is Bronzino's *An Allegory of Love.* When I look at Van Gogh's *Irises* I see some irises and I am ready to yield to those who see more. But when I look at *An Allegory of Love* I see not only a picture of transfixing beauty, but a mass of ideas, suggestions, warnings, and jokes, and I don't know how you could get all of that into a picture unless you were a Mannerist. One of the figures in the composition is called Fraude—Fraud, Deceit, Double-dealing, Deception. It is the figure of a girl of delicate beauty, who holds out her hand in which there is a honeycomb; it is only when you look more closely that you see that she has the feet and claws of a lion, and a dragon's tail with a dart on the end of it.

Have you ever, in your own love life—and you must have one—met with this figure? Have you ever wondered how Van Gogh would have painted it? Of course he didn't want to. But Bronzino wanted to say his say about the nature of Love, and this aspect of it—deceiving, cheating Love—and he had to be a very great Mannerist to do it.

He says so many things—far more than I can possibly talk about now. He says to the central figure, who is Venus—"Take care; that youth you are kissing so voluptuously is your son." He shows us Jealousy raving. He shows us Old Time and his daughter Truth, drawing aside the curtain to reveal what the world would like to keep secret. And Bronzino could not have shown us all these things if he had not been a Mannerist, and free from the chains of photographic reality.

May one talk of Mannerism in the writing of fiction? I don't see any reason why not. Some very great writers have worked in that mode. One of the greatest was Rabelais, whose name is known to everybody, but who is not much read, though he has splendid things to say to the world today, and especially to the academic world. To come nearer to our own time, and to name a writer who is very widely read, I would certainly call James Joyce a Mannerist, for he casts aside the chains of realism in order to show us, in his best-known novel, how the life of a Dublin advertisement salesman can follow the pattern of the travels of *Ulysses* in the course of a single day. The effect is funny, tragic, astonishing, and wholly magical.

I write as I do because I need the grotesques, the Classical and Biblical echoes and the high colour to say what I have to say, and what I call reality. Some kind people have added the word *magic*. What is magic? Is it not the production of effects for which there appear to be no causes? Behind all magic there is an explanation, but it is unwise to seek it too vigorously; there are lots of things in life which are more enjoyable when they are not completely understood. A good piece of magic is a work of art and should be respected as such; it is a flower, not an alarm clock, and if you pull it to pieces to find out what makes it work you have destroyed it, and your own pleasure.

That is where fiction and the art of the theatre meet; they are to be enjoyed first; and any discussion as to what they are and how they work must take second place to that initial pleasure. In our modern world we are very eager to explain everything, codify everything, and reduce everything that is complex to whatever may be comprehended by the greatest number, because anything that is mysterious is undemocratic, and "elitist." That is a pitiful attitude when it is allowed to infect the world of art.

World of Wonders is just that: The book and the play were made for your pleasure, and your pleasure will be greatest if you accept them simply as what they are.

16

Lewis Carroll in the Theatre

In the celebrated writers series at the Stratford Festival, Davies gave a lecture related to the production of *Alice Through the Looking Glass*, on July 10, 1994. The lecture was given in the morning with a production of the play in the evening. As you can see from the Theatre Diary entry that follows, Davies enjoyed the performance enormously, finding that it roused in him the Welsh sensation of *hiraeth*, or nostalgic longing.

Davies wrote on June 2: *Set to work on the Lewis Carroll lecture and find as I expected that the amount of material I have prepared must be handled with great care if the piece is not to be a mere jumble; I want it to be a pleasing* causerie; *no use bludgeoning a Sunday audience of holidaymakers, nor yet insulting them …*

And on July 10: *I give my lecture on Lewis Carroll in the Festival Theatre; very large audience, all downstairs sections filled except the two extreme sides, and a substantial number in the balcony. Lecture goes very well; great laughter and prolonged applause. But it was a bit too long, and as we began late it was noon when we finished and there was no time for questions.*

P.M. Alice Through the Looking Glass *at the Avon, directed by Marti Maraden and very well dramatized by James Reaney. Sheer delight! Fine theatre art and accomplishment wedded. Splendid Alice (Sarah Polley); never put a foot wrong. A procession of greatly gifted actors in the familiar roles (e.g., Douglas Rain as Humpty Dumpty). Imaginative devices; after Tenniel but not slavish: e.g., a magnificent, alarming Jabberwock. Transporting. Roused in me* hiraeth *as the best theatre does.*

The English have long been famous for their eccentrics. I speak of the English particularly among the peoples of the British Isles because they recognize eccentricity and glory in it. The Scots do not admit that anything a Scotsman does is other than logical and inevitable. The Irish regard logic and inevitability as themselves evidence of eccentricity. Welsh eccentricity, like so much else that is Welsh, is apt to be dark and of the spirit. But the English are proud of their eccentrics because the centre toward which they face, spiritually, morally, and often physically, is different from that of their fellow countrymen, and the English people cherish them and indulge them because of their oddity and whimsicality. The English, we must remember, are very fond of pets of all kinds.

Eccentricity takes many forms. There are people who, like Dr. Samuel Johnson, are impelled to touch every post they pass in the street, or perhaps to avoid stepping on cracks in the pavement. There are people who cannot, or will not, sleep unless the head of their bed points toward the magnetic north. But these are trifles. There are other eccentricities that verge on madness, except that they do not inhibit the eccentric person from meeting the ordinary obligations of life. But the really great eccentrics are all inimitable; they are not possessed by a single oddity; they are, in their deepest selves, unlike the generality of mankind.

It is about one of these, Lewis Carroll, that I am to speak to you today. It is not part of his eccentricity that he is known to most people by a name that was not his own; that is because he chose to write under a pen name, and Lewis Carroll is, by one of those logical tricks in which he delighted, a rearrangement of his own name, which was Charles Lutwidge Dodgson. He was, in fact the *Reverend* Charles Lutwidge Dodgson and his status as a clergyman influenced virtually every aspect of his life. He was not fully a priest of the Church of England; he chose not to advance beyond the rank of deacon because he had an inhibiting stammer which would have made the task of preaching very heavy for him and disagreeable for his hearers. He was known to many of his friends as Dodo, because he pronounced his own name as Do-do-dodgson. So, although he often assisted at church services, he was never a parish clergyman. He was, instead, a teacher of mathematics at Christ Church, Oxford, where he had been an undergraduate. All told, he spent something like fifty years in Christ Church, and a pleasanter place to live it would be hard to find if you were a retiring scholar, a bachelor, and—an eccentric.

Perhaps I should explain that, in the nineteenth century, it was necessary that he should be a clergyman to hold his position as mathematics don in the college. All those who ruled and taught in Oxford in those days had to be ordained, for the hold of the Church of England on both Oxford and Cambridge was still absolute, and Nonconformists and Jews were not admitted. Those of you who have visited Oxford know what a busy, crowded, noisy place it now is and you might perhaps not guess that it was a university town if it were not that, now and then, the traffic is halted while the Vice-Chancellor, preceded by his two mace bearers, crosses the street. It must be one of the few places left in the world where self-assertion, covetousness, and the whole world of the combustion engine must come to a halt because somebody distinguished for his intelligence is going about his business. But in Dodgson's day it was a quiet university city where, it was said, grass grew through the cobblestones of the streets during vacation time.

Of course it was full of learned men who passed their time in teaching, study, and writing and in the evenings consumed extraordinary quantities of the excellent wines which were the pride of the college cellars. Dodgson, by the way, was extremely fond of sherry and was considered an admirable judge of it. If there are any of you here who have grown up under the barbarous illusion that sherry is a drink for old ladies, I advise you to drink a few glasses of the real thing, and learn better. Sherry is generously fortified with brandy. Dodgson, by the way, liked to drink his sherry while walking about the room. He never ate lunch, but at midday he got through a fair amount of sherry, while walking a quarter of a mile or so.

As a teacher he had the reputation of being dull. On the very few occasions when he preached, the report was that he was earnest, logical—and dull. A great many of his Oxford colleagues, where Common Room conversation was expected to be simultaneously learned and witty—which is by no means easy—found him dull. But was he dull? Dodgson seems to have been so, but why would you have come here this morning to hear me talk about a dull teacher of mathematics who lived from 1832 until 1898 and was dull every minute of it? No, you have come to hear about this eccentric man's *alter ego*, who was Lewis Carroll.

It is important, I think, to emphasize that he came of what used to be called "a good family," in Yorkshire. The Dodgsons could trace their ancestry back before Tudor times and they had always lived in the upper-middle range of society; since the early eighteenth century they had been chiefly clergymen, sometimes attaining to high office. They had large families, and a trick of marrying cousins, which was not so odd then as it might seem now, for when families were very large, and visits were confined to the distance a horse could travel in a day, cousins were the sort of people one met. Lewis Carroll had a positive army of cousins, uncles, and aunts and he knew them all and valued them as friends all his life. He himself had three brothers and seven sisters, and a lively and highly intelligent household they seem to have been. The photographs we have of them reveal an extraordinary degree of family likeness; there is a picture of Dodgson's seven sisters, every one of whom might have been taken for Charles "in drag." Not that he looked in the least effeminate; it was that the girls had the strong, rather distinguished features that marked him.

He was born into, and seems never to have questioned, that English "class system" which has been so much abused in the present century. Indeed, several governments have announced their intention of abolishing it, and the most recent prime minister to retire showed her egalitarian principle by accepting the title of Baroness Thatcher. Certainly it had its objectionable side, but it also had its virtues, and it is notable that in England it was possible to climb up the class ladder if you had the brains and determination to do so, and this was because the English always had a tender spot for anybody with money, which they associated, by no means mistakenly, with energy. This was not so in France, for instance, where rank was everything.

Dodgson's family were gentlefolk, and never forgot it, but they had a high notion of what was expected of people in their position, and everybody who spoke of Dodgson's parents and his family, said how kind and generous they were to less fortunate people. The gentry did in those days what the state does now for those who cannot take care of themselves, and Dodgson was a generous man all his life long.

His childhood was very happy and—what is not always the case—his schooldays were reasonably happy. I mention this because so many writers have been unhappy at school, and in our century many have told us about their unhappiness at length and with bitterness. Of course nobody is *very* happy at school; if you meet anyone who says otherwise, you may know that you have met someone who is stuck in childhood, like a cow stuck in a swamp. Childhood may have periods of great happiness, but it also has times that must simply be endured. Childhood at its best is a form of slavery tempered by affection.

It is in Dodgson's childhood that we find the first traces of Lewis Carroll. The family of eleven children amused themselves with a magazine, most of which he wrote. They acted plays and presented puppet shows, and these were his work. As a boy he showed the inclination toward light verse and nonsense verse which later made him famous. This sort of family invention and family entertainment was not forced upon the family of the Reverend Charles Dodgson by poverty for they were privileged children; they were inventive because they were of more than average intelligence.

After schooldays at Rugby, Charles—so named after his father—Lutwidge, which was the name of his mother, who was his father's first cousin—went to Oxford, to Christ Church, as so many of his family had done before him, and in 1852 he achieved first-class honours in mathematics and was immediately appointed to a studentship—that is to say, a Fellowship in Christ Church—and in 1854 he took his B.A., proceeding in 1857 to an M.A., and assumed the duties of mathematical lecturer. In effect he never left Christ Church, which suited him exactly, until he removed to the home of some of his sisters in 1898, and died there, at the age of sixty-six. We do not think that a great age now, but he had begun in his fifties to speak of himself as an old man.

I don't want to bore you with biographical detail or load you with an account of everything Dodgson wrote. Because, as Dodgson, he wrote a considerable number of technical treatises on mathematics, which were received with respect, if not rapture, by the people who could understand them. One of these, called *Euclid and His Modern Rivals*, which he brought out in 1879, was a serious and excellent contribution to Euclidean geometry, but the mathematical world was offended by it because it contained a number of jokes, and the mathematical world does not admit the existence of jokes. This seems to have been a case in which Dodgson and Carroll became dangerously mingled.

So far we have talked a good deal about Dodgson, and said little about Lewis Carroll. Where did he come from and who was he? He came from an aspect of Dodgson's character that I must approach with caution, because I do not want to be misunderstood. He was extremely fond of little girls. Not of children in general. He detested little boys, and in one letter to a child friend he actually suggests that she should open the penknife which he has sent her for her birthday, and stick it up her brother's nose. In the present age, when everybody is an amateur psychoanalyst, and where the newspapers are filled every day with tales of horrible crimes committed against children and by children, such a suggestion as that must be jumped on and worried until some horrible secret has been squeezed out of it, but I do not propose to get into that sort of work this morning. I shall say no more than I have evidence to support, and that amounts to this: Lewis Carroll was enchanted by little girls, fell in love with little girls, and never laid a wicked hand on one of them. He was a gentleman and a Christian clergyman and it was on those principles that he lived his life.

We know who most of the little girls were, and there were a great many of them. The one of special interest to us was Alice Pleasance Liddell. She was the second of the three daughters of the Reverend Henry George Liddell, who was appointed Dean of Christ Church in 1855, at which time Alice was three years old. It was a family of intellectual distinction for the Dean was, with Robert Scott, then Master of Balliol, the author of the great *Greek Lexicon* which is still a standard work. Alice was a lovely child, and all the Liddell family had unusual good looks. She was a beauty—a *stunner* in the language of the time—even as a child, and she grew to be a beautiful young woman. But there is a revealing entry in Lewis Carroll's diary for May 11, 1865: "Met Alice and Miss Prickert [she was the child's governess] in the quadrangle; Alice seems changed a good deal and hardly for the better—probably going through the usual awkward stage of transition." Alice at that time would have been thirteen, and Carroll's judgment was right; she was becoming a young woman, and thus of no further interest to him.

Lewis Carroll was an expert photographer, at a time when photography was a vastly more complex pursuit than it is now. But all the drudgery of preparing the plates, and subsequently developing them, and of coaxing results from the huge cameras, whose focal length was determined by the most careful management of the extensible bellows, and the most exact adjustment of the heavy and very valuable lens, was a delight to his scientific, mathematical spirit. To make the work even more difficult, it had to be achieved by daylight, and this required very exact judgment and artistic talent as well as luck, to achieve a good result. We have great numbers of the photographs Lewis Carroll took, both of his child friends and of adults, and they show him to have been a man of quite unusual gift. Some of them, like his portraits of Tennyson, of Ruskin, of Christina Rossetti and her brother Dante Gabriel, of Ellen Terry and of Millais, are among the finest achievements of that early period of the photographer's art. And of course there were pictures of Alice.

They come as a surprise. We are accustomed to think of Alice as she appears in the accepted illustrations of the books by John Tenniel. There Alice is a self-possessed, charming little girl with long fair hair brushed back from a serious face, whose normal expression is serious, and sometimes darkens into a frown when something especially outrageous is happening. But the real Alice was not fair, but dark, and the dominant feature of her lovely face is the mystery of a pair of wonderful dark eyes, which seem to see far more than a child might be expected to see. This is certainly a face to fall in love with. Speaking for myself, and as the father of three daughters, I am not more than ordinarily susceptible to the charm of little girls, but when I look at the portraits of Alice, I can sense what it was that enthralled Lewis Carroll, and inspired two books that are undoubted classics, not simply of children's literature, but of that small portion of literature that is held dear by countless readers of all ages.

We know when the story first came into being. We have Dodgson's diaries, and on July 4, 1862, he records: "I made an expedition up the river to Godstow with the three Liddells; we had tea on the bank there and did not reach Christ Church until half-past eight." The Liddell children were Lorina, Alice, and Edith, and Alice at that time was just ten years old. The other member of the party was another young don, the Reverend Robinson Duckworth, who remained a friend of Carroll for the whole of his life. He says of the great occasion: "The story was actually composed and spoken over my shoulder, for the benefit of Alice Liddell who was acting as 'cox' of our gig. I remember turning around and saying, 'Dodgson, is this an extempore romance of yours?' I also remember well how, when we had conducted the three children back to the Deanery, Alice said, as she bade us goodnight, 'Oh, Mr. Dodgson, I wish you would write out Alice's adventures for me.' He said he would try and he afterwards told me that he sat up nearly the whole night, committing to a MS his recollections of the drolleries with which he had enlivened the afternoon. He added illustrations of his own and presented the volume, which used often to be seen on the drawing-room table at the Deanery."

It was not until 1865 that *Alice* appeared as a book. If you want to see what that original MS looked like, it has been reprinted in facsimile in a paperback; the later published story is a good deal enlarged and augmented. But if you have any ambition to possess a first edition of the printed book, I advise you to consider your next move very carefully, because Dodgson and his illustrator, Tenniel, were not satisfied with it, and recalled it, so that only about thirty of the first edition exist, and the last one to come on the market sold for one million, eight hundred thousand pounds. The second edition is also quite an expensive book. If you want quite a lot, but not all, of what Lewis Carroll wrote, you can get a fat book called *The Complete Works* (it isn't, but publishers have no shame) in The Nonesuch Edition, and I truly think it is all that any reasonable person could ask for, because Lewis Carroll was not always an enthralling writer, and I assume that you do not want his numerous mathematical writings.

He himself had no high opinion of *Alice's Adventures in Wonderland*, and was rather surprised when the first edition—which, as I have explained, is really the second—was a resounding success and quickly achieved the reputation it has since maintained as the finest book for children ever written. I will not weary you with the details of how many times it has been republished, and in how many languages. It made Lewis Carroll instantly famous, and it was characteristic of him that he maintained his privacy and his quiet life as an Oxford don in spite of all the admiration that was evoked by the book.

His popularity with children, of course, became almost overwhelming, and his children's parties were famous. They were very much along Victorian lines. Children came with their mothers or governesses, and there was always plenty to eat of the kind of thing children like—or liked in Victorian times—which seemed to mean a great deal of rich confectionery. The entertainment, which Lewis Carroll directed with total control, was likely to include conjuring, by the host, a magic lantern show, directed by the host, and games, led by the host.

These games give us most interesting information about Carroll himself. A great spinner of fantasy he might be, but he was a mathematician first and foremost, and one of the games he delighted to play with his child guests was called Symbolic Logic, and that was exactly what it was—but adapted to the child mind. The method is that familiar to Bertrand Russell and Alfred North Whitehead, but as Lewis Carroll uses it, the results are absurd. Was he demonstrating that logic is itself an absurdity? I don't know but I wouldn't put it past him. Here's an example: Three concrete propositions are offered, thus—1. Babies are illogical; 2. Nobody is despised who can manage a crocodile; 3. Illogical persons are despised. What is the logical conclusion? That babies cannot manage crocodiles. How do you like this one? 1. No one takes in *The Times*, unless he is well-educated; 2. No hedgehog can read; 3. Those who cannot read are not well-educated. What is the logical conclusion? No hedgehog takes in *The Times.* Can you stand one more? 1. Nobody, who really appreciates Beethoven, fails to keep silence while the Moonlight Sonata is being played; 2. Guinea pigs are hopelessly ignorant of music; 3. No one who is hopelessly ignorant of music, ever keeps silence while the Moonlight Sonata is being played. Logical conclusion—Guinea pigs never really appreciate Beethoven.

Would you like to try some of those when next you have a children's party? Or do you ever give children's parties? Or are you permitted to attend the parties your children give? But Carroll's parties were immensely successful and invitations to them were eagerly sought. He was keenly interested in everything relating to proper conduct and good manners, and even wrote some *Hints for Etiquette.* Here is one: "In proceeding to the dining-room, the gentleman gives one arm to the lady he escorts—it is unusual to offer both." As we read of those parties now, we must conclude that Victorian children were, in some respects at least, quicker in the wit than the children of today. But as I said earlier, much was expected of the children of the upper classes. Girls, I mean. Boys were expected to be rather thick in the head. Try some Symbolic Logic on your little Couch Potato, when you go home, and see what happens.

I have spoken of children's parties. When he was amusing a single child, Carroll was somewhat more exacting. One little girl, who spent a weekend with him, was driven almost to despair, because he insisted on teaching her to play chess. But not ordinary chess; it was a form of chess he had himself invented, in which all the rules were changed, and the moves of the pieces were determined by new rules. All children seem to have thought Mr. Dodgson delightful, but there is no record of any one of them who found him easy company.

Of course, Victorian children *were* bright. I am fond of the story about Carroll, who was entertaining a child friend of his who was visiting Oxford. She was a child actress, and she was appearing in the university city in a comedy now forgotten called *Bootle's Baby.* This is what Carroll records in his diary for June 12, 1889: "Again took Maggie about. We called on the Evans, Chapmans and Symonds and I introduced her to the Bishop of Oxford! The Bishop asked her what she thought of Oxford. 'I think,' said the little actress with quite professional aplomb, 'it's the best place in the provinces!' At which his Lordship was much amused." If that story puzzles you, remember that Maggie was a small actress, and that "the provinces" was a somewhat patronizing term used in her profession to describe any place that was not London, hub of the theatrical universe.

Lewis Carroll's popularity did not affect his work in Christ Church. Indeed many of his colleagues thought it somewhat below the dignity of an Oxford don to be associated with such frivolous stuff. But he showed a surprising practicality in dealing with his fame. He insisted on excellent contracts with his publishers, and he was quick to invent a number of games based on *Alice* which brought him in a lot of money. Indeed, he became quite rich.

Of course that did not happen at once. And Alice's family do not seem to have been overjoyed by the fame that had touched their small daughter. Indeed, Mrs. Liddell became cold and almost hostile toward Dodgson, who must have been rather a nuisance, for he hung around the Dean's house at all sorts of hours, and often visited the nursery without Mrs. Liddell's knowledge—though of course the governess was always present—and he wrote innumerable letters to Alice. These have not survived, for when she grew up Alice Liddell—who became Mrs. Reginald Hargreaves—refused to exploit her association with the popular book in any way. We assume that they were humorous love letters, such as might be written to a child, and we may be glad that they have not endured to be picked over and theorized about by insensitive scholars and psychoanalysts.

We understand Mrs. Liddell's concern. One of Dodgson's hobbies, which we must approach with care, was a passion for photographing the little girls he knew, sometimes in fancy dress, as fairy tale characters, but sometimes in the nude. None of these nude photographs have survived, for at his death his heirs distributed them to the ladies—now grown women—who were the subjects. We must try to understand this in Victorian terms; Dodgson repeatedly expressed his feeling that a naked girl child was the loveliest thing on earth, and from his other photographs we can divine that they were not erotically or provocatively posed. It was a fact, too, that he took these photographs always with the mother of the child present, and never a word of complaint was ever raised. But it remains an odd hobby for a bachelor clergyman, and we can understand the concern of Mrs. Liddell, who was by no means green. I have no doubt whatever that Dodgson never permitted a hint of adult sexuality to enter his mind, but such thoughts cannot be kept out of our twentieth-century minds. Nabokov's astonishing novel *Lolita* cannot be banished from consciousness. We are the inheritors for good and ill of what may be called the Freudian Revolution.

We must take into account Dodgson's extraordinary—one is tempted to say absurd—concern with female innocence. One of his projects—never achieved—was to produce a special edition of Shakespeare from which any reference that might even slightly blemish the innocence of a child had been deleted. This would have resulted in a somewhat ragged volume, for Shakespeare does not seem to have been aware of innocence as Victorians understood it, and even some of his most delightful heroines—Rosalind, for instance, or Beatrice—have very free tongues.

That purified Shakespeare was only one of the books for children that Dodgson wanted to produce, but did not do so. He had a plan for a child's Bible, from which any reference to God's anger or punishment for sin had been removed. It was pointed out to him that this would have meant cutting out Noah and his Ark, so popular with children, because Noah was escaping from God's wrath. The only departure from strict Christian orthodoxy of which we know Dodgson to have been guilty was his declaration that Jesus could not have believed in an eternal hell of punishment for sin, and that if he found that Jesus did entertain such a dreadful notion, he would declare himself to be no longer a Christian.

But this is all Dodgson. Lewis Carroll seems to have had extraordinary access to the imagination of a child and when he is writing the *Alice* books he never takes a stupid step.

What is even more astonishing is the hold that the *Alice* books have exercised over the minds of millions of adults. They have become what we may call "cult books," known to people who quote them slyly in conversation, hoping that someone else present will notice the quotation and perhaps offer another in return. This can be embarrassing. I recall an occasion in my youth, when I was at Queen's University in Kingston, when the English Club assembled one afternoon to hear the university librarian, a gentleman named Cockburn Kyte, address us on T.E. Lawrence's *Seven Pillars of Wisdom*. Mr. Kyte, who was immensely tall and thin and might well have come from one of Tenniel's illustrations for *Alice*, rose and with a smile of ineffable archness began: "'It was the *best* butter,' the March Hare meekly replied." And then he paused, plainly expecting us to fall about and slap our thighs at the aptness and witty allusiveness of his introduction to his subject. But we were a group of cornfed hicks who stared at him, thinking that he must have gone off his head, and his speech began with one very lame leg. We had read everything that was on the curriculum of the English Department, but I think I was the only one who had read *Alice* and I could not imagine how Mr. Kyte expected to make her relevant to T.E. Lawrence.

But since then I have been in company where the quotations and references to *Alice* flew about so swiftly that the oxygen in the air seemed seriously exhausted and we were in danger of ascending into what Shelley called "the intense inane." It is still—or it was so until quite recently—impossible to read a serious English newspaper or magazine without finding some *Alice* reference in it. Tenniel's illustrations have been a treasure house to cartoonists, and particularly to political cartoonists, who have delighted to portray the Emperor of Germany as the Jabberwock, or various prime ministers as the Mad Hatter, and always with the solemn figure of Alice, making one of her sensible and taking-down comments.

It has remained an upper-class book. Let me read to you a passage from a play that was immensely popular between the two great European wars, called *Journey's End*; it first appeared in 1928, and was acted all over the world. The scene is a dugout on the Allied front, and an officer named Trotter enters from the trenches above, to find another officer, named Osborne, reading a book. Trotter is what was called a "ranker" officer, meaning that he had been an enlisted man who through his ability had been promoted to officer status; Osborne is a gentleman, formerly a schoolmaster. Trotter says: "What are you reading?"

OSBORNE: *(wearily)* Oh, just a book.

TROTTER: What's the title?

OSBORNE: *(shows)* Ever read it?

TROTTER: *Alice's Adventures in Wonderland.* Why, that's a kid's book!

OSBORNE: Yes.

TROTTER: You aren't *reading* it?

OSBORNE: Yes.

TROTTER: What—a kid's book?

OSBORNE: Haven't you read it?

TROTTER: *(scornfully)* No!

OSBORNE: You ought to. *(Reads)*

How doth the little crocodile
Improve his shining tail
And pour the waters of the Nile
On every golden scale!

How cheerfully he seems to grin
How neatly spreads his claws,
And welcomes little fishes in
With gently smiling jaws!

TROTTER: I don't see no point in that.

OSBORNE: *(wearily)* Exactly. That's just the point.

TROTTER: You are a funny chap!

Now, I think the author, R.C. Sherriff, has made a brilliant exposition of the charm and magic of *Alice* in that short scene. There is nothing in the world wrong with Trotter; he is a man of ability and great good sense, brave and good-natured in adversity. But his mind is not tuned to that curious pitch that is most frequently found in what used to be called the upper classes, which seems to hanker after an irrationality, a freedom from the chains of logic and reason, and a holiday in a world where the ordinary concerns of life have no validity. The English form of this cast of mind is brilliantly caught in the two volumes of *Alice's Adventures in Wonderland* and *Through the Looking Glass*, where unexceptionable logic gives rise to a totally inexplicable but logical chaos, and a freedom from the domination of dull reason. Why does this assert itself chiefly among the educated upper class? It would be politically incorrect to attempt any hint of an explanation.

People who do not know the *Alice* books, or have read them superficially, are apt to miss their poetry and also their dark side. There are portions of each book that can be frightening to a small child. As for poetry, I can only suggest that you study carefully the poems in the books, which are usually parodies of morally improving poems of the sort that Victorian children were expected to get by heart. But there is a gripping quality in some of the original poems that qualifies them, in my opinion, for identification as true poetry, which stirs the imagination and the emotions.

One of the finest of these occurs in *Through the Looking Glass*; it is called "Jabberwocky." You probably recall the first stanza:

'Twas brillig, and the slithy toves
  Did gyre and gimble in the wabe:
All mimsy were the borogoves,
  And the mome raths outgrabe.

What does it mean? Because it does mean something, and if you wish to make a close study of Lewis Carroll you can read his own explanation of what he called, in the beginning, *A Stanza of Anglo-Saxon Poetry.* He will tell you that "brillig" means "the time of broiling dinner, i.e., in the close of the afternoon." You will learn that a "tove" is a species of badger that has short horns like a stag and lives chiefly on cheese. It is "slithy" because it is smooth and active. What is a "borogove"? It is an extinct form of parrot which in its heyday lived on veal. And "outgrabe" is of course the past tense of the verb "outgribe" which means shrieked or creaked. The whole stanza, translated into modern English from Anglo-Saxon means, "It was evening, and the smooth active badgers were scratching and boring holes in the hillside; all unhappy were the parrots; and the grave turtles squeaked out." Are you still with me? And if so, are you edified and happy?

That first verse was written sixteen years before the heroic poem of the conquering of a monster called the Jabberwock was added to it.

"Jabberwocky" cannot be denied the name of poetry. It invites the imagination to explore a world that is complete within the poem. It arouses wonder. It tells a story which might easily have come from an Anglo-Saxon source or from one of the great German legends that inspired Wagner. A brave youth faces a dreadful monster, kills it, and returns in triumph to his father who is overjoyed. Perhaps we think of the hideous Grendel rising from the mere, slain by the dauntless Beowulf. But just a moment—there is something in the tone of "Jabberwocky" that tempts us, not to mock at the exploit of the heroic youth, but to see it somewhat askew; a child may feel terror on hearing the poem, especially if it is looking at Tenniel's splendid illustration of the creature, part prehistoric, part inspired by the wonderful paintings which show St. George slaying the dragon; but the triumph of the Jabberwock slayer is the triumph of a child, as we see him in the picture, valiant with his sword. What is the child slaying? The psychoanalysts have had their say, and some of what they say prompts us to assent. We share in the father's cry:

"And hast thou slain the Jabberwock?
    Come to my arms, my beamish boy!
O frabjous day! Callooh! Callay!"
    He chortled in his joy.

Have we all, at some time, slain the Jabberwock? Or, sad to say, have we failed to do so, or merely wounded the creature? I am not a psychoanalyst, and have no right to say, but I may be allowed my strong personal opinion. Lewis Carroll had seen something to which most of us are blind and had put it in a form of which only he knew the secret, and we can penetrate the secret—perhaps—by intuition.

The hold which this poem has had over countless readers is evidence of its power. Incidentally, it presents a pretty problem to those heavily burdened souls, the translators. It is the problem they face with James Joyce. But several of them have met it as bravely as the child hero met the Jabberwock. I will not trouble you about many of them, but it may amuse some of you to hear how a scholarly diplomat, the late Lord Vansittart, rendered the tricky first verse in his Latin version:

Coesper erat: tune lubriciles ultravia circum
Urgebant gyres gimbiculosque tophi:
Moestenui visae borogovides ire meatu
Et profugi gemitus exgrabuere rathae.

The rest is every bit as good, but I don't want to spoil your appetite for the play with too much pleasure now.

I promised somewhere, did I not, to talk to you about Lewis Carroll and the theatre? Apart from photography, it was his greatest pleasure and enthusiasm. It has been suggested—though I think wrongly—that he declined to accept full ordination into the priesthood because attendance at the theatre, though not actually forbidden, was not encouraged for the clergy of the Church of England. But whenever he could, there in the theatre sat Carroll, in his clerical dress, an enchanted playgoer and often a friend of some of the actors and actresses on the stage. (Perhaps I should say a word about clerical dress. He lived before the Roman collar was the usual wear for clergymen; in his day they wore white bowties with black clothes of clerical cut, which meant that they had no lapels. I can remember, when I was an undergraduate, seeing very old clergymen around Oxford, who still dressed like that.) So that is how you must imagine Lewis Carroll, as he sat in his favourite theatre, The Princess's, watching Charles Kean and his wife in Shakespeare, or perhaps a stirring melodrama. The pinnacle of his theatre experience, he wrote in his diary, was Kean's production of *Henry VIII* the scene (it is act 4, scene 2) in which the much-troubled Queen Katherine falls asleep and has a vision of angel visitors of whom she says:

Saw you not even now a blessed troop
Invite me to a banquet, whose bright faces
Cast thousand beams upon me, like the sun?
They promised me eternal happiness
And brought me garlands, Griffith, which I feel
I am not worthy yet to wear: I shall, assuredly.

This is the Queen's vision before her death. Apparently the scene, as Lewis Carroll saw it at the Princess's Theatre on January 22, 1855, was a splendidly imaginative piece of stage illusion. This is what Dodgson wrote in his diary:

Oh, that exquisite vision of Queen Catherine! I almost held my breath to watch: the illusion is perfect, and I felt as if in a dream all the time it lasted. It was like a delicious reverie, or the most beautiful poetry. This is the true end and object of acting—to raise the mind above itself, and out of its petty every-day cares—never shall I forget that wonderful evening, that exquisite vision—sunbeams broke in through the roof and gradually revealed two angel forms, floating in front of the carved work on the ceiling: the column of sunbeams shone down upon the sleeping queen, and gradually down it floated a troop of angelic forms, transparent, and carrying palm branches in their hands; they waved these over the sleeping queen, with oh, such a sad and solemn grace—So I could fancy (if the thought be not profane) would real angels seem to our mortal vision, though doubtless our conception is poor and mean to the reality. She in an ecstasy raises her arms toward them, and to sweet slow music they vanish as marvellously as they came.

Here's enthusiasm, indeed! I have seen *Henry VIII* several times, and I have never seen anything to touch that; Dodgson was no simpleton who knew nothing of plays; he was a man of extensive culture and a seasoned playgoer and this vision remained with him as one of the great artistic experiences of his life. It reminds us, if we need reminding, what splendours the Victorian theatre offered, with its magnificent painted scenery and the magic of its gaslight. Modern directors, of course, don't believe in angels. Indeed, one often wonders what they do believe in. But this was Shakespeare done for an audience who had few reservations about angels and it was, it seems, splendid. So splendid that this playgoer cherished it all his life.

And yet it was stagecraft—a combination of art and illusion. Lewis Carroll knew a lot about that. He and his brothers and sisters had possessed two toy theatres, for which they wrote plays and performed them with great seriousness. Stage illusion was in Dodgson's blood and we miss something if we do not understand the dramatic qualities of the *Alice* books, the sudden appearances and disappearances, the transformations, and above all the rapidity with which the action takes place.

Dodgson's approval of the stage was not total, and he seems to have enjoyed farces and comedies of the most witless sort; I can speak with feeling because I have read some of them, and they speak of a theatre utterly gone, to be replaced by a witlessness agreeable to our own age. But there were plays to which he objected, and one of these was *Faust*—one of the many butcheries of Goethe's great play which he saw in 1857, and about which he wrote: "I think it is a play that should never have been put on the stage—it is too horrible, and too daring in its representation of the spirit world." The presentation of Mephistopheles "made my blood run cold." Yet, even here, great stagecraft and great acting could win him over. In 1886 he saw Henry Irving's version of *Faust* and wrote: "It is magnificently put on the stage and Irving as Mephistopheles is wonderfully good. Ellen Terry is of course exquisite as Margaret." You see, it was the great stagecraft that won him over. It was in the same year, 1886, that Lewis Carroll had the joy of seeing a stage version of *Alice*, the work of Henry Savile Clarke, opening on December 23, at the Prince of Wales Theatre. It was a great success, and Lewis Carroll's fame was extended in a new direction.

It would be beyond my powers to mention all the stage versions of *Alice* that have appeared since that triumph, and you would quickly be bored by the recitation. Some have been very good: There was one, with the text adapted by Clemence Dane, in 1944, with a cast that included Sybil Thorndike as the ferocious Queen of Hearts and Rima Beaumont, who was a splendid reminder of the beauty of Alice Pleasance Liddell. Not surprisingly, it is in the casting of the central role of Alice that so many productions have come to grief. The desire to make her cute, or pert, or a giggler, or a wisecracker, or sexy, is the downfall of countless actresses and their directors who are convinced that they need to make Alice more interesting than she appears in the book—which is, of course, to mistake what Alice is really like, for Alice is a very serious, self-respecting little girl. It appears that the first stage Alice, whose name was Phoebe Carlo, filled the bill perfectly and won the admiration and gratitude of Alice's creator.

Alice has been made into a ballet—more than one, indeed. And of course *Alice* has inspired countless films, not one of which has been really satisfactory. They include a complex version devised and directed by Dr. Jonathan Miller, in which was explained—for Dr. Miller is nothing if not an explainer—that all the figures in the stories represented Victorian adults, as they appeared to the eyes of a child. I have never been able to track it down for it did not enjoy wide distribution, but I am sure it was interesting, as everything Dr. Miller does is interesting, and I fear that it may have been too clever for its own good, which is a trap into which Dr. Miller has occasionally fallen.

At the opposite end of the intellectual scale lies the Hollywood film of 1933, which was made accessible to the kind of people for whom everything must be blatant and vulgar, and its success was thought to be assured by a cast that included Cary Grant as the Mock Turtle (why?) and Gary Cooper as the White Knight (somewhat more credible) and W.C. Fields as Humpty Dumpty, which was total disaster to all except those who thought Fields funny whatever he did. This was a thoroughly illiterate film, made by people who had never been children, and perhaps had never seen a child. Their worst choice was in casting Charlotte Henry as Alice. I must guard my tongue, but perhaps I may say that she was a thoroughly democratized Alice. But one movie critic wrote of her, "she's as pert a piece of jailbait as ever fell down a rabbit hole." *Alice* has been filmed performed by puppets. It has been filmed as a musical. There was a version made in 1951, with a fine cast, but somehow the story went askew and turned out to include Queen Victoria as the Queen of Hearts. A film called *Dreamchild* showed us Alice, grown old, remembering Dodgson and the story at Oxford. *Alice* has been very well done on the stage, but the movies have never come near it.

As Lewis Carroll and the Reverend Mr. Dodgson grew older—they never grew very old in modern terms for he died when he was sixty-six, convinced that he was an old man—the split between the two became more pronounced. Inevitably his success in the theatre was deplored by very serious people who thought it was unfitting in a clergyman. He was not to be shaken, and defended the theatre boldly—but not without reservation. Consider this passage, which he wrote in 1889 when he was fifty-seven:

Let me pause for a moment to say that I believe this thought, of the possibility of death—if calmly realized and steadily faced—would be one of the best possible tests as to our going to any scene of amusement being right or wrong. If the thought of sudden death acquires, for *you*, a special horror when imagined happening in a *theatre*, then be very sure the theatre is harmful for *you*, however harmless it may be for others; and that *you* are incurring a deadly peril by going. Be sure that the safest rule is that we should not dare to *live* in any scene in which we dare not *die*.

That passage occurs in the preface to Lewis Carroll's last work of imagination. It is a novel called *Sylvie and Bruno* (1890). I am sorry to say it is a very bad novel but it is of great psychological interest because in it the Reverend Charles Lutwidge Dodgson and Lewis Carroll are struggling for supremacy. Neither emerges as the winner. It is a broken-backed novel, for the plot leaps dizzily to and fro over the abyss that divides two stories. The one is about two children; Sylvie, a delightful little girl but obliged much of the time to adopt a maternal or perhaps governess-like attitude toward her little brother Bruno. Sylvie is sweet as Alice never is; indeed she becomes cloying all too easily. As for Bruno, I find it hard to speak with moderation. Evelyn Waugh said of him that he was "a creation of unique horror." If you think that harsh, let me give you a sample. Impersonating children is not one of my gifts, but I shall try my best.

"Really, Bruno, you must come and do your lessons."

"I *wiss* oo wouldn't say '*really*, Bruno!'" the little fellow pleaded, with pouting lips that made him look prettier than ever. "It *always* shows there's something horrid coming! And I won't kiss oo, if oo's so unkind."

"Ah, but you *have* kissed me!" Sylvie exclaimed in merry triumph.

"Well, then, I'll *un*kiss oo." And he threw his arms round her neck for this novel, but apparently not *very* painful, operation.

"It's very like *kissing*," Sylvie remarked, as soon as her lips were again free for speech.

"Oo don't know *nuffin* about it! It were just the *conkery*," Bruno replied.

There is really an extraordinary amount of kissing in this book, and we know that Carroll was a great kisser. He might well have been more reserved in print.

It would take too long to tell you the tale of these two children who dwell most of the time in Elfland, where their father is King; they also spend some time in Dogland, which you will not be surprised to hear is full of dogs. But by means of elephantine contortions their story is intermingled with that of some adult humans—because Sylvie and Bruno seem unable to determine whether or not they are fairies. The other story is about an impossibly beautiful, pious, and refined girl called Lady Muriel, who has two lovers. One is a doctor who thinks he is too old for her, and thus disqualifies himself, and the other is a Captain Eric Lindon who is a heroic, splendid fellow, who has one grievous defect in the eyes of the lady. He is a convinced atheist. The author wrote, "Whether it is better, or worse than the *Alice* books, I have no idea; but I take a far deeper interest in it, as having tried to put more real *thought* into it." But thought, alas, is no substitute for genius. The careful planning of *Sylvie and Bruno* cannot match the inspired improvisation of *Alice.* The book is filled with painful religious arguments, in which Lady Muriel tries to bring the atheist Captain into a better frame of mind. But it won't do, so she marries the doctor, who thereupon destroys his health by heroically fighting an epidemic of some unspecified illness in a nearby town. It is Captain Eric who nobly brings him home, a wreck, and Lady Muriel settles down to one of the happiest fates that could befall a Victorian heroine—that of devoting herself to a hopeless invalid. Endless love but no hint of sex. If you want to find how Sylvie and Bruno become involved in this high-minded affair, you must read the book yourself. It is sad that after the genius of the *Alice* books, and of *The Hunting of the Snark*, Dodgson should have fallen to this, but nothing can take those splendid works from us, nor should we suppose that even as Dodgson gained strength in his latter years, Lewis Carroll became a shadow of what he had been. It was Lewis Carroll, the inspired mathematician, who replied, when he was asked to contribute to a philosophical symposium—

And what mean all these mysteries to me
Whose life is full of indices and surds?
x squared plus seven plus fifty-three
equals eleven-thirds.

Making Speeches

17

The Deadliest of the Sins

Queen's University, in Kingston, put its mark on me in two inexpungeable ways; first by its kindness in taking me in when I had no real right to expect it, and second, by strong moral doctrine that was implicit in all its teaching. To have attended Queen's during the Depression of the thirties was to know that life was stern in its exactions, and austere in its rewards. As the recipient of an honorary degree in 1962, it would ill become me to be frivolous, even though cheerfulness would keep breaking in. So I talked about one of the Deadly Sins—the deadliest, indeed, for it is such a slow and subtle killer.

It is with a feeling of very special pride that I stand here at this moment, for I have just received my first degree from Queen's University. Queen's, for the second time in my life, has shown extraordinary kindness toward me. Many years ago it looked as though I should never go to a university, because I had made a miserable hash of my Matriculation examinations. I had failed—not by a hair's breadth, but utterly, abysmally, and catastrophically—in both algebra and geometry. I can easily recall the exact mark I made on both those papers. It was zero. There was no question of having another try. I had been getting zero in mathematics for a full three years. I exhibited in an awe-inspiring degree that quality which theologians call "invincible, ignorance."

I am now able to speak of this with calm, but at that time I was terribly depressed by my failure. It was not unexpected; indeed, I had foreseen it for months. Nevertheless, I was very miserable, because in those days it was necessary to pass in twelve papers to get into a university, and I wanted to go to a university very much. It seemed to me that if I could not go to a university I should undoubtedly drift into some despised employment, take to drink, and die by my own hand within a few years. My failure was abject, my condition was wretched, and the midnight sky of my prospects showed not a single star.

It was then that Queen's University took pity on me, and I recall my sense of relief and gratitude when Dr. W.E. McNeill, who was the vice-principal at that time, suggested that I might attend lectures and write examinations as something mysterious called a Special Student. I could not hope for a B.A. but I could learn what other B.A. students learned. So I passed three busy years here; I even became something called a Tutor. A Tutor is to a professor what the boy who cleans his brushes is to a painter. And at the end of my three years I had scraped together enough academic respectability to get me into another university which did not set great store by mathematics. It lay, I may tell you, beyond the shores of Canada, where mathematical enthusiasm burned with a kind of hellfire for several years afterward.

Queen's came to my rescue when my future was dark and forbidding, and treated me with royal generosity. And now Queen's has done so again. If ever a university showed itself a bounteous mother to a poor varmint, Queen's was so to me, and I can only say that I shall ever be grateful. In the words of the Presbyterian hymn, I stand before you—

> Pavilioned in splendour
> And girded with praise

—but I tell you most sincerely that I am the humblest man within these walls.

Allusion has been made to a university called Waverley of which I have written in some trivial and jejune productions of mine; certainly I have made merry at the expense of a university of that name.

Nobody has ever successfully identified it with Queen's. Indeed, nobody who really knows Queen's could believe that the two were the same. Where does the resemblance lie? The whole suggestion is distasteful to people of refined feeling. Let us dismiss it.

What shall we talk about, you and I, who are getting our first degrees from Queen's today? The problem is a little easier than is usually the case, because we are both going into new jobs. I have been an author for many years, and I intend to go on being one. But being an author isn't a job—it is a state of mind; also, it is not a gainful occupation except in a rather restricted sense. I have been earning my living as a journalist for twenty years, and now I am giving up that sort of work to take a different sort of job in a university. I shall be very green at it, and I expect I shall do a lot of things the wrong way. Perhaps I shall be a failure, but I have failed at several things already, and somehow I have lived through it. Failure at a specific task is always disagreeable and sometimes it is humiliating. But there is only one kind of failure that really breaks the spirit, and that is failure in the art of life itself. That is the failure that one does well to fear.

What is it like, this failure in the art of life? It is the failure which manifests itself in a loss of interest in really important things. It does not come suddenly; there is nothing dramatic about it, and thus it works with a dreadful advantage; it creeps upon us and once it has us in its grip, it is hard for us to recognize what ails us.

It is not for nothing that this failure was reckoned by medieval theologians as one of the Seven Deadly Sins. I suppose you know what they were. Wrath, Gluttony, Envy, Avarice, and Lechery are not very hard to recognize and are perilously easy to justify by one means or another. Pride is an extremely subtle sin because it is so clever at disguising itself as something else, and those astute men St. Ambrose and St. Augustine thought it the most dangerous of all the sins. But it is the seventh which I think is particularly prevalent in our day; medieval theologians called it Sloth.

Sloth is not really a suitable name for it now, because the word has come to mean a sluggishness and inactivity which is chiefly physical. But the sloth the theologians meant, the sloth which can damn you in this world and perhaps in the next, is spiritual. There was a better name, a Latin name, for it; it was also called Accidie, and it meant intellectual and spiritual torpor, indifference, and lethargy.

To be guilty of Acedia it is not necessary to be physically sluggish at all. You can be as busy as a bee. You can fill your days with activity, bustling from meeting to meeting, sitting on committees, running from one party to another in a perfect whirlwind of movement. But if, meanwhile, your feelings and sensibilities are withering, if your relationships with people near to you are becoming more and more superficial, if you are losing touch even with yourself, it is Acedia which has claimed you for its own.

How can it be recognized? Anatole France said that the great danger of increasing age was that the feelings atrophied, and we mistook the sensation for the growth of wisdom. It is true that as one grows older, one's sense of proportion may become greater, and things which troubled us or wounded us deeply in our youth seem less significant. But that is a different thing from feeling nothing deeply, and leaping to the conclusion that therefore nothing is really very important. As one grows older, one learns how to spare oneself many kinds of unnecessary pain, but one is in great danger if one ceases to feel pain of any kind. If you cannot feel pain at some of the harsh circumstances of life, it is very likely that you have ceased to feel joy at some of the satisfactions and delights of life. When that happens, one lives at all times under a mental and spiritual cloud; it is always wet weather in the soul. That is Acedia, and it was called a Deadly Sin because it dimmed and discouraged the spirit, and at last killed it.

I am sure that all of you know some people who have yielded to Acedia. They are the dampers, the wet blankets of life. Unfortunately some of them have a great attraction for the young. Their chronic lack of enthusiasm looks so much like sophistication. They are often clever people, who are adept at putting a chilly finger on the weak spot in whatever attracts their friends. They seldom make mistakes, because they never put themselves in a position where they are not complete masters of the situation. They take a sly pleasure in the failure of others, and they are always ready to say "I told you so." They have made just one great—indeed monstrous—mistake: They have died to joy and pain, and thus to feeling.

The opposites of these people are not, of course, those who allow every enthusiasm to run away with them, whose hearts always rule their heads, who go a-whoring after everything that is new. They are, on the contrary, people who take pains to keep their common sense in repair, and who keep their intelligence bright, but who also make daily efforts to meet experience with a fresh vision, and to give to everything that comes their way the measure of feeling, of emotion, of charity and understanding—yes, and also of pain—that it needs in order to understand it.

Because you are university people, I assume that you are people in whom mind is more prominent and better trained than is feeling. If you had not had some intellectual bias—even of quite a mild sort—it is unlikely that you would be here today to receive a degree. Therefore you must take special care that, in the years ahead of you, feeling is not neglected.

The temptation to neglect feeling is strong. You see—I say this knowing that it is blasphemy within university walls—it is really very much easier to think sensibly than it is to feel sensibly. We all know what messes people get into when they feel too much and think too little; but those people do not compel my pity so much as the hundreds of thousands whose lives are cast in a mould of midget tragedy because they think a good deal, in a strangulated, ill-nourished fashion, but hardly feel at all. These are the victims of Acedia.

Therefore I charge you, whether you are struggling under the burden of a mighty intellect, or perhaps just shuffling along with a pretty well-trained mediocre brain, to take pains not to lose your capacity to feel.

How is it to be done? I have some practical advice for you in this struggle, which is one of the great battles of life. Take some time every day—*every* day—to examine what you have been doing in the light of feeling, rather than of intelligence. It may be before you fall asleep at night; it may be while you are walking to your work; it may be at any time when you can withdraw your attention from external matters: That is the time to ask yourself—What do I really feel about all this? Not, what should I feel about it, what does the world expect me to feel, but what do I truly feel about it? You must be honest with yourself, because self-deception is one of the commonest roads to Acedia.

Now it may happen that you will find that you are committed to some course of action which you do not like—which you may positively hate. And yet, for good reasons, it may be necessary to continue with it. We all have to do things we detest, at one time or another, because we are not free to consult our own wishes only. But if you know the truth, you are protected from Acedia.

Nor is it only the detestable things that should be carefully examined. You must look clearly at the things which make your life happy and enviable, and you must give yourself up to a grateful contemplation of them. Never take such things for granted. I have seen many a promising marriage shrivel and dry up because one or both of the parties to it assumed that happiness was something that came by right, and could never be diminished. Consciously summoning up, and consciously enjoying, the good things that life brings us is a way of preserving them. It is not in their nature to last forever; they will change, and if you cherish them gratefully, the change is much more likely to be a change for the better than if you accept them as gifts which a grateful providence has showered upon you as a recognition of your magnanimity in condescending to inhabit the earth.

I have never been able to make up my mind which it is that people fear to feel most—pain or joy. Life will bring you both. You will not be able to escape the pain completely, though Acedia will dull it a little. But unfortunately it lies in your power to reject the joy utterly. Because we are afraid that great exultation may betray us into some actions, some words, which may make us look a little foolish to people who are not sharing our experience, we very often stifle our moments of joy, thinking that we shall give them their outlet later. But alas, after a few years of that kind of thing joy ceases to visit us. I seem to be quoting theologians this afternoon. There is an old saying of medieval teachers which I recommend to your special notice:

Time Jesum transeuntem et non revertentem.

I shall translate it thus: "Dread the passing of Jesus, for He does not return." And thus it is with all great revelations, be they religious or not. Seize them, embrace them, let them engulf you, draw from them the uttermost of what they have to give, for if you rebuff them, they will not come again. We live in a world where too many people are pitifully afraid of joy. Because I wish you well, I beg you not to add yourself to their number.

Do not put off the moment of decision. Begin now. This is your hour. You are shortly to receive one of the great distinctions of your lifetime. Don't worry about looking dignified; don't be afraid that your pleasure may betray you into some lapse from that nullity of demeanour which we so pathetically accept as a substitute for true dignity. Don't accept your B.A. as if it were one more padlock on the inmost chamber of your heart. Education, if it is real and not a sham, is a releasing, not an imprisoning, thing. If you wish it to be so, the achievement of your degree is a step toward a new freedom. What is the word in your heart as you accept your diploma? Is it No—or is it Yes?

18

What Every Girl Should Know

As a schoolboy I listened to many speeches on Prize Days from older persons whose good intentions were impeccable, but whose manner and matter were tediously patronizing and stuffy. When my own turn came I determined to be as honest as possible, not to talk down, and if possible to say something that was not usually said in schools. This is what I said to the girls of the Bishop Strachan School in June 1973.

During the years when my own daughters were pupils in this school I attended many of these gatherings, and heard many speeches made by men who stood where I stand at this moment. They said all sorts of things. I recall one speaker who said that as he looked out at the girls who were assembled to receive prizes, and to pay their last respects to their school, he felt as though he were looking over a garden of exquisite flowers. He was drunk, poor man, and it would be absurd to treat his remark as though he were speaking on oath. I am not drunk, although I have lunched elegantly at the table of the Chairman of your Board of Governors; I have had enough of his excellent wine to be philosophical, but with me philosophy does not take the form of paying extravagant and manifestly untruthful compliments. Let me put myself on record as saying that I do *not* feel as though I were looking over a garden of exquisite flowers.

On the contrary, I feel as though I were looking into the past. You look uncommonly as the girls of this school looked when my daughters were of your number. And in those days I used to think how much you looked like the girls who were in this school when I was myself a schoolboy, just down the road, at Upper Canada College.

I remember that boy very well. He was a romantic boy, and he thought that girls were quite the most wonderful objects of God's creation. In these liberated days, when it is possible for anyone to say anything on any occasion, I may perhaps make a confession to you, and this is it: I never liked anything but girls. Nowadays it is accepted as gospel that everybody goes through a homosexual period of life. I cannot recall any such thing: I always regarded other boys as rivals, or nuisances, or—very occasionally—friends. I am rather sorry about it now, because in the eyes of modern psychologists and sociologists it marks me as a stunted personality. Nowadays it appears that there is something warped about a man who never had a homosexual period. But there it is. I stand before you with all my imperfections weighing heavily upon me. I always liked girls, and simply because of geography, the girls I liked best were the girls of B.S.S.

I have recovered from this folly. I have myself achieved some knowledge of psychology and sociology, and it tells me significant but not always complimentary things about you. I don't know how many of you are here today, but statistically I know that during the next ten years 58.7 percent of you will marry, and that of that number 43.4 percent will have two and a half children apiece, and that 15.3 percent will be divorced. Of the remainder, 3.9 percent will be dead, 14.5 percent will have been deserted, 24.2 percent will have spent some time in jail. One hundred percent of those who have married will have given up splendid careers in order to do so, and of this number 98.5 percent will have mentioned the fact, at some time, to their husbands. These statistics were compiled for me by a graduate student at OISE, and if you doubt them, you must quarrel with her, and not with me. I accept no responsibility for statistics, which are a kind of magic beyond my comprehension.

I have said that when I was a boy I entertained a lofty, uncritical admiration for the girls of this school. Our romantic approach in those days was more delicate than it is today, when sexual fervour has achieved almost cannibalistic exuberance, and I thought I was lucky when I had a chance simply to talk to one of the girls from this school. I never had enough of that pleasure; I yearned for more. Now here I offer my first piece of good advice to you: Be very careful of what you greatly desire, in your inmost heart, because the chances are very strong that you will get it, in one form or another. But it will never be just the way you expected. You see what has happened? As a boy I wanted to talk to the girls of B.S.S., and I always thought of doing this to one girl at a time, in shaded light, with music playing in the distance. And here I am today, talking to all of you, in broad daylight. The things I planned to say when I was a boy would be embarrassingly inappropriate if I were to say them now. Indeed, I don't want to say them; they have ceased to be true or relevant for you or for me. I know too much about you to compliment you, and in your eyes I am not a romantic object. Or if I am, you had better put yourself under the treatment of some wise psychiatrist.

Here I am, after all these years, and Fate has granted one of my wishes, in the way Fate so often does—at the wrong time and in wholesale quantity. What am I to say to you?

The hallowed custom, at such times as these, is that I should offer you some good advice. But what about? It was easier in the days when girls like yourselves thought chiefly about marriage. Nowadays when little girls play

> Rich man, poor man, beggar man, thief,
> Doctor, lawyer, Indian chief

they are trying to discover their own careers, not those of their husbands. Quite recently a very young girl told me that she did not intend to bother with a husband; she would be content with affairs, because they would interfere less with her career. That remark showed how much she knew about it. A girl who thinks love affairs are less trouble than a marriage is probably also the kind of girl who thinks that picnics are simpler than dinner parties. A first-class picnic, which has to be planned to the last detail, but which must also pretend to be wholly impromptu, is a vastly more complicated undertaking than a formal dinner for twenty guests, which moves according to a well-understood pattern. Personally I have always greatly liked dinner parties, and hated picnics. But then I am a classicist by temperament, and I think the formality and the pattern, either in love or in entertaining, is half the fun.

But you may have different views, so we won't talk about that. Let us talk about something that will be applicable to your life, whether the love aspect of it takes the dinner party or the picnic form. Let us talk about enjoying life.

Don't imagine for a moment that I am going to talk about that foolish thing happiness. I meet all kinds of people who think that happiness is a condition that can be achieved, and maintained, indefinitely, and that the quality of life is determined by the number of hours of happiness you can clock up. I hope you won't bother your heads about happiness. It is a cat-like emotion; if you try to coax it, happiness will avoid you, but if you pay no attention to it it will rub against your legs and spring unbidden into your lap. Forget happiness, and pin your hopes on understanding.

Many people, and especially many young people, think that variety of sensation is what gives spice to life. They want to do everything, go everywhere, meet everybody, and drink from every bottle. It can't be done. Whoever you are, your energies and your opportunities are limited. Of course you want to try several alternatives in order to find out what suits you, but I hope that ten years from today you will agree with me that the good life is lived not widely, but deeply. It is not doing things, but understanding what you do, that brings real excitement and lasting pleasure.

You should start now. It is dangerously easy to get into a pattern of life, and if you live shallowly until you are thirty, it will not be easy to begin living deeply. Whatever your own desires may be, the people around you won't put up with it. They know you as one sort of person, and they will be resentful if you show signs of becoming somebody else. Live shallowly, and you will find yourself surrounded by shallow people.

How are you to avoid that fate? I can tell you, but it is not a magic secret which will transform your life. It is very, very difficult. What you must do is to spend twenty-three hours of every day of your life doing whatever falls in your way, whether it be duty or pleasure or necessary for your health and physical well-being. But—and this is the difficult thing—you must set aside one hour of your life every day for yourself, in which you attempt to understand what you are doing.

Do you think it sounds easy? Try it, and find out. All kinds of things will interfere. People—husbands, lovers, friends, children, employers, teachers, enemies, and all the multifarious army of mankind will want that hour, and they will have all sorts of blandishments to persuade you to yield it to them. And the worst enemy of all—yourself—will find so many things that seem attractive upon which the hour can be spent. It is extremely difficult to claim that hour solely for the task of understanding, questioning, and deciding.

It used to be somewhat easier, because people used to be religious, or pretended they were. If you went to the chapel, or the church, or a praying chamber in your own house, and fell on your knees and buried your face in your hands, they might—not always, but quite often—leave you alone. Not now. "Why are you sitting there, staring into space?" they will say. Or "What are you mooning about now?" If you say "I am thinking" they may perhaps hoot with laughter, or they will go away and tell everybody that you are intolerably pretentious. But you are doing very much what you would have been doing if you were your great-grandmother, and said that you were praying. Because you would be trying your hardest to unravel the tangles of your life, and seek the aid of the greatest thing you know—whatever you may call it—in making sense of what will often seem utterly senseless.

I am not going to advise you to pray, because I am not an expert on that subject. But I do know that it is rather the fashion among many people who do pray to think that it is pretentious to pray too much for yourself; you are supposed to pray for others, who obviously need Divine assistance more than you do. But when I was a boy at the school down the road, we were taught that prayer has three modes—petition, which is for yourself; intercession, which is for others; and contemplation, which is listening to what is said to *you.* If I might be permitted to advise you on this delicate subject, I would suggest that you skip intercession until you are a little more certain what other people need; stick to petition in the form of self-examination, and to contemplation, which is waiting for suggestions from the deepest part of you.

If I embarrass you by talking about praying, don't think of it that way. Call it "pondering" instead. I don't know if you still learn any Latin in this school, but if you do, you know that the word *ponder* comes from the Latin *ponderare*, which means "to weigh." Weigh up your life, and do it every day. If you find you are getting short weight, attend to the matter at once. The remedy usually lies in your own hands. And in that direction the true enjoyment of life is to be found.

There you are. I promised your Headmaster I would not speak for too long. But I have done what a speaker on such occasions as this ought to do. I have given you good advice. It is often and carelessly said that nobody ever takes advice. It is not true. I have taken an enormous amount of advice myself, and some of it was extraordinarily helpful to me. I have passed on some of the best of it to you this afternoon, and I have enjoyed doing so. Because, as I told you, it was my ambition for years to have a chance to talk to every girl in B.S.S. and today I have achieved it. Not quite as I had hoped, but then, in this uncertain world, whatever comes about quite as one hopes? I have enjoyed myself, and for what I have received from you I am truly thankful.

19

Insanity in Literature

It is understandable that insanity should be a frequent theme in poetry and fiction and drama; it is one of the most arresting evidences of the frailty of that reason on which civilized man so prides himself; we all stand much nearer to unreason than we suppose. The exploration of insanity that has taken place during the past century has told us much, and has offered some improvements in the alleviation, and sometimes the cure, of mental disorder. All my life I have been keenly interested in what medical science can do in this realm, and I have been greatly complimented by invitations to talk, first to the medical staff of the Clarke Institute in Toronto in 1976, and later to the Department of Psychiatry in the medical faculty of the University of Ottawa in 1977. On both occasions I was rewarded by the opportunity to talk to psychiatrists about their work, without being under the constraint of making them a professional visit.

When I was asked what I would speak about tonight, I suggested airily that "Insanity in Literature" might provide a topic. It was not until I put myself to the task of composing an address that I realized that I had bitten off far, far more than I could possibly chew in the compass of an after-dinner speech; I had proposed a subject that would provide material for quite a thick book. As I toiled on, wondering what I might choose from the mass of material at hand, it occurred to me also that you might wonder why I had chosen such a theme. I know something about literature; that is how I get my humble living. But do I know anything about insanity? Anything, that is to say, that would entitle me to speak on such a subject to such an audience as this?

The truth is that I have been fascinated by insanity since I was a child. By the time I was three years old I was aware of it, because our village madwoman lived directly opposite my parents' house. Every village has its madwoman, and ours was of special consequence because she was also rich. Her heirs were waiting for her to die; they visited her frequently, and sometimes they might be seen coming down the steps in haste, followed by her abusive screams. She lived in a Victorian house—a tall house, painted grey, and with plenty of those ornamental windows which such houses have—windows that one cannot imagine opening inward into any pleasant or ordinary room. The heirs did not interest me, because I did not know what they were, but Miss Ferguson herself was the star of the drama of my childish world, because from time to time she would escape from the big, strong woman who was her keeper, and dash out into the road, throw herself down in the dust—because it was a dirt road—and throw up a cloud like a hen having a dirt bath, meanwhile screaming in a terrified voice, "Christian men—come and help me! Christian men—come and help me!" As indeed they did. Men—more or less Christian—used to assemble quickly and assist the keeper to get Aunt Ellen—which was what everybody called her—back into her Victorian Gothic prison. When you think of this drama you must imagine a small figure, transfixed in wonder, standing at one side of the wide movie screen with its back to the camera. Me.

I recall that once, when my mother was haling me off to bed at what I thought an unreasonably early hour, I threw myself on the floor and shouted "Christian men, come and help me!" and my mother was displeased; she said I was not to make fun of Miss Ferguson, who was to be pitied. But it was not my intention to make fun of her; I simply wanted to be like her. She was the most dramatic character in my world, and I accorded her the compliment of imitation.

My family had an insane member of its own, as I suppose many families do. He was a cousin of my mother's who had qualified as a medical doctor, but never practised, because he had fallen in love with a young woman who refused his suit, and he went strange for several months. Doc, as he was always called, was a victim of unrequited love, and you may judge how romantic a family mine was when I say that this was accepted as a perfectly valid reason for losing his wits. He recovered some of them in time, but never fully; he did not work in the ordinary way, but he devoted himself to mechanical and physical experiments, the purpose of which was to discover the principle of perpetual motion. He never found it, but he lived in a houseful of wheels and springs and water engines, seeking for it, until he was almost ninety. He sustained life almost entirely on a diet of oatmeal porridge, and was buried in what was to have been his wedding suit. When I became a writer, he used to secure copies of all my books from the Public Library—because he was extremely tight with his considerable fortune—and would write to me, as each one appeared, a letter that never varied in form. It went:

> Dear Cousin—
> I have read your book
> I presume you know that there are typographical errors
> on the following pages.
> Yr. affct. cousin,
> O.A. Langs

I used sometimes to wish that I could achieve the Nobel Prize, just to see if it would jolt a compliment out of Doc. But alas, he has gone where there are no typographical errors, and I shall never know.

You see that my interest in insanity began early, and it has never abated. When I was at Queen's University I was taught by a psychologist who later achieved a substantial reputation, and who was a wonderful instructor. His name was George Humphrey, and for many years he was Professor of Psychology at Oxford. I sometimes discussed with him an ambition I then held, which was to be a psychiatrist. He advised against it. Be a ditchdigger, he said, or make a profession of pulling up tree stumps with your bare hands, but do not be a psychiatrist; the work is brutally hard, and the rewards are meagre. If you are a psychiatrist you will have to spend many hours each day talking to, and listening to, people whom nobody else can stand. I don't think you have the temperament for it. I heeded his advice, and became an author; the work is brutally hard and the rewards are meagre, but at least you can choose your own company.

Literature, however, only emphasized my concern with madness. Literature is full of it, and it is a matter of endless fascination to me to observe how various authors have dealt with it. Some of them know a great deal about the subject; the concern of others is merely romantic. They use madness to get rid of characters whom they cannot quite persuade themselves to kill. In my time I have read countless novels, usually from the Victorian period, in which characters succumb to an illness called "brain fever," which is usually brought on by overwork of an intellectual kind. Now I understand that there really is a brain fever, more properly called encephalomyelitis, and if I am not mistaken it is truly an inflammation of the brain. But the brain fever of the novelists sounds more like mononucleosis, accompanied by fatigue and depression which, under the care of a Victorian doctor who believed in a low diet, bleeding, and heavy purging, might very well present all kinds of distressing complications. But brain fever was generally invoked by novelists when they wanted to get a character out of the way for an unspecified period of time. Recovery was common; the afflicted person reappeared in the novel, pale and interesting, in time to play his allotted part, which was frequently to reveal a secret known only to himself, which would have brought the novel to an abrupt end if it had been made known too early.

Shakespeare knew a great deal about madness, as he knew about so many things. His most famous madman is unquestionably Hamlet, and the fascination of Hamlet is that we cannot be sure whether he is mad or not. He pretends to madness, certainly, and talks irrationally in order to annoy people he does not like. Sometimes his despair—as for instance when he discovers that Ophelia is acting as an agent for the King and her father, in order to trap him into damaging confessions—verges on madness. When he has killed Polonius he exhibits symptoms that look like madness, but which are really a combination of despair and cunning. We who sit in the audience know that in whatever is of great importance Hamlet is not mad; he is the sanest person in the play. But I need hardly tell such an audience as this that keen insight may alternate with apparently irrational behaviour in people who are under extreme emotional stress, and that to call this madness is altogether too simple a solution to the problem.

The unquestionably mad character in *Hamlet* is Ophelia, and the reasons for her madness are plain: The man she has thought of as her lover rejects her and kills her father. In some modern productions of *Hamlet* it is also suggested that she is pregnant. This seems to me to be quite needless and unjustified. But what is of interest to us here is not the fact that Ophelia is mad, but the means Shakespeare uses to show us that she is so. He chooses a typically Shakespearean device, which is music. Ophelia does not rave, though she says some mystifying things; she sings, and it is the choice of her songs that tells us her story and the emotional confusion that has robbed her of her sanity.

Her songs are sharply contrasted, and have two themes, death and unfaithful love. One seems to spring naturally from her mourning for her father, because we have seen that she was an attached and dutiful daughter—more dutiful, perhaps, than was good for her. The other song is a rowdy piece about seduction, and for a moment we may wonder where such a girl would learn such a song. But as we all know, the most carefully brought up girls come to know things that we might imagine were unsuitable for them, and the song Ophelia sings she might easily have heard soldiers singing in the royal castle of Denmark. It is amazing how much we can forget, however often we are told, whereas a dirty limerick, once heard, clings to the mind like a burr. It satisfies something in us of which we may be ashamed, but which we disown at our peril. Ophelia in her madness displays the most touching pathos linked with a coarseness which is even more touching because it seems to be so much out of character. But is it? I do not need to tell you what jarring and extraordinary elements are to be found in apparently normal human beings.

But I must not tell you what madness is: That would be the grossest impudence on my part. I want to give you some instances of madness in literature, and in this case I am demonstrating the extraordinary art and compression with which Shakespeare has shown us the destruction of a mind, told us the reasons for it, and wrung our hearts in a scene of 219 lines. And how did he do it? With music, primarily, and we know the power of music to evoke feeling without offering tedious justifications. Music was sometimes used in past ages as a palliative for mad people. Probably the most famous patient was Philip V of Spain, who suffered from melancholy depression. Every night for ten years (1736–46) the famous *castrato* singer Farinelli sang the same four songs to the king: We know what they were: he sang them rather more than 3600 times. He saved the king's reason and he received a fee of fifty thousand francs a year. Any of you who have pleasing voices might reflect on this story.

But to return to the case of Ophelia. Was this genius unaided by science, or did Shakespeare know anything specific about madness? I think he knew a good deal of what we might now call the clinical aspect of insanity, because a great deal more was known about madness in his time than we sometimes realize. One of the greatest books on madness that has ever been written in any age was the work of a man who was thirty-nine when Shakespeare died. The book is *The Anatomy of Melancholy* and its author was Robert Burton, an Oxford scholar; it first appeared in 1621, and it ran through five editions in the author's lifetime. Shakespeare, who died in 1616, could not have read it, but if its contents were in the air, so to speak, he might have been aware of much that Burton describes. Sir William Osler called this book "the greatest work on medicine ever written by a layman." Sir William meant that as praise, but I think the book is not the work of a layman; it is the work of a clergyman who was himself seriously affected with what he called melancholy, and what we might nowadays call neurosis; "I write of melancholy," he says, "by being busy to avoid melancholy"; as a neurotic Burton was no amateur; he knew what he was talking about. There is strong suspicion that he died by hanging himself, but I do not see how that would be, for he is buried in the Cathedral at Oxford and I cannot conceive that the Dean and Chapter would permit a suicide to be buried there, especially with a rather showy monument which displays, among other information, the astrological chart of Burton's nativity. I mention the matter of suicide simply to show that Burton was the kind of man about whom such a thing could be said; he was a melancholy man, and everybody knew it.

I am sure that some of you know Burton's book, but I should be surprised if all of you had read it. What has he to say about melancholy? It would be easier to tell you what he does not say about it. The book is long, but none of its admirers—in which number I count myself—think it too long. I first met it when I was twenty, and I read it through; since that time I do not think a year has passed in which I have not reread some substantial portion of it. In the true sense of the word it is a delightful book. Not because it is quaint—though certainly it seems quaint when first one encounters it. Not because it is a repository of all sorts of queer information, obscure belief, and remote classical reference—though some of its charm lies there. Not because it affords us the trashy pleasure of laughing at some unquestionably exploded and absurd ideas—though there are plenty of these. No, the delight of *The Anatomy of Melancholy* lies in its splendidly humane scholarship and penetrating wisdom, which make it a book that is a friend for a lifetime. When I read it now I am not the student who read it when he was twenty, nor am I the man who read it when he was engaged in the often-melancholy work of editing a daily newspaper. I have read it married and unmarried: I have read it when childless, when a father, and when a grandfather, and it has shown something new and valuable to me in these and all my other conditions of life. If I am lucky I shall read it as a very old man, and I am sure I shall find things in it then which elude me now.

But I am growing enthusiastic, and I can see you becoming restless, as you long to be through with me, and rush out to the bookshops to acquire this phoenix among books for yourself. If you do not know it already, be careful, I beg you. Your first acquaintance with the book may be like biting a peach and breaking a tooth on the stone. For one thing, it is a long book. For another, when you open it you will find that it is crammed with quotations in Latin. And you will find the rhythm of it somewhat unfamiliar, for Burton writes headlong, as if he wanted to cram all he could into a single sentence; he roars, he ejaculates, sometimes he seems to stutter. So don't rush at Burton; creep up on him slowly. I told you I read the book through when first

I bought it, but I am a book glutton, and can read anything. You may find that the book has a powerful effect on your vocabulary, and that instead of describing your patients in the proper modern scientific terms, you fall into Burtonese and tell them or their relatives that they are the veriest hare-brains, dizzards, and creatures of wit most dry and adust; if they resent this (as they most certainly will) you may condemn their scurrile and malicious obloquies, flouts, and calumnies, and scorn them as railers and detractors. Because, you see, one of the charms of Burton is that he never uses one word when five or six will do, and his words are of a Jacobean directness and splendour. Like everybody else worth knowing, Burton takes a little getting used to. But once you have fallen under his spell, you are his forever.

Am I recommending mere quaintness, or has he anything to say to the modern psychiatrist—or, as he would say, mad doctor? Yes, he has everything to say to you. Read him with care and you will find the basic ideas of Freud and Jung set before you in seventeenth-century terms. You will find recipes for drug therapy. The *Anatomy* is divided into three principal partitions, each of which is, in its turn, divided into sections, members, and subsections. The first part deals with the causes and symptoms of melancholy; part two tells of the cure of melancholy; part three deals particularly with love melancholy and religious melancholy. There is much in the book which is at present unfashionable, and about which we may fittingly be reminded. For instance, Burton pays detailed attention to jealousy as a cause of melancholy. Jealousy is much out of fashion; we do not hear it mentioned as a factor in professional life, or the world of business, or as an element in politics. Where is the modern critic, either in the arts or in the sciences, who will admit that jealousy plays any part in his judgments? Is this because jealousy has suddenly and mysteriously disappeared from our world? Is it, of all sins, the one we have conquered and banished? I do not think so. But when did you last hear jealousy mentioned as the mainspring of any mean action, or plot, or public or private attack? Read Burton on jealousy, and be refreshed.

Indeed, read Burton on almost anything. Dr. Samuel Johnson said that this was the only book that ever took him out of bed two hours sooner than he intended to rise. Sir William Osler, who was a good bookman as well as a good doctor, delighted in Burton. So, if you do not know him already, let me introduce you to this great master of your healing art. Let me offer a word of advice, however: If you are not thoroughly proficient in Latin, begin with the Everyman edition, which has translations of all the Latin passages included in the text. It makes the going very much easier.

I introduced Burton because he was for thirty-nine years of his life a contemporary of Shakespeare. There is no evidence that they knew each other, but the writer of *King Lear* would have been much at home with the writer of *The Anatomy of Melancholy*, and as they both understood jealousy to the uttermost depths of that powerful and destructive passion I am sure that they could have exchanged fruitful opinions about it.

I leave Burton only because I want to talk for a few minutes about the frequency with which we meet with scenes of madness in the theatre. The dramatists of an earlier day saw madmen in the streets—the Bethlehem men, as they were called, because they were in a sense outpatients of the Hospital of St. Mary of Bethlehem in London, commonly called Bedlam. They wandered about in search of charity, and it is to the credit of mankind that they seem to have found it. Indeed, they were often accorded a special indulgence because it has for centuries, and in many lands, been a belief among simple people that madmen speak truth. It was as truth speakers that Bedlamites often appeared in the drama of the seventeenth and eighteenth centuries. But the dramatists knew something that has always been acknowledged, though never trumpeted abroad, among the medical profession. That was that gross insanity among the poor and unfortunate becomes neurosis, or oddity, or eccentricity among those who are more fortunately placed in society. To be poor, and mad, is utter misery: To be mad, but to have well-to-do friends or family, is still misery, but it is not usually so gross in its manifestations. If you want to know what the eighteenth century thought of moneyed madness, look at Congreve's comedy *Love for Love*, in which young Valentine Legend pretends to be mad, because he is unlucky in love, and unlucky in money, as well. His disguise of madness makes it possible for him to speak truth as no man in his right mind would dare to do.

That is a comedy. But there is much madness in the tragedy of this era, as well. One of the greatest unjustly neglected tragedies in English is Otway's *Venice Preserv'd*, written in 1682—forty-two years after Burton died. It is neglected now, I think, because during the Victorian era it was not fully understood. It is essentially a tragedy of homosexual love, in which a man stakes his whole life, including the wife whom he dearly loves, in order to prove himself to a male friend as a worthy partner in a conspiracy to overthrow a government. The woman, whose name is Belvidera, suffers horribly in this dreadful predicament, and at the end of the play she loses her reason; in the final desperately affecting scene we see her torn between the ghosts of her husband and the man whose esteem he values even above her affection. It is great tragedy, and its greatness owes much to the sufferings of its author, who spent a part of his life in the most painful subjection to a woman whom he loved to the pitch of madness, and who did not love him. I do not need to tell such an audience as this what that sort of love implies—a love which is in fact a bondage to an ideal that has nothing to do with the woman upon whom it is projected. The drama of the inner life is not something that has been discovered within the past century, as some people appear to think, and the complexities of homosexuality did not appear on the world stage at the end of the reign of Queen Victoria.

The tragedy of the seventeenth and eighteenth centuries abounds in mad scenes, and where there is tragedy there will also be comedy. The greatest comic mad scene in English drama, in my opinion, is in Sheridan's farce *The Critic*. The heroine, Tilburina, is crossed in love—precisely like my cousin, whom you will remember—and as the author observes, she comes in stark mad in white satin. A friend says, "Why in white satin?", to which the author replies, very properly, "O Lord, sir, when a heroine goes mad she always goes into white satin!" And Tilburina has her great mad speech, which was one of the things a leading actress demanded of a leading part. Here it is—

> The wind whistles—the moon rises—see,
> They have killed my squirrel in his cage!
> Is this a grasshopper!—Ha! no, it is my
> Whiskerandos—you shall not keep him—
> I know you have him in your pocket—
> An oyster maybe crossed in love! Who says
> A whale's a bird?—Ha, did you call, my love?
> —He's here! He's here!—He's everywhere!
> Ah me! He's nowhere!

And the author inquires, with satisfaction, "There, did you ever see anybody madder than that? You observe how she mangled the meter?" To which his friend replies, "Yes, egad, it was the first thing made me suspect she was out of her senses." There were many serious mad scenes in eighteenth-century plays that were not very different from that one. But by the end of the eighteenth century we had seen the end of the exploitation of madness for comic effect; during the nineteenth century it was regarded much more solemnly—which is not the same thing as taking it quite seriously.

The nineteenth century was pre-eminently an era of Romance in drama, poetry, and the novel, and the approach of the age to madness was deeply romantic. The squalor and destructiveness of lunacy were overlooked. Romance was itself often equated with madness, and a characteristic attitude is that of Matthew Gregory Lewis, who describes Romance as a "fair enchantress"; one seeks her among

> … graves new-opened, or midst dungeons damp,
> Drear forests, ruin'd aisles and haunted towers,
> Forlorn she roves, and raves away the hours!

A very pretty picture, but it suggests a woman not so much mad as delightfully and self-indulgently melancholy. The figure of the beautiful lunatic—always female and young—is a common one in all romantic works. Where it arose, I cannot tell you, but it seems contrary to the experience of those who know most about the insane, and who do not find that insanity is a beautifier—is, indeed, quite the opposite. But now and during the nineteenth century common sense and common observation assert themselves, as they do in Charlotte Bronte's *Jane Eyre.* The description of the mad Mrs. Rochester in that book is not glamourized, and the horrible moment when the heroine wakes from sleep and finds the madwoman looking down at her, about to set fire to the bed curtains, is brilliantly described, but in well-controlled terms.

I should like, however, to direct your attention to a nineteenth-century writer whose name may be strange to many of you. Indeed, I find it is strange to all but inveterate book gluttons like myself. His name is Henry Cockton, and he was not a very good writer; my amateur diagnosis of him, from reading several of his books, is that he was even more paranoid than authors generally are. His books abound in plots, schemes, treachery, and double-dealing, all on a strictly domestic scale. His heroes and heroines are rather disagreeable people, though he obviously wants us to like them. One of them is a tedious practical joker, whose name is Valentine Vox, and as you might guess, he is a ventriloquist, and uses his gift to make a thorough nuisance of himself. But it is not the jokes of *Valentine Vox the Ventriloquist* that interest us now, but the subplot of the story, which is about a man named Grimwood Goodman, whose relatives imprison him in a private lunatic asylum in order to get control of his money.

Would you believe that possible? It was quite possible in 1840, when the book appeared. In those days anybody in England could be committed to a private asylum if two medical practitioners certified him insane. Medical practitioners might mean apothecaries, and it was not even necessary for both of them to see the patient at the same time. The means by which Mr. Goodman is spirited away seem farcical, but they were founded on fact; two medical men visited him, tormented him with questions as to whether or not he claimed kinship with Queen Victoria, and drove the irascible man to such a pitch of rage that he ordered them out of his house; very soon afterward he was picked up in the street by two toughs, and whisked away to Dr. Holdem's private asylum, certified insane and violent by the two doctors who had provoked him. Dr. Holdem is a splendid character, described as having a fiendlike smile—an invaluable possession for any psychiatrist, as I am sure you will admit. Once inside, how was Goodman to get out? The attendants included bruisers who took care of any complaints from patients and any attempts at escape. There were officials, also medical men, who were called Commissioners in Lunacy, whose task it was to visit such private asylums periodically, and inspect them. But when the Commissioners were expected Dr. Holdem had Mr. Goodman strapped down, and one of his assistants tickled the poor man's feet while the Doctor repeatedly asked him whether or not he had received a letter from the Emperor—no mention of which Emperor—recently. At last, to be released from torture, Goodman admitted to receiving such a letter, and when the Commissioners arrived, Dr. Holdem displayed poor Goodman to them, with the information that he had said that he had received a letter from the Emperor the day before. Perfectly simple, and quite horrible. Quite true, what is more, for the painstaking Cockton declared publicly that every outrage he described in his book he could swear had happened at a private asylum within forty miles of London. The book, though no great work of art, was instrumental in bringing about some reform of this abuse, though private asylums were a scandal in England for a long time afterward.

Valentine Vox contains a beautiful lunatic, by the way. She is kept in a special part of the madhouse, which is described as a "den," and from which Goodman hears "harsh screams and bitter imprecations." So dreadful are these that he supposes the inmate of the den must be a raving maniac "whose former life had been spent among the vilest and most degraded." Not at all. Her case resembles Ophelia's. She is "a fair girl, whose skin was as pure as alabaster, and whose hair hung luxuriantly down her back in flaxen ringlets." Nevertheless, she was "running round, shouting, screaming and uttering the most dreadful imprecations that ever proceeded from the lips of the most vicious of her sex." It emerges that this girl has been locked up in the madhouse because she is an heiress who is a nuisance to her relatives. But what is perhaps most interesting about her to such an audience as this is contained in this very brief exchange between Goodman and one of the keepers. "The character of her disease," he says, "is I suppose, very dreadful?" And the keeper replies: "No: there ain't much the matter with her; she only wants a husband." The theory of the sexual origin of neurosis was not so original with Sigmund Freud as we may have been led to believe. Indeed, he learned of it from J.M. Charcot, and as Cockton implies, it was part of the mythology of madness many decades earlier.

Not all nineteenth-century asylums were as dreadful as this. Bernard Shaw had an uncle who ended his days in an asylum, where the young Shaw and his father sometimes visited him. Upon these occasions he would not speak, or show any sign of recognition, until they were about to leave. Then he would take up his flute—for music was his great solace—and play "Home, Sweet Home." A typically Irish story. But it demonstrates the fact that Shaw's uncle was contented and well cared for where he was, and perhaps had lost his taste for family life.

I do not want to weary you with detailed information about books in which insane people occur; my purpose, indeed, is simply to throw out a few hints as to books you might like to read if you are curious to discover what literary people have thought about madness. There is one modern novel which you should certainly not neglect, if your curiosity reaches so far. It is *The Ordeal of Gilbert Pinfold* by the late Evelyn Waugh. It appeared in 1957, and it is a classic of its kind. What gives it unusual interest is that it describes experiences which the author himself underwent during a period of stress in his life, and these are described with an economy and eloquence which I dare say are uncommon among the case histories your profession requires you to read. People of great talent have sometimes been mad, but only rarely have they written about it.

In 1954 Waugh was in bad shape, and in search of better health he went on a voyage to the Mediterranean and Ceylon. He had suffered disquieting symptoms, and on board ship they became worse. He heard voices in the night, calling his name, and jeering at him; he became aware of plots against his peace and even against his life; he suspected that the cables he sent home from the ship were being delayed by the radio officer, and circulated among the passengers for their amusement. His predicament is funny, and it is also horrible, because we know that Waugh underwent this confusion himself. His reason was not in good order, and his troubles were aggravated by the fact that he was taking massive doses of several sorts of medicine. He was taking some very strong pills for his rheumatism, and because he could not sleep he was taking a mixture of bromide and chloral; as it was ineffective he doubled and trebled his dosage. To quiet the nagging of his nerves he drank large quantities of port, gin, and brandy. More—he drank far more crème de menthe than most of us could possibly choke down, because he liked it. Let me repeat that these terrible dosings were not the cause of his doubtful sanity; they were little frills and arabesques which he added to it. The miracle is that he was able to write such a brilliant book as *Pinfold*, which I do not think has ever been equalled as a description of a man whose reason remains active, although the information on which it is acting is delusory. If you have not read it, read it. I do not suppose that you get many patients like Evelyn Waugh, but it can do you no harm to recognize the possibility.

I cannot pretend that I have done more than touch lightly on some of the high spots in the immense range of literature which deals with insanity. I have not spoken of writers who were acknowledged to be insane but whose work was of rare beauty—such poets as Christopher Smart in the eighteenth century, whose "A Song to David" I commend to you; and John Clare in the nineteenth century, whose poem "Written in Northampton County Asylum" is of a terrible pathos. I have not mentioned Thomas De Quincey's *Confessions of an English Opium Eater*, which is one of the great literary accounts of an addiction persisted in to the point of madness. I have said nothing of William Blake, a very great visionary poet who seemed mad to many of his contemporaries. I have purposely said nothing about my own novels, in which quite a lot of madness and borderline madness occurs, and occurs in a way which particularly interests me—that is, madness as, just possibly, a means of perceiving another sort of being from which something of great value may be learned. My most recent work is a trilogy in which a madwoman is one of the central characters because, although she is demonstrably insane, her insanity releases trains of thought and feeling in other people which are immensely fruitful. This is the way an author may look at unreason. I know it cannot be your way, but I think it has its purpose, for anything that coaxes us out of the beaten paths of thinking and feeling has value, and also presents us with great dangers.

I hope, however, that I have persuaded some of you that your work is not solely clinical, but has links with the world of art. A neurosis, as Dr. Freud often reminds us, is a form of creation—not the best kind, or an especially attractive kind, but undoubtedly one kind. And I hope that I have persuaded some of you that you are not the only people who look long and hard at insanity. Writers do so, too. Very often they think of it in relation to their own work. Thomas Mann, especially, wrote brilliantly about the relationship of art to madness, and of art to criminality. This is a direction in which several writers have tried to follow him. Of course some of them are silly and trivial, but not all. As Jung once said, the writer may see out of the corner of his eye what the grave clinician misses. And if I have trodden on anybody's toes, or seemed to intrude, as a layman, where I should have kept my distance, I can only say what Robert Burton says in *The Anatomy: Nemo aliquid recognoscat, nos mentimur omnia.* That is to say, let no one take these things to himself, they are all but fiction.

Youth

20

Ham and Tongue

The following speech was given for The Cosmos Club of Washington, D.C., a distinguished group with a special interest in Literature, on April 6, 1977.

When I was asked to speak to you tonight I inquired, as speakers always do, what you wanted me to talk about. The first answer was the most daunting that can possibly be made to such a question: It was "Feel at liberty to talk about anything you please." Such an answer, so obviously intended as a courtesy, springing from a high-bred assumption that anything that came into my head would necessarily be welcome to such an audience as this, had the effect of driving every possible theme out of my mind. Or rather, to be more truthful, of driving out of my mind any theme upon which anyone could possibly wish to hear an after-dinner speech. Ponderous themes, depressing themes, themes so minatory as to partake of the character of prophecy suggested themselves to me, only to be dismissed with disgust and sinking spirits. But at last the idea came to me: "Why not talk about making speeches? Why is it done, and how is it done?"

The more I thought about that subject, the more it appealed to me. There are, I believe, something like three hundred millions of people on this continent at this moment. I have added a few additional millions, to include visitors from abroad who are here for the express purpose of making speeches. I estimate very roughly that of those three hundred millions, at least three hundred thousand are on their feet at this moment, talking to various groups drawn from the others. Speech-making is one of the principal pursuits of the Western World, but although everybody does it, nobody seems to talk about how it is done. We have keen critics of the techniques of all sports and pastimes, but who criticizes the technique of the speaker? Every art—drama, music, painting—comes under the reducing lens of the critic, except the art of making speeches. Literature, even on the lowest levels, is the fodder for thousands of critics, and the subject of countless graduate-school theses, but the body of a public speech is rarely examined as if it were a literary creation. The content of a speech is frequently chewed over, but the manner in which it is delivered and the circumstances of its delivery go undiscussed. One wonders why.

In part, I think, it is because there is a widespread belief that a public speaker is a more or less inspired creature, who is making up what he says as he goes along, and that he should not be held accountable for his grammatical muddles, his inaccurate facts, and his uncouth delivery. In my lifetime I have seen the growth of what might be called The North American Myth of Sincerity, a myth which suggests that anything that is done skilfully, or with accomplishment, is of less worth than what is botched. This Myth applies very strongly to the public speaker; the botcher is thought to be a worthy fellow, who is searching his soul for every word that falls maimed and bleeding from his lips. The reality is otherwise; sincerity can be as much a mannerism as anything else, and I am always suspicious of speakers who appear to be struggling for every sentence. They are frequently crooks, who have mastered their barbarous style just as, in an earlier day, they would have mastered the elements of rhetoric.

In my boyhood I heard many speakers of that earlier day, who prided themselves upon being spellbinders and silver-tongued orators. I have heard speakers of whom it was said—the remark was by no means original, but it never failed to give pleasure—that when they were infants the bees had clustered round their cradles, to sip the honey from their lips. In retrospect, I wonder if any bee ever came back for a second sip. They were very strong on manner, those spellbinders, but they were no better stocked with matter than their less gaudy contemporaries. At the time I heard them, their day was passing. The Age of Sincerity was dawning; I hope that I may live to see the sun set on the Sincere Speaker. There is only one way to make a speech, and that is to have something to say, and to say it as clearly as you can, in a fashion that does not insult or patronize your hearers. Easy to say: not in the least easy to do. Nor is the fault all with the speakers. The passion for public speaking that possesses us on this continent, the unquenchable thirst for everything from full-scale oratory to what is misleadingly called "a few words," makes public speakers of thousands who would do better to remain silent, and drives those who have some knack for speaking to speak altogether too much.

Consider the situation in which we find ourselves. I am greatly complimented to have been asked to speak to you; I am delighted to be here. But common decency compels me to recognize that you would be far better off if you were being entertained by a first-rate conjuror, or a talented clown, or perhaps even by a ventriloquist. There was a time when this fact was given due consideration. When I was a boy I used often to go with my parents to political rallies, where candidates for Parliament appealed for votes. Those men were no fools. They included in their entourage an entertainer, who put the audience in a good mood. After the entertainer had delighted us with his comic songs and his imitation of a Red Indian reciting "The Charge of the Light Brigade," we were softened up for the political address. As a boy, I had no vote; if I had been enfranchised, I should unhesitatingly have voted for the entertainer. I learned a lesson at those meetings, and it was this: If you haven't got a professional entertainer on your side, you should do your best to be entertaining in your own person.

I put this lesson into practice at an early age. At my school many prizes were offered, and two I regarded as my personal property; they were the prize for reading aloud, and the prize for public speaking. I sought them, not for glory, but for money. Each contest carried a prize of a finely bound book but, in addition, the right to buy twenty-five dollars' worth of books. Fifty dollars! It was the riches of Ali Baba in a day when a very good book could be bought for three dollars and fifty cents. The unappeasable lust for books which has been one of the glories and the nuisances of my life made it absolutely obligatory for me to get that money. How? Other boys had similar ambitions. But I had a degree of low cunning that was beyond my years, and I reduced the arts of reading and speaking to a formula drawn from the world of the sandwich-maker. It was, very simply, Ham and Tongue.

How well I remember those school contests! My rivals, who were fine boys and have since grown up to be fine men, went in very heavily for Sincerity. They knew where the wellspring of sincerity was; it resided in their fathers. They would admit, though of course not to the judges of the contest, that they had received some help from their fathers in preparing their speeches. In consequence the physician's son was apt to harass the audience with addresses on Man's Struggle Against the Common Cold, and the chartered accountant's son pontificated on Municipal Taxation—Whither? They shouted and waved their fists; the cords in their necks stood out with strain. But I was not a fine boy; looking back, I think I must have been rather a horrid boy, because I adopted a conversational manner, cracked a lot of jokes, and sometimes—I blush to recall—made fun of the other speakers. These were very probably the promptings of the Evil One, but the Evil One was a good friend to me, and I always got the fifty dollars.

I think that the Evil One must have whispered something to the Headmaster of the school as well, because during my time he changed the rules, and demanded that the speeches be extemporary, on subjects drawn from a list he prepared himself. The experts on the Common Cold and Municipal Taxation were flummoxed. But Ham and Tongue carried me through. My affectation of naturalness was precisely that—an affectation; my apparently conversational delivery was in fact quite a loud, carefully articulated yell; I could make myself heard over a brass band.

The Headmaster's purpose in changing the rules was to give us some experience of thinking on our feet. And so it did. It could not, however, do much for a boy who never by any chance thought in any other posture. Personally, I mistrust the notion of thinking on one's feet; I have known many speakers who prided themselves on that ability, and I am sorry to say that many of them were blatherers; they did not know when to stop. This took me some time to realize, because my father was a great admirer of these extemporary speakers; it was the fashion of his day to value length of oratory, and he exulted over political figures who could hold forth for two hours, without a note. My father particularly stressed this: "Without a note!" he would cry, fixing me with a glowing eye. So when my turn came, I naturally tried to speak without notes, but I soon found that it was not for me. Not merely notes, but a prepared script was what I liked. Of course I did not know it, but I was part of a movement toward the prepared speech, with a typescript for the assistance of reporters who cannot write shorthand.

The prepared script also has its dangers. Politicians were probably the first to discover that the script might as well be prepared by somebody else. But no—I wrong them; credit for that discovery belongs to the clergy. Politicians—slapdash fellows with a boundless faith in the gullibility of mankind—all too often gave speeches which were as new to them as to the audience, and not infrequently they came upon words that were unfamiliar to them and ideas that surprised them.

I know all about that. My own political career was a very quiet one: I was a backroom literary hack. I recall writing a series of broadcast speeches for a political aspirant whose fame had been gained as a professional hockey player. Nothing could persuade him to look at his speech before going on the air, and although I did my level best to write in his own style and vocabulary, such as it was, every now and then he would gag over something—a subordinate clause, or a crumb of unfamiliar punctuation—and reveal himself in all his pitiable insufficiency. Once I gave him a joke, and that was a very great miscalculation, because the cast of his mind was not jocular. Having uttered the joke, and being dimly aware that something untoward had happened, he tried—if I may so express it—to suck the joke back out of the microphone. His committee were displeased with me, but as they were not paying me anything and I was writing simply out of political loyalty, I could afford to ignore their huffing and puffing.

Another experience as a political ghost writer found me preparing speeches for a man who had been, thirty years earlier, a modest success as a baseball player. He was convinced that his small fame was still resounding in the minds of the youth of the day, and he kept urging me to get it into the speeches. "Tell them I'm a straight shooter," he would say. So I did, but without conviction, for he was so plainly not a shooter at all; he was a magazine of blanks, and he lost the election. He seemed to think that I was a contributing cause. You cannot make a Demosthenes out of an old ballplayer; you cannot even cloak him in the grey mantle of Phoney Sincerity. If he has no conception of Ham and Tongue, you are beaten, and so is he.

When I speak of Ham, I hope that you do not think I recommend a grossly histrionic style of delivery. That used to be popular. There were speakers who wept, speakers who were immense in their indignation, speakers who were hugely sarcastic. At the very bottom of the list came the speakers who told funny stories.

A funny story is, in itself, a good thing, but we have not the appetite for them that existed in our grandfathers. Their taste now seems to us to be gross; their delight in stories involving dialect or racial characteristics is out of fashion. But there was a day when a speaker who rose to his feet and declared that the situation in which he found himself reminded him of the Scotchman, the Irishman, and the Jew who went to a funeral could hold an audience in the palm of his hand. Scotchmen, Irishmen, and Jews were all, by definition, funny, but the real gold of the story lay in the funeral. In Canada forty years ago funerals were surefire.

Let me recall one of these rib-binders. A Scotchman was attending the funeral of his wife, and when the ceremony was concluded, and everyone had left the graveyard, he was to be seen standing by the grave, looking into it with a countenance set in what might have been taken for deep grief. A friend approached him, and said, gently: "Well, Jock, so Margaret's gone." "Aye," said the bereaved husband. "She was always a good wife to you," said the friend. "Aye, so she was for fifty years and more," said the widower and then, after a moment's reflection, "but ye ken I never really likit the wumman."

I have seen that joke throw an audience into paroxysms. Scotchmen and their wives nudged one another in ecstasy and slapped one another's thighs as they laughed at it. Irishmen and Jews laughed, at the same time wondering how they could adapt the story to their own races. But of course that was out of the question; there was something resolutely Scotch about it, and you could no more change it than you could hope to bleach a piece of tartan.

All of these modes of oratory depended heavily on Ham, that quality of histrionism without which a public speech is as piffle before the wind. Ham is out of favour in our age of sincerity, except for the assumption of fake modesty of which I have already spoken. When I left the world of journalism to become a university professor I quickly discovered that Ham was nowhere so deplored as in the academic world. The professor who calls upon the arts of rhetoric and oratory to make his students pay attention quickly wins a name as a charlatan. I have always been glad of my twenty years in the newspaper world, because it taught me many useful things, and one of them is that the public has no particular objection to a charlatan if he does not overstep the bounds of modesty and artistic restraint. Better the charlatan you can hear than the sincere scholar who lulls you to sleep with a sound like the moan of doves in immemorial elms. My own education was prolonged and various, and my best professors were all hams.

I recall with particular affection a Scotsman who was lecturing about the Romantic Poets; he was trying to give us some understanding of the stress of soul and intolerable pressure of imagination that made those men great, and I suppose we looked uncomprehending. He paused, and walked to the window, and looked out at the snowy landscape for perhaps a full minute, and then he said, in a sorrowful voice: "I don't suppose there is one of you mutts who has the slightest idea what I'm talking about." What happened? Did we rise in indignation? Did we rush to his office and burn his library, and demand that he apologize on his knees before we would consent to hear another word? No; we sat up straight and listened very hard and loved him forever after. About two weeks ago I sent a contribution to a fund to create a scholarship in his name. Greater love hath no student than this: that he lay out hard cash to memorialize a dead professor.

That was Ham. What about Tongue?

To me, it is almost wholly a matter of vocabulary. We have all met those excitable, exuberant people who assure us that they just love words. People who just love words too often delight in the showy siftings of the dictionary. I would rather listen to somebody who loved meanings better than words themselves, a speaker who would remain silent rather than use a word he did not truly know. People who just love words are all too often the people who talk about "meaningful interface," and spend a lot of time on "marginal variables" whenever they set out upon an "in-depth overview." Doubtless these expressions have some original meaning, but as the people who just love words use them they are gaudy toys, bearing the same relationship to a perceptible meaning that a Christmas tree ornament bears to a fine jewel.

The true word-lover must be constantly on the alert to changes in language. When I was a young man at Oxford I took heed of the fate that befell an American friend of mine, who was reprimanded on his oral examination because he dearly loved the word *motivate* and used it often. The examiner who rebuked him was an old man, who explained courteously and patiently—but oh, the courtesy and patience of Oxford can burn like a refiner's fire!—that the word had no respectable ancestry, that it could not be derived from Latin and had sneaked into the language from France and Germany; it was a low word which my friend would do well to scrub from his tongue with acid. I took warning by my friend's experience, and I shrink from "motivate" still. But much time has passed; "motivate" is now in the *Oxford English Dictionary* and I have become a fossil, in this respect at least. My recollection of this incident makes me cautious about rebuking my own pupils when they say "prestigious" when they mean "distinguished." To me "prestigious" means, and always will mean, juggling tricks, because it derives from *praestigiae*, and when it is used in the modern way I feel as though a rusty sword had been thrust into my—well, not perhaps into my heart, but into some sensitive part of my body. But I do not want to parade as a conservator of endangered species in the world of words. Let the unlettered yahoos ravish the language; what do I care? But I refuse to join in the gangbang.

I refuse for what I consider a good reason. I am not one of those tedious people who writes to the papers correcting other correspondents about English usage. No, my concern is that of a writer, and on occasion a formal speaker, who wants to be as careful and even pernickety about meanings as he can. Without precision of meaning we damage not simply language, but thought. The language we share is beautiful and alarmingly complex. Try as we may, we are all likely to make mistakes, and very few among us can claim to know the English language in perfection. But we can try.

A humbling lesson for me came about a few years ago when I had an Oriental student of great promise who was terribly worried about English idiom. Blithely I undertook to help him, and we set to work to go right through Fowler's *Modern English Usage*, I to explain and he to learn. It was not long before I was over my head in difficulties and my Japanese friend was in gales of laughter. I was embarrassed because of my ignorance and he was embarrassed because it was wholly against his code to laugh at a professor. What do you say when someone asks: "Why do they say 'Let's drink toast,' when they are drinking wine? What does it mean, 'By hook or by crook?'" But we managed to laugh our way through from A to Z with great benefit to us both; the difference is that he has remembered most of what we learned, whereas I have lapsed into my old bad habits. To this day I cannot be sure when I should use "that" and when I should use "which," but my secretary knows, and between us we keep up some sort of pretence.

It is the idioms that ensnare us, and never so fatally as when we have learned them by ear rather than by the eye. Some years ago I was being introduced at a dinner where I was to make a speech, and the man who had undertaken this dangerous work had the easy fluency of a politician. Having told his hearers my age—which is something about which all audiences feel an unseemly curiosity—and all the jobs I had held, he announced solemnly: "Mr. Davies is a man of many faucets." There was a little coarse laughter, but most of the audience looked at me with new respect.

Ham and Tongue are the essentials of public speaking, and ideally they should be balanced in roughly equal quantity. Shakespeare supplied a splendid object lesson in the Forum Scene in *Julius Caesar*. The first speaker is Marcus Brutus, and he is a skilled rhetorician; schoolmasters and professors delight in demonstrating how finely balanced is his address to the mob. But Brutus was wholly a patrician; he was too much a gentleman to stoop to emotional appeals. The second speaker of the day, as you recall, was Mark Antony. He was no mean rhetorician, but in addition to Tongue he had a splendid endowment of Ham, and we all know what happened. Brutus won respect, but Antony started a riot.

Now I must make a confession. It is many months since I was invited to speak to you, and in the interval several letters have passed between your club and myself. It was in one of the earliest of these that the suggestion was made that I speak about any subject that took my fancy, and a few weeks ago I fished that letter out of my files and set to work. Not until I was well launched did another letter work its way up through the debris on my desk, asking me to speak about my books. What was I to do? Should I discard Ham and Tongue, and prepare a new speech? That would have been the proper course of action, but for some time I have hankered to talk in a public speech about public speaking, and I could not quite persuade myself to give up the chance. So I decided to do both, and now I am going to talk for a while about my books, and then, I understand, we are to have a period of questions.

It is a queer business, being an author, and I do not fit into any of the well-known categories. To begin with, I never meant to be one. I did not, as a child, write stories; I greatly preferred to read them. Later, in my schooldays, I wrote verses—I do not regard them as poetry—because my school had a prize for the best poem written every year. I wanted that money, because it was awarded not in cash, but in a credit on a bookshop. Other boys wrote from the heart; very frequently they wrote about girls. The girls I knew were not very good subjects for poetry, because they laughed a lot, and poetry addressed to themselves would have put them into fits. So I wrote about my school, and instead of writing with the kind of poetic freedom that was popular at the time, I wrote in heroic couplets. I knew that I had only the slightest lyric feeling, but I was a demon on technique, and I could mint a couple of dozen couplets, given time and hot chocolate, which was the favourite tipple of my Muse. I always won, and I know now that it was morally wrong that I should have won. A boy who had bled a bad lyric was a poet, even if a bad poet, and I was just a deft cabinetmaker, a technician. Here again the Evil One stood at my elbow, but in my defence I must add that he seems to have been at the elbow of the judges, as well, and made them prefer technique to passion.

What I really wanted to do was to write plays. And I did. And most of them have been acted, and some of them have been acted several times. But until quite recently, being a playwright in Canada was uphill work, and there was no money in it whatever. Like most persistent playwrights, I eventually achieved some productions abroad, and even joined the grey, inglorious army of those who have failed on Broadway, but I knew that there must be some other, more effective way of grabbing the public by the windpipe and making it listen to what I had to say. So I tried my hand at writing a novel, and lo! it worked. Of course all the critics of novels said that I wrote like a playwright; now that my novels are reasonably well-known, and because I still write plays, the critics are apt to say that I write plays like a novelist. Critics, of course, have no such problems; they all write a peevish, falsely jocose prose which, like all literary styles, is a mirror of their souls.

The novels of mine which have been most warmly received are the three last to appear; they are called *Fifth Business*, *The Manticore*, and *World of Wonders*. They are usually referred to as a trilogy, and I am quite in agreement with that, but honesty demands that I say that I never meant to write a trilogy. I wrote one book about three men, and it was well liked, especially by a large and generous group of readers in the United States. But I still had things to say about another of the men who was essential to the story, so I wrote a second book. It was never my intention to follow it with a third, but at last I did so, because the matter of the third book was still troubling me, and there was only one way to get it out of my mind. But there was no planned trilogy, I assure you.

Why did people like it? I think it is because I have discovered, over the course of the years, what I am. I have already told you that as a boy I was without the fervour that inspired my rivals in the public-speaking contests. I have confessed without a blush that I am no poet. But I seem to have emerged as a moralist; my novels are a moralist's novels.

It sounds dreadful, does it not? But if we are faithful to that careful use of words that I was talking about earlier, we quickly set aside the notion that a moralist is a sad creature who points to the right as the rest of mankind rush blindly to the left. A moralist is one who looks at human conduct with as clear an eye as he can manage, and says what he sees, drawing, now and then, a few tentative conclusions. He is not necessarily someone who beats the drum for a particular code of conduct, someone who rebukes what he believes to be sin, someone who looks down on people who are driven by passion, craving, or fear. But if passion, craving, or fear are what ail them, he will not pretend that it is otherwise. He is compassionate but he strives not to be deluded.

Of course he will be driven now and then to come to a few conclusions, but he will be cautious about giving them a too general application. He will observe that quite often people reap what they have sown. If he is honest he will admit that it is sometimes very difficult to know what they have sown, or to be certain about what the harvest is.

That is the principal theme of my trilogy. I began it because for many years I had been troubled by a question: To what extent is a man responsible for the outcome of his actions, and how early in life does the responsibility begin? I concluded, not without long debate, that it began with life itself, and that a child was as responsible as anyone else if it chose a course of action knowingly. In *Fifth Business*, in the first few lines, a boy makes a choice: He wants to hurt his companion, so he throws a snowball at him, and in the snowball is a stone. The snowball hits somebody else—a woman who is brought to bed prematurely of a child whose struggle for life is long and heroic. The consequences of the snowball with the stone in it continue for sixty years, and do much to shape the lives of three men, and in a lesser way to influence the lives of many people whom they encounter. One man becomes a speculative scholar with a touch of the saint about him: one man lives a sensual, self-serving life and dies, at the age of seventy, because he is suddenly faced with the reality—or one of the realities—of what he is: the third man lives heroically, in the sense that his life is a struggle against severe odds, and achieves a queer kind of fame. Any of the three is a man whom we might like, or detest, if we met him casually. All three are, in various ways, liars. All three do some good in the world and some evil. But it is in the inner life that one is almost a saint, one a failure, and one a hero.

Because I do not think it part of a novelist's task to bamboozle and puzzle his readers, the novels are written in a fashion that makes them seem to be simpler than in fact they are. I strive to write as clearly as I can. Because of this limpid quality in the prose some readers think they have understood what in fact they have missed. Teachers ask young people to read the books who are not really ready for them, and the results are sometimes amusing. A couple of weeks ago a very nice young man of seventeen came to see me because he had to write an essay about this trilogy, and when he appeared he was equipped with a list of questions. He fired the first one at me as soon as he sat down. "What do you consider the chief structural weakness in your trilogy?" he said. I looked him in the eye and said: "I don't think it has any structural weakness; I think it's just great." He was not prepared for that; his teacher was training him for criticism, and of the monstrous vanity of the artist he knew nothing. But he was a nice boy and he said: "Well, you see, there's no unifying theme that runs through all three books." "Is that so?" said I, and suggested that the theme of the single action that bore results for sixty years might meet his need. He had not noticed that, but he was very severe with me about my unhappy proneness to coincidence, which was, he said, not like life. But, I countered, "This is a novel; if you want life, you can find it on the street, and an incoherent mess it will be; a novel is a work of art, not *cinéma vérité*. And I am an artist, not a child with a Kodak and a tape recorder." We parted on very good terms, and I was so bold as to suggest that his teacher might not be doing him a favour by making him take novels apart with a critical apparatus of the approximate delicacy of a wrecking iron.

These teachers are a queer lot. A few years ago a whole class of high school students came to see me to talk about my work. I explained to them that I wrote first of all to entertain my readers, but that I did not think that entertainment was necessarily trivial, and that I had been lucky in finding readers who wanted to be entertained just as deeply and seriously as lay in my power. But the teacher who was with the class would have none of that; he knew where my weakness lay. He demanded if my books were not sometimes funny. I admitted that I certainly hoped that was so. Then he moved in for the kill. He demanded, sternly, "Don't you think your use of humour will keep your books from living?"

It was hard to reply because the question opened up so many unexpected realms of speculation. For one thing, it had never occurred to me to wonder whether my books would live or not; I was simply pleased to get them born and before the public. But then—"your use of humour." What did he mean? It was spoken as if he suspected me of injecting myself with humour, as with some vile drug, and, then sitting down with peals of maniac laughter to write so long as the fix lasted, without a prudent regard for my claim on immortality, which notoriously wants no truck with humour. I don't know what I said. He stopped me cold.

It was because I have never consciously "used" humour in my life. Such humour as I may have is one of the elements in which I live. I cannot recall a time when I was not conscious of the deep, heaving, rolling ocean of hilarity that lies so very near the surface of life in most of its aspects. If I am a moralist—and I suppose I am—I am certainly not a gloomy moralist, and if humour finds its way into my work it is because I cannot help it, and am not strongly conscious of it. Certainly I do not "use" humour, but there are times—several times every day—when I am conscious that I am possessed by it, and a man possessed is a poor commentator on his possession.

21

A Chapter of Autobiography

Sadly, we will never see an autobiography by Robertson Davies, although the fragments that exist show that the world has lost a great book. Yet for his admirers there is much to be learned from what exists; from Judith Skelton Grant's 1994 biography, *Robertson Davies: Man of Myth*; from the scenes in his novels that clearly draw on his experience of life—this, after all, is the man who states later in this book that "to ask an author who hopes to be a serious writer if his work is autobiographical is like asking a spider where he buys his thread"; from the talks or essays in this book and elsewhere that resonate with the voice of the man; and, perhaps most directly, from the autobiographical fragments that tell us about how he recalled aspects of his life, recollected in tranquility.

Davies attended Upper Canada College in Toronto from 1928 until 1932. The distinguished private school's founder Sir John Colborne, whose statue stands at the current school's core, gave Davies the perfect name for its close fictional equivalent, Colborne College. There Dunstan Ramsay taught, and three boys who were to play important roles in *The Cunning Man*—Brochwel Gilmartin, Charles Iredale, and Jonathan Hullah—met and became friends.

Davies's account of his school days, published in the school's alumni magazine *Old Times* in 1979, is vivid and requires little explanation. The Headmaster, W.L. "Choppy" Grant, was the son of a legendary Principal of Queen's University in Kingston (the Salterton of Davies's young manhood and early novels) and a member of a family that continues to contribute much to Canadian life and letters. By contrast, the mysterious initials "OISE" represent the Ontario Institute for Studies in Education, an establishment founded in the 1960s that continues to attract the scorn of traditionalists like Davies.

Convocation Hall, mentioned here as the setting for the *St. Matthew Passion*, is the great hall at the centre of the University of Toronto. It was there that the public Celebration of the Life and Work of Robertson Davies was held in the week after his death. The speakers included other writers such as Margaret Atwood, Timothy Findley, John Kenneth Galbraith, Rohinton Mistry, and Jane Urquhart. All of the platform party—unaware of the entrance's significance for the young Davies seventy years before—came in by "The Artist's Door."

He wrote in his diary: *September 11: Make start on my piece for UCC, which is more serious in tone than I had foreseen. September 13: Work most of the morning on the UCC piece and finish it except for rounding-off paragraph. Have tried to be honest, and neither to knock the place nor pretend it was what it was not.*

It has long been fashionable for writers of autobiography to abuse their boarding schools, at which they declare they were unhappy, misunderstood, bored, and ill-used. Only fools expect to be happy all the time. Only people of primitive perceptions think that youth is a time for unalloyed enjoyment. Occasionally I meet people who assure me that their school days were the happiest time of their lives, and I pity them; I wonder what they have been doing with the years that have passed since they left school forever.

My earliest days at the school were clouded by several rebuffs. Not more than three days had passed before I was summoned to the Headmaster's office, and I recall still exactly what he said to me: "Davies, I think you ought to know that you won that scholarship for which you competed, but I decided to award it to Blank instead of you; his mother, as you perhaps know, is a clergyman's widow, and your father can well afford to send you here." My contribution to the conversation was "Yes, sir," but I wished afterward (and I wish still) that I had the courage to say, "Why not give Blank the money and award me the scholarship?" I should greatly have liked to be a scholarship boy, and I think it would have made a difference to my school years, because UCC respected brains, and I thought I had enough to take my place with others who bore the scholarship mark.

Perhaps it was this rebuff which led me to make a stupid mistake a few days later. New boys were given an intelligence test that now seems to me to have been of a primitive and arbitrary kind—but intelligence tests were then in their infancy. It consisted of a number of problems in mathematics, in which I knew I should fail dismally, but its other side was a series of word tests, in which I was confident I could do well. One of them, I recall, was a short story in which candidates were asked to fill in the missing words in a paragraph which begins rather like this: "One fine——, Little Red—— was walking through a deep, dark——, carrying a——of——to her——." Aha, I thought, here's where I show 'em! And I filled in the missing words in such a way as to give the story a wholly new meaning.

I had reckoned without the sort of mind that delights in intelligence tests. I was put in the lowest form, IIIB, and the master in charge of the test called me in and told me in sorrowing tones that I had failed abysmally. How badly, I asked. He would not assign a numerical mark, but said, "The result shows that if you entered the Army as a private, you could never hope to be promoted to corporal." This was a heavy blow, and although in a week or two I was pushed up to the Lower Fifth, where I more or less belonged, I never quite recovered, and there were a few masters who persisted for a year or so in regarding me as a cretin. Fortunately there were others who understood that I had simply not acquired the knack of doing the expected, which was at that time—and is still, to some extent—the secret of passing tests.

Membership in the College Rifle Battalion was obligatory, and as I had some musical training I tried to get into the band. No buglers were needed, but there were openings for drummers. I could not drum; stiff wrists. So out I went to the parade ground with an old and impotent rifle, where I was a painful spectacle because I tend to become confused when shouted at.

Add to this that I was put to share a room with Blank, the son of the needy widow, who had been given my scholarship. He was an uneasy companion. He walked in his sleep, and twice took my clothes while in the trance and put them in a room on a lower floor, so that I had to trace them in the morning. Nor was that all. Somnambulism—which he attributed to disturbed nerves—upset his digestion, and while sleeping he vomited in the washstand basin. Every night. This sounds like grossly farcical invention, but I swear by all I hold sacred that it is strict truth. I asked the housemaster to move me, and told him why, and he took pity on my wretchedness.

Blank further distinguished himself that first autumn term when the school doctor gave the boarders two lectures about sex, in the Prayer Hall after classes. The doctor was not a gifted lecturer, his subject embarrassed him, and he was afflicted with an opacity of vocabulary that made it hard for us to know what he was talking about, much of the time. But he did manage to say that self-abuse was a grave matter, attended by dire consequences, and that he was personally able to tell a boy given to this enormity simply by looking at him. At that moment Blank fainted, to the doctor's dismay, and the extravagant delight of all the rest of us.

It gives me keen pleasure to add that Blank was expelled before the end of his first year. I think it was because of gambling, on which the School cast a cold eye. He was last seen by me driving down the avenue in a taxi, smoking a large cigar. This was educational: I have never trusted the son of a deserving widow since, nor has this principle ever failed me.

Perhaps my worst handicap was that I had no cousins. UCC seemed to me at that time to be peopled entirely by WASPS whose interrelationships were more complicated than those of the gods of Olympus. I had no known relatives, my family was not notably rich, and instead of being a WASP I was rather obviously a Celt. But so was the Headmaster, thank God.

Quite soon I acquired a reputation for eccentricity. This was not surprising, for if you tell a boy he is odd, he is likely to become odd, even if only to be obliging.

These things, and the total lack of privacy which was a dominating factor in school life, made my first year a difficult one. It was wholly out of the question for a boy to be alone, and when once we had left our living quarters in the morning, we were forbidden to return to them, even for a book or a handkerchief, until the end of the school day, when we went up to change for sports. One never knew the luxury of a moment's silence or solitude. I took refuge in music lessons; when one is practising the piano one can be pretty sure of being left to oneself. It was possible to practise scales while reading a book.

The school building was a curiosity, and even I could see that it had not been built to house a school; a school was imposed upon a building which had formerly been, I believe, a military hospital. It had the air of jerry-building and gimcrackery which one associates with buildings put up under government contract; it was a congeries of unexpected draughts, unaccountable noises, and inconvenience. In winter heat was sporadic; at about five in the afternoon the radiators were boiling, and this was the time when many boys dried their sweaty long underwear, worn for football or hockey, on the coils, so that the frequent icy blasts through the loose window casements were a relief. Heat ceased at nine, when the boarders went to prayers and the smaller boys went to bed; the older boys who had another hour's study, and went to bed at eleven, often sat with rugs over their knees at their desks, before creeping into beds under the mattresses of which they had put a thick layer of newspaper, for warmth. The rule was that at night every window must be open as wide as it would go; more than once I have wakened with snow on my bed.

The washing arrangements were old-fashioned; every room, in which two or three boys lived and slept, had a washstand, with a white crockery basin and a jug, in which hot water could be fetched from a tap up the hall. Bathing was a public affair, and the water closets were in booths which had no doors. There were not enough tubs—showers were unknown—so that there was a schedule to arrange bathing times for everybody, and the schedule was subject to constant and elaborate change. It was not, I suppose, worse than Rugby in Doctor Arnold's day.

In high winds the school tower moved perceptibly. It was inhabited by junior masters, and on windy nights they were all extremely cold and some were noticeably nervous.

I was told that the food at UCC now is good. In my day it was not. It depended heavily on starchy dishes, like macaroni and cheese, tapioca, rice, and a variety of hashes. There were two high moments in the year; the first was in autumn, when an Old Boy sent venison to the school, and we feasted royally, and the other was late in the Spring term, when the cook provided extraordinary quantities of asparagus. At night, before going to bed, we could, if we wished, have milk, and some boys mixed it with a powder distantly related to chocolate, called Toddy. There was a boy from the West Indies who made himself late-night tea, out of tea leaves sodden in hot water from the tap. In the cold weather I suffered frequently from neuralgia, and perhaps at this late date I may confess that I treated it by going to the music room where the music master kept a bottle of Scotch hidden (as he supposed) behind a chair. I have had a fondness for a snort of neat Scotch ever since.

No account of UCC fifty years ago would be complete without reference to the code of behaviour to which we were expected to conform. Masters must invariably be addressed as Sir, and it was said—not quite truthfully—that no Master should ever see a boy seated, except in classroom or assembly. We leapt to our feet as if galvanized whenever a Master appeared, and stood with hands at our sides—*never* in pockets. The Headmaster, who had a keen zest for etiquette, lectured us about this, and gave vivid imitations of boys who lounged, who chewed gum, who were all the things a UCC boy must never be. He insisted that when we met our seniors in the streets we must raise our hats (for we all wore hats, and, except for games, caps were anathema) and we must raise them high enough for him to see a patch of sky under the hat. I do this to the present day, sometimes to the amazement of my juniors, who know nothing of hats. We must converse in sentences and paragraphs, and slang was the mark of a low and vulgar contempt for language.

It was a black day for the Headmaster when there was a brief craze for a thing called a Whoopee Hat, which was a hat in the Fedora style, but of cherry red or canary yellow. Boys with a sense of the vogue began to wear these things to school, until a ban was placed upon them, as it was placed on the use of cars. We were reminded sharply and often that we were expected to be gentlemen, and precisely what a gentleman was formed the basis of at least one talk in Assembly every week.

A gentleman, as defined by Dr. W.L. Grant, was one who claimed his place in the world by devotion to high standards of honesty and courtesy, and maintained his claim by unrelenting hard work for some aspect of the public weal. We were told, in the plainest possible words, that we were a privileged group, and every crumb of privilege had to be paid for in the coin of public service. And simply to pay for one's place in the world was the least that was expected; we must strive to do better than that and leave the world a better place than we found it. Good manners were merely the external sign of the inward man; fine manners unaccompanied by fine principles were worse than unenlightened bad manners, because they were a fraud.

This, as you see, was the "character moulding" against which there has been so much protest in recent years. Dr. Grant was the son of the great Grant of Queen's, and his father-in-law was Sir George Parkin, first secretary of the Rhodes Trust, so the apostolic line as it came to us was as unclouded as it could well be.

All three were men of admirable character and distinguished mind, worthy of imitation. But this line of thinking could lead to absurdities. Strenuosity, for its own sake, may be counterproductive, and the best efforts of a fool result only in more folly. I recall my housemaster, William Mowbray, assuring us that we harmed our characters irreparably if we wore our slippers to breakfast, because Sir George Parkin had said that a man who did so revealed a sad lack of moral stamina. Later I was to learn from one of Sir George's granddaughters that he could hardly have said anything of the kind, because he was himself a committed slipper-wearer, and had to be kept up to a suitable standard of dress on public occasions by the efforts of his wife and daughters. The doctrine as expounded to us was pure Mowbray, disguised as Parkin. But there were more sinewy adjurations to live well. I recall a Sunday evening service of prayers where Dr. Grant startled some of us by shouting the great cry of Luther: "Live in the large: avoid sin if you can, but if you must sin, *sin nobly!*" Life was never dull when Choppy Grant was near to charge it with his extraordinary enthusiasm and pedagogic zeal.

He was the source of energy for the School. Sometimes he was wrong-headed and occasionally he was silly, but most of the time he was a vivid and inspiring element in our daily life. He was an admirable teacher and sometimes in the winter months when so many masters were ill that classes were without teachers, he would fill in, teaching with a richness of reference and personal knowledge that made languages splendid, history a revelation of human greatness or depravity, and any literature a key to the mysteries of the human spirit; exact subjects—maths and sciences—were not within his range, but anything that could be illuminated by a far-ranging mind was his by right.

As a disciplinarian and administrator he was capricious—not meanly capricious, but whimsical; we never knew what he would decree. I think that there is much to be said for such an attitude; even-handed justice is for democracies, and UCC under his rule was undemocratic, in that a stupid offence by a boy who obviously knew better might be severely punished, whereas the same breach by an oaf who knew no better could be treated lightly. He was charitable toward what he called, in the term of Catholic theology, "invincible ignorance." Dr. Grant backed his own judgment of boys, and so far as I could observe, he had uncanny instinct, most of the time.

He treated us as men, as so did those who worked with him. I recall an occasion when a master, goaded beyond endurance by a boy whom we all knew was not merely third-rate but thirty-third rate, called the boy a shit—in private rebuke, not in class. The boy made a self-righteous fuss to William Mowbray, who was acting as Headmaster during Dr. Grant's absence. Mowbray, a notably just but not a humorous man, pondered the complaint briefly, then said: "Considering the matter in fairness, do you think the word was ill-chosen?" As a way of dealing with boys who are supposed to be intelligent, I think that goes to the root of the matter in a way undreamt of by Student Grievance Committees or Staff-Student

Disciplinary Boards, or any of the other elaborate means of avoiding the point devised by recent educational theorists.

Discipline could be rough. Boys had their hair pulled and their heads smacked when direct action seemed called for. One Master, Mr. Darnill, kept a boxing glove filled with some heavy material on his desk, attached to a leather thong; when a boy was stupid or impudent, Darnill threw the glove at him, and never missed; he then retrieved it, hand over hand, amid applause from the class. I was once hit in the face with a banana skin, flung by a master who thought I was not so well up in my Latin translation as I ought to have been. I bear him no grudge; his action was direct and made its point.

Boys are variable creatures, sensitive about some things and barbarous about others. I recall a very young master, woefully ill-suited to the teaching profession, which has its mystical link with lion taming. The rumour in the school was that he had to be given a job because he was a relative of the Governor General—at that time Lord Bessborough—and the G.G. was our patron. Poor Mr. Ponsonby's classes were Chaos and Old Night; now and then the uproar was so dreadful that the Headmaster would have to send someone to cope. He grew tired of doing it himself, and he could not always send another master, so he took the fearful course of dispatching a prefect to do the job, literally sending a boy to do a man's work. I suspect that he was sick of poor Ponsonby. Once I was given the task. The order was plain: "Go to Mr. Ponsonby's class and restore order." It was not difficult. Poor Ponsonby was in a corner looking like an aristocrat (which he was) under threat of a Paris mob, and when I appeared the mob fell silent. I gave Mr. Ponsonby some trumped-up message from the Headmaster about a special Assembly the following day, and left, signalling to the class by my glance that if they did not let up on poor Ponsonby the Head would wash them in steep-down gulfs of liquid fire. They were no more brutish than most boys, but they could not resist torturing a helpless creature.

Corporal punishment, though not frequent, was always a possibility. We had a system of Punishment Drills, and a boy who piled up too big a number of these was Gated—that is to say, he could not have weekend leave and must spend the time in study, under supervision;

day boys had to come to school on Saturday for this punishment. But a grave offence could bring a caning, usually of six strokes. Impudence amounting to serious ill manners was the commonest cause. If this seems a trivial reason for a punishment that is now regarded with horror by many apparently sane people, reflect on the nature of the School: Nobody was compelled to go there and the parents of those who went paid substantial fees to have their sons taught as well as possible, and trained in the code which the Headmaster urged upon us in his talks at morning prayers. A boy who rebelled against some school custom would be given a hearing, but a boy who was simply a bloody-minded nuisance and disturber of the peace was beaten. No obloquy clung to him; he had wiped out his offence and he was in good standing afterward. He was not a hero to the other boys; he was simply someone who had incurred a debt and paid it.

At the root of the punishment system lay the principle that boys were not treated as adults unless they showed adult responsibility. We were being trained for maturity; it was not assumed that we brought it with us in our trunks.

Now and then we were given surprising adult treatment. I remember one afternoon, when I was walking in the grounds, the Headmaster met me, and said, "Walk with me and I'll tell you what I remember about the downfall and trials of Oscar Wilde." Which he did, laying true schoolmasterly stress on the objectionable character of the Marquess of Queensbury, who was a bad speller and wrote a note to Wilde calling him a "somdomite." What astonished me was that he had compassion for Wilde and thought he had been hardly used. I felt that I had been invited into the adult world, just as I did when the music master, Richard Tattersall, asked me to come to a Sunday rehearsal of the *St. Matthew Passion* at Convocation Hall, saying, "Come in by the Artist's Door; I think it's time you did." I grew several inches in the instant. The masters at UCC knew how to treat boys, when to rebuke and when to offer them the Keys of the Kingdom. They were men of character, old warriors, ripe scholars, men who knew not OISE and its fashionable follies.

I was grateful to many of these men, and one I hated. He taught mathematics, and for two years his daily litany of contemptuous abuse, directed at my stupid head, was worse than anything I have had to endure since—and writers become acquainted with bitter criticism. At last the Headmaster excused me from maths, on the grounds of "invincible ignorance." (I can now, by the way, do simple reckoning far better than most bank clerks.)

Of the many who taught me well, I can pay a tribute only to Mr. Wright (I never knew his first name) who taught English and demanded of me that I read Browning's *The Ring and the Book*, which was not required by the curriculum but which he thought was my cup of tea. It was my bottle of brandy, for it revealed to me that between great poetry and depth psychology there is no division but that determined by the presence, or lack, of imagination, for imagination is not dream spinning, but insight.

It was such men as these I bore in mind when I was describing the character of Dunstan Ramsay in my Deptford Trilogy.

My time at the School coincided with the worst days of the Depression, and we felt something of its chill, for many parents were hard hit; and I now know what we were not supposed to know then, which was that many parents were in default for fees, and the School bore the default bravely. Several masters who had considerable sums of money in the fairy gold of Stocks Purchased on Margin discovered that the gold had turned to withered leaves.

Although I am not certain that market troubles were the whole cause, one of the housemasters committed suicide, and a suicide in a school must be tactfully handled. Two prefects had heard the shot, and rushed to his study to find him already dead; they were sworn to secrecy and I believe they did indeed keep their mouths shut, but matters of that kind have a way of making themselves known. I remember his funeral clearly, because on a Saturday morning I was detailed to carry funeral wreaths to the Prayer Hall as they arrived, and after an hour or two I was to be seen mounting the stairs, laden with flowers and weeping uncontrollably. It was not grief, for I had not known the man; it was rose fever, to which I am a victim still.

More cheerful occasions marked the celebration of the School's Centenary. Prize Day that year was of a special magnificence, for the Governor General was present; he was Lord Willingdon, a figure of impressive distinction and splendour of dress. But splendid dress was not confined to him alone; the procession of masters to the dais was notable for the variety of morning dress that appeared under the silk gowns and the gaudy hoods. One or two masters had no degrees, and I recall Commander J.N.B.P. de Marbois in splendid naval kit; it was like UCC at that time that geography should be taught by a sailor, who had actually visited the strange lands he talked about and who had, it was said, eaten human flesh among the savages of Tierra del Fuego.

Most of the masters wore heavy bands of war decorations, and some of them—Mr. Parlee, Mr. Potter—bore graver evidence of service in a war we were never allowed to forget.

We were not unaccustomed to Governors General. I recall a later visit from Lord Bessborough, to whom we paid scant attention because he was accompanied by his beautiful French wife, who gave the prizes to the boys of the Prep and kissed each one. There were many seniors, and I was among them, who wished for the first time on that occasion that we were younger.

No great celebration passes without some element of farce, and our Centenary was marked by a football song, composed by one of the junior masters and sung to the tune of "John Brown's Body." It went thus:

St. Andrews, welcome here today
You've come to meet your doom;
For UCC, with no delay
Will leave you little room,
To harbour doubt about the play
We'll fill you full of gloom
In our CEN-TEN-A-RY!
Charge team, and hit them with your HEADS low!
Play fair and square until they ALL know
U.C.College fights just like a TRUE foe,
In her CEN-TEN-A-RY!

I shall not reveal the name of the writer of these lines, for he later attained to academic distinction, and I do not wish to shame him.

Many of the boys, who believed they had some taste in verse, were aware that this was not simply doggerel; in Stephen Leacock's words it sank even lower, and was describable only as chickerel, or possibly piggerel. We roared it with ironic delight on every conceivable occasion, knowing full well that the School could not very well condemn literary criticism as ordinary impudence.

Such reminiscences as these, however, are not sufficient to sum up the atmosphere and quality of the School as I knew it. Its dominating characteristic was that the relationship between the masters and the boys was that of adepts to aspirants, not that of retailer to consumer, or employer to unionized worker, which sometimes seems to be the ideal of our state schools. The authority they had was maintained by their superiority of learning, experience, and intellect; whatever rights we achieved we had to earn by showing our fitness to use them wisely. And the influence of the Headmaster, that learned, enthusiastic, vivid, mercurial man, set the tone for everything. We were encouraged to live in the large, and some of us had a shot at it.

22

My Early Literary Life

On January 27, 1988, the distinguished Canadian magazine *Saturday Night* celebrated its one hundredth anniversary with a gala dinner in Toronto. As the equivalent of American publications such as *Harper's* or *The Atlantic*, the now-monthly magazine continues to play an important role in Canadian intellectual life.

At the time of the celebration the magazine's editor was John Fraser, who in 1995 followed in Robertson Davies's footsteps to become the fourth Master of Massey College in the University of Toronto. It was appropriate that he should invite Robertson Davies, a former literary editor of the magazine and possibly its oldest ex-employee, to deliver the toast to the magazine that was at the centre of the evening's festivities. Few of those present suspected that Davies's memories of the magazine would extend back to the time before he could read, or that his memories of working there from 1940 to 1942 would be so clear. Or, indeed, that he still bore ink-stained scars from that time; the insensitivity of the evil Mr. Croucher in his words "still rankles here in me buzzem!"

On July 16, 1988, Davies noted: *Write to John Fraser whose August issue of* Saturday Night *displays my speech toasting the old paper very handsomely though there are some drawings of what a bad artist imagines me to have looked like in my twenties, and the wedding picture of Brenda and me which we both dislike.*

When I was first asked to propose this toast, I was horrified to discover that my association with *Saturday Night* goes back for seventy years. It began in my childhood, because *Saturday Night* used to come to our home. My father was a journalist, my mother was a writer—a newspaper writer—so the whole family was in the trade. And when I was a very little boy I remember that on Sundays my parents sat reading a very large newspaper printed on glossy, coated stock which, I understood, was called *Saturday Night*. That was during the years of the First World War and I learned to write from *Saturday Night*. But I did not learn to read from it, because what I used to do when my parents had finished with the paper was to get a pencil and copy the big headlines and work out the letters in that way. I never understood what they meant and nobody ever told me, but that was what I did.

I recall that my father used to read the first section of the paper, which was full newspaper size; that part was about international affairs and primarily, of course, about the Great War. I was very much aware, from what he read, and what he said, and what he read aloud to my mother and to my brothers, that this conflict was between two extraordinary antagonists: one, a Mr. Lloyd George, who was of overwhelming nobility and splendour because he was Welsh, like my family; and the other was a monster, an incarnation of evil, who was the German emperor, Kaiser Wilhelm II. I used to see, in the *Saturday Night* pages, caricatures of Lloyd George, hair flying splendidly with the excess of his zeal and patriotism as he exhorted other people to fight. And also, the picture of the cringing, evil German emperor, wearing a helmet with a spike on the top of it, with extraordinary upturned moustaches and a sneer that would chill the blood of a crocodile. There were occasionally caricatures of his son, Prince Louis Ferdinand, who was always referred to as "Chinless Freddie."

My mother, meanwhile, as my father was reading this inflammatory stuff, was reading the section of the paper that was given over to fashion and society. Because in those days, *Saturday Night* devoted a great many pages to society and everybody was interested in it. I should like to think that the editor would reinstitute that enthusiasm and that in Canada we would get some real society and not just a coven of committees devoted to the assistance of the dystrophic and the paraplegic and the AIDS-ridden and *les misérables* who seem to have taken the forefront in our world at the moment.

Later on, I began to read *Saturday Night* myself, and I was particularly interested in the middle section, which was devoted to literature and the arts. And what I especially liked were the theatrical pictures that were printed of actors who were going to appear in Toronto in the week following the date of publication. They were splendid; indeed, splendid in a sense which the younger among you cannot conceive at this moment. It was an era when the theatrical profession was either beautiful or distinguished. The ladies were elegant, beautiful, stylishly dressed, marvellously coiffed, splendid creatures, inspiring even to a very young boy (mind you, young boys are very easily inspired). And the men had an air of hauteur and distinction, a height of white collar and a splendour of cravat, that has utterly disappeared from the theatrical profession, which has become now, I fear, a congeries of scabby detrimentals who never seem to wash their hair, and I don't want to look at their pictures any more. But, in those days, the pictures of the theatre people were transporting, and I looked at them with the keenest interest. And also, I read the theatrical reports by Hector Charlesworth, which were witty and charming and interesting and never cruel, though sometimes pointed. And I read the work of a man, who is not much remembered nowadays, called Peter Donovan. The thing about Peter Donovan was that he was funny; and in those days it was permissible for publications like *Saturday Night* to be funny. Peter Donovan (whose famous pseudonym was P. O'D) was very funny indeed. I wish the spirit of those days would return, when somebody in *Saturday Night* could be knowingly and intentionally and pointedly funny.

Well, now we hasten on in our story to the year the war began, 1939, when things were very, very bad in the theatrical profession, of which I was a member. I remember vividly waking up one morning in London, in England, and discovering that the government had closed all the theatres indefinitely and that over five thousand actors in London alone were out of work, and I was one of them. There was no job for me there, so I came back to Canada, where I thought I might conceivably get employment, and it was not easy to find. *The Globe and Mail* was going through a mid-life crisis which has existed with it for fifty, sixty, and seventy years, and in wartime could not bring itself to appoint anybody to such a frivolous position as that of a theatre critic. So, although I banged upon their doors, I got no job there.

While this was going on, I was summoned by my country to be considered for military service. Well, now, I didn't respond with a whoop and a holler, because I had heard about people getting killed in the First World War and I had no particular interest in following their example in the Second. However, I went along and got examined. I assure you I went into the examining pavilion a young Hercules and I came out an ignominious wretch. I was utterly rejected. I had been aware that, sometimes, my apprehension of things at a distance was dim, but I had not expected to be condemned as blear-eyed. I knew that, occasionally, I didn't catch everything that was said at great distances, but I didn't know that I was really rather tediously deaf. And I had had occasions of exaltation which I put down to the mercurial nature of my temperament, but I didn't realize I had vertigo. I was turned down on these points because the Canadian army had all the blind, deaf, and dizzy people it needed already.

I assure you, I crawled out of the doctor's office almost on my hands and knees. I still had not got a job and I needed one very badly. Then, suddenly, something extraordinary happened. These coincidences—Jungian coincidences—occur from time to time in my life. The news appeared in the papers that the literary editor of *Saturday Night* had died in a boating accident on a lake near Ottawa. He was a man named Hal Sutton. Well, I thought, now there's a job I might conceivably aspire to. But, you see, I had been so well brought up that I thought the death of a literary editor such a grievous affliction that for two or three weeks, certainly, the magazine would close down entirely, and it would be shameful to intrude upon their grief. But I met a friend of mine in the street, and I told him what my intentions were and what my feelings were, and he said, "Don't you believe it: You get in and apply right away. And don't send your letter through the mail, take it down and put it through the letter box at

Consolidated Press." I thought he knew what he was talking about so that's what I did, and the very next day I received a phone call from the editor, Mr. B.K. Sandwell, asking me to come and talk to him about this application that I had made.

I went. I was terrified of Mr. Sandwell, but Mr. Sandwell was charming, pleasant, and put me greatly at my ease. We talked for a very short time. I'd expected to be grilled, but I wasn't grilled. And then Mr. Sandwell said, "Well, that seems very satisfactory. Let's go and talk to the publisher." So, we went to talk to the publisher, and I've never talked to such a publisher in my life before or since. We went into a magnificent office which was panelled in some splendid, I expect exotic, wood. And there sat, not a grim-visaged male, but a charming lady. She was Miss Sutton, and she was the publisher of *Saturday Night*, and she was, indeed, the aunt of the man who had so recently died. I expected her to be suffused with grief, but she was not.

So I talked to Miss Sutton and I very quickly discovered that Miss Sutton was not interested so much in my literary qualifications as in my personal life. "Are you married, Mr. Davies?" she said.

"Yes, Miss Sutton. I am."

"Have you any children?"

And I, blushing deeply, said, "Well, no, Miss Sutton, but it is now early November and my wife and I hope that before the end of the year … um …"

Miss Sutton became all smiles and we got on admirably, and the interview, again, was uncommonly short. Miss Sutton said, "Now, there is only one thing still to consider: What salary would you expect?"

Well, I was prepared for that one, because I had consulted my father by telephone and my father said, "I know for a fact that B.K. Sandwell gets five thousand dollars a year for being editor of *Saturday Night*. Now you must not consider that you are worth as much as B.K. Sandwell, so you must put your salary somewhere slightly below half what he gets, but not too far below."

So, I was ready for Miss Sutton and I said, "Well—ah—I think that perhaps forty-two dollars and fifty cents weekly would be about right."

And Miss Sutton looked grave, as publishers always do, and said, "Well I think, possibly, we could agree on that."

And so we did.

I said, "When do I begin?"

And Mr. Sandwell said, "You begin at once. You come in the day after tomorrow. Tomorrow is press day; come in the day following."

So I did. And I met the staff and the staff were delightful people. There was Mr. Sandwell himself, of course, who was the editor. And there was Pat Richards, who was the financial editor and a very big wheel in the affair because he gave advice about how you invested your money. In those days, you could still write to *Saturday Night* and ask, "What do I do with my money?" and Mr. Richards would send you a personal reply telling you what to do with it. Mr. Richards, I always thought, was a man of extraordinary self-denial because he never worked upon his advice to get rich himself: He just let other people get rich on what he suggested. Mr. Richards had an assistant called Wessely Hicks, who did the layout of the paper. He was very kind to me and showed me the ropes. And there was Miss Bernice Coffey, who did fashion and society and what were then called, reprehensibly of course, "women's affairs."

That was the whole staff except for the secretary, Miss Watson, who like all good secretaries cloaked her steely core in boundless charm. One of her main jobs was to protect Mr. Sandwell from the bores, time wasters, and certifiable lunatics by whom he—like all editors—was beset all day. I began to realize why they needed somebody in an awful hurry. If you reduce a staff of six by one, you're in considerable trouble.

But there were all sorts of people who appeared who worked on the paper occasionally. One was Karsh, the photographer, at that time very much at the beginning of his career, who was doing a lot of photography for *Saturday Night*. There was the photographer who worked regularly for the advertising department, whose name was Jaycocks, a delightful Englishman. Jaycocks taught me a lot of things about photography, which I've never forgotten. One time I said to him, "Jay, all the food that you photograph for the food advertisements looks so absolutely delicious. Why is that? You know that most of it is awful."

And he said, "Well, it's simple, you see. They get everything ready and then I get a can of varnish and pour it over the whole thing, and it brings out that wonderful, delicious gleam which everybody admires in the pictures."

Now, *Saturday Night* at that time was not an independent journal. It was a publication put out by a firm called Consolidated Press; it had a very large group of papers, which are what are called "trade papers." They were *The Canadian Founder and Die-Sinker* and *The Canadian Leather-Pounder and Fuller* and *The Canadian Nail-Drawer and Wire-Pusher*, and all those things, and they were money-makers, every last one of them. *Saturday Night* was the black sheep of the family, because, although it was the most illustrious paper of the group, it lost money pretty consistently. And for that reason we were perpetually under pressure from the group who ran Consolidated Press. You see, Miss Sutton had established a sort of Byzantine Empire and she was the empress at the top of the heap. Below her were a group of palace eunuchs, so to say, who did all the work, and these were, some of them, very curious people indeed.

I remember the first day that I was at work on *Saturday Night*, I filled out a lot of papers about what pension I would get when I was seventy, and all those things you do when you go to work in your early days on a paper. Very shortly afterwards an extremely small, but globular, man appeared in my office, a man full of self-esteem, obviously, and he said, "Here are your forms."

I said, "Yes?"

He said, "Well now, look at them. I can read every word you've written."

I said, "Yes?"

He said, "Well now, I'm going to tell you something, because I'm a man who's achieved a good deal of success in the world of business, and you are a young man just entering the world of business. And I want to tell you that nobody who succeeds in the world of business ever writes legibly." And he then proceeded to scribble something on a paper and he said, "That's my signature."

And I looked at it and I thought, "Yes, that's his signature. I don't know what his name is, but that's his signature." And then he marched away, having conferred upon me this inestimable boon. I've never forgotten it, and I have gone right on writing as clearly as I can.

There was another man who quickly appeared in the door of my office, hissing strangely, and I later on discovered that this was evidence of an inveterate malignance against literary editors. He was the assistant business manager and he bore the Dickensian name of Croucher. Mr. Croucher was the thorn in my flesh and the bane of my life, because Mr. Croucher would appear on publication day with an advertisement which simply had to be squeezed into the literary pages. He would insist that this be done and it had to be done, because I was junior to Mr. Croucher and could not say him nay. And I remember my lowest hour was one day, when we were just about to go to press, and Mr. Croucher came in and said, "I've got to have three inches, a column wide, for an ad on your page, your first page." He got it, of course. It was an ad for "Pussy-foot Closet Tanks." In order to wedge it in I had to cut three inches of deathless prose by myself. I resented that. I resent it still. It still rankles here in me buzzem!

I made other acquaintances very quickly in those first days at the paper. One was the compositor who took care of the literary pages. He appeared, suddenly, a gigantic man, and made strange noises, and pointed and jabbed and made signs, but I knew exactly where we stood. He was a type of printer that you don't see any more, because printing has ceased to be that kind of trade. But in those days a great many people who were deaf-mutes became printers, and this man was a deaf-mute. He was a wonderful fellow, a first-class printer and a great friend. He was understanding and amusing and we got on admirably. He would point, sign, make motions, and I would write in my ridiculously legible handwriting and, in that way, we got along splendidly.

I also got on not very good terms, but on very intimate terms, with the proofreader, who was an Englishman, and a demon grammarian. He was much distressed by me, but I didn't worry too much, because he was much distressed by everybody. He was distressed by Mr. Sandwell; he was distressed by the whole paper. None of us seemed to know any grammar as he understood grammar. He was particularly dismayed by what he called my objectionable abuse of the colon. He explained this further: It was a kind of syntactical AIDS he was talking about, a deficiency syndrome. He wrangled with me about this all the time that I was at *Saturday Night*, which was well over two years. We never reached an agreement.

But I eventually found out how things went, and I remember the very first review that I wrote as book editor was of a collection of Ogden Nash's poetry and the headline which I wrote for it was "Golden Trashery of Ogden Nashery." And a lot of people thought that was very un-*Saturday Night*. But Mr. Sandwell thought it was just fine.

A lot of people had odd ideas about what the literary pages in *Saturday Night* should be like. In my very first week, a dignified and beautifully dressed gentleman suddenly appeared in my office without a by-your-leave, and proceeded to select books from the shelves and set them aside, obviously about to put them into his briefcase and carry them away. I made inquiries. What did he think he was doing, I asked.

"I am going to review these books," he said.

Well, I thought, this is Waterloo. And I said, "You know, really, when I want you to review a book, I will see that it is sent to you in plenty of time for you to get on with it." Meanwhile, I snatched the books and put them back on the shelves. This was terrible, because he went away looking daggers. And I discovered, because Miss Watson was looking white and shaken, that this was no less a grandee than Professor Pelham Edgar, of the University of Toronto, and it was as though, in modern terms, I had shot Northrop Frye. Nobody that I was, I had given Pelham Edgar the bum's rush! He never darkened the door of *Saturday Night* again during my time there. But I felt that I had not entirely missed the mark, because I noticed, when I went out to look around and see what the carnage was like, that Mr. Sandwell, whose door was always open, was shaking with laughter. And so I decided that everything was all right.

One of the pleasures of my work was a weekly chat with Hector Charlesworth. He had been editor, had then become one of the earliest broadcast administrators in the country, and had returned to journalism, as music critic of *The Globe and Mail* and as a reviewer and occasional critic for us. He was a splendid figure, of Edwardian elegance; he loved to tell how in his younger days he had often been mistaken for the Prince of Wales (later Edward VII). Indeed, he had sometimes shown himself on a platform on the prince's train, when the prince himself was on another platform, causing some confusion among the loyal souls gathered at country railway stations. Two princes! It was like an *Uncle Tom's Cabin* company with two Topsies. He was always handsomely dressed, and every week he had his beard trimmed by a female barber whom he spoke of as "Madame Queen"—the name of a character in the *Amos 'n' Andy* radio program.

He was a fountain of anecdotes about the theatre of the late nineteenth century, and as this was an enthusiasm of mine I became his disciple. As a critic, I think he was strong as a judge of acting, rather than of plays, and his recollection of differences in the performance of *Hamlet* by a variety of leading players was detailed and perceptive.

He was wonderfully courteous to women, and a great, and respectful, celebrator of the beauty of actresses. I remember that once, when we had become strong friends, he said, "I want to show you a picture of my wife," and he drew from his pocketbook a Victorian photograph of the kind that used to be called *"carte de visite"*; it was of a wonderfully pretty girl of not more than twenty wearing one of those tight bodices down the front of which marched a procession of charming little buttons. This was Kate Ryan, who, at the time we were talking, was a bedridden invalid whose chief entertainment was the pursuit of innumerable lawsuits—something she had inherited from her father, Peter Ryan, a brilliant Liberal politician who was, it appeared, irrepressibly litigious.

Hector belonged to a bygone age, and a very good age it must have been. His kindness to me was all the more warming because there was no reason why he should have paid any heed to me whatever. Indeed, when I look back at my days on *Saturday Night* it is of the kindness of Hector Charlesworth and B.K. Sandwell—gentlest and firmest editors—that I think first and last.

And so, on and on it went, and I enjoyed my time at *Saturday Night* immensely. One of the things that I did was to try to popularize

Canadian wine. We were getting out a Christmas edition. B.K. said, "What can you think of that would be novel?"

I said, "Well, somebody saying something good about Canadian wine."

He said, "You go ahead and try that."

So, my wife and I tried a number of recipes, and I printed an article under a pseudonym, a feminine pseudonym—it was the custom in the paper at that time—saying that if you heated it, and put enough spice in it, and added a few glasses of brandy to it, it made an admirable punch. And this was an absolutely fiery success. I became the white-haired boy of the Canadian wine industry and I can still feel the caress of Noah Torno when he talked to me about that article later on.

In the course of time I left *Saturday Night* to take up other employment which was necessary for one reason or another—reluctantly, because I loved the place.

It is, par excellence, Canada's intellectual paper. It has been so for a hundred years. It has, at its very best and sometimes when it wasn't at its very best, been a mountain breeze among the smogs and miasmas and hypocritical fug of Canadian life. We must treasure it for that reason and, as we look back to its past with admiration and affection, we must look forward to its future with expectation, with very great hope.

And so I ask you to drink a toast not to *Saturday Night*. Let us call it "our paper."

23

My Musical Career

Robertson Davies felt that music, which turns the thoughts inward and is conducive to contemplation, was a route to self-knowledge; a journey he described many times as the most important of all. He loved many forms and styles of music and had done so from his youngest days. Therefore, when the Royal Conservatory of Music at the University of Toronto invited him to become a Fellow, he was very grateful for the honour, being acutely aware that he was not an accomplished musician. He made this speech at the ceremony on November 26, 1994, and noted the event in his daily diary:

Rest in P.M., *and set out to dine with the Principal of the Royal Conservatory (Peter Simon) and his wife at a restaurant high up Yonge Street which we had great trouble finding, as the numbers on that miserable thoroughfare run both ways—one up and one down! Pleasant dinner and the Simons are both charming. To the Recital Hall at the Centre, and greet Lois Marshall. The ceremony well managed, and my speech goes admirably, for they had not expected to laugh, and I had determined that they should, and succeeded in the highest degree. Enjoyed the affair which I had not expected to do. But Simon is reviving and putting new dignity on the Conservatory, and is succeeding very well … A young man and his father both received degrees; the son, a Canadian, had the characteristic Canadian pie-face; the older man, a European, had a well-formed and distinguished face. This so often happens. Why? Can it be a matter of climate?*

I am more grateful than I can express for the honour which you have done me; it is totally unexpected and it comes from a source which I have long held in awe. My admiration for this institution goes back to the days of Sir Ernest MacMillan who, among other accomplishments, made Canadians a perceptive and sophisticated audience for music. That I should, on this occasion, be linked with Miss Lois Marshall, whose art has been one of the great pleasures of my musical experience—as indeed it has been to hundreds of thousands of others—is to me a truly wonderful experience. I thank you warmly, and I wish I could say that I shall strive to be worthy of this distinction—but I know that will be utterly impossible.

Let me explain. It is not that I am ignorant of music, or that I have no career in music. But alas, that career has been so obscure, so ignominious that it hardly deserves to be regarded as a career at all. You are all of you this evening receiving awards that mark your musical achievement, in some degree; doubtless music will be your profession, and doubtless some of you will achieve great things in the musical world and bring refreshment, and perhaps enchantment, to a new generation of listeners. I could never have been included in such a group as yours, because I have, all my life, been among the very worst musical performers in a profession which is not lacking in failures.

I come from a family that was devoted to music and I was brought up in an atmosphere in which music was a very special interest. Everybody sang. Everybody played something. My father played the flute; my mother the piano; one of my brothers was a by no means inglorious performer on that now almost forgotten instrument, the cornet. We were a Welsh family and song was as familiar to us as speech. It was decided that I should excel all the rest as a musician, and as soon as I could sit on a piano stool without falling off I was set to work on that appallingly difficult instrument, and I was kept at it for years, and years and years.

It was obvious to me from the beginning that I had no talent, and the piano, with its array of grinning teeth, was my tormentor. But simply by the process of growing older, I made something that looked like progress, and in my teens I was despoiling the works of Beethoven and Chopin and Schumann. I had, you see, no scrap of that quality which psychologists call "the sensation function." I never knew where anything was. I would place myself at the piano, and bring my hands down on what ought to have been a commanding opening chord, and foozle it every time.

My mother's idol among pianists was Paderewski. I knew that I would never be a Paderewski, so I searched among the other great pianists of the day, looking for a model, and I found one at last who seemed to be just right for me. He was Vladimir de Pachmann. His style was refined, and so was mine. He was distinguished for the fact that especially in the works of Chopin he struck a great number of wrong notes. It was here that I knew I could rival him, and perhaps even excel him. You see, he struck his wrong notes in extremely rapid passages: I worked at my technique until I was certain that I could strike great numbers of wrong notes *in very slow passages*.

Nobody appreciated my style. I remember the dark day when my teacher, who was a very kind and patient man, but also a musician of a high order, said to me: "You know, Davies, it's perfectly clear that you will never be able to play the piano acceptably even if you live to be a hundred. Why don't we stop wasting time and settle to some serious study of musical literature, and it's just possible that after a while you might make some mark as a music critic."

You will understand my dejection. A critic! Could any greater ignominy befall someone so devoted to music as I was? It was as if I were an aspiring tennis player and had been told that some day I might be a ballboy. But I did as I was told. I tried to understand what I could never hope to perform.

Not, mind you, that I did not have my triumphs. When I was an actor in my young days I was often asked to provide music for plays in which I appeared, and I did. I suppose nobody listens critically to such music. My finest hour came when I was working in a play which was set in the time of Henry VIII, and some offstage music was required on an instrument called the virginal. I expect you all know what a virginal is: It is a young and inexperienced piano. I twangled out a few easy pieces, some of them written by Henry VIII himself, and all went well. Then, suddenly, the British Broadcasting Company decided that it would like to have some parts of our play broadcast over the air, and again I was required to provide the musical accompaniment.

I cannot forget my dismay when I went into the studio and was confronted with a large harpsichord. It was a huge affair, with two sets of teeth and a bewildering variety of pedals. I assumed an air of nonchalance, and tinkered with the thing until I had subdued it to, roughly, the status of the virginal to which I was accustomed. And I got away with it! Nobody found me out and I listened to the subsequent broadcast with a good deal of satisfaction.

And what do you suppose happened? The play was scheduled to go on for an hour, but when it ended there were still ninety seconds before the end of the hour. My guardian angel was hard at work, because some kindly soul at the BBC filled in the time with a record by Yella Pessel, who was one of the great harpsichordists of the day! Afterward, several people said to me, "I never dreamt you could play like that."

I am not a liar. But I am not a fool, either. I always replied, "I'm glad you liked it."

That was the high point of my musical career. After that, I did indeed become a critic, but I wasn't much good because I couldn't bear to write nastily about some wretched performer who had played far better than I had ever been able to do myself. If you can't spray the acid around you are no use as a critic, so I had to take to other forms of writing in which I was able to say what I really felt about music, without having to provide personal examples.

There it is, you see. I stand before you as a failed musician, upon whom nevertheless this kindly institution has bestowed an honour. You are not failed musicians. You are the real thing. Speaking, as it were, from the sidelines, I wish you every success and happiness in a career to which I was never able to aspire.

Age

24

A View in Winter: Creativity in Old Age

A few days after the previous selection, Davies took part in a symposium on old age at Johns Hopkins University. On November 4, 1993, he gave the speech that follows on the subject of creativity late in life. He wrote to a friend: *My news is chiefly concerned with growing old. But does that mean that I am sinking into an armchair, dozing and thinking of times past? It most certainly does not! I do not think I have ever been busier in my life. I am not looking for things to do. They are looking for me. I seem to make a great many speeches, and they all take time to prepare and I do not become less nervous as I grow older. Since last summer it seems almost as if I had never shut up. But the last two ventures were entertaining. I went to Baltimore to the Johns Hopkins Medical Center, where they were having a series of meetings about old age; they asked me to speak about creativity in old age, and as I am now eighty, and still working steadily, I was assumed to know something about it. What I told them was simply that if you have never been creative in your younger days you must not expect to write, or paint, or compose music simply because you have grown old. But if you have done these things when young, you will probably go on till you drop. Who ever heard of a "retired" painter?*

I have been asked to lead off this afternoon's discussion with some remarks on creativity in old age, and while it may appear obvious to you why I was chosen for this task, I assure you it is not so plain to me. It is true that I am old, and it is true that as a writer—primarily a novelist—I continue to work up until the present time, but to me there seems to be nothing extraordinary about it. I simply continue to do what I have done all my life, and I see no reason to stop. I am not tired. I am not wanting in ideas, and for me writing has always been my principal worldly task. Why would I cease?

The answer might be given that I wanted to rest. There is a widespread belief in our Western world that after the age of sixty-five *everybody* wants to rest. But I do not want to rest. For me to cease writing would not be a rest, it would be a deprivation. I should become one of those tedious men whom one meets among people who are retired, who is a social nuisance because he has nothing to do. Inactivity and deprivation of all accustomed stimulus is not rest; it is a preparation for the tomb. But I shall not base my remarks entirely on my own opinions, and in preparing to talk to you today I have done quite a lot of research into the matter of creativity in old age, especially as it concerns writers.

I shall not bore you, however, with a recital of all the writers I have found who have continued their work into old age. There are literally scores of them, but many belong to earlier periods of general culture and their names would probably not be resonant to a modern audience. Shall we allow two great names from this century to suffice? Thomas Mann, a towering figure in the world of the novel, died at the age of eighty (1955), having just completed what has been described as Germany's greatest comic novel, *Confessions of the Confidence Trickster Felix Krull.* And in case you do not think a German comic novel an especially thrilling achievement, astonishing though it may be, I refer you to the list of very fine novels, ranging from the ironic to the tragic, which had occupied him since the age of twenty-five. The other figure to whom I call your attention is, of course, Bernard Shaw (1950), who lived to be ninety-four and was writing up until his final illness. There are critics who point out that Shaw's later work is not on the same level as that of his writing until the age of seventy-six, when he wrote *Too True to Be Good*, a play of remarkable experimental characteristics; what he produced after that time he himself called "Shaw's Dotages." For many years during my life as a university teacher I gave a seminar on the works of Shaw, and every year my students read these last works with astonishment, and agreed that many of us would be happy to have such *dotages*.

You may object that the two examples I have given you are men of genius. But of course. True creativity in old age does not appear in mediocrities.

Here I may be treading on contentious ground. It is an illusion of our modern concept of democracy that virtually everything in life that is good may be attained by virtually everybody. If some people can be creative in old age, obviously everybody can do so, if they can acquire the knack. There must be some secret, some formula, which will open the doors of autumnal creativity to everyone, and for them the Winter View will be a revelation.

This is the point at which we may ask ourselves what we really mean by creativity. My desk dictionary says it is "showing imagination as well as routine skill." That is a very broad definition and not quite what we want. That definition is partly useful in describing the work of children in kindergarten, because what a child does with its crayons is inevitably imaginative because the child does not, for instance, look at a chair, or its mother, or a tree when it draws these things; what it draws is an inner vision. But the child has no routine skill, no technique. It is when it begins to develop these qualities—observation and technique—that it discovers that its symbols for chair or mother or tree do not correspond to what it sees. For our discussion of creativity here I think we might consider the definition that Frank Barton employs in his essay "The Psychology of Creativity," where he says it is "the ability to bring something new into existence." But even that does not cover the ground. When Rembrandt paints an old woman, he does not bring the whole race of old women out of the everywhere into the here; he does not even create the old woman who sits before him in his studio; but he creates the old woman *in the picture* and in so doing he shows us aspects of that particular old woman, and of old women in general, which we had not observed. It is his inner vision and special perception. Creativity is something new brought into existence by someone with a special power to conceive, or describe, or reveal.

Not the most determined social philosopher can pretend that this special power can be aroused in great numbers of people by the acquirement of a knack.

But—*Hope springs eternal in the human breast; / Man never is, but always to be blest*—as a poet of unquestioned creativity has told us. There are on this continent great numbers of people who optimistically assure others that they too can be creative, even if they are not creative on the highest level. They can paint—not as well as a Renoir, perhaps, but they will never know unless they try. They can write—and although they may not challenge Thomas Mann or Bernard Shaw they may have a very pretty talent which they have not yet employed. It is significant that these optimists never urge their admirers to try their hands at the art of music; they recognize that music requires the discipline of a whole new language of expression, and that there is already as much mediocre music in the world as can be endured. But they urge their listeners to unbridled daubing and word processing, and they assert boldly that what appears is genuinely creative. And they are right in that nothing like what results has ever been seen in the world before and with God's mercy will never be seen again.

Here I must declare a personal prejudice; I am doubtful about the employment of art as a means of therapy for people who are bored and seek something to distract them—as a pastime for the idle. Of course great paintings have come out of asylums for the insane—the astonishing work of Richard Dadd leaps to mind at once—but as a usual thing the doctors and analysts keep the work of their patients for their own inspection. But in the realm of writing the proliferation of sadly mediocre work is the despair of publishers and agents and of authors like myself, who are asked to pass judgment on these undistinguished productions. Somebody—very often a social worker or a healer of some sort—has suggested to these people that they should write, either pieces of fiction, or verse, or personal reminiscence. So far, so good. But human vanity is such that virtually nobody can write anything without feeling impelled to show it to somebody else; the writer is so astonished to find that he or she can indeed fill pages with material that looks like writing that they cannot rest until they have tested it against the taste of somebody who is supposed to know what good writing is. I shall not waste your time with an outburst of personal grievance, but I cannot forbear to say that every week my desk is littered with writing of this kind, sent to me for an opinion by people who do not often enclose an addressed envelope for return, and to whom the concept of return postage is wholly unknown. I have tried to be charitable and understanding about it, but many years as a professor supplied me, in the form of student essays, with all the innocently bad writing that I can cope with in a single lifetime.

What has caused this outburst of yearning for creativity? It is said that after the Second World War the United States became alarmed and discontented because Russian scientists were outstripping them in the field of space exploration. It seemed to me that Bob Hope hit the nail on the head when he said that it was because their Germans were better than our Germans. But the huge world of the educational theorists thought it was because American education was too confined in its syllabus, that too much had to be learned by rote, and that intellectual freedom was not encouraged. Children must be urged to make discoveries for themselves. The belief in the boundless spirit of intellectual adventure in the very young is one of the unchallenged myths of educational theorists. Every tot is thought to be a genius in embryo. Anybody who has ever been a child knows very well how conservative, how dull and intellectually corseted children can be, and one can only conclude that educational theorists have never been children.

The new approach to education was not confined to science; it spread over the whole curriculum. Classics were out; children had to read about people like themselves. This has led to a new school of novel writing called *Teen Tales*, with such titles as *Mary's First Abortion*, or *The Faulty Condom*; and *Jimmy's Tough Luck, or the Dirty Needle*. These cautionary tales have slight literary worth and are valueless in encouraging literary taste.

Rote learning was abandoned because it stifled the creative spirit. IQ tests were suspect because they might suggest that one child was in certain respects superior to another, with supposedly disastrous effects on the self-confidence of the lesser child. *Out flew the web and floated wide; The mirror crack'd from side to side*—and the curse was upon us all, for we in Canada follow American fashions in educational theory with a deadening faithfulness.

In the world today there are great numbers of people who were children when that educational revolution took place and who are now in late middle age or in early old age. They have not lived lives distinguished by any special creative zeal, but they can now be persuaded that creativity lies within their reach, and that it will enlarge and brighten what some social scientists so hideously call "the twilight years."

I fear that these trusting souls are doomed to disappointment. You cannot decide that you are going to be creative at that age. Unless creativity—I don't like the word but there is no precise substitute for it—has made itself manifest in their lives long ago, they are not going to discover that they have it now. It is too late. They must not be deceived by the bombast of Longfellow:

> Ah, nothing is too late
> Till the tired heart hath ceased to palpitate;
> Caro learned Greek at eighty, Sophocles
> Wrote his grand Oedipus, and Simonides
> Bore off the prize of verse from his compeers
> When each had numbered more than four score years.

That is all very well, but Cato had been an intellectual all his life, Sophocles was a poet of mighty renown, and Simonides had been writing epitaphs since he was a child. When he wrote those lines Longfellow set himself on a level with writers in *The Reader's Digest* and kindred popular publications which urge old people to discover their hidden creativity just as they urge them not to give up sex, but to keep banging away, however loudly outraged nature cries for rest. The idea of hidden creativity is a delusion, like talk of "mute, inglorious Miltons." If there is any genuine creativity it will assert itself early in life, and if someone is mute and inglorious it is foolish to call him a Milton. If you are prepared to put up with that sort of nonsense, I am a mute inglorious Beethoven.

The trouble, I think, arises because many people confuse creativity with intelligence. They are not at all the same thing. It may very well be that in advanced years many people discover aptitudes and abilities which are related to intelligence of which they had not been conscious before. But creativity is not directly associated with intelligence, and may indeed exist where intelligence is not strong. Artists and poets and musicians are notoriously unskilled in their approach to practical matters, and are disastrous in their handling of money. Sometimes, like Balzac, they acquire great fortunes and then lose them in some hare-brained scheme, or blow them in absurd extravagances; this is not what the intelligent person does. Creative people are often victims of bad habits which they cannot control; intelligence is a safeguard against such folly. I have often declared, to be greeted with incredulity, that it is possible to possess creative power in the highest degree without having intelligence above a modest level.

The intelligence testers come to my assistance. A scientist in this sort of calculation, Catharine Morris Cox, has applied her skill to the work of a great many writers. I am not wholly convinced of her ability to assess their level of intelligence when she has only their published work to go on, and her more exact tests cannot be applied to people long dead; nevertheless, she has made known her findings and seems to have no misgivings about them. And, among authors, who do you suppose she declared to be the most intelligent of all? John Stuart Mill. He was a political economist, and unless you are one of those mocking persons who regards political economy as whimsical, fictional, unfounded vapouring, you will not be likely to think of him as powerfully creative. Out of all his voluminous writings, he has left only one phrase that has crept into common use—and it is "unearned increment." But out of the 200 marks that are possible in intelligence tests, Mill scores a superb 190, five points above Goethe. It is interesting that Lord Byron scores 150, whereas Wordsworth and Keats and Shelley are nowhere. Shakespeare does not even get on the list below the 100 mark. Balzac, of whom I spoke a moment ago as a reckless spendthrift, scores 130. These findings are based on the Terman Intelligence Quotient index.

I confess that I take some comfort in Shakespeare's inadequacy, for many years ago when I was fourteen I was subjected to an intelligence test as I entered a new school. When the results were posted my name was not on the list, and I asked the master in charge why that was so. "I hardly like to tell you," he said. With sinking heart I inquired, "Was my score very bad?" "I won't give you the figure," said he (he was a kindly man), "but I will tell you this. It is a score which, if you were in the army, would mean that you could never rise above the rank of private—not even to corporal." This was bad news indeed, and it affected me for a long time and saddens me still. (But after all these years, I venture to think that if I had spent my life in the army I might have at last risen to be a corporal. Indeed, in a war where men fell like flies and promotion was rapid and haphazard, I might even have become a temporary sergeant.) But as things were I had no choice—it was literature, or starve. So without measurable intelligence I became a writer and, although I have done other things on the side, so to speak—been an actor, edited a daily paper, directed a college for graduate students, lectured as a professor—it was scribble, scribble, scribble all the way. Witless wretch that I was, it was my destiny.

I know that in saying that I am offending those among you to whom the idea of destiny, or fate, is repugnant. You are Americans and your country has prospered in the belief that anybody can do anything if he tries hard enough. And indeed that is, in a measure, true. But common sense must not be snubbed. It is obvious that President Clinton can be the chief executive of your country, and it is possible that he had his eye on that office long before it came within the range of possibility. But it was his fate to be President. If he had set his heart on being a greater tenor than Pavarotti I don't think he would have made it, although it is known that he has some humble musical skill. I do not put forward a dreary doctrine that everybody has his place and cannot rise above it; rather, I say that the place he has attained, and in which for a thousand reasons he is fixed and above which his best efforts will not lift him—that is his destiny. It is a commonplace to say that character is destiny: I think it equally true, but bitterer on the tongue, to say that destiny is also character.

Whose destiny is it then, to be creative and to continue being creative throughout a lifetime? If it is not intelligence, what is it? It gets us nowhere to say it is a gift of nature. How does nature manifest the gift?

Because it is what I know best, I speak principally of writing, and of writing on the level which commands respect above what we are ready to accord to trivial verse, or fiction that is consciously written to pass the time and then be forgotten. But what I am going to say applies also to creative people of other kinds—to musicians, to painters, sculptors, architects, to creators of all sorts who bring something new into existence, or who remind us of something old that has been forgotten or neglected. What sort of people are they?

I hope that the scientists among you do not think that I have forgotten your creativity. By no means. Do we ever forget that it was Einstein who said that the truly creative scientists are those who have access to their dreams? What did he mean by that?

I am certain he did not mean the access to the world of dreams that may be achieved by psychoanalysis. In that mingling of science and art the dreams of the patient are given the most careful consideration and the patient becomes aware of his or her dreams as never before. But to undergo psychoanalysis does not make you creative. Einstein must have meant something else.

What he meant, I think, were not entirely the dreams of sleep but those curious and often startling images and spoken messages, and hints of music, that occur when we are in that state of reverie that lies between sleeping and waking, and in which problems are sometimes solved which have defied the best efforts of the awakened mind. Scientists are familiar with August Kekulé's famous dream of the snake with its tail in its mouth—the uroboros of myth—which gave him his solution to the problem of the benzene ring. It was in such a state of reverie that Coleridge, assisted perhaps by his accustomed dose of laudanum, composed the poem "Kubla Khan," which he was able to recover and write down after he woke up. It is one of the gems of poetry in English, and as we read it we too are taken into a different world, in which nothing is familiar but in which everything is somehow marvellously clear.

Another instance of a similar sort concerns the composer Richard Wagner. He was composing his opera *Das Rheingold* and he had for some time been searching fruitlessly for the theme of introductory music that would call up the whole splendour and majesty of the river

Rhein. One day, very much worn out by the stress of his creative work, he laid himself down for a rest, hoping to sleep. But, as he says, he could not sleep but fell into a somnolent state, a reverie, indeed, and then he became conscious of a chord of music which persisted in the hearing of his mind as other, fantastic variations formed themselves about it. He knew that it was the chord of E-flat major. He wrote: "I awoke in sudden terror from my doze, feeling as though the waves were rushing high above my head. I at once recognized that the orchestral overture to the *Rheingold*, which must have long lain latent within me, though it had been unable to find definite form, had at last been revealed to me. I then quickly realized my own nature; the stream of life was not to flow to me from without, but from within." This is no mere figure of speech; what flowed to him on this occasion were 136 bars of superbly evocative music, rooted in the major triad of E-flat. There was nothing fanciful or vague about it.

This sort of thing is familiar to innumerable creative people, and Wagner puts the matter clearly when he says that the flow is not from without but from within. Every writer knows the experience of having somebody tell him a story or describe a character which is supposed to be exactly what a writer is looking for. But it isn't. Writers can be cantankerous, and any attempt to prime their pump, or insert a story into them, is likely to be met with resistance and sometimes with contempt. It is of course true that writers pick up hints from what they hear which may in time turn into completed stories. But a hint is all they want; they resist detail. Henry James has written revealingly about this aspect of his art; the hint is all, and too much corroborative detail interferes with the amplification which is the writer's own work. The hint must be absorbed, perhaps forgotten, but somehow "put into the works," so to speak, and in time it may reappear and be used.

The creative process cannot be forced. Sometimes I am visited by very young people, students in high school, whom I have, for one reason or another, agreed to talk to about writing because they study some of my books. It is not a sort of encounter that I meet with enthusiasm, because a book one has written undergoes strange metamorphoses by the time it has been accommodated to a class of students of widely varying capacity by a teacher who may not be a perceptive guide. One of the questions I am most often asked by such visitors is, "Where do you get your ideas from?" My answer is always the same: "I do not get my ideas, they get me." Students think I am being facetious and don't want to tell the secrets of my workshop, but what I say to them is no more than the truth. Unless an idea rises from within, it is of no use to me as the groundwork of a story. It must have some connection, probably indirect but by no means beyond discovery, with me and the inner world where I chiefly live, as do we all. It has been said with truth that virtually all fiction is disguised autobiography, and sometimes the disguise is very thin. But more often it defies the external searcher or the critic, because it is associated with the writer's fantasy life, into which the researcher, the biographer, the critic, cannot intrude.

So I repeat: The creative process cannot be forced. Of course we read exciting stories about Mozart writing the overture to *The Marriage of Figaro* on the day of the first performance, or about Sheridan writing superb pages of comedy almost as the actors are about to go on the stage. But we would be more accurate to say that Mozart and Sheridan are putting on paper the overture, or the scenes of comedy; these things have been in existence before but have not been put in tangible form. Mozart and Sheridan may have been lazy, but they have not been uncreative. Many creative people can tell you of the work that can be done under the pressure of necessity, but the work lies ready to be brought forth; it cannot be dragged into existence from nowhere at all. I suppose psychoanalysts could tell us about the desire to retain something until the precise moment comes for its appearance, but psychoanalysts have not, on the whole, been especially good at explaining the secrets of creativity. I think it is because to them the quality of art is not important, and we all know how ready Freud and Jung and their followers have been to choose second- or third-rate literature as the subject of their investigations on this subject. What is mediocre is more easily dissected and scrutinized than what is first-rate. It is easier to apply psychoanalytical theory to something like *Gradiva* or an adventure tale by Rider Haggard than to go to work on Goethe's *Faust*. When Ernest Jones writes about *Oedipus* or *Hamlet* it is instructive how little his opinions enlarge or increase our pleasure in the plays. It may be that psychoanalysis is hostile to art, which is markedly resistant to systems of analysis.

So, if the creative process cannot be forced, can it be encouraged or assisted? Yes, it can. Elaborate theories in elaborate language can be produced to describe this process, but in the end it comes down pretty much to the artist's ability to get out of his own way. He must not force; he must not strain. In his encounters with the creative process within him he must not dictate, or bully, or make conditions. He must, in fact, give up control and abandon himself to what happens. It is surprisingly difficult to do this in a world where so many of us have been subjected to strenuous education, with its emphasis on the virtues of hard work, and its insistence that virtually anything can be achieved by determined effort. Many people find any such abandonment of control, any non-interference, is impossible.

Artists, if they have the root of the matter in them, know what to do. That is why so many people think of them as idlers, loafers, people without decent ambition and application. The fact is, of course, that they are often working hardest when they seem most idle. They are getting out of their own way and allowing the creative process to take over. Everybody knows how strange it was to see Einstein standing, sometimes for hours, watching men work on a construction job, or digging one of their innumerable holes in a busy road. Watching other people work is, for the creative mind, wonderfully evocative of all sorts of reflections, some of which are useful. This is a characteristic of the creative person that can be maddening to those around him, and is a great source of domestic disquiet.

Knowing that this is true, high-minded institutions have brought into being places where artists can be creatively idle, living in pretty little cabins, having everything they need (and much that they merely want) provided by their kindly patrons, and perhaps appearing only at dinnertime to chew the rag and pass the wassail bowl. But I cannot find any evidence that these retreats bring forth important artistic work, and I think that the reason is that they are in their benevolent way urging, expecting, hinting, coaxing. It is in contact with the world at large that artists—idle lookers-on though they may appear—are most impelled to do what they do—which is to listen to the inner voices.

Does the artist really do nothing during these periods of apparent idleness? No. He politely and reverently asks for the help he needs. In the language of religion, he "waits upon the Lord." Sometimes he must wait a long time. He must learn patience. Nothing can be forced. The growth of what is excellent is slow. The mushroom growth of the third-rate has little to do with real creation.

I have given a good deal of time to talking about how creativity works, insofar as I understand the matter. I have not said much about old age. I hope I have made it clear that I do not think creativity makes a sudden appearance when a man or a woman has laid down the task that has engaged them for fifty or more years. If you don't have it when you were young, don't hope for it when you are old. It is a gift, and if that is elitist and undemocratic, I am not myself responsible.

A gift—yes, but what sort of gift? I have said that the creative person is not necessarily highly intelligent, as the world understands intelligence. On the other hand, the creator, the artist, is not an *idiot savant*—a simpleton with an inexplicable knack. What is the gift?

I think it has been very well described by a writer of great achievement, the late Vladimir Nabokov. When he was discussing the writing of André Malraux, he said: "The longer I live the more I become convinced that the only thing that matters in literature is the (more or less irrational) *shamanstvo* of a book, i.e., that the good writer is first of all an enchanter." The word *shamanstvo*, a Russian friend tells me, means "enchanter quality." Much is contained in that definition. "The only thing that matters"—this suggests that style, ranging from the stately prose of Samuel Johnson to the seemingly unstudied prose of Mark Twain, is a secondary consideration. "More or less irrational"—this suggests that the writing takes its quality from an inner source and not from a rigid conscious control. And then, of course—"The good writer is first of all an enchanter." If you are an enchanter, the gift may develop and undergo refinement, but it is present from the beginning; it will not suddenly manifest itself at the age of retirement. And to be an enchanter—what is that? I shall not attempt to tell you, because you can meet the quality and fall under its spell, and analyze and explain it if you can, by reading literature of the first order in which it is to be found.

Let me give as an example one great poem, which combines enchantment, art, and thought of a superior order, and which concerns old age. It is truly a View in Winter. Many of you will know it. It is Robert Browning's "Rabbi Ben Ezra." The first lines are very familiar:

> Grow old along with me!
> The best is yet to be,
> The last of life, for which the first was made:
> Our times are in His hand
> Who saith, "A whole I planned,
> Youth shows but half; trust God, see all, nor be afraid!"

The suggestion that life should be seen as a whole falls heavily on the ears of many people today, who worship youth and the pleasures of youth (especially sex) and are determined to prolong youth so far as possible for as long as possible. After which, who knows what horrors! The poem praises youth, but not as the best part of life. The poem tells us to look indulgently on youth and forgive our youthful follies, but never for a moment pretend that they are not follies and unbecoming the later years of life. Only life seen as a whole reveals any meaning or intention in whatever Power originated the life, and whatever measure of understanding there may be comes with age.

The poem declares that God works as a potter, and man is the pot he fashions. The potter's wheel is the time and circumstances in which man finds himself and the clay is what is man's essence, his spiritual being. Only the totality, the finished work, can be judged if one hopes to find purpose in the work, and that judgment is the work of old age.

The poem has been harshly criticized because it seems to say that man has no free will. Maybe it does say that, and maybe it is right. I do not propose to argue the point, except to point out that Browning is speaking, as he so often does, in the character of another person, in this instance a twelfth-century theologian and philosopher, whose theme is old age. For many years I have made it a point to read "Rabbi Ben Ezra" on my birthday.

These are the reflections of a writer. I make no particular claim for them, except that, for obvious reasons, they are truly "A View in Winter."

Canada

25

What May Canada Expect from Her Writers?

The personal struggle of Aleksandr Solzhenitsyn and his utterances when he had at last been permitted to leave Russia affected me deeply, and made me think afresh about what it means to be a writer. Personal ambitions are given great importance in North America, and attempts to take writing with a more than personal seriousness—to regard it in fact as a vocation and a trust—may gain the writer a reputation for inflation of the ego. Canada is no friend to seriousness of this kind, among writers or, indeed, among people in public life. A profoundly Canadian story was told me by a friend who was at a party in Vancouver in 1957 when someone came in with the news that Lester B. Pearson had been awarded the Nobel Peace Prize. There was silence for a moment, broken by an elderly lady who spoke, trembling with indignation: "Well—just who does he think he is?" she demanded. Mr. Pearson had offended against her Canadian demand for the appearance (not necessarily the reality) of humility.... The speech that follows was made in 1972 to a society of Industrial Accountants, who had asked me to say something about writing.

Since 1901, when it was founded, the Nobel Prize for Literature has carried greater distinction than any other international literary award. It never fails to arouse widespread interest, even among people whose concern with literature is slight. Never did it give rise to so much discussion as in 1970, when the award was made to Aleksandr Solzhenitsyn, the Russian novelist.

Much of this excitement was created by the refusal of the government of the USSR to permit Solzhenitsyn to go to Stockholm to accept the prize, and by a later refusal to grant a travel visa to a representative of the Swedish Academy who sought to visit Russia in order to award the prize on the spot. The Russian government does not like Solzhenitsyn, and with reason; he is unquestionably one of its most outspoken critics. Being a novelist of sombre emotional power, whose work is translated and read everywhere in the Western world, he is something more than just a nuisance; he is a protesting voice, heard everywhere. He enjoys the special immunity of the great artist—for any attempt to get rid of him or silence him would bring about an international outcry.

Nor is Solzhenitsyn crippled by modesty in the claims he makes for himself. The splendid confidence in his own greatness that is exhibited by some European writers—the name of the late Thomas Mann comes to mind, as well as that of Solzhenitsyn—speaks of a culture very different from our own. A great writer, he has said, is like a rival government in an oppressed country, and the official government cannot be expected to like him. He knows himself to be a man of heroic courage, living constantly under threat; a single unwise move on his part, or a failure of discretion on the part of Russian authority, could bring about his death. He has no wish to die; he wants to go on living, and writing, and making his widely read protests against the tyranny that would reduce him to silence, or compel him to join that group of biddable writers who ensure a safe and profitable career by working within the limits considered permissible to artists in the USSR.

Because of his special status, people everywhere who are interested in the cause of literary freedom waited anxiously for what Solzhenitsyn would say about the award of the Nobel Prize for Literature to himself. It was only within the last few weeks that his speech of acceptance could be made public. On August 25 it was released to the world, and, as was expected, it was yet another powerful protest, not so much against the Russian government as against all forces, everywhere, that seek to harness, censor, and diminish the opinions of men of letters, who must, above all artists, have freedom to say what they have to say without hindrance. For the work of the writer, whose medium is words, may come under fire from any government official who thinks he understands words, and is ready to excerpt passages which he considers, for one reason or another, to be offensive or dangerous.

Solzhenitsyn's speech caused little stir in Canada. For indeed, when has anything concerned with the world of literature ever caused a stir in our somnambulistic country? There may have been some comment in our press; if so, I did not see it. But I read some newspapers that come to me from outside Canada, and there the speech was reported, discussed, and sifted for what this extraordinary, courageous being had dared to say in the teeth of a government which might crush him, and where, as he said, "a whole national literature was buried, cast into oblivion not only without a grave, but without even underclothes, naked, with a number tagged onto its toe."

What I have said up to now may strike you as a rather ominous beginning for a speech which you may have hoped would be light in tone—perhaps even funny. Don't worry: The funny part is coming now. As I read, and reread, what Solzhenitsyn had risked his freedom and possibly his life to say to the writers of the world, and to people who value the free exchange of ideas, and not only of ideas but of feelings, emotions, and shades of sensibility, I asked myself again and again: "What does this say to me? I am a Canadian writer; this man is talking to writers; what do his words mean to a Canadian?" There were two possible responses: laughter or tears. I chose to laugh, but it was not what people mean when they speak of "a good laugh." It was a bad laugh—one of the very worst laughs I have ever had in my life. For I realized that my own country had not yet progressed to that point of development where literature is a serious matter.

Do not misunderstand me. I do not long to live dangerously. I do not want to lie awake at night wondering if the soft knock of the agents of the secret police will come before dawn. I have no yearning to see in Canada any increase in what we already have of the violence of which Solzhenitsyn says that it "is brazenly and victoriously striding across the whole world." But I should like to think of myself as a writer in a country which demonstrably and undeniably had a serious concern with serious things, which saw itself from a world view and not from a parochial view, and which could distinguish between what things in life are serious and what things are merely solemn. I should like to think of myself as a writer in a country where a writer is recognized as a man with a vocation and not merely as a man with a hobby. I should like to think of myself as writing for fellow countrymen in whose personal consciousness I might hope to form a part, however humble, and not simply as an entertainer whose value rises or falls by the estimation in which he is held by *The New York Times* Book Review or the Book-of-the-Month Club. Are these desires of mine unrealistic? I read and reread what Solzhenitsyn had written to the world and I realized that he and I were worlds apart. He, living in a country where to be a writer was as dangerous as to be a spy in the employ of a foreign power: I, living in a country where to be a writer is as innocuous, as laudable without being in the least significant, as being a manufacturer of yogourt.

I spoke of Solzhenitsyn as living in the USSR as a spy in the employ of a foreign power. But every writer of any significance in any country is a spy in the employ of a foreign power, and that power is the supranational power of free, unresting, probing intelligence. If that power is foreign to Russia, is it not also foreign to Canada? But Russia seems to know that it exists and dreads it: Canada has but dimly guessed that such a power exists. When I speak of Canada I speak of the educated and intelligent men and women of the whole country: I do not speak of a few hundred intellectuals who are indeed aware of this external world power, and who owe it their chief allegiance. A few hundred quiet intellectuals do not make an awakened country; only an aware, alert, tirelessly curious middle class can do that, and it is greatly to be feared that in our country the middle class rarely stirs in its sleep. And yet to say that as a nation we sleep is not really accurate, for to sleep is often to dream, and Canada, in the national sense, does not dream. Our condition is stuporous; dully contented and stuporous.

Did I say that Canada does not dream? That again is not *quite* true. Canada does dream, but it pays very little heed to its dreams. I do not know how much attention you pay to modern advances in the investigation of the mind, in health and in sickness; the people who are engaged in that work pay great attention to dreams, and they are familiar with the patient who, when asked if he dreams much, replies, "I dream now and again, but I don't remember what I dream." Not to remember one's dreams can be a danger signal, because it means that one of the routes by which the deepest promptings of the spirit reach the intelligence has been closed off. Not by accident but because of indifference or, worse, fear as to what the dreams might hint at, or give a riddling voice.

The literature of a country is in many ways like the dreams of a man. Some dreams are so fleeting, or so trivial, or so obviously caused by a draft from the open window, or an unwise snack before going to bed, that we quickly put them aside. Similarly some books are so inconsiderable, or so obviously touched off by some trivial circumstance, that we are quickly tired of them. But there are other dreams which cannot be attributed to external causes, and which are so vivid in their purposeful statement that we puzzle over them, and remember them for years afterward. Sometimes, if we are persistent, they yield up a secret; they tell us something about ourselves that we are well advised to heed, and grateful to learn.

So it is with books. There are even dreams which, without being themselves prophecies, contain the form of something that is yet to come. The writers of such books are not prophets, except in the sense that they are sensitive to national attitudes and generally accepted points of view in a way that most men are not. They can, as the saying goes, see through a brick wall. The reason is simple: The wall has long since ceased to exist, but it is the writer, rather than some other man, who notices when it came down.

I hope you will not think me immodest if I offer an example that concerns myself. For many years the question occurred to me at intervals: What would Canada do with a saint, if such a strange creature were to appear within our borders? I thought Canada would reject the saint because Canada has no use for saints, because saints hold unusual opinions, and worst of all, saints do not pay. So in 1970 I wrote a book, called *Fifth Business*, in which that theme played a part. Several people suggested to me that I misjudged Canada in supposing that it would not know a saint when it saw one. But only last summer it was drawn forcibly to the attention of the people of Canada that they had possessed one man, Dr. Norman Bethune, who was certainly considered a great humanitarian, of virtually saint-like stature, in Red China. Canada had pretty well succeeded in ignoring Dr. Bethune, who unquestionably held unusual opinions. But all of a sudden Dr. Bethune began to pay; he was the strongest sympathetic link between Canada and a country with which Canada hoped to do some profitable business. And as soon as Dr. Bethune began to pay, political figures hastened to the scene of his birth, a memorial plaque was unveiled there, and Canada was assured from several sources of undoubted respectability that Dr. Norman Bethune had been a Great Canadian, and that we had at last overcome our natural modesty about saying so.

I told you that there would be some funny parts in this speech, and that is one of them. I was understandably pleased that a book of mine had dwelt, certainly not in a prophetic but in an allusive manner, with a theme which so soon asserted itself in our national life. A new novel of mine appeared on October 20, and I can hardly wait to see if anything I have written in it will make a subsequent appearance in the daily news.

I said that I would talk on the theme: What Does Canada Expect from Her Writers? The question is easily answered: Canada expects nothing from her writers. Let us rephrase the question to read: What May Canada Expect from Her Writers?

Canada may reasonably expect what other countries expect and get from a national literature. First, a sense of national character. Not, I hasten to say, of aggressive nationalism, of scorn-Britainism, of anti-Americanism, for these are negative qualities upon which nothing can worthily be built. Nor do I mean a projection of the picture of a typical Canadian of any kind, for literature of the first order does not deal with types, but with individuals. But as a people we are neither Englishmen who have been exported to the New World, nor are we Americans who, having been assembled on Canadian soil, pass as a native product while still looking like something conceived in Detroit.

We have our own concerns, our own secrets, and our own dreams. Sometimes, to the Canadians who remember and ponder them, these dreams are restless, disquieting, and fearsome; sometimes they are foreshadowings of what is yet to be; sometimes they are assurances of personal conquests and new heights seized and held. It is upon these deeply personal things that our national character rests.

Second, we may expect from our writers that vigilance on behalf of intellectual freedom and moral vigour which Aleksandr Solzhenitsyn has shown heroically and in isolation in a country where those qualities are endangered. Endangered, as I have pointed out, because the government of his country fears them. Endangered and abraded in our land because it appears so often that Canada hardly realizes that these qualities exist, and does not know where to look for help in making them matters of acute and untiring national concern.

Last, we may expect from our writers a true depiction of what our life in Canada is. And of course I speak of the essence of that life, not its externals. That life cannot be described in terms of the problems of other countries, for even when we share those problems, they appear in our country as Canadian matters. Nor can our national life be described without saying some things that will distress tender-minded people who shrink from what is disagreeable. A great poet has said:

> If way to the better there be
> It exacts a full look at the worst.

But not, of course, at the worst alone. There is much in our life that lies in realms that can brace us, elate us, and make us laugh.

Canada has a literature now, and some parts of it may well be objects of national pride, and as I am myself a novelist, and must not therefore speak of the work of novelists, let me refer you to the work of some of our poets, which is poetry of a special fragrance, for it is our own. And in the future, we may, if Canada asks for it, expect from our writers works of the kind Solzhenitsyn speaks of in the great declaration to the world of which I have already spoken. They are, he says, works of pungence and luminosity, with completely irrefutable power to convince, works which cause the reader to be visited, dimly, briefly, by revelations such as cannot be produced by rational thinking.

Works like the looking-glass in the fairy tale, he says; you look into it and you see not yourself but, for one second, the Inaccessible, whither no man can ride, no man can fly. Ah, yes, but to have glimpsed the Inaccessible is, however imperfectly, to have gained access to it. Once we have *found* the mirror, we can return to it again and again.

And that, ladies and gentlemen, is what your writers can give you, if you want it, and let them know that you want it. But that decision rests not with the writers, but with you. And before you can ask us for what we have, it is first necessary to understand what we are.

26

The Canada of Myth and Reality

He must be a rare Canadian indeed who does not feel himself moved, from time to time, in and out of season, to comment on some aspect of his country's fortunes, spiritual being, government, arts, sciences, economics, virtues and shortcomings, and any and every aspect of the national life. Such comment is a national sport even more popular than hockey. It is a different thing, however, to be asked to talk about one's own country in another land, to people who know little about it. This was my daunting experience when I was asked to talk about the myth and reality of Canada at a symposium promoted by the Association for Canadian Studies in the United States, the theme of which was Twentieth-Century Canadian Culture. There was only one thing to do—to speak truth insofar as it is given me to perceive truth—and this is what I said on April 5, 1977.

What qualifications have I that excuse my temerity in appearing before you to talk about Canadian Myths and Realities? It sounds, doesn't it, as if I possessed some splendid certainty about which Canadian attitudes were the stuff of myth, and which were indisputable fact. But I have no such confidence; in my time I have seen realities dissolve at the first touch of serious investigation into myth, and I have seen myths given the validity of reality, and acted upon as if they were matters of accepted fact. So—who am I to draw distinctions?

Well, to begin with, I am a Canadian by birth, and, on my mother's side, by long descent. I have lived by far the greater part of my life in Canada, and I have some factual knowledge of it that I have gained first as a journalist and latterly as a university teacher; I have also another knowledge of Canada that I can only call a feeling in my bones, a congeries of intuitions and hunches belonging to my calling as an author. I am neither a politician nor an economist, and I cannot speak with any of the splendid authority that belongs to such people. But I am a Canadian right enough: I share all the Canadian perplexities and doubts: I approach them, however, with one eye cocked toward the concept of myth, which has been my study for many years, and the other eye clear, I hope, of that cataract growth of unwarrantable pride which is such a hindrance in any sort of national self-inspection.

What do I mean when I speak of myth? In national terms I mean the sort of attitude which most people take for granted, the belief that nobody questions because nobody troubles to put it in concrete terms. The myth of national character is familiar to us all: In your country it is summed up in the figure of Uncle Sam, a Down-East Yankee in the dress of 1830 or thereabouts, totally unlike most of your citizens in every way, though now and then, on the streets or in a photograph, one spies the reality on which the stereotype was founded. We all know John Bull, who is not at all like any Englishman we have ever met, and Marianne, that generous-hearted, big-breasted female who is such an incongruous symbol for modern France. But where is the Canadian stereotype? We had one once, a grinning fellow called Jack Canuck, who looked as if he were engaged in wheat farming on a large scale, but we got rid of him because he simply didn't do. Of late years two stereotype figures have arisen from the pressures of our political situation; one is a wistful, large-eyed, pitiful girl in the peasant dress of the eighteenth century, and the other is a coarse-grained, large-footed, evil-visaged Scotch banker, to whom she is bound in a hateful marriage from which she seeks to escape. The mismated pair are, of course, Quebec, La Belle Province, and the other part of Canada. A queer song-and-dance team they are. But whatever reality they may have in Canada—and certainly they have some roots in popular belief, which is not to say roots in fact—they are not recognized outside Canada, and the essential point about national stereotypes is that they should have a wide acceptance among people of other nations.

Does this mean, then, that Canada has no national character, no myth by which it lives and from which it approaches the rest of mankind? No, it does not. It means only that Canada achieved adulthood comparatively recently, in an era of the world's history that has been immensely complicated by universal education, international social and political concern, and the sort of sophistication that relates to a highly developed technology. I do not mean that we are a young nation; we used to say that, but we are now aware that we are not really very young, and that in terms of some of the emerging nations of the Third World we are positively venerable.

Perhaps we have been a little late in coming to self-recognition. Sometimes when I think of the great world family of English-speaking peoples, I think of Canada as the Daughter Who Stayed at Home. I mean that in 1776 Columbia, a self-willed girl with a strong sense of her own independence, left her mother's house, after some high-pitched family rows, and set up a household of her own. At that time Canada elected to stay with Mother. It was not a simple decision, for Columbia offered us all the inducements that naughty girls have at their command; we have not forgotten the bags of gold (we suspected that they were of French origin) with which some of your very persuasive citizens—including that extremely persuasive, somewhat ambiguous character Benjamin Franklin—visited us, hoping that we might be bought. But, to continue this simplified version of history, we said: "No, Mother needs us, and we shall always be true to Mother; so long as she needs a faithful daughter, we shall never desert her." So what happened? Just what everybody with a knowledge of family behaviour might expect to happen: Columbia, the naughty daughter, prospered mightily and Mother (who always had a sharp eye for success) became very fond of her. And the Good Daughter Who Stayed at Home became, in the course of time, rather a bore. Many years have passed since that decision and that outcome: Mother has been having a rough time, and has taken up with all sorts of rowdy Continental companions. And the Good Daughter has begun, somewhat belatedly, to have very serious thoughts about her future. Where does it lie?

It does not require a very acute political sense to see that it lies with the North American continent, and there are those who say that the Good Daughter ought to have listened to Columbia two hundred years ago, and made a break with Home. Such attempts to unscramble historical omelettes are a waste of time, and it is too late now for us to throw in our lot with you as ten more, very large, states. We have become too set in our ways, and in some important respects our ways are not your ways, nor are our thoughts your thoughts. Our ideas about education are not like yours, and although you have done very distinguished things in education on the top level, I think that on the middle level we have done better than you. In matters relating to the administration of justice we are accustomed to a system that it is fair to call more rigorous than yours, somewhat less open to political caprice. And particularly in political matters our system is markedly different from your own, apportioning power more evenly, and affording the means of getting rid of elected persons who do not please us with considerable dispatch. In many other respects we are manifestly your inferiors, and we borrow from you and copy from you without shame. In financial affairs our great defect is an extremity of caution; we seem to have been settled by a more penny-pinching class of person than you were, and we are, on the whole, resistant to feats of financial daring.

It is too late for us to change our spots now, and if some of our spots are manifestly blemishes, there are others that we consider rather becoming.

In one respect we are, if you will permit me to say so, more realistic than you. We have recognized that all nations of the first rank nowadays are socialist in their general political trend, and we act on that knowledge, sometimes ruefully, but with a philosophical determination. When you visit us, you may not immediately sense that you are in a socialist country. You see remnants of an old order—courts conducted with considerable ceremony and an antique form of dress; the majority of the populace according special treatment to persons who are representatives of the Crown; legislatures bound by ceremonial observance and a special kind of language. These things have an agreeable quaintness, and also a profoundly practical purpose in maintaining a proper decorum in the discharge of social and political affairs. But beneath all of this we are a people firmly set in the socialist pattern. We have bitten the socialist bullet, and it is a long time since we felt any perceptible toothache because of it.

One obvious way in which our socialism shows itself is in our government support for the arts and sciences. We have made it work, not always to everybody's satisfaction, but still with a kind of rough and perceptible justice. Insofar as public encouragement *can* support art and science—and admittedly such support can only be very general and cannot be expected to produce wonders—we accept such a plan as part of the responsibility of the nation as a whole.

But where, you may ask, are the myths? Demonstrable differences are easily understood: What have you to say about those things which are more truly divisive, because they exist not in politics or law or banking or even in the arts, but in the less accessible realm of the spirit?

Our myths, or "life-supporting illusions," as your great scholar of the mythic world Joseph Campbell calls them, are many, and I cannot explore them all. There is, for instance, our Myth of Innocence or Moral Superiority: Deep in our hearts we Canadians cherish a notion—you see that I do not call it an idea, because an idea may be carefully formulated, whereas a notion is an elusive thing that takes form from every mind that embraces it—we cherish a notion that we are a simple folk, nourished on the simpler truths of Christianity, in whom certain rough and untutored instincts of nobility assert themselves. Now, of course you are rather in that line yourselves, so you will readily understand what I am talking about. But you will not understand it quite as a Canadian understands it, because of course such a Myth of Innocence is really a manifestation of pride, and it means Innocence in comparison with the flawed virtue of somebody else. And for us the somebody else is you.

When I was a boy, when history was still a compulsory subject for children, I learned some things that would surprise you. I have alluded already to one of them, concerning the war of 1776. You may be surprised to learn that for generations of Canadian children, you were the Bad Guys in that war, and you may think yourselves lucky to have won it, because if you had not, George Washington would have been hanged as a traitor. Of course as I grew older, and learned more history, I moderated this idea, but at my Canadian university nobody suggested that you were in the right. The Revolutionary War was a struggle between pig-headed Englishmen on both sides. England behaved badly, and you behaved badly, but there was one figure in that struggle who behaved with propriety and perhaps with nobility, and that was Canada.

Later on, in the War of 1812, you once again behaved in a manner deeply distressing to our feelings. Let me give it to you as it was given to me, when a child, and ready to accept whatever was said with sufficient authority. Set on by the French, in order to create a diversion on the North American continent and to divert British troops from the European struggle, you attempted to invade Canada. Perhaps you did not try very hard: We, with inferior numbers, drove you back home again. Of course the Sword of the Lord was on our side. I do not suppose that the Battle of Stoney Creek bulks very large in your national consciousness, but it is tremendous in mine, because much of it was fought on the farm of one of my forebears, and in that battle we wiped your noses rather roughly.

Why were we able to do it? Reason suggests that your forces had been misinformed; you thought we would welcome you as liberators; it is quite a common error of invading armies. When the farm boys on your side saw the farm boys on our side as mad as wet hens and firing hot lead out of farmhouse windows, they very sensibly decided that it was time to go home and reconsider the whole thing.

It was not a very terrible war, but the people who died in it were just as dead as any other soldiers who were trying to do what they were told, and we are still proud of them. I greatly admire the United States, but I am a creature of irrational passions just like everybody else, and when I visit the battleground of Queenston Heights, where the names of some of my ancestors appear on the monument, both as foot soldiers and as officers, I am extremely glad we licked you, and if the grass grows green there, it is not just the Canadian blood, but the Yankee blood, that gives it a special coppery lustre. Our Myth of Innocence, of having behaved well under stress, haunts those battlegrounds. And, alas, where Innocence flourishes, her shadow, Moral Superiority, is to be found as well.

Please do not misunderstand me; I have not come to Washington to fight the War of 1812 over again, but I cannot talk of our Myth of Innocence without speaking about it. I was also taught in school that in our dealings with the Indians we were greatly superior to you, because you cheated them and killed them and were thoroughly miserable to them, whereas we explained to them about the Great Mother beyond the sea, who loved them so much that she had prepared lovely reservations for them; the Indians understood perfectly, and sent the Great Mother presents of war bonnets and tomahawks (which, so far as I know, she never wore in public). It is only in comparatively recent times that the Indians have suggested that perhaps our Myth of Innocence needs a few footnotes, written by themselves.

Perhaps you are ready to say that my Myth of Innocence is nothing but a disagreeable self-righteousness, and certainly that plays its part in the myth, though I do not think it is the whole thing. But self-righteousness is part of the blood and bone of this continent, and I think it is somewhat stronger in Canada than it is among you. Self-righteousness is bound to be a characteristic of colonizing peoples; a grabber always wants moral backing when he grabs. If the grabber is an aristocrat in feeling, he justifies his grabbing on the simple ground that he is the stronger and therefore the superior, and that what he can seize he will hold. You had some aristocrats among your forefathers. Very few of the early settlers, or the later ones, of Canada were of aristocratic antecedents. They were humble people, who came to a new land because there was nothing for them in the old land, and it is a bitter Canadian saying that, of those who came, the only ones who stayed were those who did not have the return fare.

Humble people: How we exalt them in our history books and in our popular literature! And rightly so, for to their bravery and endurance we owe much of what we now are. They are, unquestionably, the salt of the earth. But as my own ancestry was indisputably humble, I may be permitted to say that a small quantity of salt is enough; it is the manifest duty of humble people to stop being humble just as fast as they can, because the shadow of their humility is a know-nothing, cantankerous self-righteousness. The very moment that humble people realize that they are humble and that humility is a very fine thing, their goose is cooked. In Canada we have had more than enough of such vaunting humility, and the neglect of intellectual and spiritual aspiration that it fosters. I do not suggest that the alternative is the grasping, self-serving spirit that is the shadow of aristocracy, but surely we can find a model for Modern Man that avoids both these extremes. We must rid ourselves of the Myth of Innocence on both sides of our border, for it is a potent source of mischief and a breeding ground for many dangerous sorts of stupidity. Innocence preserved too long sours into ignorance.

What other myths have we? I could talk of our Myth of Frugality, which is another pioneer inheritance, and like our Myth of Innocence degenerates rather too easily, and becomes mere pettiness and, in the world of the spirit, a mean mindedness.

But I shall not linger over our lesser myths, because there is one, very apparent in our national life now, and a mighty mischief-maker, on which I wish to spend some time. It is our Myth of Difference.

We are more like you than we are like any other nation on earth. Yet how quick we are to contradict an Englishman, let us say, who calls one of us an American. And when he says, as he often does, What's the difference? we are puzzled to give a short answer. If you ask a Swiss how he differs from a Frenchman, or an Italian, or a German, he can tell you at once, and probably he will say that, long years ago, he fought for his difference. I have spoken of the War of 1812, in which we fought for our difference; Canadians have fought in many wars (we once mustered a regiment to go to Italy to defend the Papal States) but we have only fought on that one occasion to preserve our own land and our own difference. In the light of what was going on in the world at the time, it was not a fight that bulks very large in the chronicles. But there is more than one kind of fighting, and anybody who reads the newspapers with his eyes open knows that the great battles of our time are the psychological battles, though these are often disguised as ideological battles. You made a great advance in your nationhood when you fought an ideological battle—for that was what it was, though it was fought with shot and shell—at the time of your Civil War. We are fighting our Civil War right now, and we are fighting it on what appear to be ideological grounds. Below that level, however, it is a psychological war, and the contestants are not only the Province of Quebec against the remainder of Canada, but the provinces against the Dominion government, the rich areas against the poor areas, and an unformed New Canada against an Old Canada that has served its turn. We are fighting the psychological war without revolution, though we may have to come to terms with some devolution, and the fullest stress of the psychological war has still to make itself known among us.

It is a war of immeasurable importance to us, and we fight it very much alone, because we cannot expect other nations to understand it deeply, nor could we tolerate any interference from them. We do not understand it wholly ourselves, and sometimes it seems that several wars are being fought. Those who can see only the wrangle with Quebec do not give full importance to the struggle that is going on between the industrial East and the newly rich West. And there are great numbers of us who think that the war is with you. You are supposed to have seized effective control of our primary resources and our industry. The fact that, if this is so, it happened because we had not wit enough or pride enough to keep what was our own only makes your wickedness more dreadful. There are also people who think that you have smothered our intellectual development and robbed us of our identity. Again, if this is so—and I beg you to note that I am not saying that it is so—it must have been because you were smarter than we were, which of course is intolerable. These deeply offended people want our identity back, and they often seem to think that it can be returned by you if only we abuse you loudly enough.

To my mind, all these struggles are part of a great struggle, comparable in its rigours to your Civil War, but fought very differently, inflicting different wounds, creating casualties of a different order, and leaving scars no less terrible. But the outcome will be—must be—a different Canada.

Many Canadians expect that it will be a Canada with what they call "a recognizable identity." We have, you see, been undergoing what is fashionably called an Identity Crisis. It is supposed that we do not know who we are, and that we wallow in an intolerable morass of self-doubt. This belief is attaining to the stature of a myth. It does not seem to occur to the people who talk most about it that only a minority of people, not to speak of peoples, have complete certainty about who they are and where they are going. Earlier I spoke of the national figures who serve as a cartoonist's shorthand for many nations—Uncle Sam, Marianne, John Bull, and the like; it sometimes seems that our Identity Crisis people want to secure one of those figures for us. They are the kind of people who attach immense importance to external things—to national costumes, folk arts (those dreary enthusiasms of the aesthetically stunted), national shrines, and the like. But surely everybody knows that such things are manifestations of a national spirit, rather than the origins of it.

People who look deeper into our national predicament desire more durable evidences of identity. They seek it in the arts. Science is of no help because scientists, benign or malignant, refuse to play the national game. Music is a lost cause, because the time for national schools of music seems to have passed; music is of international worth or it is nothing, and some of our contemporary music has won gratifying acceptance in the larger musical world. Painting is a different matter, and certainly some of the painting done in Canada in the present century has strong national inspiration and individuality. But it is in poetry and fiction that the questers repose their greatest hopes. A Canadian literature, recognizable as such at home and abroad, is what they want. But the creation of a national literature is almost as slow as the building of a coral atoll; toil as we may, the recognizable island will not rise above the waves in a very great hurry. But we are working at it, and we have made rather more progress than some of our most anxious Canadian watchers seem to understand.

Here I walk on dangerous ground, for I am myself a Canadian writer, and my work has been treated with friendliness and generosity outside my own country, and with special generous friendliness by your country. I have always had a friendly reception from a body of readers in Canada, but upon the whole the label of "satirist" has been attached to me, and countries that are not sure of their own identity are understandably suspicious of satirists. I have never thought of myself as a satirist: I do not sit down to my work sniggering with malice and muttering, "Here goes with the acid!" But I have certainly been strongly aware of the power of myth in Canadian thinking, and I do not share or admire many of our most popular myths; there are, however, other mythical elements in Canadian life and the Canadian ambience which I think deserve greater attention than they get, and I have tried to bring them into prominence. This is not what satirists do, and the recognition of what I am really attempting has been swifter and more sympathetic abroad than at home, and I am deeply grateful for understanding from any quarter.

One of the tasks of the Canadian writer is to show Canada to itself. He is not obliged to do this, but it is one of his options. Canadians—perhaps I should say the critical and academic world of Canada—are anxious for this kind of revelation, and so there is a strong temptation to fake it. Very few people seem to be aware how strong the pull of public opinion and public expectation is on an artist of any sort, and when he tries to give his public what it wants he is not perhaps a conscious faker, but what he produces is certainly a fake. The artist who binds himself to what might be called the national service can only do worthy and effective work if he is wholly true to himself: If his allegiance is to some form of public expectation, he is not serving his country as an artist should. An extreme example of this sort of dilemma is to be seen today in Russia, where public expectation and what the artist is driven to do by his true self are often widely at odds, and where the artist may suffer grievously if he does not toe the line.

To show Canada to itself—a serious and heavy task, and it cannot be undertaken by anyone whose determination is to wipe out the past. The odd thing is that so many Canadians who are eager to bring forth a new spirit seem to think either that we have no past, or that it is unworthy of consideration. I do not speak of an historical past in terms of lands seized and conquered, battles fought, and political crises endured, because nobody can deny the existence of such things: I mean a cultural past. Canada has a cultural past, and in my opinion it is a curious and interesting one, in which we were like the younger member of a large family who appears incongruously and somewhat comically in the cut-down garments of his elders. The young Canada during the whole of the nineteenth century wore a strange rig-out that we might imagine as a pair of pants cut down from Uncle Sam's very long legs, and the Union Jack waistcoat of John Bull, arranged with safety pins to fit a figure that lacked the John Bull paunch. Very often, instead of Uncle Sam's gaudy pants, a Scottish kilt, stained with the blood of age-old grievance and betrayal, shrouded the lower part of the body. And oh! the hats! A shabby tricorne in Quebec; the battered chimney pot of the Irishman in Ontario; the forbidding black puritan stove lid of the Mennonite in the West. We had hats for all seasons. It was a scarecrow outfit, beyond any doubt, but it was surprisingly warm, and when worn with an air it was by no means unattractive. Now that we are in a position to afford a new cultural suit I don't think that we should pretend that we never wore cultural castoffs when they were all we had. But we need not make our new garments fashionable versions of the old.

I remember these cultural castoffs with clarity and with affection, because when first I went to school every child was coursed through a variety of "readers" whose purpose was to extend his vocabulary and grammar and sense of rhetoric, and also to instruct him in what the world expected of him. Longfellow's "Psalm of Life" told us about footsteps on the sands of time, and Ben Jonson told us that

> It is not growing like a tree
> In bulk, doth make men better be.

Benjamin Franklin, whose *Reader's Digest* morality disgusted me even as a child, warned us not to pay too much for our whistle (as if you could pay too much for a really enchanting whistle), and Sir Henry Newbolt adjured us to "play up, play up, and play the game," though as the game was cricket we were not very clear about how it was to be done. We read about the heroism of Grace Darling in saving shipwrecked mariners off the coast of Scotland, and we read about Brave

John Maynard, who perished with his ship on Lake Michigan in order to save its passengers. People say now that we were badly used because none of the heroes, and moral gurus, were Canadians, but I can tell you truthfully that no such thought ever entered the heads of the children with whom I went to school. To us a hero was a hero and a guru was a guru and we felt no overmastering desire to know any of them personally.

My parents were great consumers of periodicals, and printed matter crowded into our house from England and the United States every month. They even took in two magazines for me, which gave me a confused notion of international boyhood. One was *The Youth's Companion*, originating in Boston, and it abounded in tales of boys with splendid characters who could not lie or steal, spoke in elegant periods, and earned their own pocket money by methods of unimpeachable honesty. The other, called *Chums*, came from England and it was about boys whose sole aim in life was to reduce their schools to a state of anarchy, and their masters to sobbing idiocy. Many of these English boys were conjurors, hypnotists, and somnambulists; when I came later to study English political history I understood exactly who its principal characters were, and how they had been educated. But my schooling, and my companions, did not belong in either of these categories. I was reconciled to the fact that life in Canada was rather a quiet experience.

As I grew older, like many young Canadians, I did not wholly accept this quietude, and I sometimes fretted against the ill-fitting old clothes that—in a cultural sense—we all seemed to be wearing. I was troubled by a question that one of our present Canadian cultural leaders, Professor Northrop Frye, has reduced to the query: "Where is here?" In modern terms, I wondered, why isn't Canada getting a piece of the action? And like thousands of young Canadians, when the time came I tried to solve the problem by leaving Canada and going to where the action seemed to be. And like thousands of young Canadians, circumstances and inclination led me back to Canada, hopeful that some of the action might be generated there.

That is what is happening now. The younger Canadians are vastly more impatient than was my own generation, but in the world of cultural growth you cannot make things happen merely by wishing to do so. A Canadian poet of my grandmother's generation summed it up in one of those lines of leaden obviousness and undoubted truth, when he said

> The growth of what is excellent is slow.

Cabbages can be grown quite quickly; an oak takes longer, and I do not think my country should be contented with a cabbage culture.

Nor will a cabbage culture suffice for us, however many persuasive political and literary people of the truck-garden and greengrocer persuasion may appear among us. We are, in our innermost hearts, too good a people to settle for cabbages. But at present the uproar is for a Canadian identity. What is it, and where is it to be sought?

We have many people who like the question so much that they do not seem to trouble very much about the answer. But there is an answer. I have known it, and many other Canadians have known it, for a long time. But it is not an answer that I can give you in blunt language; like so many of the important answers, it must be approached by indirection.

For me, for many years, the answer has best been formulated in a Canadian poem by one of our finest poets, who has already spoken to you in one of these meetings, Douglas LePan. It is in a poem, published in 1948, called "Coureurs de bois". It speaks of only one Canadian, but as a true poem should, it speaks also for many thousands. Here it is:

> Thinking of you, I think of the *coureurs de bois*.
> Swarthy men grown almost to savage size
> Who put their brown wrists through the arras of the
> woods
> And were lost—sometimes for months. Word would
> come back:
> One had been seen at Crève-coeur, deserted and
> starving,
> One at Sault Sainte Marie shouldering the rapids.
> Giant-like, their labours stalked in the streets of
> Quebec

Though they themselves had dwindled in distance:
    names only;
Rumours; quicksilvery spies into nature's secrets;
Rivers that seldom ran in the sun. Their resource
Would sparkle and then flow back under clouds of
    hemlock.

So you should have travelled with them. Or with
    La Salle.
He could feed his heart with the heart of a continent,
Insatiate, how noble a wounded animal,
Who sought for his wounds the balsam of adventure,
The sap from some deep, secret tree. But now
That the forests are cut down, the rivers charted,
Where can you turn, where can you travel? Unless
Through the desperate wilderness behind your eyes,
So full of falls and glooms and desolations,
Disasters I have glimpsed but few would dream of,
You seek new Easts. The coats of difficult honour,
Bright with brocaded birds and curious flowers
Stowed so long with vile packs of pemmican,
Futile, weighing you down on slippery portages,
Would flutter at last in the courts of a clement country,
Where the air is silken, the manners easy,
Under a guiltless and reconciling sun.
You hesitate. The trees are entangled with menace.
The voyage is perilous into the dark interior.
But then your hands go to the thwarts. You smile.
    And so
I watch you vanish in a wood of heroes,
Wild Hamlet with the features of Horatio.

It is all said there. The Canadian is the *coureur de bois* who must understand—understand, not tame—the savage land. And is it the savage land of rocks and forests only penetrable by the patient explorer? Only in the sense that this is a metaphor for that equally savage land of the spirit—"the desperate wilderness behind your eyes,

/ So full of falls and glooms and desolations, / Disasters I have glimpsed but few would dream of …" The Canadian voyage, I truly believe, is this perilous voyage into the dark interior of which the poet speaks. It is a voyage in which many are lost forever, and some wander in circles, but it is the heroic voyage of our time. In our time, when men have journeyed to the Moon, and returned quite unchanged and only scientifically enlightened, the dangerous voyage is the voyage into man's spirit, our knowledge of which is still very much at the point that geographical knowledge had reached when Magellan, Vasco da Gama, and Columbus dared greatly and enlarged the world of man.

But why Canada? Why should this nation so wanting in the rich sense of the past—of an individual self-made past—that is the prized possession of other nations be specially suited to undertake explorations that belong to all men? Because, I think, the Canadian travels very light; he can strip off the castoffs and the lendings of the other nations more readily than they can rid themselves of garments that have taken on the quality of skins.

Who is this voyager? Again the poem tells us. "Wild Hamlet with the features of Horatio." There is the Canadian. The appearance is that of the secondary character, the hero's friend, the confidant; but the opportunity and heart—if he has the courage to trust it—is that of one who may be a hero, and a new kind of hero, a hero of conscience and spirit, in the great drama of modern man.

27

A Canadian Author

"Even now when I visit New York, I have a haunting fear that I may be detected as an unrepentant Tory, and tarred and feathered." When he was awarded the Medal of Honor for Literature by the National Arts Club in New York on February 24, 1987, Davies was conscious that he was the first Canadian to receive this signal honour. It was as a representative of his country that he chose to speak, and his reference to his own unrepentant Loyalist forebears and to tarring and feathering will resonate with all readers who are familiar with the New York scenes in *Murther & Walking Spirits*, in many ways the most personal of his novels.

Among the friends and dignitaries mentioned in the diary entry that follows, "Nick Meyer" is Nicholas Meyer, author of *The Seven Percent Solution* and a Hollywood film-maker; Jean Sutton Straus was then the province of Ontario's representative in New York; and Robert MacNeil, an expatriate Canadian, was a respected New York television newsman who has gone on to become a distinguished author.

His diary records the following impressions: *Dress and are ready when called for by Leslie and Joanna Garfield, who drive us to the National Arts Club, on Gramercy Park, a New York area unknown to us and reminiscent of London. The Club House is on old mansion, hideous in the nineteenth-century manner, but also dignified and impressive and admirably suited to the sort of Club this is. Large, handsome rooms. A large crowd; they have had to have an annex to the dining room; this is a great compliment … After dinner, speeches: Robert Johnstone our*

Consul General who spoke admirably briefly, and in terms that made me blush: said I was doing what Joyce had done—"Forging in the smithy of my soul the uncreated conscience of my race"—very flattering—but I think it's true, and brilliant of Johnstone to discern it ... Nick Meyer speaks with surprising eloquence and grace. Jean Straus speaks charmingly and elegantly. Robert MacNeil says what he thinks I have done for Canada. All this reduces me almost to speechlessness, but speak I must. And I do, and it is received with blush-making kindness.

On such occasions as this, the speaker has obligations he cannot neglect without gross discourtesy. He must express his pleasure and gratitude for the award he has received at your hands, and I do that, with unfeigned enthusiasm. He must say how complimented he is by your presence, and once again I do so heartily. He must thank those who have spoken so generously of his work—and again I do so; their generosity is warming and encouraging, for I am at the beginning of yet another book and I need encouragement as much as if it were my first. He may suggest that he is unworthy of the award and of your friendly encouragement, but he would be unwise to do so with too much conviction for he may inadvertently carry his point, and you may feel that there had been some mistake. I accept this award without false modesty or demurral, because I think that it reaches beyond me toward a group of writers in my own country whom you have seen fit to recognize through me, and I respect and honour your intention.

Canada has come into the larger world of literature rather suddenly. We have always had writers, and some of them were good, though few gained a hearing beyond our own border. But in something like a quarter of a century Canadian writing has begun to take a place in the very large world of literature written in English (on this occasion I do not pretend to speak of what our writers have done in French). Nor has our writing been confined to the English-speaking world; we have travelled widely to many lands, in many languages. Last month *The Times* of London said of our writers, "they have crammed a century of change into a generation." During a period when so many Canadians have been chattering in fashionable despair about a "crisis of identity" for our country, Canada's writers have been examining that identity and presenting it to the rest of the world. As Aldous Huxley has said, poets and novelists do more to form the idea of a national character than any other group in society. A national literature is a mirror in which the nation sees its face. Canadian writers have been busily silvering and polishing the mirror for home use, and at the same time painting a portrait which other lands have inspected with interest and friendly approval.

Geography is a great creator and conditioner of literature, and if there is one thing we Canadians have in undiminishing abundance, it is geography. Ours is the second-largest country in the world, the largest being, of course, our near neighbour, Russia. In our huge land mass we have a population not quite half the size of Poland. Our other near neighbour, yourselves, has a smaller land with ten times our population, but even so you are by no means crowded. Some Canadians, and some of them in high places, cannot stop comparing us with you, and demanding to know why we do not do some of the things you do, the way you do them. The answers these people give, when they choose to give an answer, are usually concerned with economics. But there are elements which go into the making of a people that are vastly more important than economics. The land itself is one of them, and the greater part of our country is more ancient than, for instance, the land of Manhattan, where we are at this moment. I cannot believe that this extraordinary antiquity—not antiquity of man, for it extends beyond the era of man—does not affect our people, and do much to determine our character. With the land goes the climate, and ours is a climate that makes men watchful, reserved, and somewhat disposed toward melancholy. We have the chilly distinction of possessing the coldest national capital in the world, compared with which Moscow seems positively Californian. The land and the climate are all-pervasive, and we know that the blackest or most turbaned newcomer to our country will have descendants who will, within three generations, be Canadians in spirit.

Our history is not like yours, for you were born of revolution, and our roots are deep in a dogged loyalty. The people who first settled our country were not like your Pilgrims, or the handful of powerful aristocrats who settled in Virginia and thereabout. The stories of most of our earliest settlers were sad ones, and not the least unhappy was the tale of those supporters of the British cause who, at the time of your Revolution, were compelled to go north and begin life afresh. Many of my own forebears were of that group, and even now, when I visit New York, I have a haunting fear that I may be detected as an unrepentant Tory, and tarred and feathered. There is an element of loss and betrayal in our history which even yet tends to make us an introverted people, with the particular kind of inner strength that introversion implies. No, we are not like you, though if you come to our country on a visit you may not be strongly aware of having left the United States. But stay with us for a year, and the difference will be amply apparent. We do not wear our hearts on our sleeves.

Out of such people comes the literature I represent at this moment and which you have chosen to honour. Once again I thank you. But although I feel that I stand here for many others I must necessarily speak in my own character, and I should like to say something about what it means to be a Canadian author, from my own experience.

I imagine that it is something like what it must have been to be an American author a century or a century and a half ago, when your country's literature was still young. Louisa Alcott wrote amusingly about the curiosity she provoked as "the woman that wrote the books." Of course, as a woman, she was a double oddity, for it was a time when people spoke patronizingly of "lady novelists." People rapped at her door when she was trying to work; they peered in at her windows; sometimes they managed to get into her house and stole pens from her desk; she was asked for advice on a variety of unlikely subjects; it was assumed that she lived a life of adventure and very possibly of dubious morality. It was assumed also that she had time to devote to any cause that anybody wanted to promote, and that she would be delighted and honoured to drop her work and hurry off to make a speech. It was also assumed that she was an ever-flowing source of her own books which, as she obviously got them for nothing, she would be happy to give away.

Times have not changed greatly, but in our day the post office and the telephone have added new terrors to the writer's life. "Do you get many letters?" people ask me. Yes, I do get many letters. Not as many as if I were a film star, but sometimes more than I can cope with, because I have a conviction that every letter should be answered. If someone is kind enough to write to you saying that they like your work, common courtesy demands that they should be thanked. But it is not these courtesy letters that are vexatious. The troublesome ones are those that hold out offers of a position as a writer-in-residence at a university, somewhere—often very far away. Such a position would, writers explain with disarming enthusiasm, give me a chance to be among young people and encourage young talent—possibly even to discover a genius. It is not easy to reply in evasive terms. The people who write such letters know very little about authors. What author wants to leave his workroom, where he is surrounded by happily familiar mess and disorder, to live in a university residence and eat residence food? He knows that he will get no work done while he is surrounded by young people, who may be delightful in their uninhibited youth, but scare off the Muse by their noise. As for encouraging young talent, most of the writers I know are doing their uttermost to preserve and encourage middle-aged or even elderly talent, and if they met an undoubted young genius they would probably poison him, as Salieri is supposed to have poisoned Mozart. Indeed, the dark side of the literary character, the shadow of the man of letters, seems to be unknown to the people who seek writers-in-residence. They think authors are jolly good fellows, and I cannot bear to tell them the truth.

Then there are the people who are looking for somebody to make a speech, and they think an author would be just the right person to fill a "slot"—they always talk about "slots"—in their program. Very often these speeches are to be made far away—as far as California or Texas—and the writers generously offer to pay the fare of the author, as well as a generous fee. Their goodwill and their generosity are overwhelming. But one must not underestimate their craftiness. They write now, in February, to ask for a speech to be delivered next February. Therefore the writer has to be ingenious in his refusal. It is no use saying that he is writing a book: Surely he cannot make such a task stretch over a whole year? It is futile to say that on the date mentioned he must attend his grandmother's funeral; they will set detectives to work to discover that his grandmother is in robust health and shows no signs of decline. It would never do to write and say that the author does not really like making speeches, that he is of a shy and reticent character, and that the thought of facing an audience arouses all the skin diseases, catarrhs, and mysterious aches that he includes in his hypochondriac's repertoire. A man who is prepared to expose himself on paper must surely have no objection to facing an audience? Come on, man, rouse yourself and fly to Texas, where an eager audience awaits you!

What these kind people do not understand is the profound physical inertia of authors—and by authors I mean producers of fiction, and not explorers, or people who have written a book explaining how to attain sainthood by some special diet. Authors hate to move. Authors are Stoughton bottles.

Are there any among you who do not know what a Stoughton bottle is? Many long years ago, on this continent, there flourished an elixir, a cure-all, which had been devised by a man—I think he was a pharmacist of some sort, or possibly just a tent-show witch doctor—called Stoughton, and he presented his nostrum in a bottle of a squat, broadly based appearance which seemed not to sit upon the druggist's shelf, but positively to have taken root there. And thus the Stoughton bottle became a byword for sullen inertia. My grandmother used the term frequently, and more than once she applied it to me. "Don't just sit there like a Stoughton bottle," she would say, unaware that she was addressing an embryonic author.

Ladies and gentlemen, behold a Stoughton bottle! I assure any of you who may feel some uneasiness about what I have said when I speak of speech-making in these terms that I do not include the sort of speech-making in which I am engaged at this moment. To speak to a sympathetic audience of literary people is quite a different thing from flying—O, most dreadful of all forms of travel!—to speak to an audience of strangers in Texas. In such circumstances as these I am quite a different creature—a Stoughton bottle transfigured. A Stoughton bottle with wings, you might say. Authors, or perhaps, I should say this author, will certainly make speeches, but not to fill slots.

The telephone is something quite different. Now and then I meet people who say, "Why don't you have an unlisted number?" There are two reasons. The first is a modesty which I know you will understand. Lord Byron once remarked that he did not mind having his portrait painted, but he felt that sitting to a sculptor for a bust was like making a pretension toward immortality. I feel the same way about an unlisted telephone number. To refuse to speak to people who want to speak to me demands a thickness of crust that I simply do not possess.

There is another reason—I said there were two—and it is this. The telephone certainly permits people to gain entry to your house whom you would not dream of admitting through the door. But it may also be a herald of unexpected good fortune. When my telephone rings, it is always possible that it is somebody bringing me good news, of a magnificent inheritance, or an offer to dine with the great or even the merely wealthy, on equal terms. Sheer curiosity, without which an author cannot exist, demands that I be available by the phone.

Calls announcing good fortune do come over the wire now and then, but less often than calls from high-school students who want help with essays; often they say encouragingly that they are studying a book of mine in class, and are at a loss to understand it. About a year ago I had a typical call, at nine o'clock at night, in which a young man whose voice was changing, said, "Say, are you the fellow that writes the books?" When I admitted that I had certainly written some books, he continued: "I've got to write this essay, and I have to hand it in tomorrow morning, and I wonder if you could give me some help with these-here Jungian archeotypes?" To hang up the receiver at that moment would have been the act of a stony-hearted monster; here, obviously, was a soul in torment, and so I proceeded to get myself into a proper mess. I explained that Dr. Jung's theory of archetypes was complex and not easily explained in a few words. Then, with goat-like and fatal stupidity I went on to say that an archetype was a pattern of experience common to all of mankind, and that the pattern was greater in its power than any individual experience of it. I said, thinking he would know about such things, that falling in love was an archetypal experience. "Like how?" said the boy at the other end of the line. I plunged even deeper. I soon became aware that what I was saying was, in Shelley's fine phrase, "pinnacled dim in the intense inane." I found myself trying to imagine, from the sound of his voice, what my inquirer looked like. With the awful folly of an author, I tried to shape my answer about falling in love to what I supposed he might have experienced. I attempted to enter into his feelings. "You have surely fallen in love?" I said. "Naw, I can't say I have," was his reply. Here was a Romeo who had not even met his Rosaline. How long I floundered on I do not know, but it seemed an eternity. His answers took on a tone of incredulity, changing to hostility. He seemed to think that I was evading his question, that I was toying with him in a whimsical and unfeeling fashion. "Am I supposed to tell that to my teacher?" he demanded. A vision of his teacher swam into my consciousness, and I lost my self-control and told him in unsuitable terms what he could tell his teacher, who had encouraged him to get me on the phone and make my life intolerable. "I guess what you're trying to say is—" he began, and I gave a scream of pain. "I'm not trying to say it: I've said it as best I can," I roared. He hung up in disgust and, I am sure, disbelief.

As a novelist I have been described by many critics as a moralist. I find no fault with that. One of our finest Canadian writers, Margaret Laurence, who died a few weeks ago, said that every serious novelist is at heart a moralist. My notion of a moralist—the belief on which I base my writing—is someone who observes the vicissitudes of life and tries to discern in them some patterns, some lasting truths that govern what happens to us as we meet whatever fate has in store for us. A moralist is not one who teaches a system of morality. He is someone who points out as interestingly as he can that if you play with fire you will get burned; that the dog returns again to his vomit and the sow that was washed to her wallowing in the mire; that two and two do not merely make four, but just as often they make twenty-two; that God, or the First Cause, or the Life Force or whatever you want to call it, is not mocked, and that the mocker will unfailingly get his lumps, and it is vanity to think that he may not get them in some other world than this, or in some aspect of this world of which he has no understanding. That is what I am saying, and saying it as entertainingly as I can manage.

Because, you see, I am strongly of the opinion that a novelist's job is to be entertaining, not in a trivial or shallow way, but in such a way that his readers will want to finish his book, and perhaps think about it. I know it is old-fashioned, but I do not myself like novels that set puzzles for readers, or snub readers, or determinedly abuse and bamboozle readers. Some years ago when Vladimir Nabokov was asked what quality he thought was of the greatest importance in writing, he replied that it was something he described by the Russian word *shamanstvo*, which he interpreted as meaning "the enchanter quality." I agree with my whole heart. As a boy I was captured, and have been held forever, by Sir Philip Sidney's description of a real, unmistakable writer: "he cometh to you with words, set in delightful proportions.... and with a tale, forsooth, he cometh unto you with a tale, which holdeth children from play, and old men from the chimney-corner." My dearest hope is that when all else has been said, that might be said of me.

Thank you for this award. I assure you that I shall cherish it.

28

Literature in a Country Without a Mythology

Strong transplanted Scottish (or, in the usual Canadian usage, "Scotch") characters abound in the fiction of Robertson Davies, from Dunstan Ramsay's fierce mother in *Fifth Business*, who might never have left her Dumfries home, to the philosophical journalist Hugh McWearie in *Murther & Walking Spirits* and *The Cunning Man*, whose view of human nature is formed by his background as the son of an Edinburgh policeman, not to mention the advantage of an education at the University of St. Andrews. In *What's Bred in the Bone* the key fact about the town of Blairlogie is that "the best of the town's money and business was firmly in the hands of the Scots, as was only right and proper."

In his own everyday life Davies did not minimize his own "fine confusion of Scottish blood," his winter headgear being adorned with a pin reproducing the McKay family crest. So it was no surprise that he relished the invitation to give the lecture named after the Scottish novelist Neil Gunn (1891–1973), in the capital city of Edinburgh. The May 27, 1988, lecture gave him the opportunity to speak to an understanding audience about the difficulties of maintaining a distinctive national culture in the face of an overwhelming neighbour to the south. He speaks very directly about the then-current debate about the Free Trade deal with the United States and specifically about his fears concerning its long-term effect on Canada's culture, "turning the link into a shackle."

In his diary he writes very enthusiastically about this trip to Scotland and about Walter Cairns, who was the head of the Scottish Arts Council at the time, and who had invited him to speak. In a piece written in August 1995 called "Remembering Walter Cairns" he tells the following story of his visit to the other great city of Scotland, and an emergency that called for the powers of a Magnus Eisengrim:

Walter joins us later in the day, in time for tohubohu and brouhaha at our Glasgow hotel, where, when we go to our room, we find the housekeeper, the manageress, a maid, and a boy with a ladder and a flopping towel attempting to cope with two alarmed pigeons, who swoop and dive alarmingly, and have become copiously incontinent with fright. This circus goes on for quite a while, the manageress grieving "Oh, what must you think of us?" as the housekeeper dashes at the birds with an umbrella which she opens and shuts rapidly; it was Walter, I believe, who suggested that the boy's towel might better be used to trap the birds, and that if the housekeeper would stop gunning with her umbrella, the birds might come to rest. This is the plan that works: The boy creeps upon the pigeons like a poacher, traps them, and thrusts them out into the great world of Glasgow. We retire, while the room is put in order—no small task.

Does anyone, I wonder, ever begin a lecture like this without being overwhelmed by misgiving that he has totally mistaken his subject and based his remarks on assumptions that are groundless? I do not know what you expect of me, but because you have asked me to come from Canada to fill this distinguished lectureship this year I assume that you want me to speak as a Canadian, and that you want me to say at least something about my own work. It is by no means visitor's flattery when I say what pleasure it gives me to be here, for, like so many Canadians, I carry in me a fine confusion of Scottish blood—mostly, I may say, from the Highlands—and a number of my forebears received their education in the famous university of this city. But in Edinburgh you have no lack of Robertsons or Mackays, so it is as a Canadian I shall speak. I shall even attempt the daunting task of saying what a Canadian is. And though I hope that what I may say will have some wider application to literature, I shall set off from a Canadian point of view.

These are days when literature and writers are much in the news, because there are so many countries where free expression is forbidden, and writers—who are a rebellious lot, as a usual thing—are forced to take political stands, espouse causes, and stand by principles which are often only slightly associated with their real work. This worries me because, though I admire the courage that is demanded of writers in, for instance, South Africa and in many parts of South America, I cannot persuade myself that such political action is a writer's first duty, and I fear that the increasing emphasis on the Author As Hero may be harmful to the greater task of the Author As Fabulist, Moralist, and Visionary. Sometimes, when I am talking to students, they ask me what I think a writer is. I know that often they want me to speak of the author as he leaps upon the barricades carrying the red flag of freedom, because young people understand and admire action—would, indeed, rather act than think. But I say to them: The author today is the descendant of the storyteller who went into the marketplace, sat himself down upon his mat, and beat upon his collection bowl, crying, "Give me a copper coin and I will tell you a golden tale!" That is what I truly believe. All honour to the Author As Hero, when firm necessity demands that he be a hero or lose his honour. But let us not, in the heat of these troubled times, assume that a Hero is what an author must be or he is no author. It may seem harsh to say so, but the golden tale may save a thousand lives when the heroic death has been forgotten.

In Canada we are, upon the whole, free from grave political trouble of the kind I have mentioned. Oh, we have a lunatic group in Parliament who want to impose an absurd Censorship Bill on art of all kinds in the country, but we can mock them into silence, I think. The prudery of the half-educated is always with us in Canada, but no worse than it is anywhere else. Indeed, until quite recently, Canadian writers were so little heeded that they could have written almost anything they pleased, without official interference. Our censors were so sure that all evil would enter Canada through the Customs that they never thought of looking for the homegrown variety. The myth of our innocence and purity was very widely believed.

I have spoken of a myth, and the title of my address is "Literature in a Country Without a Mythology." That is a Canadian paradox, and it is the title of a poem by one of our finest living poets, my old friend Douglas LePan. In his poem he writes of a lone adventurer travelling in his canoe along the West Coast of Canada, where the only traces of human life to be seen are the occasional Aboriginal villages. The poem concludes:

> … not a sign, not an emblem in the sky,
> Or boughs to friend him as he goes: for who
> Will stop where, clumsily constructed, daubed
> With war-paint, teeters some lust-red manitou?

It is a poem that speaks of the sense of isolation felt by the Canadian of today, at most only a few generations from Europe, in a land which still declares itself to be strange, and if not unfriendly, certainly reserved and only partly comprehensible. It is a land where there is no easily accessible guide to the past, no widely accepted tale of our beginnings, no friendly jumble of things that are taken for granted. A country, in fact, without a mythology.

What is a mythology, after all? A body of ill-assembled religious belief, a cosmology, a muddle of superstition and folk belief? It may be these things to people of crudely rational mind, but if we look deeper we see that a mythology looks very much like the unconscious mind of a people, that area which is accessible only in dreams and visions, and where extraordinary energy resides. It is what a people calls on when rationality seems exhausted, and it does not fail those who call. The word *soul* has a bad savour to many people today, but it is hard to avoid it when we talk of these matters. A mythology is one of the evidences of the soul of a people. Can it really be that Canada has no such thing? No soul?

Oh yes, Canada has a soul right enough, but it has until recently been exceedingly cautious about letting it show. Nor was this simply because Canada was shy, though reticence is a national characteristic; it was because Canada was spiritually lazy, and was perfectly happy to borrow soul, if it might be needed, from Britain or the United States. Noble, haughty Britain: vigorous, freedom-loving United States. Who needed to bother about a soul when these two countries had so much, and were so ready to let their souls hang out, and to let Canada make do with whatever slopped over from their vast, intoxicating tubs of emotion? But those days of dependency are over. We have come to the time in our history when we must find and possess our own soul. And how are we going to do that?

Are we indeed a country without a mythology? The phrase is a provocative one, but it talks of an impossibility. The base and ground of all mythologies is human experience, which does not vary immeasurably from one people to another; mythology is the way in which a particular people has chosen to state its experience, not to impress other people but in the hope of understanding itself. Mythologies are not coherent structures, except when they are regularized for children's reading. Mythologies are huge cairns of anything and everything that helps to explain a people to itself; some of the rocks in the cairn are ugly boulders and others may be quite smooth pebbles. It doesn't matter so long as the cairn rises above the level ground and serves, in some way, as a home of the gods. Canada has a mythology, but it is only now, after about four hundred years of history, forced to decide what it is going to do about it.

The pressure comes from outside. Canada was for long a British colony, never the favourite colony because it is a land that has never appealed powerfully to the European imagination. The French have never thought well of it. The early explorer Jacques Cartier wrote quite seriously that it was "the land God gave to Cain." Voltaire called it a few acres of snow. Napoleon, when he was reduced to giving advice from his seclusion on St. Helena, said that England would be better off without it. British administrators who were sent there tended to regard it as a place of exile. Things have not got better. It is asserted that our name comes from the remark of a Spanish explorer, "Aca nada"—nothing there. Kingsley Amis nominates *Canadian Wit and Humour* as one of the world's shortest books. I could go on for a long time in this strain, for Canada may say with Falstaff: "Men of all sorts take a pride to gird at me." But whatever outsiders may say to the detriment of Canada, we say much worse things ourselves. Indeed, in an early play of mine, I once said that Canada was not a country one loved, but a country one worried about, and to my dismay I now find that remark enshrined in a book of quotations.

And yet, somehow, by sheer weight of geography, and the passage of time, and a slow accumulation of national wealth, we seem to be forcing ourselves upon the attention of the world, and we are now in the uncomfortable position of having to discover, and in some measure to define, our national soul.

Are we late in the day? Not really. I suppose if we were to assign sizes to national souls, as we do to shoes or hats, we might agree that the largest, most powerfully defined national soul in all of history—the unquestioned Number Nine—would be Russia, but it was not until the nineteenth century that anybody began to talk about the Russian Soul. We are a little bit slow in getting off the mark, but we have begun, and the talk of the Canadian soul has begun for us, as it began for Russia, with our writers.

Talk about the Russian soul was not utterly rejected by the Russian people, because a great many of them assumed that the national soul was in the care of the Orthodox Church. Of course Orthodoxy was not the whole of what the Russian writers were talking about. Not even Dostoyevsky thought that all that made Russia Russian was to be found in the Church. In Canada we have no such generally accepted caretaker for the national soul, and consequently talking about it is hard work. Telling Canada that she has a soul used to be rather like telling a stupid and unsophisticated girl that she was beautiful; she laughed coarsely, and kicked you on the shins. A great deal of persuasion was needed before she would pay attention to what you were saying, and stop calling you a fool. But during the last year or so something has happened which has made the stupid girl listen a little more seriously.

I will not bore you with detail: Simply, it is the desire of the present Canadian Government, and particularly its leader and our Prime Minister, to enter into a Free Trade agreement with the United States. The Government, and the world of big business that supports it, insists that such an agreement would enormously enlarge Canada's national wealth, create a great many new jobs, and open up the country to the sort of development that would bring in American capital.

As I have said, the business community is, in the main, delighted by this idea and supports it as big business usually does—by laughing at its opponents as people who do not understand how the world wags, and who should be content to trust their betters in such supremely important matters as money and trade. But there is substantial opposition to the Free Trade proposal on both sides of the border for a variety of complex reasons, but in Canada by a strong misgiving that a Free Trade agreement would threaten and eventually wipe out any indigenous Canadian culture. Loud and clear, a lot of Canadians are saying that there are things in our national life that are more important than money and trade, and the word *culture* is being used on the street, so to speak, in a new sense.

The new sense confuses the tycoons, because they think they know what culture is. For them it is art galleries and ballet companies and opera companies, and theatre companies, to which some of them contribute quite generously. But they still live in a world where pictures and ballet and opera and theatre are heavily dependent on imported goods, and they do not really understand that the fostering and production of such things within Canada could mean anything very much, or employ any important number of people. They are determined that the worth of an activity is related to the number of jobs it creates.

The Canadians who resist them know better. These cultural activities which the tycoons understand, now have a local habitation in Canada, and the people they employ are important to the country in a way the tycoons have not yet comprehended. When we send a symphony orchestra or a ballet company abroad, they make Canada known in an international world that is of the highest importance because it shows that we are part of the *internationale* of cultivated people, and that, insofar as international cultural exchange favours a climate of world peace, we are doing not at all badly. Furthermore, we are submitting ourselves to the judgment of the world on a level that asks for no favours, and is not directly hitched to the world of business.

It is a matter of history, of an inherited governmental system, and of a national psychology. The questions of the governmental system may be dealt with most easily. What virtually all Americans, and too many Canadians who deal in the international world of money, fail utterly to understand, is that Canada is that political oddity, a socialist monarchy. We have created an elaborate and very successful welfare state under a monarchical set-up which is itself a declaration that there are things of national importance that are above politics and above simple matters of finance. The U.S., for historical reasons, mistrusts the concept of a welfare state, and this mistrust shows itself nakedly under present U.S. government, which commits uncounted billions of the national wealth to what it calls defence, and is close-fisted in giving money to plans which would ameliorate the grinding poverty of a great part of its people. Quite simply, in Canada you could not get away with that. We have been accused of being half-hearted in our defence system, and although we blush slightly under such accusations we know in our hearts that our gigantic country—the second largest in the world in land mass—is wholly indefensible, and so we would rather compromise and debate than get into wars we know we could not win. Is this want of national pride? No, it is want of a bellicose spirit that would seek to impose its ideals on any other people. We have other fish to fry, and they are fish we catch in our own waters.

That's enough about our governmental system and whatever it implies and includes. What about our history?

Canadian history is supposed to be dull. I would rather say that until the present century it has been such a sad story that we remember it, but do not choose to dwell on it.

Who are we? The naked fact is that virtually all of us are descended from people who never wanted to go to Canada, and who did so under the lash of grim necessity. Our first European settlers, the French, came to Canada more than four hundred years ago, because life at home was hard and without hope; there were adventurers, and traders, but the farmers and tradesmen knew they were exchanging a bad way of life for another which they hoped, by determination, to make less bad. The vigour and intransigence of their spirit is still a powerful factor in our national politics.

The French are not a majority. What about the others? I know a good deal about them, not from the history books, but because I feel it very deep in my bones. Some of them had to leave the British Isles—many were Scots, but many also were Irish—because the cruelties of history made it impossible to stay in their homelands. I do not have to tell their story here; it is part of your history. Harsh landowners, having displaced them from their bits of land, sold them aboard emigrant ships at about a guinea a head, and they found themselves in a country of which they knew nothing, but where the choice was survival or death. Their sufferings were pathetic in the highest degree. Some of them—usually men from the British armies—had been given grants of land by gentlemen in Whitehall who had utterly inadequate maps, and when the settlers arrived they found that their new holdings were either masses of rock, or unproductive muskeg, or were even under water. For a time I lived in a community whose earliest settlers were Irish peasants from the city of Cork who had been transported to Upper Canada to be farmers. They knew nothing of farming, and pathetic tales were still told of wretched men and women hanging about the doors of taverns, offering to dance a jig for a penny. The ability to dance a jig was all they had brought with them.

My mother's father was descended from a Scottish group for whom I have a special sympathy. Their origin was the uttermost northern part of Scotland, and so the gentlemen who arranged for their transport to Canada assumed that they would be best suited at a latitude comparable to the homes they left behind them. So these wretches were deposited on the shore of James Bay, and if you do not happen to know where it is, I can assure you that it is a brutal place even for people from Sutherland. A great many of them died, of course, but some managed the long trek to more southerly Canada, and survived. But when I look at photographs of my grandfather today, I think I can see something of the desolation of those early settlers in his face still, a century later.

But the immigration from Scotland and Ireland is not our only hard-luck story. After the American Revolution Canada received many thousands of political refugees from the new republic. When I say refugees I use the word in its fullest sense, for they had been deprived of civil rights, of land and money, their children were driven from the schools, and they were subject to all the harassment of the losers in any war. They got to Canada as best they could, sometimes on foot, sometimes by the waterways, often assisted by Americans who felt some sympathy for these outlaws who were given and gladly received the name of Loyalists. Many of them were people who had been prosperous in the American Colonies before the Revolution, and in Canada they were tireless in their labours to re-establish the economy, the education, and the religious institutions that they had been forced to leave behind in the land of the free and the home of the brave.

To this day they have not forgotten that they had to make a run for it in the post-Revolutionary days, and though they are unfailingly polite to Americans, they do not look southward with any particular warmth.

Does it seem to you that I am talking about a nation of losers, of exiles and refugees? Modern Canada is a prosperous country, but the miseries of its earliest white inhabitants is bred in the bone, and cannot, even now, be rooted out of the flesh.

Which brings me to the third element of which I spoke earlier, which is the psychology of Canada. Is it fanciful to ascribe a psychological character to a country? If that were so, how would we know the French to be French, and Germans to be Germans—and the Scots to be Scots? These people, of course, exhibit obvious and sometimes even farcical national characteristics, but such things are not what give them individuality. In Canada we have nothing that marks us outwardly as what we are, but the inward character is something very clear, when you know what you are looking for.

In psychological terms Canada is very much an introverted country, and it lives cheek by jowl with the most extroverted country in the world, and indeed the most extroverted country known to history. Let me explain the terms. In personal psychology the extrovert is one who derives his energy from his contacts with the external world; for him, everything lies outside and he moves outward toward it, often without much sensitivity to the response of that toward which he moves. The introvert, on the other hand, finds his energy within himself, and his concern with the outside world is a matter of what approach the outside world makes to him. It is absurd to say that one psychological orientation is superior to the other. Both have their value, but difficulties arise when they fail to understand one another.

The extroversion of the United States is easy to see. It assumes that it must dominate, that its political and moral views are superior to all others, and that it is justified in interference with countries it thinks undemocratic, meaning unlike itself. It has also the unhappy extrovert characteristic of seeing all evil as exterior to itself, and resistance to that evil as a primary national duty. This is what makes so much trouble between the United States and the USSR; the fact that the USSR is, and has been all through its history, a strongly introverted state makes for continuous trouble and ill will, and assertions of moral superiority on both sides.

Canada, the introverted country, feels no impulsion to spread its domination beyond its own boundaries, and has shown itself generous and sometimes absurdly permissive in its acceptance of the behaviour and customs of the numberless refugees that seek our shores. We are prepared to put up with almost anything to avoid trouble. This looks like weakness, and sometimes it is. But it also brings the introvert trait of selfishness. Americans are generous to a fault: We sometimes behave as though it were a fault to be generous, and we are used to being rapped over the knuckles because we do not give enough to have-not countries of the Third World. We wonder, deep in our hearts, how they are ever to make a place in the world if they are always on the take. That was not the way we had to do it. Deep in our hearts we are what you might choose to call a thrawn people. Such a description is not wholly justified, but it is not without some grounds. Now, suddenly, we are faced by a desire on the part of our Government and our powerful and vocal business community, with the likelihood of what many of us see as, eventually, a takeover not immediately political, but cultural and indeed spiritual. We have built up our arts by means not approved in the States; a lot of public money goes into the support of, for instance, our national broadcasting company, which is one of the things that knits together a vast land still sparsely populated. We have a flourishing National Film Board. Music, opera, ballet, and theatre receive public support in a measure which is not adequate—when have artistic people ever considered any degree of support adequate?—but which recognizes their significance in our national life. Although the performing arts are important and are easily seen to be important, it is by our literature that we have made our deepest impression, and I do not need to tell this audience that the state cannot beget a literature, and can do very little to support it, except for grants-in-aid to writers who are thought to be promising. But grants cannot ensure public acceptance, and the acceptance Canadian literature now enjoys all over the world rests simply on the quality of the work—quality and individuality.

How gratifying this is to Canadian writers I cannot begin to express. A couple of years ago I was asked to attend a conference on Canadian literature in Vienna, and I went, though I am not temperamentally a conference-going sort of man. At the opening dinner I sat next to a Hungarian scholar who proceeded to quote to me from the poems of my old friend Douglas LePan, of whom I spoke earlier. I was abashed to find that he knew my friend's work with a completeness and depth of penetration far beyond my own. Nor was this an isolated instance. I have travelled a good deal in Europe during the past five years, and everywhere I go I am astonished and somewhat breathless to find how much we mean to friends abroad of whom we know nothing. My own work has been pretty widely translated, and I am always surprised to hear from readers in South America—a world utterly unknown to me. The last news I had of a translation of my work came from Israel. Not ungratefully, I assure you, but in utter amazement I wonder what people in Israel would find to engage them in my work. Now, if I were to hear that some things of mine were to appear in Arabic, I would be convinced that I was indeed internationally recognized. I have never appeared in Chinese but English editions of my work are pirated in Hong Kong, and that is, I suppose, a compliment in the Oriental manner. Canada, through its writers, has suddenly come under international literary scrutiny.

You may ask why I suppose, that a Free Trade agreement with the United States, and all that it implies, would alter or endanger this situation. But I can remember, and many other Canadian authors can remember, being offered publication in the United States on the condition that we would make a few alterations in our text that would transfer the scene of our novel to the U.S.A. To this day that is virtually a condition of having a moving picture made of a Canadian novel. We have a Canadian film industry and our films are much respected at international festivals. But we cannot get distribution for them in the U.S. because they are seen as a form of competition with Hollywood, and Hollywood is not the most generous or culturally conscious part of the great Republic, and doesn't like any sort of competition. All the film distribution of the North American continent has been in American hands, and a Free Trade agreement is not going to change that.

May I interrupt the thread of what I am saying for a moment to tell you a story that gives great delight in Canada? Because it is cheaper to make films in Canada, many U.S. companies come north to make portions of their films, and last year a group appeared who wanted to film some scenes in a street. But there was a problem: Our Canadian streets are much cleaner than American city streets, so the property people were sent off to get some suitable dirt and rubbish with which to Americanize our Toronto street. When the trash had been distributed to the liking of the director, the crew broke for lunch. While they were away, some of our street cleaners appeared and were greatly affronted. What a dirty street! So they cleaned it up, and when the film crew returned all their splendidly atmospheric dirt had been carted away, and they were furious. That sounds like a Swiss story, but I assure you it is Canadian.

Nor is a Free Trade agreement going to be friendly toward our publishing industry, which is a substantial one, and has had to maintain its position by adroit manoeuvring and some government assistance of an indirect kind. Such governmental assistance would undoubtedly be protested by American publishers as a restraint on their freedom of trade, and unfair competition.

Would it matter? Yes, it would. Not long ago a popular Canadian writer, Pierre Berton, wrote a history of Canada's involvement in one of the great battles of the First World War—the Battle of Vimy Ridge. The book sold seventy thousand copies in hardcovers, and another one hundred thousand in paperback, and for Canadian publishing that is a triumph. Would any American publisher have produced such a book? Of what interest would the Canadians at Vimy be for U.S. readers? But that book is a solid contribution to Canadian pride and nationhood, and we don't want to throw such things away for the satisfaction of car manufacturers, and other forms of Big Business. Canada is waking up. Canada, where Biblical references are still understood by quite a few people, sees itself suddenly as Naboth's Vineyard. You remember that the great King of Samaria coveted Naboth's vineyard, and made him an offer for it. Naboth replied, "The Lord forbid it me that I should give the inheritance of my fathers unto thee." Poor Naboth lost the fight, and was traduced and stoned to death. But those of us who have Canada's newly found nationalism and national culture near to our hearts have hopes of reversing that nasty story, and keeping our vineyard for ourselves and our children.

This dispute is a particularly difficult one because one of the parties to the difference does not see that there is any dispute at all. An American tycoon, commenting on the Free Trade proposal, said, as if he were disposing of a trivial objection, "It's all business, isn't it?" But that is precisely what it is not, and why it is not so is extraordinarily hard to make clear to what may be called the extroverted Front Office Mentality. A couple of months ago a friend of mine, an important Canadian publisher, spoke on this theme to an influential group in New York called The American Society. The members, who were all important figures in business, are worried because Canadian investment in the U.S. is becoming a factor in their economy which they regard, probably quite rightly, as a threat. Within the last two years the largest single holding of Manhattan property has passed into the hands of a Canadian company; the largest moving-picture distribution complex has become Canadian-owned; the largest association of retail stores in the U.S.A., of which Bloomingdale's is the best known, now is owned by a Canadian entrepreneur. To the business mind, this is almost the equivalent of a Russian invasion. My friend the publisher was trying to explain why a distinctively Canadian culture was important and why we were determined to preserve it. After she had done her best she was astonished to be asked by the wife of an American publisher: "I don't get it. You keep talking about *Canadians.* Aren't you all Americans, too?"

Americans are precisely what we are not, and what we don't want to be. And the Americans, charming, extroverted, certain of their acceptance everywhere, simply cannot understand it. And of course it is a problem. A Canadian historian, Arthur Lower, said once that we Canadians love England but don't like Englishmen, and that we love Americans but can't stand the United States. I have been trying to explain to you why this is so. There was an embarrassing war in 1812, which Americans tend to ignore, because it was the first occasion when their armed forces were defeated, and they were defeated by Canada. The Americans, urged by their friends the French, attempted to invade Canada, in order to create a diversion and draw some British troops away from Napoleon's difficulties on the Continent. Being Americans, they had to have a high-toned reason for their invasion, and they let it be known that they were going to free Canada from the hateful British yoke. To their incredulous dismay, they found that, although Canada was not abjectly devoted to the hateful British yoke, we preferred it infinitely to the flabby American yoke, and we fought fiercely to repel the invasion, and were indeed so successful that we made a sally into the States and burned the city of Washington. We had the good sense, of course, to return to where we belonged, but we made our point. Several of my forebears fought in that war and some died in it, a fact in which I take a good deal of pride.

Why are we so obstinate in this matter? What are we defending? In part it is our land, so much of which is a part of that Great Laurentian Shield that extends across the Atlantic and rises again in Northern Europe. I believe strongly that the land upon which one lives influences one's character, and our land has given us qualities that are more akin to the Scandinavian countries than any part of the U.S. except the New England States. I have spoken of our national introversion, and I see sympathies in our national feeling that attach more strongly to the lands of Ibsen and Strindberg than to anything to the south of us. And as our land makes us what we are, it of course gives its quality to the best of our literature. The poet I have already quoted, Douglas LePan, speaks in one of his poems of the Canadian as

> Wild Hamlet, with the features of Horatio.

It is a striking figure, and one I have pursued in my own work.

I should like to speak to you now about my own work, because it is characteristically Canadian, and I assume that you expect something personal from me, or you would not have asked me to be here today. I could certainly talk of the work of several other Canadian writers, but I feel that might be to refine modesty to a point of needless scrupulosity.

I have been a writer all my life, not because I ever felt any overmastering urge to be one, but because I was born to the trade. My parents and brothers were writers, usually as journalists, but as literary craftsmen as well. I assumed that writing was something that everybody did, and I think I was at least twelve years old before I realized that not everybody does write, that there are people who find writing insuperably difficult, and that there are people who aspire powerfully to be writers but don't know how to begin. I am frequently asked for advice by young people who are in this latter quandary, and all I can honestly tell them is that if they don't know how to begin they had better reconsider their ambition to write. Beginning is simple. You write at the top of the page: "Once upon a time." If nothing comes to mind to follow that introduction you are not a writer. A critic, perhaps, but not a writer.

I have no belief in the power of anyone to teach someone else how to write, and although I am aware that universities everywhere now offer instruction in what is called Creative Writing, I have no idea how they go about it, nor have I observed any astonishing flow of brilliance from those who undergo such instruction. Being a writer is somewhat like being double-jointed. Either you have it or you don't. Of course you can work upon what nature has given you, and perhaps become a Boneless Wonder, or Indiarubber Man of literature, but without the initial endowment you are not likely to do it. If you are very, very lucky, you may be born a very good writer—perhaps a poet—but there is a disagreeable corollary to that piece of good fortune; you may die young, while the roses in your chaplet are still fresh. Or, even less desirable, you may live on, without any perceptible development of your powers, and the rose leaves in your chaplet fall off, with your hair. Lucky writers get better as they grow older, like wine, and die rich in fruitiness and delicious aftertaste, so that their works survive them.

My work was not very warmly received in Canada during my early days. I was criticized as being unCanadian. I think now that what bothered critics was that it was simply not Canadian as they conceived Canadianness to be. I began writing during a rather gloomy period in Canadian literature. As one of our best writers, Margaret Atwood, has said, Canadian literature has a strong pull toward what is sombre and negative. It is allowable to be a humorist, a relentlessly funny writer, who writes the kind of book you take to people in hospital, but the idea of humour as an element inseparable from writing even on serious subjects, of humour as the light that plays on a writer's mind, was not understood and was rebuked in my early work. But it was out of the question for me to change. I was born very much under the influence of the planet Mercury, and my outlook on life is mercurial. Not, I assure you, frivolous, or trivial; not jeering or contemptuous, but most assuredly not solemn for the sake of solemnity—a quality which critics are apt to confuse with seriousness. I was indeed serious, but not solemn.

In time the critics became used to me. And at last, when I was fifty-seven years old, I wrote a book that made even the most reluctant decide that I was a serious writer, however regrettably flawed by humour, and that my subject was indeed Canada. Not Canada simply as a geographical expression, but as a climate of being, an ambience, an inescapable psychological fact.

The book in which I made my serious intentions so clear that it could not be misunderstood even by the most perfunctory reviewer, was called *Fifth Business.* I did not write it, I assure you, to prove anything or demonstrate any thesis, and I shall speak of that later. But I was surprised and pleased many years afterward to read some remarks made by Eugene O'Neill, the American playwright, and this is what he said:

The playwright of today must dig at the roots of the sickness of today as he feels it—the death of the old God and the failure of science and materialism to give any satisfying new one for the surviving primitive religious instinct to find a meaning for life in, and to comfort its fears of death with. It seems to me that anyone trying to do big work nowadays must have this big subject behind all the little ones of his plays or novels, or he is simply scribbling around the surface of things and has no more real status than a parlour entertainer.

That is what I was trying to do in my book: to look at what O'Neill—not a notably cheerful man—called the sickness of today, but which I would rather call the spiritual predicament of today. But I was not, I assure you, attempting any such thing consciously. I was simply writing a book that demanded to be written. I wrote "Once upon a time," and there it was.

Does that sound grandiose? Was I visited by some Muse who urged me on? No, but I was certainly impelled to write that book because I was troubled and haunted by an image. Doubtless you know how these things happen. When we are unoccupied, and perhaps somewhat tired, pictures arise in our minds which we would be troubled to explain. In my mind, for several years during which I was much occupied with other work—I was setting a new college going in the University of Toronto—I was troubled by such an image. It was a simple one: In a village street, at about six o'clock on a winter's night—the night of Boxing Day, I was sure—two boys appeared who had quarrelled while playing; one boy was walking some distance in front, and the other boy threw a snowball at him, and I knew that concealed in that snowball was a stone and that if it hit the boy it might hurt him badly. And that was all the picture told me.

This happened so often that I became aware that I must investigate that image if I was ever to have any peace. This is what I did, and the novel *Fifth Business* was the result.

I shall not give a long account of what the book is about. Briefly, the stone-laden snowball did not hit the boy it was meant for, but hit a woman who was out walking with her husband, and it affected her so badly that she miscarried the child she bore, and never regained her reason—as the world of that village understood reason. She became the local madwoman, and did a number of things that the village could not endure. As for the child who was born prematurely, he became a neglected and pitiable but unusually self-reliant and surviving sort of man who later achieved a good deal of celebrity as a conjuror, and illusionist, and psychologically a trickster.

But the first boy, whose name was Dunstan Ramsay, was plagued by overwhelming guilt, because he was convinced that the woman had suffered in order that he might survive. In her seemingly mad behaviour he saw saintliness, and his life was dominated by an absurd problem: Could such a woman be a saint in the true sense of the word? Indeed, what *was* the true sense of the word? Heroic virtue? Miracles? As a Presbyterian he had no experience of saints, but his obsession drove him to become a well-known expert on saints, a hagiologist, and when the madwoman was without friends in the world he made himself responsible for her care. His profession—for being a hagiologist is not a paying task—was that of a schoolmaster, and to the world in which he lived he seemed no more than a somewhat eccentric teacher in a boys' school. But after many years, he contrived a meeting—not a confrontation, simply an encounter—between the boy who had thrown the fatal snowball, and who had become a very rich and influential industrialist, and the famous illusionist. Neither was known to the other, and when Ramsay made it plain how they were involved, they were cool and polite. But when, shortly afterward, the great industrialist was found in his car at the bottom of Toronto Harbour, with a stone in his mouth, it was Ramsay, who had preserved that stone for fifty years, who knew what had really happened, and indeed who had killed Boy Staunton. Was it the magician? No: not really.

As I worked on that book I became aware that one book was not enough to explore the story as it demanded to be explored. So in the course of the next five years I wrote two other books: One was the story of the rich industrialist, and the effect his character had exerted on everybody around him, and particularly his unhappy son. The rich industrialist was not what the world calls a bad man; but he was very much an extrovert, and he had edited out of his memory anything that might be damaging to his idea of himself. That was his self-image until he ended up in the harbour with the stone in his mouth.

The third book was, of course, the tale of the illusionist, whose life had been one of dreadful privation and servitude until, by lucky chance, he met the woman who transformed his destiny, and who in time lifted the load of Presbyterian guilt from the heart of Dunstan Ramsay.

As I told you, in the beginning this story was not warmly received in Canada. But when it gained very warm commendation in the United States and elsewhere, Canada changed its opinion. Many Canadians began to see in the tale of Dunstan Ramsay some relevance to themselves and to their country. Began, indeed, to think that perhaps the Canadian is Fifth Business in the affairs of the world.

And what is Fifth Business? It is an expression from the world of the theatre, and especially of opera. This is how it was defined for Ramsay by the woman who at last brought him to a sense of what he really was:

"Who are you? Where do you fit into poetry and myth? Do you know who I think you are, Ramsay? I think you are Fifth Business.

"You don't know who that is? Well, in opera in a permanent company of the kind we keep up in Europe you must have a *prima donna*—always a soprano, always the heroine, often a fool; and a tenor who always plays the lover to her; and then you must have a contralto who is a rival to the soprano, or a sorceress or something; and a basso, who is the villain or the rival or whatever threatens the tenor.

"So far, so good. But you cannot make a plot work without another man, and he is usually a baritone, and he is called in the profession Fifth Business because he is the odd man out, the person who has no opposite of the other sex. And you must have Fifth Business because he is the one who knows the secret of the hero's birth, or comes to the assistance of the heroine when she thinks all is lost, or keeps the hermitess in her cell, or may even be the cause of somebody's death if that is part of the plot. The *prima donna* and the tenor, the contralto and the basso get all the best music and do all the spectacular things but you cannot manage the plot without Fifth Business! It is not spectacular, but it is a good line of work, I can tell you, and those who play it sometimes have a career that outlasts the golden voices. Are you Fifth Business? You had better find out."

I SPOKE EARLIER of what Eugene O'Neill said about the necessity for the writer to explore the malaise of our time—the changed conception of what God is and how God is encountered in the life of man, in our day. It is not easy work to present that malaise to the modern reader in a way he will accept. My novel *Fifth Business* is written in the form of an extended letter from Ramsay to his Headmaster, apparently to explain why he is not such a dull dog as the world at large thinks him. It is vital to the understanding of the book to recognize, as the story proceeds, who this Headmaster is. Do you know that not once since that book was published in 1970, and has been the subject of a great number of critical essays and considerations by academic critics of the most impeccable qualifications for being critical, has any critic recognized who the Headmaster is? Quite simply, and to me obviously, the Headmaster is God, to whom Ramsay is saying—this is what my life has been, what my destiny has made of me, where your hints and nudges have taken me. Judge me, for I am your creature. Ramsay has lived his whole imperfect and eccentric life in the constant awareness of God, and in the end he knows, like a true introvert, that God is within him and not external to him and that in that consciousness he is saved or damned—to use the Presbyterian terms familiar to him from childhood. In the end he knows that he is saved, which is to say that he has come to terms with his destiny as honestly as he knows how. And he recognizes that the means by which he has been saved are not those that had ever been made known to him by the religion of the past. The knowledge of God must begin with self-knowledge; where it goes after that is every man's task to find out.

I thought I had said that as clearly as anyone could, without being rudely and inexcusably didactic—without hitting the reader over the head with that most objectionable of literary appurtenances—a Message. I hate books with Messages. Though I am beguiled by the magnificent style of *Pilgrim's Progress* I can never really like the book because Bunyan was obsessed by his Message. I have never liked *Robinson Crusoe*, despite its enviably plain style, because Defoe could not hold his peace, and must always be preaching and nudging his reader to accept his Message. Tolstoy, that splendid barbaric giant, almost discredits himself by the frequency, the simple-mindedness, and the remorseless nagging of his Messages. The real author, in my view, is the one who approaches his hearers with a Golden Tale.

Real readers can understand what a book is saying without having it spooned into them like brimstone and treacle. Of course, not all readers are real. My books are frequently recommended to students in Canadian schools, and from time to time students come to see me, to talk about them. Often this is an experience agreeable to them and to me. The ones who try my patience are those who, when I have explained some point in a book, look me in the eye with all the confidence of youth and say, "What you're *really* trying to say is—" To that I have a well-worn reply, and it is this: "My dear young friend, I am not *trying* to say anything: I am *saying* it as clearly as careful consideration and my not wholly inconsiderable art permit me to do. Your job is to understand it." But I have many readers who do understand, and the letters they write me are one of the foremost satisfactions of authorship.

A country's literature is a crystal ball into which its people may look to understand their past and their present, and to find some foretaste of their future. The pictures are never simple, never wholly clear, and certainly never didactic. They need interpretation; not the interpretation of the literary critic, unless the critic is a person of gifts comparable to the writer, but the interpretation of the heart, the sympathy and understanding that are the partners of insight. Canada has, over the years, produced such a literature, and during the past quarter of a century that literature has grown to an extraordinary maturity. It has done so with the encouragement of a growing body of readers who want to hear what their writers have to say, and make it part of their national consciousness. I avoid the term *national culture* because it has been abused by people who think of culture as a commodity, separable from the rest of the national life. Culture is an ambience, a part of the air we breathe. That special ozone is now to be breathed in Canada, because it arises from the land itself—not a few acres of snow, but a country of immensely varied beauty of landscape and of season, including our lovely and dangerous winters. It arises from our history, not dull, but covered, sombre in palette but with wonderful flashes of brilliance. It arises from our psychology, which takes its colour from the land and the history. The fear that it might be lost if we entered into a closer financial link with our southern neighbour is, I think, exaggerated, for the land and the history and the psychological direction cannot be wholly changed by anything so superficial. You, in Scotland, know that political unity with a more aggressive and powerful country is not the death of the essence of your own country. But such a link could be dangerous and in some respects depleting, and I hope we have the self-preservative good sense to declare against it. A strong link already exists, and it is sufficient without turning the link into a shackle.

As I said at the beginning, I have no idea of what you expected or wanted me to say. But I have given you what our grandparents called "a piece of my mind"—not, I hope, too disagreeably. I have attempted to show you something of the wild Hamlet who lurks behind the features of Horatio.

29

The Value of a Coherent Notion of Culture

This lecture was given as part of The Walter Gordon Series of Lectures in Public Policy at Hart House in the University of Toronto on Wednesday, September 23, 1992, chaired by the Master of Massey College, Ann Saddlemyer. It was the third of the series and the participants were Carlos Fuentes and Robertson Davies, with Fuentes speaking first. The title of the event was "An Emerging North American Culture," and Davies took the opportunity to voice the general Canadian weariness with the attempts of the unpopular government of Brian Mulroney to amend the Constitution through apparently endless negotiations conducted at places like Meech Lake and Charlottetown. The audience roared their approval as he laid into the politicians and their "tiny minds."

On August 24, 1992, Davies wrote to a friend: *Next month I have to join in a public discussion of North American Culture (what a pompous title) with Carlos Fuentes, the Mexican writer (and a very fine one). Both Canada and Mexico know what it is like to live side by side with the U.S.A., and to be taken for granted by its government and its people. I expect we shall have a lively time and I look forward greatly to meeting Fuentes.*

Ever since I was told that the subject of this discussion would be "An Emerging North American Culture" I have puzzled over the implications of that title. It cannot mean that there is no North American culture at present; any community has a culture of some kind. Does it mean that something lurks in the womb of the existing culture, something markedly different, which is going to leap upon us after the millennium which is now a mere eight years away? What does it mean by "culture"?

I presume that it means the civilization, customs, artistic and scientific achievements of a people, or group of people, in this case Canada, the U.S.A., and Mexico; the word is often extended to mean simply a way of life. After all, the life of an entire continent is influenced by a similarity in culture; but in a certain degree also national cultures are inescapable. The most determined hermit would have trouble escaping completely from the culture that encloses his solitude.

If that is so, North America unquestionably has a culture, and it is rooted in the European culture which is the dominant aspect of civilization among the principal countries of our time. We have developed and altered some aspects of that European culture to suit our own needs and tastes. Are we here tonight to discuss the possibility that something wholly new will appear on this continent in the course of—let us say—the next five hundred years? Frankly, I think that anything of that kind is most unlikely.

Very soon, however, in a mere two or three hundred years (which is nothing in terms of the growth of a culture) we shall surely find that the culture of North America will have taken on several attitudes and developments which come from the Orient. I cannot guess how many of you are familiar with Oswald Spengler's remarkable and prophetic work, *The Decline of the West*, in which he foresees the decline of the Western world and a corresponding rise of Asiatic and African powers. He puts forward a theory of cyclic progression, according to which great cultures and continents undergo a period of growth, followed by maturity and then decline. The theory is briefly expressed in Bishop Berkeley's "Westward the course of empire takes its way"; it is interesting to recall that the Bishop wrote those words in a poem called "On the Prospect of Planting Arts and Learning in America." But Spengler had less faith in arts and learning than in industrialism and technology. I cannot claim any authority in such matters as these, but we are all aware that it is common talk now that the United States is losing its industrial and technological supremacy to Japan, which is unquestionably establishing itself as a dominant force in industrial and technological affairs. If Japan takes the lead in industry and technology, this continent will certainly adopt, perforce, many Japanese characteristics.

Things which seem in themselves to be trivial may often be straws which show the way the wind is blowing. In the great days of Rome the mark of a truly influential citizen was the possession of a Greek secretary; since the end of the Second World War the mark of distinction in the U.S. is the possession of an English secretary; the modern Japanese produce admirable secretaries of their own, but they show dominance by the possession of a few pictures by Van Gogh and a cellar of the finest French wines. Draw what conclusions you will. When the cultivation and elegance of one nation become the coveted possessions of another, it seems that the clouds are beginning to gather over the skies of the nation which provides the greatly desired toys.

Please do not assume from what I am saying that I am wholly pessimistic about the Western world of which we are a part and whose industrial, technological, and artistic achievements we not only share, but to which we make an honourable contribution. Unfashionable as it is nowadays to say so, I firmly believe that there are attributes which belong to blood and race which cannot be copied with total success. Imitation, even on the highest level, is not creation.

I think of the world of music. Some of the finest executants on our concert stages and even on our operatic stages are now Orientals. They come *very close to the best*, but if you will allow me to express a personal opinion—music has been a lifetime preoccupation of mine and I think that my opinion is not uninformed—they are not *quite* the best. Our own artists, in the performance of our Western music, have still that quality which makes the difference between the admirable and the transcendent; it is the quality which distinguishes the uttermost that can be achieved by intelligence from that which is the essence of spirit, and, if I may use an unpopular four-letter word, of soul.

This is to speak of musical performance only. What about the writing of music of a high order? This is an area in which the East has not excelled. It would be absurd to say that it may not yet do so, but it is mere fact to say that it has not done so yet.

So: Does the course of empire really take its journey westward until it arrives at last in what we have been used to call the East? I am inclined to think that it is so, but I do not think the movement will be completed in our time or in our children's time or in our grandchildren's time. Our decline, if decline we must, will be slow, and for some of us the best may be yet to come.

Doubtless you have been wondering when I would get to Canada, because these lectures are expected to have a Canadian relevance. In what I am about to say I beg you to believe that I am not lambasting my country because I scorn it; I speak as I do because it has long been the privilege of a country's authors to speak of what they see with the special vision which is theirs. If I utter warnings, you must think of me as akin to the sacred geese who warned Rome that the enemy was attacking the Capitol; by their clamour and their scolding they saved Rome. Can our writers save Canada? We can try but we must not expect that Canada will like us for it. We all know the fate of the prophet in his own country.

In discussing this matter of a North American culture it is obvious that Señor Fuentes has been asked to join us because his country and ours may be said to enclose the United States, which is of course the dominant power on this continent. Mexico and Canada are in a sense parentheses around those words *The United States of America*. Parentheses are used for many purposes and sometimes they confer a hint of irony. The United States of America—it is a somewhat vaunting title, for those states do not yet include Mexico or Canada, but we overlook it. We pay it no mind, just as we do not worry that a small local baseball contest is vaingloriously named The World Series. The parentheses—Mexico and Canada—are used to our great neighbour talking always at the top of his voice. Do we parentheses have anything of importance to say? Señor Fuentes has spoken for Mexico; let me say something about Canada, though I shall certainly not forget Mexico.

We Canadians are all, I think, a little exhausted by the hullabaloo, the brouhaha, the powwow that has gone on in our country about our Constitution. We have wearied of the incessant pitter-patter of tiny minds trotting across our land to say, at one place or another, what they will or will not put up with as the structure of our country. But we may have missed, in our irritation, something of great importance that is not at once apparent. This constitutional wrangle is our version of a civil war. It is a psychological rather than a military conflict but nonetheless important because it is a war of ideas, fought somewhat ineptly with words. When we think of civil wars we think of the Roundheads confronting the Cavaliers, and making their point by beheading a King; we think of the Blue and the Grey involved in bloody struggle to maintain the Union. Our Mexican friends have known many civil insurrections, and, like ourselves in 1812, have fought the United States on land to preserve what is their own. Those wars are embalmed in the glory of military exploits and their story can be stripped down to make a chronicle understandable on a low level by children. But our present conflict is a Canadian version of a civil war, and dowdy and dispiriting though it may appear, it is nonetheless the struggle for the soul of a country and the identification of a national entity, and if what emerges is a pitiful lost soul and an entity in tatters, it will be nobody's fault but our own.

Why our own fault? Because we shall not have produced the people capable of dealing with great things in a great style. Because we have been content with a form of democracy which too readily slithers downhill into a conspiracy of mediocrity directed against a nation. Because our country, which could have boasted at one time of being one of the most politically sophisticated countries among the democratic lands, lost its way, lost its touch, ran out of gas. These things happen, and we may not pretend that they cannot happen to us. We shall have shown that those who laugh at us as a dull and spiritless people have been right.

Or is it as bad as that? I do not think so.

We are not a country populated by fools, but I fear that we are a lazy people, accepting our good fortune as though it came by divine right. The present constitutional dispute has shown, among other things, how indifferent we can be to things of the highest importance. We show no anxiety to distinguish ourselves in the world of the intellect, and in matters of business we are not, as a people, as aggressive as our southern neighbour. Except, of course, in the Province of Quebec whose leaders, armed with empurpled rhetoric which is so characteristically French, face, and face down, the tongue-tied anglophones, who sputter in terms of political correctness like damp firecrackers.

It has not always been so. In practical affairs and in the world of science we have made valuable contributions to the civilization of which I have spoken—the civilization that is known and shared by the most advanced nations on the globe. We have in our time produced statesmen of distinguished mind, great energy, noble eloquence, and devotion to our national cause, and these statesmen have come from both the dominant races of our country. Our contribution to the arts has been, until comparatively recently, confined to performers and interpreters, but there we have given the world artists whom the world has cherished. Of our contribution to the arts on the creative level I shall speak later, because it is of special significance to what I have to say this evening.

At the moment, however, it seems that we are in a trough, obviously bereft of political talent, which is the place from which we understandably expect the most potent leadership to come. I do not want you to think that I take any particular pleasure in scolding the people (men and women) who at present are in control of—no, not of our destiny, but of our immediate future—but I cannot forbear to say that they are a sorry lot. Out of the innumerable deliberations of our leaders on the present constitutional crisis have you read a solitary word that you can recall as being charged with piercing insight, or strong feeling, to say nothing of eloquence? It was reported a few weeks ago that one of our national leaders has in his entourage two speech writers, one of whom is paid one hundred thousand dollars a year and the other seventy thousand dollars, but from this gentleman—he is not our prime minister, by the way—we have not heard a word that I, as a professional assessor of words, would value at one of our base metal dollars. Even these highly paid bards, it seems, are utterly bereft of song when their theme is Canada. Nobody has any eloquence, nobody has any passion, and it is because nobody has any intellectual vigour or strength of feeling. In our political world we face intellectual bankruptcy in all the major parties.

Who is to blame? We are. These are the people we have elected to think for us and to speak for us, and if they cannot do it it is our own fault. It is not a simple matter of political expediency or political choice. Of course our electoral system in Canada, as elsewhere in the world, has become, in essence, a vast popularity contest, in which a candidate's television quality is of greater importance than his intellectual endowment or his most cherished principles. But even when that is said, what is wrong is that our choice is so limited, and our power to choose so stupidly exercised.

Any attempt to answer that question would keep us here far longer than would be endurable, so I must talk about a single element in our national life which I think contributes heavily to the malaise of which I have spoken, that rheumatoid arthritis of the intellect and of the will which is the present Canadian disease. I want to talk about education.

We are met here in a university ambience and so education may fittingly come under survey. But it is by no means only at the university level that education in Canada must bear heavy blame for what is wrong with the country. To put the matter simply, we do not take education seriously enough. We still cling to the notion, which descends from our pioneer ancestors, that education above the simplest level is an affectation, and that a limited acquaintance with the primary skills of reading, writing, and arithmetic is good enough for anybody. Anyone who confesses openly to a cultivated taste in anything whatever is regarded as an oddity, desirous of raising himself above his fellows. Our Ideal Canadian is an oaf. Of course we do not say so openly, but we make the message clear enough in our legislatures, where the first move of a government faced with financial troubles is to cut down on what the lower level of our legislators do not hesitate to call "frills," by which they mean the arts, the sciences, and education. The majority of our legislators are wholly untouched by education. Oh yes, I am sure you can produce statements to show that the chairs in our parliaments are warmed by the rumps of a large number of B.A.s and possessors of professional degrees. But would you know it if you were not told? Does their manner of expressing themselves suggest any real acquaintance with the tongue that Milton spake? (Not to speak of the manner in which Milton thought.) The plain fact is that they do not believe in education or in culture and think these things the concern of lesser, impractical, inconsiderable folk, to be encouraged or set aside as expediency dictates.

The trouble begins at the bottom. The education in our schools simply is not good enough, because it is not rooted in any coherent notion of culture. If you were to enter a classroom in any elementary school in our ten provinces and say to the teacher: "Are you laying the groundwork here for the acquirement and extension of a national culture on the level of, say, France, or Sweden, or Finland?" I wonder what the response would be, or if you would receive a response? Yet that is what we need, and what we are paying for.

What is the trouble? I think it lies in our expectations, arising from what—to use a term very popular among educators—our "role-model" is. We are imitating the United States, and not on the highest American level.

In the United States there is more than one level of education. There is what the serious people among the rich can afford for their children, and below that schools of lesser quality degenerating into schools from which one averts one's eyes in dismay. The United States has a group of universities that are not dependent on governmental whim for their maintenance, and are thus free to give education above the level that politicians can understand. In Canada we have no such universities and the sad consequence is that our universities are at the mercy of uneducated people who have no idea of what education really is.

What is that? What *is* education? Let me tell you an illustrative anecdote. Some years ago, when I was Master of Massey College in this university, I knew a young man, a member of the college, who was a first-class student of history. He wrote an excellent thesis, and got his Doctorate of Philosophy in history. But then he needed a job, and the world of history offered none. So, to keep bread in his mouth, he took a minor post in a financial house dealing in stocks and bonds.

He rose rapidly. When I met him about four years later, and asked him how things were going, he said, "I've learned one important thing, above all others; there's nothing in the financial world that a good grasp of history doesn't help."

There spoke a really educated man. He was not educated in finance, but I gather that in that world it is possible to learn by practical experience. To learn, if you already know what learning is. If you know what real mental application is. If you have something in your head that conditions your outlook on the world that is more extensive than the confines of the stock market. If you are, in fact, a truly educated person and not simply a trained peasant. But are politicians aware of this concept of the educated man? Have they any awareness of a mental capacity that extends beyond the boundaries of the job in hand, whatever it may be? Of low cunning, they have some awareness, because they employ that in their own lives. But of real education, what do they know?

A few weeks ago I was at the Stratford Festival, which has, for forty years, been one of the cultural glories of our country, and I was watching a performance of *Love's Labour's Lost.* There came that splendid moment when the curate, Sir Nathaniel, says of the stupid oaf Costard:

> Sir, he hath never fed of the dainties that are bred in a book. He hath not eat paper, as it were; he hath not drunk ink; his intellect is not replenished; he is only an animal, only sensible in the duller parts.

At that moment I wanted to leap to my feet and cry: "Say it again! Say it again! Send a fax to every member of a provincial legislature and to every Member of Parliament and let him remember it when next he hears the word *education.*

You think that I am speaking in extreme terms, don't you? Remember those sacred geese that saved Rome; did they restrain themselves? My dear friends, how carefully do you read your daily newspaper? Do you not recall that earlier this year a Member of Parliament from North Vancouver told the legislators of our country that their poor assistance to the Canadian publishing industry was money wasted? Why? Because, he said, only ten percent of Canadians read books; he himself was a great reader (and at this point he gave the names of two writers of mingled crime and pornographic books as his favourites) but he read no Canadian stuff because it just wasn't good enough. There was nothing whatever to be gained, he said, by giving any assistance to literature in his country. The honourable member's name was Chuck Cook.

Is there anything to be said in support of Chuck Cook? I am afraid that there is. A recent survey under the auspices of the United Nations to discover how many people read books in forty-four literate countries revealed that Canada ranked forty-third. We were ahead of only one other country, and that was the United States. But we have still a claim to the lowest rung on the ladder because we tax books, and no other civilized country does so.

Where does the blame lie? With our systems of education, surely. And what is the remedy? Not to press on with the present prevailing attitude toward education, which seems to be that all subjects must be made diverting and easily mastered, and that what used to be called The Play Way in learning should dominate our educational ethos. Tell young people that something is easy, and they will certainly treat it easily and regard it as trivial. Reduce the tough chewing of history to vague generalities called Social Studies, lower the sights of literary instruction to exclude Shakespeare and the Bible as the foundations of English prose, teach mathematics as a collection of puzzles rather than as a mode of thought and reasoning, and you reduce the foundations of education to rubble. Education is hard work, not play, and its rewards are a seriously informed, wide-ranging attitude toward the whole of life, and the beginning of a great adventure, which, without it, can sink into an incoherent mess.

I imagine that there are among you university teachers who are familiar with the dispiriting work of teaching university students basic things that they should have learned before they appeared in your classes, to say nothing of teaching them what logical argument is, and the necessity to express considered opinions in concise and literate prose. But you are too often faced with young men and women who have no experience of intellectual rigour, and no conception of the root of all education, which is the thirst for knowledge which can only be slaked through self-education.

But to return to Chuck Cook, a man whose name fascinates me as a novelist, because only the highest inspiration could find so appropriate a name for a man who holds his opinions. Is he right in saying that there are no Canadian books worthy of intelligent attention? I confess that in such a matter I am a biased witness, and I am biased because the reception of my own writing by my fellow Canadians has been, on the whole, generous. But if I depended for my livelihood on my earnings within Canada, I should certainly live in a manner of humble restraint. However, like a number of other Canadian authors, my books appear in many countries and in twenty or more languages, and the reception they receive is warming and encouraging.

I do not say that boastfully but in refutation of what Chuck Cook implies when he says that Canadian books are not "good enough." They are good enough to carry the name of Canada and the ideas of Canada and a Canadian way of thinking and feeling to the rest of the world where they are received with respect and pleasure. They are good enough to make Canada appear as a country with something to say that the civilized world wants to hear about the condition of mankind and the way in which man's hopes and man's fears are encountered in the northern reaches of this immense continent. They have an individuality of viewpoint which is not that of the United States, but a soberer, darker, and, I venture to say, richer point of view than that which pertains to our south. I am not knocking the literature of the U.S.; that would be absurd. But I am asserting that our Canadian writing at its best has a flavour of its own and that the literate world enjoys that flavour and finds it reassuring as evidence of unity amid the diversity of civilized people the world over.

This is what a national literature does. This is what our guest, Señor Fuentes, has done so splendidly for Mexico, and it is what perhaps a dozen Canadian writers are at present doing for Canada. Canadian literature is a travelling ambassador of incalculable influence for what is best in this country. It is a message to the world that the intellect is not dead here, whatever the Chuck Cooks and the whole rabble of half-baked politicians, whose vision does not extend beyond the next election, may be signalling from their legislative buildings. The wine of political thought in Canada is a very watery tipple at the moment, but the brandy of Canadian literature is well over proof.

Limitations of time have compelled me to restrict my remarks about Canadian art to literature alone, but our sister arts can, and do, speak eloquently for themselves. I have been severe, but not, I think, too severe, about the Canadian people as a whole. Like our neighbours to the south we are self-declared seekers after happiness, but again like our neighbours to the south, we have no firm idea of where happiness is to be found.

Around the Great Hall of the neighbouring Massey College, these words are written, and I commend them to you: "Happiness is impossible, and even inconceivable, to a mind without scope and without pause, a mind driven by craving, pleasure, or fear. To be happy, you must be wise." Perhaps Señor Fuentes recognizes those words. They are by the Spanish American philosopher George Santayana; he is not much in favour at the moment, but he is nonetheless a perceptive and potent thinker.

Our neighbour to the south exhibits in its political world (using that phrase in the broadest sense) what happens when honest wisdom gives place to pleasure, craving, and fear. Can we learn the obvious lesson and abandon those delusive attitudes insofar as they have already seized upon our governors? Can we not demand of them that they state their opinions more clearly on matters of the highest importance—and certainly our national culture is of the highest importance. We should do so, because if we do not do so we shall go the way of all stupid, greedy, covetous, frightened peoples.

And it will be nobody's fault but our own.